FAR WORSE THINGS

"Maybe you should come back during regular *daylight* office hours," the detective said through the partly opened door.

"Except time is of the essence, Mr. Micale. We must speak now or not at all. May I come in?"

His eyes narrowed suspiciously. "Do you require permission?"

"I'm merely trying to be polite." I had a very charming laugh. I'd practiced it. "I'm afraid you're thinking of vampires, with the whole not being able to cross the threshold thing."

"Yeah...That's just silliness from the movies." Except he still didn't let me in. "So who are you?"

Some humans were easier to manipulate than others. Some required a more *direct* approach. "I am someone who can answer some of the questions that keep you up at night. I know about your map...The one with all the missing people on it. Help me and I will help you."

He was quiet for a long time. "My mother used to say I was too dumb to know when to quit." Then he stepped aside and opened the door. However, he did not specifically give me permission to enter. He was still testing me.

I walked through the doorway, and nothing happened. Thus destroying his foolish delusions about Nosferatu. He seemed relieved. *Silly man.* Didn't he realize there were far worse things lurking out there than mere bloodsuckers?

—from "Allegation of an Honorable Man"
by Larry Correia

NO GAME FOR KNIGHTS

Edited by
LARRY CORREIA &
KACEY EZELL

NO GAME FOR KNIGHTS

Copyright © 2022 by Larry Correia & Kacey Ezell

"Larry's Introduction" © 2022 by Larry Corriea; "Kacey's Introduction" © 2022 by Kacey Ezell; "1957" © 2022 by Robert Buettner; "Faint Heats" © 2022 by Griffin Barber and Kacey Ezell; "The Lady in the Pit" © 2022 by D.J. Butler; "All in the Family" © 2022 by Nicole Givens Kurtz; "Sammy Oakley and the Jewel of Amureki" © 2022 by Laurell K. Hamiliton; "Utopia's Sheep" © 2022 by Craig Martelle; "Pandemonium" © 2022 by Sharon Shinn; "Pagan" © 2022 by S.A. Bailey; "The Hound of the Bastard's Villa" © 2022 by G. Scott Huggins; "Midnight Ride" © 2022 by by Chris Kennedy; "The Incomparable Treasure" © 2022 by Rob Howell; "Storm Surge" © 2022 by Michael F. Haspil; "Gutter Ballet" © 2022 by Christopher Ruocciho; "Allegation of an Honorable Man" © 2022 by Larry Correia

A Baen Books Original

Baen Publishing Enterprises
P.O. Box 1403
Riverdale, NY 10471
www.baen.com

ISBN: 978-1-9821-9290-7

Cover art by Dominic Harman

First printing, September 2022
First mass market printing, September 2023

Distributed by Simon & Schuster
1230 Avenue of the Americas
New York, NY 10020

Library of Congress Control Number: 2022024197

Printed in the United States of America

10 9 8 7 6 5 4 3 2 1

For all of the men in the arena, the world-weary

paladins, the gray knights, the anti-heroes.

We see you. Keep fighting.

Contents

Larry's Introduction

This was Kacey's idea. Our first collection of noir-themed fantasy and sci-fi stories was called *Noir Fatale*, and it came out amazing. For that one our theme was the femme fatale. For our second volume we decided to focus on the next big noir archetype, the detective.

I think Raymond Chandler provided the best description of this type of character:

But down these mean streets a man must go who is not himself mean, who is neither tarnished nor afraid. The detective in this kind of story must be such a man. He is the hero; he is everything. He must be a complete man and a common man and yet an unusual man. He must be, to use a rather weathered phrase, a man of honor—by instinct, by inevitability, without thought of it, and certainly without saying it. He must be the best man in his world and a good enough man for any world. I do not care much about his private life; he is neither a eunuch nor a satyr; I think he might seduce a duchess and I am quite sure he would not spoil a virgin; if he is a man of honor in one thing, he is that in all things.

He is a relatively poor man, or he would not be a detective at all. He is a common man or he could not go among common people. He has a sense of character, or he would not know his job. He will take no man's money dishonestly and no man's insolence without a due and dispassionate revenge. He is a lonely man and his pride is that you will treat him as a proud man or be very sorry you ever saw him. He talks as the man of his age talks—that is, with rude wit, a lively sense of the grotesque, a disgust for sham, and a contempt for pettiness.

The story is this man's adventure in search of a hidden truth, and it would be no adventure if it did not happen to a man fit for adventure. He has a range of awareness that startles you, but it belongs to him by right, because it belongs to the world he lives in. If there were enough like him, the world would be a very safe place to live in, without becoming too dull to be worth living in.

—Raymond Chandler,
The Simple Art of Murder 1950

And that is what these authors have strived to deliver. We assembled a crew of extremely talented storytellers. Their stories are all in wildly different settings, from sci-fi, to fantasy, urban fantasy, or alternate history, and they vary greatly in tone and feeling, but all of them feature characters who are solvers of crimes or righters of wrongs, with their own—sometimes peculiar—code of honor.

I hope you enjoy reading these as much as Kacey and I did while putting them together. I'm proud of this anthology.

If you find a story in here you particularly enjoy I'd encourage you to check out more of that author's work. Half of the fun of anthologies is discovering new writers to read, and we've got some amazing ones here. It's been an honor to work with them.

—Larry Correia

Kacey's Introduction

There are two sides to every story.

I'm not exaggerating when I say that editing *Noir Fatale* was a huge milestone in my career. Like bucket list huge. Working on that project gave me the opportunity to edit some of my very favorite authors and create something incredibly cool dedicated to my all-time favorite character archetype.

But like I said, there are two sides to every story. And if the femme fatale is my favorite, then her foil, the hardboiled, lone-wolf detective is a very, very close second.

Larry and I were, of course, thrilled with the positive reception that *Noir Fatale* received. I cannot begin to express how grateful I am to everyone who picked up a copy, whether in print or e-format, or the amazingly well-done audiobook. Thanks to all of you, Larry and I now have the opportunity to bring you the other side of the story, as told by fifteen amazing authors.

Among those fifteen, we've got veteran, bestselling authors and new voices alike. Every one of their stories has a unique and interesting take on the detective archetype. Personally, I found it fascinating that many of the characters are not technically detectives at all, but each of them has the distinctive feel of an honorable man doing his best to uncover the truth in a dishonorable world. Whether the story is set in a far future science fiction reality, an alternate version of our own history, or a fantasy realm we've never known, they all speak of a hero—battered and bloody as he may be—who just won't quit. And as we dig yet again into the darkness that lies within our own minds, it's comforting to know that somewhere, in that darkness, the truth-seeking hero still fights on.

I hope you enjoy these stories. We've definitely enjoyed bringing them to you. As Larry said, it's been an honor.

—Kacey Ezell

NO GAME FOR KNIGHTS

1957

Robert Buettner

1957

Seven nights a week extraordinary blondes, on the arms of tuxedoed blond Nazis, decorated the crowds that packed Berlin's Aces American Bar. The crowds overpaid to drink, dance, and sweat, and this November Thursday night was beginning just as sweaty and as profitable as every other night in 1956 had.

Some said the blondes drew the crowds. Some said it was the club's aeronautical theme.

Most said the crowds came for American whiskey, backroom gambling, and the Negro musicians who played American rock 'n' roll and rhythm and blues. Even though, or perhaps because, all of those things were officially illegal in Berlin.

For that matter all of those things were illegal across the Greater Third Reich. Which in 1956 stretched north beyond the Arctic Circle, south across the Mediterranean into North Africa, west to the English Channel, and east beyond Hitlergrad, formerly called Moscow.

Robby Ritter liked to think Aces' success had a lot to do with its owner's nightly presence on the balcony that overlooked Aces' dance floor. Although the blondes did make keeping an eye on his investment less a job than a pleasure.

Tonight one particular blonde who entered drew his eye. He had to peer around the prewar American Gee Bee racing plane that hung from the ceiling, and the contortion aggravated the scar tissue in his neck. But the view was worth it. She slithered out of her wrap, and the backless sequined emerald sheath she wore underneath clung like paint. She handed the wrap to the silver-haired fat man who had brought her so he could check it.

She turned, surveyed the club, and Robby's view improved from magnificent to breathtaking.

The fat man also turned, took the goddess's gloved elbow, then spotted Robby on the balcony and waved.

Robby blinked. "Of all the Nazis in Berlin she's with Tauscher?"

Robby trotted downstairs from his perch and met the couple as they reached the bar.

Max Tauscher was the gauleiter of Berlin. Technically that meant he was the head of the Nazi Party for the region that contained Berlin. Practically that meant that Max was the man to see if you wanted anything in Berlin done. Or not done.

Max already smelled of bourbon as he bear-hugged his host and Robby felt the Knight's Cross with Leaves and Swords that gleamed on Max's tuxedo's lapel. Max pushed him back to arm's length then hailed Hitler.

At the moment there was whispered doubt whether Hitler was still alive, but even if he were dead Germans would hail him forever.

Tauscher shouted to be heard above the band. "Robby, it's been so long!"

Robby shouted, "You were here last night, Max."

Tauscher cocked his head. "So I was."

The woman hailed Hitler with her right hand then extended it to Robby and smiled. "I insisted Max bring me here to meet you. Margarethe Kohl, Mr. Ritter."

A diamond-rimmed black-on-red swastika brooch, denoting Nazi Party membership, was strategically pinned on her gown's décolletage. Robby smiled, bowed, then kissed her extended hand. "I'm flattered, Miss Kohl."

She raised her big blue eyes to the stubby red-on-white Gee Bee. As the music boomed the plane trembled at the ends of the cables it hung from. Everything else in the club shook too, from the air-racing trophies and memorabilia that lined the club's walls, to the bottles behind the bar, to the jitterbugging Germans.

She said, "I'm impressed with what you've created here. It exceeds its considerable reputation."

Tauscher turned his head in response to a shout, shouted back, then pointed away from them. "It's a toady of Himmler's. I must go genuflect!" He winced as the band's American guitars screeched louder. "Robby, don't you have a quiet table where Margarethe and I can talk with you?"

Before Ritter could answer Tauscher disappeared into the crowd.

❖   ❖   ❖

Table 3 was a linen-draped island in the corner, an acoustic dead spot that Robby reserved for business meetings.

Thomas saw them coming, seated the lady, lit a Chesterfield for her, then asked Ritter, "What'll it be, boss?"

Kohl smiled at Robby. "I'll have whatever the boss is having."

Ritter said to her, "Straight-up Manhattan's the house specialty. We import the best bourbon Kentucky makes, bitters from Trinidad and Tobago, and we marinate our own Washington State cherries."

Robby raised two fingers, and Thomas disappeared.

Robby asked her, "When did you leave the States?"

She blew smoke, then peered at him through it. "I didn't mention where I was from. And I've been told my accent is indistinguishable from a native Berliner's."

"It is."

"Then how—?"

"Your legs. German women wear Axis-made Japanese silk stockings even though nylons wear better. The tariffs on American nylons are deliberately confiscatory. But a lady can bring in a reasonable quantity for personal use."

She laughed. "I was warned. I stocked up last year before I left Los Angeles. Maxie told me you know the black market as well as you know flying. But what piqued your interest in women's stockings?"

"Puberty. What piqued your interest in a draft-dodging saloon keeper?"

"I'm not interested in your politics or your saloon keeping except as they relate to your flying. By the way, one American to another, let's speak English. And call me Peggy." Peggy Kohl pointed at the drinks-and-smokes menu clipped into a stand on the table. Her English had a midwestern twang Robby hadn't heard for far too long.

She said, "This is the swankiest club in Berlin, but you sell top brand American booze and cigarettes for half what the cheapest dive in town charges for tap water and peanuts. How do you manage that?"

Robby shrugged. "I keep costs down."

Peggy Kohl laughed again. "Maxie already explained how you manage that. I just wanted to hear how you'd handle a question about smuggling."

"I didn't say I smuggle."

"I didn't expect you to."

What Germans today called *Pax Germanium* had kept America and the Axis powers at peace with one another for the thirty-seven years since the Great War ended in 1918. But more significantly, in 1942, the Stockholm Treaty ended the Eurasian War. The treaty confirmed the Greater Third Reich's current vast reach. So the Pax had for the last thirteen years brought widespread Peace on Earth, or at least on the parts of Earth that the Nazis considered worthwhile.

But Peace on Earth didn't equal One Big Happy World. Treaties or no, the Greater Reich secured its economy, its ideology, and its racial purity by tight trade policies and even tighter borders. So smuggling, in both directions across what the British politician Churchill called the Iron Curtain, had been a lucrative, but risky, business for a while.

Robby narrowed his eyes as he pointed to her Nazi Party pin. "My turn to see how you handle a question. How and why does an American get one of those?"

It was Peggy Kohl's turn to shrug. "My boss values my services. And I value my job."

Before Robby could ask more Max Tauscher returned. He sat, waved to Thomas for a Manhattan, then boomed, "So! Tomorrow. Zero nine hundred. I will begin the new year high in the sky. Will you both be too hung over to keep up?"

Max was a potbellied, middle aged, glad-handing National Socialist hack. But during the short and glorious Eurasian War of 1939 through 1942, he had been "Murderous Max" Tauscher, lean and dashing fighter ace. His scarlet-cowled Messerschmitt Bf 109 had been the last thing twenty-nine Russian pilots saw in their rearview mirrors.

Max still crammed his body into his restored old crate and flew it at least weekly. Robby hangared and maintained Max's Messerschmitt, free of charge, at Aces Air Park. He hangared his own two-plane special-purpose air force there too.

Still, Robby wrinkled his brow as he looked from one Nazi to the other then said in German, "Zero nine hundred? Max, what are you talking about?"

Peggy answered. "My idea. As you were about to ask, I make films. I got my BA in film, with honors, from USC. But I found out that all career paths for women in Hollywood involve a stop on some man's couch. So last year I wrote to the only woman in the world I knew of who had any real stroke in the film business. And Minister Riefenstahl offered me my job as her personal assistant."

Robby's jaw dropped.

When film and television's influence had exploded in the 1950s, the Reich's Propaganda Ministry adapted. Goebbels remained in charge, but Leni Riefenstahl,

whose 1930s films had iconified Hitler and the Nazis,
had been appointed Minister of Graphic Information.

Robby whistled softly. "Your boss is the most influ-
ential woman in Europe?"

Max clapped Robby's shoulder. "And she's making a
movie! About me!"

Peggy smiled. "Not only about you, Max." She turned
to Robby. "Leni's given me carte blanche to create a
documentary about war heroes across the Reich who
have transformed themselves into heroes of peace. Right
now I need a chase plane and a pilot so I can film Max
air-to-air. Of course the Ministry will pay you well for
your time and expenses."

Robby already paid Max well, and often, to assure
that neither Aces nor Aces Air Park would be audited,
raided, inspected, or have its Negro employees harassed
or deported, by any entity in Berlin, from the health
department to the Berlin office of the Gestapo.

Robby smiled at his new passenger. "Lady, I'll fly
you anywhere you want to go for nothing."

The next morning Robby sat in the left-hand seat
of the de Havilland Mosquito that he normally used
to "import" contraband across the Baltic from Sweden.
The Mosquito in turn sat silent in its hangar, facing out
toward the blue-sky rectangle of the hangar's open doors.
On the airfield's apron Max Tauscher idled his red-nosed
Messerschmitt's engine toward operating temperature.
Peggy Kohl sat in the Mosquito's eccentric second-seat
position, behind Robby but staggered to his right.

She tapped Robby's shoulder. "You say our radio is
broken. So how do I direct Max so I get the shots I want?"

"It isn't broken. I just told Max that."

"Why?"

"Because I've flown with Max recently. He isn't the ace he was. I won't be party to a blonde, who an old man flying an antique airplane wants to impress, demanding aerobatics that neither he nor his airplane can deliver. Max will fly straight and slow like he usually does these days. We will orbit his plane while you take all the motion pictures you want from every angle you want."

Peggy raised her chin. "Do you have any idea how boring a plane flying straight and slow looks on the screen?"

"Do you have any idea how an overstressed plane looks when its wings rip off? But at least watching its pilot die won't bore anybody."

"You care about Max's life."

"I care about nobody's life but mine. I care about Max's influence. I've invested plenty in him to keep me out of trouble."

"Your compassion is touching." She looked around the cockpit. "This Mosquito is British, right? The Reich is so committed to 'Buy Axis' that I had to pack my own nylons. Doesn't this plane get you into the very trouble that you say you want to stay out of?"

Robby shook his head. "The Stockholm Treaty gutted the British Air Force just like the Treaty of Versailles gutted the German Air Force in 1918. Hitler loved getting even. And the German people will always love him for doing it. So the Reich had a hundred Mosquitos shipped to Germany, then scrapped the rest for replacement parts. This one sat in mothballs outside Frankfurt for years. I bought it for peanuts. All perfectly legal."

"Why not just buy an Axis-made plane?"

"A Mosquito will still outrun anything but a jet. It can carry two tons. It flies well very high or on the deck. And, like I said, parts are cheap and easy to get."

"Is the black paint so border patrol planes don't spot this one at night?"

"I just like black. And, as you see, we're about to fly just fine in daylight."

"That's an evasion, not an answer. Doesn't 'on the deck' mean so low that radar can't spot it either?"

"Are all documentary filmmakers this nosy?"

"Just the good ones." Peggy pointed at Robby's other ancient black plane, the trimotor parked to the Mosquito's right. "Your other plane looks like a corrugated shed with propellors. But it has more side windows. I could film better from it. Why aren't we flying that one?"

Robby reached up and rapped his knuckles on the segmented Plexiglas canopy above their heads. "You can film out of this fishbowl better than out of a side window. Besides a Junkers 52 can't keep up with a 109. It's an airliner made to carry seventeen people, which is why the windows. We don't need a plane like it."

"Oh. If this plane is so good for smuggling why do you even have a plane made to carry people?"

Robby shrugged and looked left, eyeing the Mosquito's silent port engine. "I never said I smuggled anything. You did. And that Ju-52 is just a sentimental indulgence. A museum piece. It rarely leaves the ground."

"Then why is that mechanic balanced on a ladder working on a museum piece's engine, like its passengers' lives depended on it?"

Out on the tarmac Max tugged the 109's canopy down, then his old fighter rolled forward.

Robby turned and studied the starboard engine.

Peggy said, "You're avoiding my questions. Is it because you're hiding something or because you think I'm a pain in the ass?"

"Some pains in the ass are worth the trouble."

Robby pressed the engine start button and the starboard Rolls-Royce Merlin coughed smoke, then thundered into deafening life. When both Merlins were singing Robby released the brakes, eased the throttles forward, and the Mosquito rolled out into the sunlight.

Thirty mostly quiet minutes later Max's old fighter and the Mosquito flew alongside one another in the sunny sky four thousand meters above the winter-brown and snow-white checkerboard of rural northern Germany. The old pilot turned his head toward them, flicked a salute, then banked away and turned back to land at the airpark.

Peggy spoke to Robby over the intercom. "I got all the shots I wanted. You fly every bit as well as Max said you did. Thank you. So now we turn back and land?"

Robby shrugged beneath his jacket. "Shame to waste such a beautiful day."

"What do you have in mind?"

"Want to see what this baby's got?"

"I think you're actually asking whether I want to see what this baby's pilot's got."

Robby nosed the Mosquito over and screamed down to the deck. Then for fifteen minutes he hedge-hopped trees and barns, and flew under a railroad trestle, at five hundred kilometers per hour. Peggy out-screamed the Merlins the whole way.

When he rolled the Mosquito to a stop and shut it down he unbuckled his harness, then turned to look back at Peggy. She sagged in her seat, panting audibly in the cockpit's sudden silence.

She smiled. "Do you seduce all your women this way?"

Robby twisted back toward her, grinning, but she stiff-armed his chest. "No."

He drew back. "I'm sorry. My radar about things like this is usually good."

Her smile returned. "Your radar's perfect. But our first time isn't going to be in a fishbowl that smells like gasoline."

On a sunny Sunday morning a month after the Mosquito landed Robby levered himself up onto one elbow, in bed alongside Peggy in her apartment. He watched her sleep, cheeks like Dresden porcelain and hair splashed golden across her pillow. She had been traveling all week, got in near midnight, and the subsequent welcome-home activities had run very late. So he tried not to wake her.

The previous month had been the happiest of his life. Every minute of every day she was in town and not at the Ministry they were together. He stayed home from the club to be with her most nights. The boss's absence hadn't hurt revenues, so maybe delegation wasn't just a catchphrase.

He eased from beneath the covers, padded to the kitchen and started coffee.

When he ran the water she called from the bedroom, "Bring me a cup?"

He called, "Sure, babe. Then I'm going out for the papers and a strudel."

"Welcome me home again first."

❖   ❖   ❖

At midafternoon Peggy, in a satin robe, sat cross-legged next to him on the couch. The Sunday papers lay jumbled at his feet, and strudel crumbs littered plates on the coffee table.

She laid her head on his bare chest. "Babe, it's time we talk."

"Agreed. I need to quit hogging the strudel."

"No. I mean cards-on-the-table talk."

His heart skipped. "Okay. You first or me?"

"Robby, I know you're not who you say you are."

"Bullshit. *You* told *me* I smuggled contraband into Germany the night you walked in my door. And you know I've paid off people like Max for years so I can keep doing it."

"That's not what I mean."

"Oh really?" Robby smirked but he knew his eyes gave him away. "And how would you know I'm not who I say I am?"

"Because I'm not who I say *I* am. Robby, when I came to Germany to work for Leni I already worked for the U.S. government. I still do."

"You're a spy?"

"A pretty fair one. But you're not Robert Ritter, minor league air racer who ran away to Portugal in 1940 to dodge the U.S. draft. Which is the fairy tale Max believes."

He shrugged. "Maybe it's not a fairy tale."

She shook her head. "For years the Nazis have been spinning their own tales about how all the undesirables in the Greater Reich just moved on and now there are none left. You know and U.S. Intelligence knows it's the biggest lie in history. And we both know surviving Jews still trickle out

of hiding in attics and cellars across the Reich and
make a run for it."

"That's a sad story."

Peggy smiled. "You know, babe, some of the run-
ners make it. Some of them make it all the way to
America. And do you know the first thing that happens
when they arrive? We debrief them because we know
fuck all about what goes on behind the Iron Curtain."

"Sounds like a happy ending for you and for them."

"And some of them told stories. Stories about an
American who smuggled Jews and gypsies and homo-
sexuals out, flying them across the Baltic to Sweden.
He refused to take a cent from his passengers. In
fact he gave them money to help them get started
in their new lives."

Robby shrugged. "Well, that can't be me. Because
he sounds like a sucker."

Peggy shook her head. "Have you been playing
a selfish jerk so long that you don't remember who
you really are?"

"I remember who brought you breakfast. And even
though I just found out that you've been lying to me
since the minute we met I still want to bring you
breakfast. Forever. Isn't that enough?"

"Robby, before I was a spy I was an analyst. Analysts
connect the dots so the real spies know what to look
for. I turned up two hundred records of Americans
who knew how to fly, who dropped out of sight in
Europe before this mystery pilot popped up. I handed
the personnel file of one of those two hundred to a
refugee who I was debriefing. A Jewish orphan who
your sucker had flown out of Berlin. She recognized
the file photo before I could blink.

"His name was Robert Roark. Trust fund kid. Graduate aeronautical engineering student. Had it made but dropped out of Purdue after the war started in Europe. Went to Canada, enlisted in the British Royal Air Force. So many Americans like him refused to do nothing while America watched the Nazis rape Europe that the RAF assigned the Yanks their own squadrons. Roark's Hurricane was set afire during an Eagle Squadron dogfight over Lille in 1941. Nobody saw a chute."

Robby swallowed.

Peggy said, "Since you probably haven't heard, Roark's squadron leader wrote that Roark saved his wingman's life by sacrificing his own. He was decorated posthumously. And the orphan told me that if Judaism had saints a thousand Jews would vote for the man in that picture."

Robby felt his lip quiver and his eyes flooded.

Peggy took Robby's face in her hands as her own eyes flooded. "My darling, you are so much handsomer than your photograph."

In the Sunday-evening twilight they walked arm in arm along the Unter den Linden, just one couple among many. The lime trees were still bare and the cold wind made eavesdropping unlikely.

Peggy said, "You never came home. Why?"

"I broke my neck when I crashed. The Germans had occupied Lille so the resistance people who hid me couldn't get it set properly at a hospital. I took months to heal. Most days I still ache.

"By the time I was healthy enough to think about going back to America to rejoin the fight, the fight was over. America never even entered the war. I had been a sucker. I wasn't sticking my neck out again. Certainly not for America. Instead I became the kind of American the Nazis would tolerate over here. Then I did what I could about the things America wouldn't do."

"The world needs more suckers like you."

"What about you? You're not really a movie professional, then?"

"Oh that part's strictly true. No spy would dare try to fool one of the world's most professional filmmakers with a legend studied up on in a couple of months. Leni hired me because I'm the real McCoy. It's the tradecraft I had to learn in a couple months."

"Tradecraft. Secret messages, that stuff?"

"Mostly."

"You could've told me sooner, babe. It would have eased my conscience to know I wasn't sleeping with a Nazi. For that matter, why did you tell me now?"

She looked up into the lime trees. "Because now I'm sure I need your help."

"Huh?"

"To fly one planeload of people out to Sweden. Basically the same thing you've been doing for years. Until yesterday I wasn't sure all of them would come out."

Robby stopped, stepped back from her and narrowed his eyes. "You put Max in your movie just to get to me."

"You thought it was because I have a thing for fat, disgusting Nazis?"

"Oh. So tell me. Which one of us have you hated fucking least?"

She slapped him so hard that he staggered.

A green-coated uniformed cop strolling the boulevard's opposite sidewalk stopped and peered at them through the lime trees.

Peggy pulled Robby tight against her and whispered in his ear, "Smile and wave or we may both wind up dead."

They both turned toward the cop, smiled and waved.

He smiled back as he touched his baton to his flat-topped helmet's brim, saluting two quarreling lovers who had made up. Then he walked on.

They walked on too and Robby said, "You exaggerated, right? If they catch Germans spying that's treason and they kill them. But if you get caught spying they just revoke your visa and ship you home."

Peggy shook her head. "If I were a spy working out of the U.S. Embassy, yes. But I don't operate under an official cover. The Nazis hang my kind of spies' bodies from piano wires after they torture us." Peggy tugged up her coat collar. "It's chilly. Do you want to stop for schnapps?"

"Jesus!" Robby paused alongside a bench and leaned against its back, then he sat.

Peggy sat beside him. "What is it?"

"You say it like you've been risking a jaywalking ticket."

"You take risks too."

"I can buy my way out of the trouble I risk."

"Which is why I didn't tell you before. If they caught me you couldn't confess to what you didn't know. Robby, you can't buy your way out of the kind of trouble I'm asking you to get into. You can still walk away from it."

"That would mean walking away from you. I'd sooner hang."

"Are you sure you understand?"

"I'm beginning to. All these trips you've been taking?

To godforsaken corners of the Reich like Jáchymov in the Sudetenland and Peenemünde on the Baltic? Any filming of heroic Nazis you did was incidental to recruiting the defectors who you need me to fly out."

"For a dumb saloon keeper you catch on quick."

"Not entirely. Why do they do it? Switch sides I mean."

Peggy shrugged. "Figuring out why is the key to recruiting defectors. For some people it's money. For some people it's ego. With men that usually means they follow their dicks. For women it may mean following someone they love. For other people it's because their country did them, or someone they love, wrong. Or they just think their country is wrong. There are as many reasons to defect as there are defectors."

Robby said, "There also have to be as many ways to get defectors out as there are defectors. The people I've flown out had no other options. But America must know about hundreds of holes in the Iron Curtain. You could slip a person out here, another there. So why me?"

Peggy said, "These people all have to leave at the same time. They're all part of something so important to the Reich, to the world, that as soon as the Nazis notice the first one missing the curtain will lock down tighter. The hunt will be on for others like them. Anyone we leave behind will die.

"We considered a complex extraction. Four times in other situations we've tried training up an aircrew to fly in, then fly just one single asset out. We've lost four crews, four planes, and four assets. Infiltrating a sub into Reich territorial waters for a pickup risks not just the sub and crew and the mission but an international incident." Peggy shook her head. "'Complex' is just shorthand for 'fuckup waiting to happen.' But you, my darling, deliver as reliably as the U.S. Mail."

"What could possibly be that important?"

She stood and pointed toward a bar down the block. "Schnapps?"

Robby smiled. "Ah. If you told me you'd have to kill me?"

"If I told you, and you got caught, the Nazis would kill you. But you'd talk first so they'd kill lots of other people too. Part of my job is minimizing death sentences."

He took her arm again and they walked. "You said you were an analyst before. How did they talk you into this death sentence of a job?"

"It isn't. And they didn't. I begged them for this job."

Robby's mouth hung open. "For God's sake, why?"

They had reached the bar and she stopped in the twilight and looked into his eyes. "I could tell you it's because I'm a patriot. I could tell you it's because I wanted to prove I was good enough. And because I wanted to work with maybe the greatest female film-maker in history. Every one of those reasons is true. And those are the reasons I presented that persuaded my bosses to let me try.

"But cards on the table? The reason is because I fell in love with the man in that file the day I read it. Not so much the picture, but the man who gave up a comfortable life to fight for what he thought was right. The man who was willing to sacrifice his own life for a friend's. The man who risked everything for people he had never met, over and over."

Robby swallowed. "Oh."

"One more thing. Max never touched me."

Robby rolled his eyes. "Come on. I know the man."

She shrugged. "Okay. He grabbed my ass. Once. I kneed his nuts so hard he cried. After that we understood each other." She flicked her eyes to the bar's door. "Do you and I understand each other well enough now to get that schnapps?"

Robby opened the door and held it for her. "After today I understand so much I'm gonna need them to leave the whole bottle."

Two weeks after Robby and Peggy had strolled the Unter den Linden Robby parked alongside Aces Airpark's hangar at midnight. He switched off his Mercedes' headlights, then climbed out. The new moon plus low, wind driven clouds deepened the darkness. That was perfect. Less perfect was the distant lightning in the west. A pilot didn't need a barometer to feel the approaching storm in the air.

He pulled down the car's gull-wing door, locked it, then ran his fingers over the coupe's low silver roof one last time. There were things the Germans did better than anyone—cars, beer, strudel—that he would miss. But there were things back home that he had been missing for so long. Mostly they were trivial, like talking baseball with someone who knew a nickel curve ball from a nickel.

The only thing he truly looked forward to was waking up next to Peggy in a place where he knew that the next morning she would still be there safe and sound.

He pocketed the Merc's keys. He would leave them in the hangar office's desk drawer. He had already left on his desk at Aces a sealed envelope stuffed with ownership documents for the car, the Mosquito, the real estate, and a power of attorney that would allow Thomas to run the club and the airpark, or sell everything and distribute the proceeds among Robby's employees. Thomas would discover the envelope when he opened up tomorrow at noon. Either way Robby's employees would be able to truthfully say they knew nothing about what their boss had been up to. He was sure he had forgotten nothing. He had better not have forgotten, because tonight's flight was one-way only.

He rounded the hangar's corner and entered the dim-lit space through the open main door. The old black Junkers was parked, angled down on its tail wheel with its three props up, in the hangar's center. The plane's fuselage entry door behind its low wing was open and its entry stairs were unfolded. The airpark fuel wagon stood alongside.

At the hangar's rear very ordinary-looking couples, children, and single men stood or sat on hand luggage and crates. Robby counted the expected seventeen heads.

Peggy stood apart from them and he smiled. He hadn't seen her for the last ten days while she traveled the Reich herding her defectors on their journey like seventeen cats.

Their journey's next leg was Robby's responsibility.

With seventeen passengers, plus baggage and document cartons already loaded, and with Peggy occupying the co-pilot's seat, Robby would fly the Junkers north. He would dodge around, or stay low enough to fly under, the ground control and coastal radars, the coastal flak batteries, and the patrol planes between Berlin and the Baltic. He knew them all well.

The isolated beach on Sweden's southwest coast was a firm, familiar friend he also knew well. He had rendezvoused there often with boats bringing him contraband or ferrying his passengers away on their journeys' next legs. Neutral Sweden's coastal authorities were sympathetic, lazy, bribable, or all three, unlike the Reich's coastal defenders.

He had performed the drill so often that it had become dull.

But tonight he would land with the luxury of marking flares set out by a shore party from an American submarine. They would off-load both passengers and cargo then ferry them to the sub aboard inflatable boats. Robby wouldn't turn the Junkers around on the beach as usual, take off into the wind, and return to Germany. He and Peggy would join her defectors aboard the sub while the shore party reduced the Junkers to unrecognizable scrap. All concerned would appear to simply have vanished not just from the Reich but from the face of the earth.

Robby ached to run to Peggy, scoop her in his arms, and twirl her in celebration. He was almost home. They were almost home.

But there were old pilots and there were bold pilots, however there were no old, bold pilots. He walked to the Junkers, then lifted the clipboard that his ground crew had hung on the Junkers' door handle before they had gone off the clock. He read the checklist as he walked around his aircraft kicking tires and waggling control surfaces.

He had climbed down from the port wing after checking the port tanks' fuel level. When he turned he found Peggy standing there.

He smiled, held up the clipboard, and ducked beneath the plane's belly to check the starboard tanks. "One second, babe. We need to get a move on 'cause a storm's coming. Just this one last thing to check before we load the cattle. We need enough fuel to make Sweden. But not so much that we're heavy on landing and sink in the sand." He paused, wrinkled his forehead, then turned and looked her up and down. She wore a business suit with heels.

He said, "Babe, the suit? We talked about this." He rapped the Junkers' old aluminum skin. "This ain't no Pan Am Champagne Clipper and we're not landing at LaGuardia. You're gonna cross a beach in the dark and wade through surf and fall into a wet rubber boat. That outfit will be a goner."

He realized her hands were clutched together and they trembled.

She said, "Don't worry about the weight. The plane's going to be fifty-one kilos lighter."

He smiled. "*You* weigh fifty-one—"

Her eyes glistened with tears. "Robby, I'm not going."

"Jesus. Babe, I'm sorry I fussed. I don't care if you wear a hoopskirt."

"I'm remaining in place in my position at the Ministry."

He realized that her face was ash gray.

"No." He shook his head. "No! I don't know what the hell you're thinking." He stabbed his finger against the plane. "But if I have to drag you aboard this ship and tie your ass into that co-pilot's seat, I will. So help me God!"

"Don't make this harder. On either of us. I'm staying. You're going."

"Oh? Okay then. If you're staying I'm staying too. How about that?"

Peggy turned and stared at the passengers. One couple's child began crying. His mother lifted him and walked back and forth rocking him against her shoulder.

Peggy pointed at the defectors. "Robby, these people have burned their bridges. Tomorrow morning across the Reich the Nazis will realize that. If you stay these people stay. If they stay they die. You've burned your bridges too. You can't stay here either."

"Shit!" Robby punched the Junkers' fuselage. "Shit!" He punched over and over until his knuckles bled. "What the hell happened?"

"While you and I were apart I learned something new. Something that changed the game. I reported it and just decrypted a response this afternoon to a request for instructions that I submitted three days ago."

Robby said, "Some tool sitting on his fat ass in Washington has hung you out to dry over here?"

"I'm the fool. Washington said extraction is my call."

"Why? Why stay? If you're determined to commit suicide at least tell me why!"

Peggy shook her head. "Staying's not suicide for me. My tracks are pretty well covered. Yes, my risk going forward will be higher. But the stakes have gotten higher too."

She tugged a handkerchief from her jacket pocket, then took his hand and dabbed the blood from his knuckles. She kissed them as she led him to the Junkers' boarding stairs then sat him on their bottom step. "The truth is a long story. It won't ease your pain or mine. But it may help you understand."

She knelt in front of him, took his hand in hers again, and looked into his eyes. "A year and a half ago a rookie intelligence analyst—me—turned up clues that the Nazis might be working on a bomb. It's a new idea. Breaking the bonds that hold atoms together."

Robby said, "The idea's not new. I minored in physics. Physicists all over the world have been theorizing about atomic fission everything—bombs, electric power stations, submarines—since Chadwick discovered the neutron in 1932. The Eurasian war heated up the discussions and the lab work. If the war had gone on longer, or if the U.S. had come in, the theorizing might have amounted to something. But the risks and the expense have kept the concept just talk ever since."

"Robby, it's not just talk anymore. The Nazis have been funding a project in labs and factories all around the Reich for a couple of years now. They're so far ahead, and the project's so massive, that these defectors from those facilities are the only chance America has to catch up."

"Maybe catching up's not a great idea. They say that a town too small to support one lawyer can always support two, because then they fight. Besides since Hitler won his empire he's spent his time building tacky museums and overdone cities. He's been taking the longest victory lap in history. He's pushing seventy. Germany's not looking for a fight."

"Robby, Hitler's dead."

"Those are rumors."

"I watched him die."

Robby's jaw dropped. "You—?"

"No. I'm not that kind of spy. But what I just found out is that the new leadership is preparing for a fight."

A lightning flash lit the hangar's interior and distant thunder followed.

Peggy stood and pulled Robby to his feet and they stepped away from the Junkers' boarding stairs.

She said, "Well?"

He didn't speak, just turned to his passengers and waved them to board. They gathered their baggage and crossed the hangar toward the future.

As they boarded Peggy took his hands again. "Robby, you were right. A storm is coming. A storm that will make the one you fought through seventeen years ago feel like spring rain. But this time America can't just watch. Neither can you and neither can I. Even if we have to fight this storm with an ocean between us."

She kissed him as the last passenger boarded.

Beneath the cloud ceiling Robby banked the Junkers.

Lightning lit the cockpit and thunder cracked an instant later. Turbulence jolted the plane and already raindrops rattled off the windscreen like bird shot. He would get his passengers to Sweden, and eventually to America, the worse for wear. But he would get them there.

He roared over the airfield one last time. In the light that spilled from the hangar she stood, face upturned toward him, small and alone in the rain.

He swallowed the lump in his throat and said aloud, "See you when the sun shines again, babe."

Ahead he saw only darkness.

Faint Hearts

Griffin Barber and Kacey Ezell

CHAPTER ONE

The noise of the crowd and the band reverberated after the relative quiet of the soundproofed office, making me wish, again, for my long-gone angel. If I'd still had the bio-integrated military-issue AI enhancing my capabilities, it could have used my modifications to mute—or at least edit—all that incessant thumping and grinding the band tried to pass off as "music."

Tongi had hired the band from out beyond the rift, and they seemed bent on slamming through their set as fast as possible. He'd said they were under contract for two shows a night, but the way they were playing left me certain there were no other stipulations in their contract about the quality of each show. I wondered for a second if they might not catch a beating for it. The big Omik club owner was rumored to have some less than savory partners, but he was hiring bouncers as well as bands, the work didn't require a functional angel, and I didn't have a lot of options. All in all, I found it best to shut up, show up, and mind my own business.

Maybe these guys were just a shitty band. A Curtain of Stars wasn't exactly the kind of high-end joint that attracted the best talent. Even if that kind of talent were available out here on the edge of the abyss, which it wasn't.

"Muck," Tongi said, the eyes that ringed his mouth beginning an asynchronous blink that always made me uneasy.

"Yes, Tongi?" I had to shout to be heard.

"I have a special assignment for you this evening, special guests that are coming tonight. A Vmog Emerita. Make certain the VIP section remains clear of any unwanted persons."

"Will do," I said.

"I am placing a great deal of trust in you, Muck. Please do not show me that it is misplaced."

"Understood, Tongi."

"I'll let you know when they arrive."

Recognizing a dismissal when I heard it, I wandered down to the main floor of the club.

It being too early for the usual clientele, the majority of people in the club were either hardcore fans or friends of the band, or maybe both. I busied myself keeping the act separate from the fans, even helping out with the eighty-sixing of a couple of mopes who believed the band was there to be pawed.

As the band finished its first set and the club grew more crowded, Tongi emerged from backstage and cornered me with his bulk. "My guest should be arriving in the next hour or so. Clear the VIP room and balcony. Tell anyone who asks that it's a private party. Once that is done, you will cover the stair whilst Amandra handles things in the VIP room proper."

"Will do," I said, edging away. I'm not considered small by human standards, and I didn't mass less than Tongi, but I experienced a gut-level aversion to being crowded by the big alien. Maybe it was the single, snaillike "foot" the Omik get around on, maybe it was the eyes or the lack of bilateral symmetry. Then again, it could have just been that I didn't want anyone that close to me. Regardless of what I thought of his management style, I needed the work. There weren't a lot of opportunities at Last Stop, especially if you have a dishonorable discharge hanging over your head.

Tongi didn't say anything else, just blinked at me in that creepy, dizzying way of his. I wonder if he knew it bugged me. Probably. He seemed to do it a lot. But since all he did was blink, I slid past him and joined the growing crowd on the main dance floor.

The music pounded through the floor and thumped up into my chest. Curtain smelled like every nightclub I've ever been in: a mix of spilled alcohol, regurgitated bile, and astringent floor cleaner. Depending on the species ratios in attendance, I'd occasionally get a whiff of various body odors, too. The ventilation wasn't great, and a dancing crowd was usually—depending on their metabolism—a sweaty one.

It was still pretty early, but the place was starting to fill up. I pushed past more than a few gyrating bodies on my way to the VIP room. I usually got one of two reactions when I did this: one, they ignored me and remained lost in that weird dance- and music-induced high—although, to be fair, there may have been other types of "high" going on as well—or, two, they turned to me with an offended growl or glare that vanished as soon as they saw the Curtain Security shirt stretched over my chest and shoulders.

Like I said, I'm not a small guy. I may not have had an angel to make me stronger than any unmodified human had a right to be any more, but I put in the work to make the best of what I still had. Even without the use of my biomods, I had a lot of muscle mass and a mug even the most charitable had to call "mean."

So it surprised me more than it should have when one particular dancer reacted in a totally different manner. He noticed me but didn't shy away. Instead, he reached out with feathered arms and gripped my shoulders with surprising strength. He was Vmog, and they'd evolved on a planet with less than Last Stop's Earthlike one G. The species fit a Terran's ideas of the "birdlike" stereotype, with long, spindly limbs and a prominent, beaklike mouth.

"Kiss me," he said, his tone insistent. "I'll pay you well."

"Ain't my type, ain't my hustle, sir," I said, grabbing his left wrist and twisting out of his grasping, taloned fingers. At least he hadn't punctured my skin, or worse, the shirt. Skin grew back. I only had the one shirt, and Tongi wasn't going to front me the credit for another.

"Please," the Vmog said, his tone high and lilting, cutting through the band's pretensions to artistry, which seemed to be based on drums, hi-hat, and little else.

"Sorry, sir, I'm on the clock. Have a good time," I said, pushing past the other dancers that crowded close and continuing my slow journey through the crowd.

As I got to the edge of the dance floor and started up the stairs toward the VIP room, something pulled my gut out of shape, some instinct for trouble. If I'd still had an angel, I'd know why the hairs on the back of my neck stood at attention. Yet another thing I missed. It sucks, relying on "gut feelings" and human-level attention to detail.

But instinct was all I had. So, after taking two steps up, I turned back and scanned the crowd in search of what had my dander up. I kept my face blank and professional—just another bouncer working the club.

The crowd continued to grow as more and more patrons packed the Curtain to see—it couldn't be to listen to—the shitty band. Even then, I couldn't understand it. Maybe if piercings in odd places and a propensity for licking the mic was your thing, they might entertain for a moment. There was no accounting for taste.

I didn't see the Vmog, or anything amiss after a good, lengthy look, so I let the feeling go, turned, and continued climbing up the stairs to the club's VIP section.

The collection of velvet and leather seats were still clear; most of the night's patrons preferred thrashing out their fandom on the dance floor.

Tongi appeared, I think mostly to check that I was where I was supposed to be, but also to drop off some premium Blovic liquorfruit for the VIP bar.

"Not for you, Muck," Tongi admonished as he slid back into the elevator that went from the main floor to the VIP area and on up to his office.

"Of course not." I'd tried the stuff before, and it got the job done, but that was the best I could say about it. Even if I were inclined to steal a taste, something in the way it metabolized made my breath stink like burnt rubber, a dead giveaway—and turnoff—for most people.

Just to be sure I couldn't be accused of hanging out rather than doing my job, I went down to the landing and assumed the position and stance human bouncers have perfected over millennia. It sometimes amuses me to think of myself as some Roman standing outside the baths, hairy arms crossed, glowering at plebs.

I was in position when the Vmog Emerita and her entourage drifted upstairs in a swirl of silks, clacking chatter, and flashing jewels. An hour passed, better music blasting from the sound system while the live band was between sets.

Shortly after the band resumed torturing eardrums, a flurry of motion from the dance floor caught my eye. Two—no, three—combatants whaling on each other, their clumsy combat causing a stir on the dance floor.

I glanced at my fellows guarding the stage, saw a large group of screaming fans had rushed it in a concerted attempt to get next to the singer. No bodies would be forthcoming from there.

I keyed my comm. "Fight on the floor. Three fighting on the floor."

Crickets.

"Fight on the floor," I repeated just as two of the combatants brought the third down and started putting the boots to them.

"Fight on the floor! They got o—"

"Deal with it yourself!" Kranz yelled over the comm. I looked back at the stage, saw the lead bouncer wrestling with an Ulgarin.

"Fuck it," I said, rushing down the stairs and onto

the dance floor. The floor was an exercise in aggravation. Without an angel watching out for me, I couldn't avoid running into people, and without my mods, my body wasn't up to automatically compensating for each impact without slowing my progress to a crawl. I gritted my teeth, turned sideways, and shoved or dragged people out of the way with every half-step forward.

A long few seconds later I broke through the ring of people around the fight. The Vmog that had propositioned me earlier was kicking the shit out—literally, from the smell—of a human on the ground.

"Enough!" I bellowed, straight-arming the upright human in the face and wrapping the Vmog up from behind with my free arm.

The human stumbled back and fell on his ass as the crowd scrambled and pushed to get away from the fight in their midst.

The Vmog grunt-clacked and dropped surprisingly strong hands to my wrist, trying to free himself. I felt skin tear under the claws. I guess I shouldn't have been surprised at the strength in his upper chest and hands. I'd read up on the Vmog. They'd evolved from soaring omnivores, where grip strength and chest power contributed a great deal to survival.

"Asshole," I grunted. Blood dripping from the wounds, I refused to let go as I snaked my other hand up under his beaklike mouth to the tiny wattle of flesh there. Seizing it, I pinched, hard. Something ground together inside before my opponent's flinch yanked the fleshy bits of my hand. It was the last resistance I had from that quarter. The Vmog went limp, a dribble of orangish foam appearing at the corners of his lipless mouth.

The one I'd knocked over was already scrambling away, bouncing off dancers and clubbers as he fled.

"Fushing shish," the—spacer, from her jumpsuit—said from the ground. She spat some teeth and more blood on the dance floor.

"You all right?" I asked, shifting the Vmog to one hip so I could look her in the eyes. The Vmog was heavy, even when he wasn't trying to rip my skin to shreds. It was a bit alarming until I felt his chest rising and falling against my arm.

"Fushing shish," the spacer repeated. Pupils tight as pinpricks. At least the pins were equally slow to respond to the constant changes in lighting, so probably drugs rather than a concussion.

I tapped my mic. "Injured human patron on the floor. Am removing one from the club."

"Stand by," Magi said. "Calling for medical services. Do we need to call Station Security?"

"No," Tongi said curtly. "Just remove the combatants from my club, Muck. By the side door, if you please."

I thought about that a moment.

The wattle-pinch I'd used was supposed to wear off after about five minutes. Once that happened, the fellow had already proved he could handle himself. If the drugged-up spacer wanted to press charges, she could ask the club to furnish recordings and I would gladly give her a statement about what I'd seen.

"Some help up here!" Kranz bellowed over the comm. Another group of fans surged up on stage, diving into the crowd.

Seeing no profit to anyone in arguing with the boss and hearing the growing concern in my co-worker's voice, I made my way to the side door and left the

Vmog in the piss-soaked alley, propped up against the wall.

Fuck if I wasn't made to regret the shit out of taking the path of least resistance.

CHAPTER TWO

The night dragged on without another dust up. By the time I finished helping Kranz get the stage cleared, the drugged up spacer had disappeared. I figured Tongi would be happy enough with that, since he'd ordered her removed, and headed back up to my post outside the VIP section just as the terrible band was wrapping up their final set.

The lead singer had just announced "Last Call" when Tongi's voice shuddered in my earpiece.

"Ralston Muck. My office. Now!"

Shit. No one had used my full name like that since I'd left home at fifteen. What else could go wrong tonight?

The crowd near the bar thickened as all of the sweat-soaked dancers and revelers fought for their last fix of the night. I sighed and headed back down to the floor to push my way through. A dozen curt "excuse me"s and one memorable patron valiantly attempting to grab my crotch later, I swam out of the press of bodies and stepped into the staff elevator.

After a short ride, the door slid open before I could touch it.

"Get in here!" Tongi said, grabbing me by my shirt and dragging me into his office.

I stumbled forward, wrenching my shirt from the

grip of his most powerful tentacle. I straightened and opened my mouth to protest, but the words died unspoken when I saw the being sitting behind his desk.

The Vmog Emerita was tall, lean. I'd seen her earlier, of course, but not up close. Her features were alien, soft proto-feathers giving her skin a blurred, almost fuzzy look, and her strong, slightly hooked beak prominent in the facial area. All in all, her beauty was undeniable, even to those not of her species. She felt me looking, and met my gaze. The weight of her despair hit me square in the gut right before Tongi *actually* hit me square in the gut.

I doubled over, coughing.

"Muck, you idiot, do you have any idea what you've done?"

"No," I wheezed. I wasn't being a smart-ass, either. It was the truth. I hadn't the faintest.

"Tongi, please," the Emerita said. Her voice was soft and lilting, like a deep baritone version of the recordings of Earth birds the Vmog resembled. "It is not the fault of your employee. My darling is a restless creature . . . restless and reckless and I worry—" She broke off, ducking her head and lifting one winged arm to hide her face.

"The Vmog you beat up?" Tongi continued in murderous tones. "He is one of the Emerita's consorts, and now he's gone missing!"

"I did *not* beat him up!" I felt an angry flush paint my skin as I stared up at him. Without an angel, I could neither hide nor control my physiological response to anger, and I felt the lack more fiercely in that moment than I had in a long time. "*You* told me to remove him from the club!"

"Yeah, well, no one has seen him since! You're lucky the Emerita is so gracious, or I'd—"

"Enough, Citizen Tongi."

The voice that spoke didn't belong to anyone I recognized. I blinked, turned and saw two humans had been flanking the door Tongi'd yanked me through. I shouldn't have missed them, even without an angel to process peripheral information for me.

One more failure in a string of them.

"Station Security Officer Keyode," the man who had interrupted Tongi said by way of introduction. He was small and dark, with hair cut close to his scalp. He pointed to the other side of the door and the tall, muscular blond man with a cruel twist to his mouth standing there. "This is my partner, Officer Dengler. Muck, is it? Why don't you tell us what happened?"

"Station Security is here already?" I asked. Then I got wise and shut the hell up. I did not like the look of the blond guy. And they might be here to close up a case they had instigated by burying me with it.

"I called them," the Emerita said, her voice wrenching. "Something is wrong. Dzavo is a free wing and a wild one, but he always tells me his plans. Something has happened to him."

"Can you tell us about your altercation with Consort Dzavo, citizen Muck?" Keyode asked, and while his expression was patient, his tone hinted he wouldn't be for long.

"Not much of an altercation," I said, hiding my wrists. "There was a fight on the floor. I was stationed at the VIP entrance, but the other staff were busy and unable to respond. So I did. The Emerita's consort was in the midst of kicking the spit out of a drugged-up spacer, so I pulled him off of her."

"Then what did you do?" Keyode asked.

I cut my gaze to Tongi. He blinked at me with all of his eyes while his mouth hole opened and closed. I pretended not to understand the message he was desperately trying to convey.

"I called it in, and Tongi told me to just get them both out of the club."

"No! I would never tell you to—" Tongi reared back on his foot, thick voice rising.

"We already checked the transmissions, big boy," Dengler said, speaking for the first time. He stepped up next to his partner and smiled widely at my boss. I immediately knew him for a dick. One of those guys who got his kicks bullying people. "Your man here"—his gaze flicked to me—"what's your name, again? Dirt?"

"Muck. Ralston Muck."

"Right. Muck here may be dumb and ugly, but he ain't lying."

"What happened to the spacer, Muck?" Keyode said.

"I couldn't physically hold them both, so I took him out the side door and went back for her. She was gone when I returned."

"But I would never, had I known! Muck didn't tell me—" Tongi spluttered.

"Tongi."

It was the Emerita. She rose to her full height and swept her wings back. Her eyes burned. It didn't take a xenologist to recognize the anger and the fear behind them as she looked at him, then my way.

"I hold you responsible," she said, enunciating each word as if it were a death sentence. Her wings spread slightly with each subsequent sentence: "Find my Dzavo. Find him quickly. Find him unharmed and I will not seek reparation from you. Is my full meaning clear?" She had fully mantled her wings by the time she was done speaking, the threat posture nearly doubling her apparent size.

"Emerita " Dengler began, holding up both hands in an effort to calm her.

If she were descended from primates, it might have worked better. As she was not, she cocked her head to turn her hot gaze on him.

He fell silent.

I half-snorted, visions of a raptor eyeing a snail dancing though my head.

"Gentlemen," she said, ignoring me. "I will return to my ship. I trust you will be quick and most of all, thorough, with your search. I will most certainly learn of it if you are not."

I nodded, thinking there must have been something about spreading her wings that worked on her chest cavity, making each word pound home like a dire threat. She carefully shrugged them back into place, had to in order to make her exit.

"Emerita," Keyode said as she passed. Even his dick partner inclined his head in respect as she brushed by us all and headed out into the elevator.

Keyode let out a sigh and turned back to me. "We're going to need a description of that female from the fight," he said. "And copies of all security recordings," he added, looking at Tongi. My boss grunted his assent.

"And don't leave Last Stop without letting us know, hey, Dirt?" Dengler said, giving me another shitty grin.

"Sure," I said, because I knew my part in his little play. So much for minding my own business.

I gave them what I had. It wasn't much, I knew. Keyode did a good job drawing out the little details. He was a fair hand at interrogation. I knew because I'd practiced the skill myself, during the War.

Before my discharge. Before my angel was taken.

"We'll be in touch," Keyode said when I'd spilled what I knew. He nodded at his partner and left.

Dengler wasn't so professional: he winked—actually fucking winked at me—before pushing out the door.

To be frank, I almost wished they would stay a while longer. I needed the job, and leaving Tongi hanging out to dry by his one foot was not likely to win the big Omik's endorsement for employee of the month.

Here we go, I thought, readying myself for a firing or a beating. Honestly, I thought it could go either way at that point.

"I ought to kill you," Tongi said, his voice weirdly thin. It was the first time I'd heard him in a murderous rage.

"You're welcome to try." In my anger, I fucking meant it, too. Don't get me wrong, I wasn't suicidal, but it wasn't like I had much going and I've always had my fair share of anger issues.

"But I cannot," Tongi said, eyes going wide with a sharp intake of air through his mouth, the Omik equivalent of a sigh. "I need you to find the Emerita's consort."

I gestured at the door Keyode and Dickler had left by. "What about Security?"

Tongi made a rattling noise with his mouth hole I figured for a filthy slur in Omik parlance. "Security? Are you serious? They're bought and paid for on every Administration Station from here to your dead Earth. Why would things be any different? And don't you dare ask by whom. That's the problem specific to Last Stop: *everyone* is in someone else's pocket. Except for you. You're too dumb to be connected, too desperate to be seen as a threat, and too angry to run. Yes, you'll do nicely. Find the Emerita's consort for us. I won't fire you and she won't have us both gutted and hung out for her young."

"She didn't look like a killer to me," I said, remembering the sadness in those beautiful eyes. I didn't mean that she couldn't, but rather that she didn't seem callous enough to resort to violence simply to get her way. Then again, that could make her more dangerous, instead of less.

Tongi let out a huff, then another, then he sucked in enough air to fill his spinal sac and let it out all at once in the Omik equivalent of laughter.

"You *are* an idiot," he said. "Don't you know who she is?"

I shook my head in the negative.

"That's Emerita Bellasanee. Look her up. She may be the deadliest being alive."

CHAPTER THREE

One of the few benefits of working nights is I typically don't have to get up early. Typically. Tongi'd made it very clear time was of the essence in finding the Emerita's lost boy, so there I was, groggy and out of sorts, but vertical and waiting outside my shitty digs for a ride.

My PID pinged just as the spherical autocab glided up to a stop beside me. I opened the door and tried not to inhale too deeply as I half fell onto the cracked polymer of the seat inside. Someone had puked in the cab recently, and the autocleaner hadn't been particularly thorough.

"Yeah?" I rasped at my PID as Tongi's face appeared above the display.

"Where are you? Why aren't you at the docks yet? The Emerita is expecting you! I had to do a lot of fast-talking to get you an appointment with her. You had better not be late, Muck, or—"

"The cab just arrived, I've got an hour, yet," I said. "And I live near the docks, so quit freaking out. You're making my head hurt."

"You live near the docks?" Tongi asked, his mouth hole twisting in distaste while his eyes blinked asynchronously, a nauseating display. "I wouldn't house a sick venoril there! Why would you—"

"You don't pay me enough," I said. "Did you call for a reason? Or just to give me shit about my apartment?"

"If you live dockside, you've got plenty of shit. You don't need more from me," Tongi shot back. I had to admit, it was almost funny.

Also, sadly, very true.

"I just wanted to be certain you were awake and would not be late," Tongi said. I hadn't worked for him long, and I didn't know Omik tells very well, but my gut said the rising pitch of his voice meant he was really fucking scared. I took a deep breath and held my tongue.

"Well, I'll be on my way as soon as we disconnect and I give the cab my destination."

"Fine. Don't mess this up, Muck." Tongi cut the call.

I stared at the empty display for a moment and shook my head.

"You can indicate your destination aloud." The tinny, electronic voice came from the cab's speakers overhead. "This vehicle will understand."

"Right." I sighed. "Dock Six B. Quickest route, please."

"Of course. Please remain in your seat at all times. Do not disengage the restraints." I sat back, let the harness enfold me, and thought about what I knew. It wasn't much.

First, the missing Vmog. He was young, by their standards, but old enough to be a consort to one of their Emeritas. Vmog didn't pair off into couple-bonds like humans tended to do. They were a race of artisans, and must focused all of their efforts on becoming the very best in the known universe at whatever particular craft or skill their parents—and there were a lot of parents for each child—trained them to. When and if a particular Vmog artisan reached the pinnacle of their chosen field, they produced a masterpiece. Once that masterpiece had been recognized or released, they assumed the title of Emeritus or Emerita, and lived out the rest of their lives being treated with near godlike reverence by the rest of their very talented race. God-like reverence that included incredible wealth, harems, and an enormous amount of clout even beyond their field. I had a hard time imagining the relationship dynamics of harem life, especially for those who did not reach the rank of Emerita. Different strokes for different species, apparently.

So, young party Vmog boy, out for a good time, gets

into a fight at the club. Why? And with whom? I had the druggie spacer chick's description pretty set in my mind after passing it to Security. I wondered if they'd found anything useful on Tongi's security feeds. Not that they would share anything with me, but I knew he had backups. I hesitated to send Tongi a request to have them forwarded to my PID, fearing he'd use the request as a reason to pester me further. I sent it anyway.

It just didn't figure. The spacer, if she was truly part of some kind of criminal conspiracy, surely hadn't carried herself like a boss, and had no entourage to prevent me ejecting her from the club. The timeline seemed too tight for someone to order a hit, too. Unless... Unless it was a planned kidnapping. From what Tongi was saying and my own research the night before confirmed, Bellasanee certainly had the money to make ransom a motive. Throw the spacer at Dzavo, knowing the fight would get both ejected so lie in wait in the alley and out front, then collect their target. A conveniently softened-up target, too.

Well. As theories went, it wasn't terrible. But I needed to know a lot more before I could say for sure. And I would need Bella to let me know if the kidnappers got in touch.

The cab glided to a stop and a chime dinged.

"We have reached your destination. Please authorize payment."

"Charge it to A Curtain of Stars, manager Tongi."

"Please wait while the charge is authorized."

I waited in the restraint system, smirking as I imagined Tongi's irritation. He knew I couldn't afford cabs, so it would absolutely *wound* the skinflint to cough up a single credit.

The Omik approved the expense, though, and quickly. The restraints whipped back into their sockets and the gull-wing-style door lifted into the heavily filtered air of the docks.

"Thanks," I said to the cab as I stepped out. I don't know why I do that shit. Guess it's just how I was raised.

I took a look around. Last Stop's docking areas are extensive. Starships, shuttle terminals, and the vast orbital elevator landings for cargo limited the view. Most stretches of the docks were noisy and crowded, and never failed to give me a headache.

But this section was different. No crowds. People moved here and there, sure, but not a single long queue of passengers or cargo handlers. It was almost pleasant without the press of people. I sniffed. Despite the better maintenance schedule on the atmospheric filters at this end, the proper heavy-metals-and-desperation stink of Last Stop Station's docks still lingered in the air. I thought the smell and the general absence of people fitting for the last, lonely haven of ships crossing the Abyssal Gap.

CHAPTER FOUR

The yacht was luxe all the way. Air filters whispered in my wake, as if my very presence sullied the air. The Emerita was a gracious hostess, inviting me to sit and plying me with refreshments before we got down to business. I refused with what I hoped was polite professionalism. I must have succeeded to a degree because the angry raptor of the night before was replaced with a cooler, more calculating Bellasanee. She confirmed that Tongi had arranged my visit, and the underlying reason—Station Security's likely corruption—for it.

I eventually got round to asking a few questions: "Was a ransom note delivered?"

"No, not yet."

"Not yet?"

"I hope such a request arrives. As proof he's alive, if nothing else."

Knowing better, I didn't contradict her. "Did he have any rivals for your affection?"

She twitched her wings, the hard edges of her mouth softening in an alien smile. "We are not human, to feel that kind of jealousy. My love is shared equally among my consorts, their adoration of me is equally individual and shared between them as peers."

I decided not to unpack that statement just yet. "Did Dzavo make a habit of using intoxicants to the point his judgment could become impaired?"

"What is this, an attempt to blame the victim?"

I decided then and there she had a far better grasp of human psychology than I did on the Vmog. "I just want to better understand his history, so that I can judge what happened last night."

"Yes," she said, looking away. "He frequently seeks the edge of control. We call such Vmog a 'free wing,' or more disparagingly, 'storm riders.' Regardless of what our wider society calls him, he is mine, and I, his."

"Does his pay allow him to indulge in such pursuits without going into debt?"

"His pay?" She shook her head, an odd point of commonality between humans and Vmog. "Dzavo has what you would call an allowance. And yes, it is sufficient for his needs."

"So he wouldn't owe anyone a large sum? Not even if he was trying to hide it from you?"

Bellasanee rustled her wings again, this time giving off an air of discontent rather than amusement. She moved her beaklike lips one over the other, which caused an odd susurrus.

"He may have," she said, finally. "He would sometimes hide things from me. I was never sure why. Perhaps it added to the excitement of his so-called 'forbidden' pastimes. I would never deny him anything, you understand. His restless spirit is part of what I love about him, but occasionally..." She let the thought trail off.

I looked away to give her a moment of privacy.

"Emerita," I said as softly as I could. "I am sorry to cause you pain. But please, if there is *anything* you can tell me about Dzavo's illicit activities, it will help."

She stared into my eyes for a long second, her raptor's pupils contracting as she studied my ugly mug. Then she seemed to decide something, because she gave a little nod and sat forward in her seat.

"There is a robotics shop," she said, pitching her voice low. "It's owned by a Cosrian named Fulu. I'm not supposed to know that Dzavo is a frequent customer."

"I'm guessing it's not because he has an interest in robotics?"

She clicked her lips together and then softened her mouth in a smile again.

"An astute guess, Citizen Muck. Go see Fulu, find out what she was selling Dzavo, and for how much. I will send you the particulars of his accounts, so you

will be able to ascertain whether or not he had some
kind of secret debt."

I got to my feet as my PID pinged, indicating a
large file transfer had begun.

"Thank you, Emerita."

"One more thing, Citizen Muck."

"Yes?" I stopped mid-turn and pivoted back to
face her. She waved a fingered wing tip and a circle
detached from the plush carpet and rose up beside
me. Under the circle, a column of slick, warship-
grade alloy held several pistol-type weapons, most of
them directed energy from what I could tell, but a
few looked like old-school kinetic projectile throw-
ers. Each weapon hung suspended by some invisible
mechanism in a lighted alcove on the column. It was
like a museum display.

Here. On her ship.

She really was rich.

"Two gifts, Rrralston," Bellasanee said, using my
first name for the first time. "Find my love and they
are yours to keep. One, choose a weapon. I fear you
will need it. Two . . ." She trailed off with a pause and
looked at me with that penetrating raptor gaze again.
"Two, I can see the war has left you scarred. Speak
with Fulu. She will have everything necessary."

CHAPTER FIVE

It felt weird, being armed once again. The contents of
the custom-extruded shoulder rig were an unfamiliar
weight. The voidfork wasn't my favorite weapon, not
by a long shot, but it was very lethal, didn't require

a lot of practice or an angel to operate, and had been designed to deceive all but the most advanced detection systems. I tried to put it out of my mind. The last thing I needed was some Security goon to notice my unease and wonder why.

Bella hadn't given any additional details, but my PID indicated the Gosrian's botshop was in the industrial sector of Last Stop, just a short walk from the docks. I hadn't much experience with Gosrians, but everyone knew the plantlike aliens were two things: utter pacifists and extreme capitalists.

I remembered a Gosrian captain I'd busted for dealing drugs from his logistics warehouse during the war, but I'd only been on the arrest team for it. The incident stood out in my memory only because it's hard to put cuffs on a viny creature that can change the thickness and length of its limbs at will. The botshop looked legit, and far less alarming than the biohazard-marked place next to it. The door opened as I approached, revealing a couple of rows of refurbished maintenance and service bots. I walked on, approached a counter that ran the length of the back wall.

A thick profusion of leafy vines shot from a door behind the counter, pulling a thicker, heavier "trunk" into the doorframe. It shook with a sound like heavy rain in a forest.

I smelled cloves and paint thinner. "Citizen Ralston Muck," a translator rig said from behind the counter. "I am Fulu Fourth Runner in the Ninth Season. You may call me Fulu."

"And you can call me Muck," I said, amused.

"I will call you Honored Customer Muck after this day. All has been arranged."

"I . . . see. I am here to ask a few questions regarding—"

Fulu's shiver interrupted me with the smell of salt and cinnamon so astringent it made me cough. "Honored Customer Dzavo Mekli Bellasanee," the translator said, "I know. Upon receiving Patron Emerita Bellasanee's communiqué, I reviewed my connections to Customer Dzavo. I was supplying him with lanklin, a narcotic and aphrodisiac preferred by some Vmog."

"Were?"

"Indeed, Customer Muck. I ran out. He was not pleased with my lack of stock and went to my competitor and received subsequent and substantial quantities of the drug. I learned today that he has fallen deeply in arrears with this competitor." A shiver and the vines contracted visibly. An acrid odor of burning soap. "This news is not good. This competitor is not known for their restraint."

"Who?"

"A human gang calling themselves the Thirteenth Revenant Army."

I had not heard of them, but the name triggered another memory: the drugged-up woman at the club having a tattoo of what looked like some undead human with a stylized 13 printed on her neck.

"Where can I find them?"

An odd scent filled the air. I didn't think it was from the Gosrian. Had the translator alerted on something? The devices were multifunction, capable of running a number of expert systems.

Fulu shivered again, casting scents too complex for me to unravel. "Customer Muck, our time grows short. I will send your PID the gang location I am aware of, but I must insist you come back here with me. I must make good on the service paid for by Patron Bellasanee."

I shook my head, wondering what the hell was going on.

Something crashed against the shop door.

More complex scents. More waving frond/vines. "Please consent to joining me here."

I nodded. "I ag—" Fulu's vines swept out before I could get the words out and yanked me bodily off the floor. Ain't nowhere near as big as I used to be, but no one would say I'm small. Fulu picked me up and pulled me over the counter like a baby.

The door crashed in. I caught a glimpse of three figures in street clothes carrying weapons. One aimed a subgun at me just as Fulu triggered some hidden mechanism that slammed a ceramo-metal shield down from the ceiling along the length of the countertop. With a sound like hypervelocity hailstones on metal, several red-white hotspots appeared. Subgun rounds stopped cold by the shield.

Fulu set me on the ground. "I apologize for touching you so abruptly, Customer Muck."

"Your competitors?" I said.

"The very same, Customer Muck," Fulu said. Her translator-device hadn't so much as risen an octave. She was also not wilting, which surprised me.

"Will this stop them?" I asked, gesturing at the shield. I hadn't seen any large caliber or heavy-energy weapons, but still.

"It will hold until Station Security arrives. Thibodeau is not with those outside."

"Who?"

"The leader of my competitors. You will find him at the address I provided."

"How do I get there?"

"You may depart this location through my compost channels to the lower levels of the station. For now, let me provide you with the order Patron Bellasanee made on your behalf."

"Order?"

"You had your angel-class AI forcibly removed as part of your dishonorable discharge, correct?"

I felt my cheeks burning, muttered a half-civil "Correct."

Fulu ignored my shame. "I have certain drugs that will restore partial functionality to most of your remaining mods." One leafy tendril rose to eye level and uncurled to reveal a portable medichine, complete with full vials of pharma.

My heart leapt, mind leaping right past the "partial" to "restore." I swallowed an addict's eagerness, said carefully, "No good if I can't afford to keep them running."

"I will continue to supply you at reasonable rates after the initial dose."

"You're that sure of prevailing against the competition? I thought you were pacifists?"

"Gosrians are indeed pacifist. There are other competitors than those presently out there. Rest assured, Customer Muck, I am partnered with those who will emerge the victors and with options to expand our market share."

Part of me wanted to walk away. I didn't want to be on the hook with Last Stop Station's underworld. Hooked up with such people, I would find it hard to mind my own business when I saw something else, something I couldn't ignore, going on.

"Do it," I said, desire curb-stomping that small,

cautious part of me into the dust. In the end, my want was greater than my wariness. Just the possibility I would become even a pale reflection of what I once was, of being that much closer to complete, was more than I could refuse.

CHAPTER SIX

With the near-euphoria of partially restored mods zinging through my system, my chest heaved as I fought to bring my breathing under control. Which was unfortunate, since I was crouched between a stinking recycler and a public autodoc. The blue light from atop the autodoc glinted from the recycler's bare metal skin. I leaned forward to look at my reflection.

Eyes wide. Pupils dilating... I was high as fuck. And damn if it didn't feel good. Like I could move in ways I'd almost forgotten. Like I'd had my full strength restored.

Like I was almost whole again.

As promised, the narrow, reeking passageways that housed Fulu's nutrient and compost cycling system had led me to one of the lowest levels of Last Stop Station. I'd climbed out through a maintenance access hatch and found myself on this cramped, neglected street. Neither one of the devices flanking me looked as if they'd been properly maintained in some time. Even though the blue light indicated the autodoc was functional, the scratched and dented exterior gave me doubts about its ability to provide the emergency life support and hospital transport such devices were required to give under Administration law. The air was redolent with the greasy-sweet stench of bioslime coming from a filtration system long overdue for maintenance and the alien critter processing plant across the alley.

Still, the location provided a view of the street and the cross alley bracketing the address Fulu'd supplied. No vehicles passing out front, no lookouts in front or rear, and no obvious surveillance blisters...which didn't really make sense. I was just beginning to wonder if I had the right place when I heard it: a scream, like the cry of a wounded avian, cutting through the oily thickness of the night air.

I held still as every instinct insisted I rush in and do something. Memories of other screams, other times, clattered through my consciousness. I took a deep breath and pushed the fragmented memories of flames licking among corpses—and those that were soon to become corpses—away.

If this was the right place—and that cry certainly made it seem like it—then barreling in there wouldn't help anyone, least of all me. I needed a way in. Too bad Fulu's compost tunnels hadn't extended this far. Then again, I would rather avoid repeating that particular experience anytime soon.

If I couldn't go down...maybe up? I craned my neck and took a good look at the upper floors and roof of the building. Sure enough, no helpful ladders or fire egress routes. There was a botwalk—a catwalk for maintenance bots—up above the recycler. Before the War, I'd have been able to make that jump from the top of the recycler, but now—

Shit.

"Not as good as the real thing," Fulu had said.

But "basic functionality" had to mean *some* increased strength, right? And hadn't I already noticed my energy kicking up on the run over here? Maybe...

Shit. Only one way to find out.

I stood slowly, glancing around to make sure that I wasn't about to be made by anyone who cared, and then launched myself at the upper lip of the recycler unit. Back in the day, my augmented strength would have let me land lightly atop the nearly two-story unit. I was satisfied with the straight leap that let me grab the edge with my fingertips. I adjusted my grip. The metal felt as filthy and slick as it smelled, but my mods responded to the pharma and my demand, furnishing extra strength to my arms and shoulders as needed. I surged up and to my feet, barely grunting with the effort.

I felt a twinge of nostalgia. It had been so long since I felt strong. It felt good.

I just hoped that the clanking sound of my boots as I scrambled to my feet didn't make too much racket.

My balance was improving beyond human norms, too. I didn't wobble once as I turned to look at the blank expanse of wall stretching above. Down here, at the station's docks, the botwalks and maintenance galleries ran above and about the businesses, and other compartmentalized "buildings" tended to be larger and more extensive than those in residential sections. I might have climbed the recycler without my mods, but only by running up part of the wall and making a lot more noise.

Even with Fulu's pharma, I *still* wasn't sure I could make that leap. I was considering finding another way in when a second scream announced I was out of time.

I took a deep breath of the reek, crouched, and leapt.

Pain exploded, searing through my nerve endings as I pushed unaccustomed muscles to, and through, the brink. My mods were suddenly aflame—an uneven burn stuttering along my nerves, like fuel igniters firing out of sequence in an asynchronous cacophony of agony so powerful I closed my eyes for an instant.

I opened them in time to see I had missed the botwalk's guardrail.

I stretched, slapping abused fingers against the lower support, slipped. My other hand scrabbled, caught on the metal undercarriage. I clutched the square spar tight, swung painfully as each edge tried to shred my skin. I hung, suspended, chest heaving as I sucked in air to try and quiet the chaos going on inside my body. The thin, extruded metal of the botwalk creaked alarmingly under my weight.

I tried to ignore the pain as I pulled my abused body up and crawled onto the botwalk proper. Fresh appreciation for the industrial noises of the district flooded my nerves as I lay still for a heartbeat and simply panted. Then I rolled over and crawled cautiously along the swaying botwalk toward the wall and the passage where the bots passed through the bulkhead into the building.

I cracked my dome on the edge of the passage as I bent to enter it. Warm, salty blood started to run into the corner of my mouth. It, combined with the scents, tight confines and heat of the enclosed space, made my stomach flip with nauseated glee. At least, I hoped it was the environment and not some side effect of the pharma.

Below me, the warehouse stretched like a dollhouse with the roof removed. Thin walls of metal sheeting divided the space into a series of small rooms on the near end, but the rest of the vast interior yawned, a singularly open, dark space.

Rather, an open, dark space with a cavity of light in the far corner. I couldn't see the source, but the glow lit up the outlines of several interstellar shipping crates stacked in long-term storage cradles and arranged to create a chamber hidden from the aisles between containers. It was probably damn near invisible from the warehouse floor.

Only I wasn't on the floor. One thing about humans: we rarely remember to look up, and when we do it's usually a nervous glance or a sarcastic eye roll.

The botwalk branched in a pattern roughly following the interior walls of the warehouse, so I continued crawling, making as little noise as possible. As I got closer, I started to pick up the sounds of harsh, labored breathing—panting, almost. And an almost subliminal whine that made the base of my skull ache.

I couldn't get directly over the space, but I got close. I couldn't see exactly what was going on, but what I did see in the light from those portable industrial lanterns made fear and revulsion war beneath my skin.

A single figure—human, like I thought—stood dressed in an old-school polymer surgeon's apron like I hadn't seen since the War. He faced the wall directly beneath me, where someone had been strapped upright against a storage rack. I couldn't see the victim, but to be honest, that was a good thing, judging by the pained keening that continued to throb in the air between us.

I reached for the Voidfork Bellasanee'd given me and slowly brought it forward. The angle was bad, given my prone position, but I squirmed around as quietly as I could until I could see the shiny wet slickness of that polymer apron through the autosights of the weapon.

The torturer stepped forward and grabbed something off a wheeled cart just to his right. I didn't see what it was, but the keening intensified, and as the figure lifted his hands, I caught the flash and whine of an ill-tuned sonic scalpel in the lantern light.

Good enough. I took a deep breath and squeezed the trigger. The targeting LED flashed briefly, the weapon's only indication that it was, indeed, forcing two rapidly cycling microwave beams on contradictory frequencies into the target.

Well, the only one other than the torturer's torso exploding as his insides became his outsides.

The torturer stumbled backwards, then inward over his exploded stomach. His flailing knocked over the tool cart with a crash. I kept my weapon in my weak hand and with my strong hand grabbed the lower edge of the botwalk and half rolled, half dived over the side. My body burned with the same stuttering, ecstatic agony as the pharma fueled my mods, but I didn't rip my shoulder out of the socket. I hung for just a split second before committing to a mostly controlled fall to the ground.

I landed on the spilled, mingled contents of the cart and torturer, which made me stumble. Good thing, too, because a flicker in the corner of my eye was the only warning I was being attacked. I let myself fall into a full crouch, and the man I hadn't seen

sitting on a stool in the corner swung another sonic
scalpel in a glittering arc that made my teeth ache
in my skull. It would have cut me, too, but seemed
to judder in the man's hand.

I straightened and backed, trying for a shot. I
threw myself aside as he rushed me, nearly losing the
front of my shirt in the process. I fired in his general
direction. The shipping crate to the left of his head
superheated and exploded in a whitish cloud.

"Stop!" I shouted, hoping to distract him.

He wiped the weird visor he wore, leaving red
streaks in the white powder slowly settling over everything. He ignored the blood and focused on me,
growled, "My lucky day! Now I have two friends to
play with."

He lunged again.

I dodged aside, maneuvering for space and time.

"With friends like you," I muttered, edging toward
an opening in the storage racks. Problem was, I couldn't
find one, thanks to the damn powder—flour, it tasted
like—still hanging in the air. But drawing him away
from Dzavo was important, too.

I glanced up at the wall of racks where the torturer
had been working. At first, my brain refused to make
sense of what was in front of me. I caught a shining
white flash of bone in a sea of mangled red meat,
and the red-brown streaks of blood running through
the Vmog's downy coat from hips to ankles.

The whine buzzed at me again, giving me a split-
second warning. This time I didn't duck. I pivoted
on one heel and raised both hands. My right forearm
exploded in pain as the jagged scalpel ripped through
the flesh and started in on the bone below the elbow.

With my left hand, I fired four shots. The first one melted his protective polymer eye shield. The next two made his eyes explode. The fourth made me turn my head away and toss my cookies.

He slumped, boneless, to the floor, the detuned scalpel striking the ground and carving a running gash into the composite before it sputtered to a stop. I hissed through my teeth and took a step back, shaking my arm out.

I brushed against something big, heavy, soft, and cold. I knew what it would be. I didn't want to look, but my boots slipped in the blood and effluvia covering the floor and I had to reach out to steady myself on the nearest object.

I figured out what I was reaching for just as my hands closed around the strong, steellike cables that formed the spines of Vmog flight feathers. Dzavo's mangled wings lay flaccid, stacked atop one another inside an opened shipping crate. They'd been amputated at the shoulder joint of the wing spar, and jagged white bone glistened through the red-brown mass of brutally pulped muscle and tendon.

I swallowed hard and looked away, refusing to think about what I'd found, and what the sight of that mangled flesh and bone meant for Dzavo. Instead, I focused on my own injury, craning my elbow around, trying to see how badly I was cut.

The wound felt Abyssal Gap-deep, but the lingering burn of Fulu's pharma kept my mods working, preserving function in my hand and slowly staunching the flow of blood. I figured I'd be all right eventually. I would have wrapped it if I could've found a clean piece of cloth in that darkened abattoir.

Instead, I turned to look at Dzavo. He still keened in pain, but it was softer than before. Weaker.

"My name is Ralston Muck," I said, for lack of a better idea. "Bellasanee sent me to find you."

Dzavo's body twitched at the sound of her name. His keening tapered to a whimpering stutter. I started walking toward him, sliding my feet along the blood-slick floor.

Gunshots exploded nearby, echoing through the empty space above us. Apparently the shooters from Fulu's had returned, and Security presumably followed.

"Shit," I spat, looking around. "I gotta get you out of here or we're both dead. Just gimme a second..." I broke off as I caught sight of the scalpel resting half-under the cart. My stomach churned, but I bent and picked it up anyway, toggling the switch to bring its infernal hum back to life.

The sound made Dzavo keen once more. He thrashed feebly against his bonds.

"I know!" I said. "I'm sorry, but it's the only thing that will cut you loose fast enough." I pitched my voice to penetrate his fear but he wasn't able to get past the scalpel's noise or the sounds of violent conflict from outside.

He dragged in a deep, sobbing gulp of air that made the vast muscles that covered the cavern of his chest ripple. His limbs stopped thrashing, but he couldn't stop the keening. I tried to tune the sound out as I brought the scalpel up and severed the first of the restraints holding him against the rack.

His fist clenched, but did not lash out at me. Good.

I went after the second arm restraint. Again, no violent response, just a vast tremble beneath my off hand. He slumped against me, a string-cut puppet, making my mods burn again as I struggled to hold him up. I had read somewhere that Vmog had, unlike terrestrial avians, quite a dense bone structure, but I was still surprised by the muscled weight of Dzavo's body draped across my bent-over back. I cut his legs free next. That done, I flung the scalpel away, happy to hear the sound of the polymer case cracking as it hit a shipping crate and smacked wetly to the floor. I grunted, feeling my overtaxed and under-trained muscles screaming as I positioned Dzavo in a fireman's carry. I looked up, judging distances. Cursing, I started the slow, painful climb up the storage racks back to my botwalk above.

We were halfway through to the alleyway when the remaining gangsters found the two bodies and their hostage gone. The sounds of their arguing and panic chased me as I pushed Dzavo through the small opening ahead of me.

Outside, the alley still stank, but after the visceral stench of that makeshift torture chamber, even the miasma of the docks was sweet.

"Come on," I said. "I know how we're gonna get you out of here."

"I can't . . . fly . . ." Dzavo said, voice Dopplering up through frequencies my battle-bruised ears would never hear without an angel.

"I know, buddy," I said between gasps of exertion. "You're still alive. Bellasanee loves you. Don't give up on her, hey?"

"Bella . . ."

Somehow I managed to get him down off the botwalk and safely to street level. The growing weakness in my shoulders and legs told me that I had burned through Fulu's pharma. I swayed there, mods stuttering. My arm hurt, a line of acid fire from forearm to hand. My fingers were growing numb. I gritted my teeth and levered Dzavo up over my shoulder for the last little bit of the way.

"Let's hope this thing still works," I said, kicking the hatch on the decrepit-looking autodoc. The inside lit up, just as it was supposed to do. A moment later the hatch slowly opened.

"Place patient inside receptacle." The autodoc's computer-generated voice was calm and soothing, and repeated the phrase in several languages. I let out a breath and eased Dzavo down to rest within the vertical cradle inside.

"Look up," I said.

Dzavo let out a groan but opened his eyes wide and stared into the optical ID scanner. A number of automated sensors took readings, while another battery of instruments slid needles into his flesh.

"Welcome, Consort Dzavo. Emerita Bellasanee has been informed of your impending arrival at the station hospital facility. Please relax as the anesthetic takes effect. Please step away from the autodoc," the calm voice said.

I closed the hatch as Dzavo closed his eyes. The autodoc whisked the cradle away through the secure tubes leading to the hospital and much-needed care.

I sighed, took off my torn jacket, using it as a makeshift bandage for my arm, which had resumed bleeding. I ditched the voidfork, stomping on it a few times to release the self-destruct nanites inside. That disposed of, I stumbled out of the alleyway opposite the entrance to the warehouse.

At least three Security vehicles were out front, positioned to form a barricade blocking off the facility. I could see Dengler's blond hair as he sighted a weapon on the warehouse door.

I turned my back on them and slipped out into the crowd of Last Stop residents moving away, carefully not seeing anything. Like draft animals with blinders on, Last Stop's denizens made it their business to mind their own fucking business.

Halfway back to my dockside place, my blood-soaked jacket started dripping. Fatigue washed over me, threatening to buckle my knees and suck me under. I kept stumbling forward, just another junkie coming down from a high. Fuck.

I shoved that thought away and pulled my PID, stabbing at it until Tongi's face appeared.

"The Emerita called from the hospital. Her consort was badly injured. You should have hurried."

"He's alive, isn't he?"

"He is, and says he would not be if not for you. You may keep your job."

Red crowded in from the edges of my vision. I didn't know if it was blood loss, fatigue, anger, or withdrawal. It didn't matter.

"Tongi, I need a medic."

"I do not—"

"Tongi, I saved the Emerita's consort. You owe me. Use your connections to find me a medic and *don't ask any questions!*"

Silence. The big Omik's mouth opened and closed as his eyes blinked in sequence.

"Fine," he said, his tone ratcheting up to annoyance again. "But then we are even."

"Whatever."

"Send your address over. Someone will meet you. And Muck?"

"Yeah?"

"Did you ever figure out who she is?"

"The Emerita?"

Tongi laughed, and I knew I wasn't going to like what he was going to say.

"Not just any Emerita. Emerita Bellasanee was the premier weapons designer of the War. She designed the Planetflare system. You know, the one used against Earth? How does it feel to know you bled for the female who destroyed your species' homeworld?"

He cut the connection. I paused for a moment, and then shook my head and shuffled forward again into the flow of foot traffic. Just like before. Nothing had changed. Eyes down, looking neither right nor left. Seeing nothing. Hearing nothing. Blinders fully on.

Minding one's own business was good for the faint of heart, and I was feeling very faint by then.

The Lady in the Pit

D.J. Butler

"I need your help."

The woman sitting across the round wooden table wore a black cloak. The hood was up, entirely obscuring her face, other than her slightly pointed, pale slip of a chin. Her voice was soft, but firm, with a whisper of silk in its tones.

Indrajit turned to look at his partner. Fix nodded. "Tell us more." Fix was Kishi, or something closely related to Kishi; he was short, with brown skin and straight black hair cut in a simple bowl shape. His voice was soft, almost girlish, belying his broad frame and the array of weapons hanging at his belt.

Their sole employee, the only member of the job-ber company called the Protagonists who was not a partner, stood across the street. Munahim was tall and had a doglike head covered in black fur, so he was hardly conspicuous, but from behind the flap of a tack shop's tent, he watched, ready to intervene if the client pulled any untoward tricks. He'd secreted himself in that station well before the client had arrived for her appointment.

"We don't specialize in damsels in distress," Indrajit added, "but it's definitely in our portfolio."

"My name is Oleandra Holt."

"Your message said that you're a priestess of the Unnamed," Fix suggested.

She purred. "An acolyte. It's unlikely I'll ever make priestess proper."

Indrajit rubbed a finger along his bony nose ridge. The ridge rose into a crest along the top of his hairless skull. It pushed Indrajit's eyes out to the side of his skull, but definitely did not make him look like a fish. Also, no fish had Indrajit's pleasing complexion, mahogany with nuanced hints of green. He was the tallest of the three Protagonists, though maybe the least muscle-bound.

"Is that because you're not an assassin?" Indrajit had no idea whether the rumors about the worshippers of the Unnamed were true, but sitting in the common room of the tavern below his own lodgings, with broad beams of afternoon sunlight and the smell of camels wafting in through the windows, he felt brave enough to ask.

Oleandra laughed. "If I deny the substance of the rumors you're alluding to, you won't believe me. An assassin-thief sworn to lie, steal, and kill in the service of the New Moon would lie in any case, wouldn't she? That's what you would tell yourself, if I offered a denial."

"And yet you deny nothing," Indrajit said.

She purred again.

"In any case, the message was eye-catching." Fix

cleared his throat and shot Indrajit a withering look, probably reminding his partner that Fix was literate, and Indrajit was not. "The devotees of the Unnamed, the Unseen, the Goddess of the New Moon, rarely disclose their affiliation in public."

"Rarely," Oleandra Holt agreed. "Not never."

"May we see *your* face?" Fix asked. "I find it disconcerting to speak to someone whose eyes I can't see."

Oleandra didn't touch her veil. "You were recommended to me by a certain...woman. A rich woman."

"Connected with the Lord Chamberlain?" Indrajit asked.

Fix said nothing, but his eyes narrowed and his nostrils flared.

"One of the scholars of the Hall of Guesses?" Indrajit tried again.

"No," Oleandra said. "But a wealthy woman and a friend."

"Will you name her?" Fix's muscles were visibly taut, as if he were prepared to leap into hand-to-hand combat at any moment. "Are she and her husband connected with the Paper Sook?"

"You ask too many questions." Oleandra stood as if to leave, her black cloak falling over her shoulders and framing a body clad in white linen. Her limbs were well muscled, but she hunched forward slightly as she stood. Was that why she covered herself with a cloak? She had a tail, too, barely visible as a bulge in the fabric around her ankles.

"Please," Indrajit said, "we're investigators by nature. I apologize if our questions are intrusive."

Fix's eyes burned.

Oleandra Holt seated herself again, slowly.

With exaggerated slowness. And she'd never really moved toward the door, and she hadn't picked up the canvas sack sitting on the floor beside her. A bluff.

"My friend said that you were bold men," she said. "The Protagonists, you call yourselves. I have heard that you are valiant fighters in the causes of other people. That you risk life and limb to rescue kidnapped and threatened people, for instance. That you uncover mysteries and bring justice to wrongdoers. That you are dogged, reliable, honest, and highly skilled."

"Ah, good," Indrajit said. "Those rumors I spread are working. Only you forgot the part about how handsome we are."

Oleandra purred again.

"Does your friend need help for herself?" Fix asked. "Rescuing from her ... husband, for instance?"

The acolyte of the Unnamed shook her head. "I come on my own behalf."

Fix slumped the tiniest bit. "Go on."

Despite their weeks of working together, Indrajit didn't know the entire story of Fix's unrequited love. He knew the woman had married. He knew Fix still pined for her, and that one reason Fix wanted to become wealthy and successful was to be in a position to woo her back.

"Like all the women of my family," Oleandra said, "I have served the Unnamed since the moon first turned for me."

"What?" Fix asked.

"You need more poetry in your soul," Indrajit said. "She means, since she reached womanhood. Only she said it in a very moon kind of way."

Fix frowned, then nodded.

"Like all the women of my family, my first encounter with the goddess was on my entry into her temple at that time. As is the custom, I took with me a votive, and deposited it there. There is a niche that my mothers before me have all used, in the temple. They passed down knowledge of it to me, and when I knelt and consecrated my votive to the New Moon, I laid it among many other objects placed by my forebears."

"This was what?" Indrajit asked. "A statue? An offering of money? A stolen item?" He didn't know what votive offerings the worshippers of the Unnamed would make. "An assassination victim?"

Oleandra hesitated.

"You don't have to tell us," Indrajit said. "Unless, of course, it matters to what you're going to ask us to do."

"It was a statue of the Unnamed," Oleandra said. "In her most traditional appearance."

"That's a paradox, isn't it?" Fix pushed back. "Her most traditional appearance is as the Unseen, without an image. The new moon is the invisible moon. Is this a riddle? Are you testing us?"

"Things that appear are visible," Oleandra said. "Her most traditional *appearance* is as a woman with no face."

"No head, in fact," Indrajit said. "I've seen that image."

"It's often scratched on the lintel-posts of shopkeepers to ward off theft." Oleandra nodded.

"Not assassination?" Fix asked.

A hint of a smile played at the edge of the shadow within the hood.

"Okay, you deposited a statue of a headless woman,"

Indrajit said. "What, twenty years ago? Don't be offended, but...maybe even thirty years ago?" It was hard to tell from just the voice and the chin.

"Among the other votive sculptures standing within my family's sacred niche," Oleandra continued, "I saw the famed gift left by my great-great-grandmother."

"An even fancier statuette," Indrajit guessed.

Oleandra shook her head. "In fact, it was a much *less* elaborate statue. My granddam found a stone, a chunk of black, smooth rock, while she was journeying around the Sea of Rains. It was a stone that had never known a chisel, but nevertheless was a clear image of the kneeling goddess. A natural idol, and obviously an item of great power."

"Obviously," Indrajit said.

Fix's jaw clenched.

"That statuette brought great power to my granddam and to our family," Oleandra continued. "We waxed wealthy, and the Lords of Kish began to give us heed."

"You attribute this to the statue," Fix said.

"To the goddess," Oleandra countered, "whom we honored with the gift of the idol."

"This is all interesting," Indrajit said. "Indeed, I'm already considering how to capture it in a pithy, moving, and yet thrilling fashion, in a few lines for the Blaatshi Epic."

"You don't have to," Fix said.

Indrajit shrugged. "But I have not yet heard anything that explains to me why you need our help."

"I am but an acolyte." Oleandra's tail swished, disturbing her cloak. "I serve the goddess in ritual ways only, and only for discrete periods of time. When it is my turn, I am permitted briefly into the temple,

and when my time of service is past, I am ushered
out again. My worship is genuine, but my appointment is social."

"You're not an assassin," Fix suggested, "you just
go to the assassins club with your friends."

"That's glib," she said.

"Yes, it is," Indrajit said, "and I'm the one who's
supposed to make the glib observations."

"Are glib observations really consonant with the
somber calling of an epic poet?" Fix asked.

"I'm wounded," Indrajit said. "And I take your point."

"Your description," Oleandra said, "however glib, is
not wrong. And my appointment means that, although
I am regularly allowed inside the Unnamed's temple,
I have little freedom within its walls, and little time."

Indrajit rested his hand on the pommel of Vacho,
his leaf-bladed sword, and nodded. "Go on."

"My grandmother's votive has been moved from
its place."

"Stolen?" Fix's gaze was cool and piercing. "Ironic."

"I think not," Oleandra said. "The family niche
became too crowded when my niece was initiated, two
new moons ago, and I believe that the temple staff
made room by throwing out older votives, including
that of my granddam."

"What, thrown out into the trash?" Indrajit gulped.
"That seems like a poor way to dispose of an item
of power."

"Or at least, a poor way to show respect to your
own tradition," Fix suggested.

"Casting out sacrifices into the trash would incur
the wrath of the goddess." Oleandra shook her head,
and the hood shifted slightly. The top of her skull

seemed to be square, and to have pointed corners. "Offered food is eaten by the priestesses, in the place of the goddess herself."

"That sounds pretty typical," Fix said.

"Old votive statues are thrown into a pit," Oleandra said.

"And we are back to the garbage heap again." Indrajit shook his head. "Why doesn't your goddess of assassins strike dead people who disrespect her in this fashion? Mother Blaat is a peaceful goddess of the sea and its life—"

"That's Indrajit's granddam," Fix said. "That's why he looks like a koi with legs."

Indrajit ignored his partner. "—and I would never spurn her so."

"The pit is a holy pit, in consecrated ground. I have seen it only once; I asked about my granddam's votive, and a priestess took me to see the pit. The pit lies beneath the temple, and is therefore itself a sacred and appropriate receptacle into which to throw such consecrated items as old votives, worn-out ritual garb, and successfully used assassins' blades."

"You saw your granddam's votive?" Indrajit asked. "Lying in this pit?"

"I saw the pit, in the shaky light of a lantern. I saw many sacred items. Before I could see my granddam's idol, I was led away. But the statuette must lie close to the surface of the mound of items in the pit, since it has only recently been removed."

"I begin to understand the picture," Fix said. "You don't have the time while you're in the temple to go after the idol yourself, so you want us to recover it."

"I can let you in," Oleandra said, "by a secret

entrance. But I only have time to open the door, I can't stand in the pit and search, or my absence will be noticed."

"A secret passage?" Fix asked. "Where's the temple? It's rumored to exist somewhere in the Dregs, but even the building is a secret. Much less some back door."

Oleandra only smiled.

"All this makes sense," Indrajit said. "But if we break in to the temple and steal an idol, won't the goddess feel...discomfited?"

"You really worry that she might feel vengeful," Oleandra said.

"Of course," Indrajit said.

"Or perhaps there are no gods," Fix said. "Not really. Perhaps they're just stories, and if you and I go into that pit, my long-limbed, green-skinned friend, we can find items of value to sell."

"Green is just one of the ones of my skin color," Indrajit said. "I am more mahogany than green."

"You're brown," Fix said. "We're both brown. That's a good shade, you don't need to be any fancier than that."

"Let's focus on the possibility that there is a real goddess here," Indrajit countered, "and a goddess of assassins, at that."

"Assassins and thieves," Oleandra pointed out.

"What are you saying, that she'll look the other way for us because she favors burglars?" That didn't sound...impossible.

"Yes," Oleandra said. "But also, you won't steal the idol. You'll find it, and hide it just within the door by which I admit you. You will just have moved the idol within the temple's sanctified grounds."

"Downgraded from burglars to trespassers," Fix said.

"Also, I'll give you sacred garb to disguise yourselves with. The goddess won't even see you."

"If the sacred garb disguises us from other believers, that's enough for me," Fix said.

Indrajit's stomach felt unsettled. "This feels like we're really tempting fate."

Oleandra set a purse on the table. "One hundred Imperials, paid now. Another hundred Imperials when I have the statuette in my possession."

"But the story doesn't quite add up," Fix said. "You're so religious that you want this statuette of the goddess back, but so impious that you will go ahead and trick the goddess to get it?"

Oleandra hesitated. "The idol is important to my family because of our history with it."

"I still don't believe it." Fix shook his head, but without taking his eyes from the woman. "You're risking some pretty big consequences for a few memories and a warm feeling."

Oleandra wrapped her fingers around the purse and gripped it tightly, until her knuckles whitened. "You're investigators, as you say. Very well. Scratched onto the underside of the idol is secret information that my family needs."

"Ah ha." Indrajit leaned forward. "Now we have a real story going."

Oleandra said nothing.

"What is it?" Fix asked. "A bank account password? A map to treasure? A dirty secret to hold over the Lord Stargazer?"

Oleandra pressed her lips together.

"Does the nature of this secret make the job more dangerous for us?" Fix asked.

"The temple staff don't know the secret," Oleandra said. "They couldn't read the secret information, even if they saw it."

"Reading." Indrajit snorted, but he did wonder what the information could be.

"If they knew what they held in their hands, they would never have thrown the lady into the pit." Oleandra spoke as if her words were final.

They sat in silence a moment. Fix turned to his partner. "And think how much more fun this is than trying to enforce the regulations of the Paper Sook."

That clinched the argument. Indrajit barely understood the language of the merchants of the Paper Sook. When the Lord Chamberlain and his spymaster Grit Wopal gave Indrajit and Fix tasks among those merchants, which was often, Indrajit found himself repeating back to Fix the words his partner said, usually without comprehending them at all. "I'm in."

Fix leaned forward. "Your friend who recommended us . . . she isn't a devotee of the Unnamed."

"But she is my close friend." Oleandra smiled warmly. "And she will hear of this bold exploit and be pleased."

"Show us where this secret door is," Indrajit said, "and tell us when to meet you."

There was no moon. The Spike rose in the middle distance, blocking out a chunk of the night sky with its knuckle of rock gripping the temples of the city's five acknowledged gods. Light from lamps and torches splashed up in yellow streaks against the tall walls of the buildings of the Crown, Kish's most elegant and exclusive quarter. The Crown was home to the palaces of the rich and the buildings of government as well as the temple district. Indrajit and Fix stood beside a small, unimportant-looking wooden door, on a dull, untrafficked side street.

"Strange," Indrajit said. "The temple to Kish's secret sixth god is located awfully close to the temples of the other five."

"Don't get cold feet," Fix said.

"I don't have cold feet. I'm just marveling at how much I still have to learn about this rotten old city."

"We're close enough to the Spike that the Temple of the Unnamed could be on the Spike itself," Fix said. "Right alongside the other five."

"Hmm." Indrajit frowned.

"Or underneath it."

Kish was an ancient city, perched on a knob of rock riddled with catacombs, in turn stuffed with ruins, strange beasts, ancient machinery, poisons, and peril. It was not an insane thought that the goddess of thieves and assassins might make her home down in that warren. But it wasn't a comforting thought, either.

Indrajit pointed. "Also, this looks more like a side entrance into that dry goods shop than a secret back door into the temple of the new moon."

"What should a secret back door into the temple look like, then?"

"Point taken. But maybe the temple isn't on the Spike, it's inside that shop. And you know, it might be that the best possible outcome for us here is that Oleandra never shows up, we don't trespass on sacred ground, and you and I get to keep the hundred Imperials."

"But then you wouldn't accomplish any mighty deeds worth recounting in the epic," Fix countered.

They were dressed in simple kilts and sandals, given the warm night. Indrajit wore Vacho at his belt, and Fix wore his falchion, his hand ax, and two long knives. He favored fighting with a spear when possible, but he'd left his spear behind, saying it might become awkward in narrow hallways. In a pocket in his kilt, Indrajit had a few items—a lantern, a flask of oil, flint and steel, and chalk.

Munahim, lurking in a shadowed doorway farther along the street, had his long, straight sword strapped to his back and carried a bow. He also had a two-handed wood ax in his possession, but it wasn't for fighting.

Munahim's role was protection. He was a selling of risk, in the language of the Paper Sook. He hung back because Indrajit couldn't quite bring himself to trust Oleandra Holt. Despite his inflamed and stricken looks, neither could Fix.

Indrajit stroked his chin. "You make a good point."

There was a triple rap on the inside of the door. Indrajit checked to be certain they were alone in the quiet street, then responded with the countersign, which was two double knocks, with a pause between.

Oleandra opened the door. She again wore her black cloak, with its hood up. "Quickly, please."

Indrajit and Fix stepped inside. The door was sturdy, and bound with iron bars. Indrajit pulled the door to, deliberately not quite shutting it, while attempting to look careless at the same time.

Oleandra yanked the door completely shut. A narrow passage descended immediately over brick steps into darkness. An oil lamp sat flickering at the top step beside a tall orange clay jar. From beneath her cloak, Oleandra produced a bundle of cloth, which she peeled apart into two smaller bundles, handing one to each man.

"Wear these to stay unobserved by the goddess." She kept her voice to a whisper.

They unrolled the fabric.

"This is a woman's dress," Indrajit said. It was the same style of dress Oleandra herself wore.

"I don't have access to the men's garb." Oleandra took down her hood, revealing a pale face with large eyes. She had no hair on her head, and four inwardly curving horns protruded from the top of her skull, making four corners. "I got the largest that I could find."

Fix pulled the dress on over his kilt. After a moment's hesitation, Indrajit did the same. The dresses were white and sleeveless. Fix's was long enough for him, but not big enough to accommodate his muscular chest, so the seams of his dress squeaked out a brief complaint and then split apart. Indrajit's dress was big enough, but short, so its waist rode halfway between his armpits and his hips, and his kilt protruded below the dress.

"Oh, we look *fine*," Fix said.

"You look right to the goddess," Oleandra said.

"When you tell your friend this part," Fix told her, "you could emphasize to her the heroism and downplay how ridiculous I look."

"That's certainly how *I* will recite this episode," Indrajit said. "Also, you will be tall."

Oleandra picked up the jar and moved it to the corner behind the door. "This is big enough for the statuette. You can leave the dresses here too, when you're finished."

"You have little time," Fix said. "Show us the pit."

Oleandra took the lamp and led them down the stairs. The air vibrated with a sound that Indrajit could not quite hear. He pressed his cheek to the wall and could make out chanting. He heard each syllable clearly, seemed to feel them in his bones, and he even felt that the syllables were familiar . . . but somehow, they didn't add up to words he could understand.

"Worship is beginning," Oleandra said. "The sacrifices are only a few minutes away, and I will be missed." She quickened her pace.

"We must be beneath the Spike about now," Fix said.

They made several turns and Oleandra didn't slow down for them. Trying not to attract attention to himself, Indrajit took the chalk from his pocket and marked the turnings. Was it a desecration to write on the temple's walls? He didn't know what sacred gesture to make to placate the goddess in case it was, but he pressed his palms together in an attitude of prayer, bowing and looking up in the general direction of where the moon might be.

Then they arrived, and he made one last mark before putting the chalk away.

The room was much larger than Indrajit had imagined it would be, and so was the pit. Seven pillars carved like headless women were spaced evenly about the walls, supporting the vaulted ceiling with their shoulders. Each of the women held a different item before her: a dagger, a garotte, a vial, a caltrop, a sword, a crossbow, and a spiked cestus. Between every pair of pillars gaped an opening and a hallway. Around all sides of the room, two paces' worth of open floor separated the walls from the pit.

The sides of the pit were steep but scalable. Within the pit lay a tangled heap of objects, including blades, trophies, clothing, and idols. There were also bones.

"This will take us some time," Fix noted.

"I'll leave my lamp," she said. "The statuette should be near the edge. Items are dropped in, not thrown into the center."

She set down the light and left them, circling around the pit to leave by a different exit.

"Is it my imagination," Indrajit asked, "or is the chanting getting louder?"

Fix cocked his head to one side. "I think you're wrong."

Indrajit eyed the shadows with suspicion. "Okay, let's do this."

They let themselves down into the pit. The climb was half again Indrajit's height, maybe seven cubits, and the handholds were generous, so Indrajit could climb down while carrying the lamp. When Indrajit stepped into the heap of objects filling the pit, he sank up to his knees.

"There are a lot more bones down here than our employer led me to expect," he grumbled.

Fix arrived beside him. "What kind of bones?"

Indrajit pointed. "The bones of men. I mean, of all kinds. Look, that must have been a Luzzazza, you can see the sockets for four arms. And these little ones everywhere are probably Zalaptings."

"Let's keep our eyes on the prize." Fix slogged inward two steps, putting himself between Indrajit and the center of the pit. Oleandra had been right that objects cast into the hole were thrown in from the sides, so the heap sank to a depression in its center. "We walk side by side, slowly, around the pit. We're looking for a black stone that looks like a headless idol. Use your imagination, people can see images in rocks and clouds with very little provocation. Anything made of black or blackish stone, we at least pick it up and look at it."

"Agreed," Indrajit said.

"If we see anything else valuable, I say we steal it."

Would that enrage the goddess? But they were helping one of her acolytes. "Yes," he said weakly.

They combed their way around the edge of the pit. Indrajit held the lamp high, because he was taller, but he occasionally passed it to Fix when the shorter partner needed to examine some object.

He noticed that the ceiling above them was pierced by a circular hole. He could see a few stars winking through it. How must that hole be disguised on the surface? Was it unseen because surrounded by buildings? Or within the courtyard of one of the Crown's palaces? Or a temple disguised as a palace?

Indrajit also took what opportunity he had to study the skeletons. They were wrapped in layers of rotting cloth, but not with the care that a mummy would be. He saw smashed skulls and deeply nicked neck bones, and three times he saw rib cages with crossbow bolts lodged between the ribs.

When he looked up to see how much progress they had made, he was disappointed.

"We're a quarter of the way around." His voice sounded huge, and it echoed. "What time is it?"

Fix shrugged.

"Where's Munahim?"

Fix shrugged.

Indrajit grumbled, but carried on.

Fix plucked jewelry from the heap, and even picked up a codex to examine it. Indrajit didn't have the nerve, and contented himself with scouring the pile of discarded temple items for any sign of the black stone idol.

Then they encountered the first body with flesh on its bones. It was a Grokonk Third, of middling height and rotting from yellow to a limpid gray. It had been strangled to death—the gashes left by a wire circled its neck, and the skin around the gashes was rotting black and peeling away from the corpse.

The second fleshly corpse was a furred Wixit, whose tongue was black and bloated in his mouth. The third, in quick succession, was a Zalapting whose chest was feathered with crossbow bolts. All three wore white dresses, rotting as quickly as the bodies were.

White dresses.

"We're getting out of here right now." Indrajit turned to climb up the wall of the pit—and saw Oleandra standing at the top.

"Too late." Her voice was hollow.

To either side of her stood two men. All four wore black trousers and shirt and a black cloak over the top, hoods hiding their faces. All four held crossbows in their hands, and they all aimed at Indrajit.

"Do you not know...?" Fix's voice was anguished. "You didn't...there is no friend who recommended us, is there?"

Oleandra shook her head.

An arrow struck one of the four men in the chest with a twang and a wet slapping sound. He fell into a puddle of his own cloak with a soft grunt, and then

Munahim came crashing out of the dark, long sword raised over his head.

Indrajit sprang forward. He jammed his foot into a depression in the stone and threw himself upward. The remaining three cloaked men turned to face Munahim, and Indrajit grabbed the man in the middle by his ankles.

Oleandra turned and ran.

Munahim slashed through the crossbow of the man in front and Indrajit yanked the second down into the pit. The man lost his grip on his crossbow and Indrajit pulled him down over himself as a shield.

He felt a satisfying thud as a crossbow bolt buried itself in the man's back.

Indrajit landed flat and hard on a knobby pile of statues and bones, all the wind knocked out of him. His peripheral vision was excellent, so despite feeling stunned, he saw Fix scoop up the dropped crossbow and shoot one of their attackers with it. By the time Indrajit rolled the dead man off himself and stood, all four attackers had been shot or cut down.

"Munahim," he grumbled. "Glad you could make it."

"Your timing was perfect," Fix said.

By a stroke of good fortune, the lamp had not been extinguished in the fracas. They climbed out of the pit.

Munahim was wounded. Blood seeped from cuts on both arms, and he had a long scratch along the side of his doglike muzzle. "They have men behind us in the tunnels. I was traveling without light, following you by your scent, so they didn't see me coming. But I don't advise going back that way."

"There have to be other exits," Indrajit said.

Fix stared at his feet.

"Okay," Indrajit said. "The woman—can you follow her scent?"

Munahim nodded.

"Then we follow her out," Indrajit said. "She clearly led us into a trap here, so for all we know, she might now lead us into another. But probably not. Probably, she's running for her life and will head for the nearest exist."

Munahim grinned. "Frightened of the Protagonists."

Indrajit clapped the dog-headed warrior, the first recruit into the Protagonists since he and Fix had formed the jobber company, on the shoulder. "Frightened of *you*. Lead out, Munahim. I'll bring up the rear."

Munahim stooped to sniff at the bricks, and then quickly jogged into one of the room's seven exits. Not, Indrajit noted, the one that he had marked with chalk.

Indrajit pushed Fix to get him in motion. Once the small man was moving, he went quickly, but he still seemed distracted.

"There's no idol," he murmured, shuddering down a staircase into a wide gallery.

"If there is, we were never meant to get it." Indrajit hesitated at the top of the stairs and shielded the lamp with his body to look back. Was that a glimmer of light behind them?

"Why?" Fix asked.

"Maybe someone took out a contract," Indrajit said. "Any number of people might want us killed, starting with Mote Gannon, who can't use his own men to do it without getting into trouble. This whole thing was clearly a trap."

"Maybe you were meant to be sacrifices?" Munahim called back over his shoulder. His voice, when asking questions, sounded like the mournful yodeling of a hunting dog to the moon.

"The bodies in the pit," Fix said.

"Maybe they were earlier sacrifices." Indrajit tried to think through what he'd seen. "Maybe we were next. Maybe these aren't really priestly dresses we're wearing. Maybe they mark us as offerings."

"I don't think maybe," Fix said.

"I don't think maybe, either."

Flowing water crossed the end of the gallery. Munahim splashed through the stream, sniffing at the opposite bank, and then picked up the scent again at the leftmost of three circular openings.

As he and Fix raced on, Indrajit pressed himself into the curve of the arch. A light appeared at the far end of the gallery. He heard slapping feet, too, but the men pursuing them wore soft-soled shoes and they had the knack of treading lightly. He couldn't make out how many were coming.

He ran to catch up to the other Protagonists.

"We're followed," he hissed.

"It could be both." Fix's voice was glum.

"Both . . . meaning, maybe someone took out a contract on us with the priests of the Unnamed, and the temple is trying to carry out the contract by sacrificing us?" It was not a comforting thought. "Uh . . . how do we terminate a hit on us?"

Munahim led them across an octagonal chamber whose floor was an iron lattice. Green light glowed beneath their feet. Indrajit had seen such light several times before, and generally thought it was a sign of ancient Druvash sorcery at work. At the far end of the chamber, they climbed a groaning iron staircase bolted into the wall. At the top, they stopped to catch their breath, and Indrajit and Fix both shucked off their white dresses.

"Oleandra is a fast runner." Munahim was panting.

"Help me get rid of these stairs," Indrajit said.

Munahim had left his great ax on the street after chopping through the door with it, but Fix had his smaller hatchet. The iron of the staircase was rusted, but solid—but when Indrajit threw his weight against the stairs, he discovered that the brick around the screws bolting the stairs to the wall was crumbling. He lay on his back and kicked repeatedly, until the stairs curled away from the wall and fell.

As the stairs crashed to the brick below, the lights of their pursuers entered the other side of the room. "Hey," Indrajit suggested to Munahim. "Let's make them put out those lights, shall we?"

Munahim fired three arrows at their pursuers, forcing them to scatter and douse their lamps. Then the Protagonists ran.

"Why does it feel like people always want to kill us?" Indrajit asked.

"Because people always want to kill us," Fix said.

"I don't think that pit was the garbage heap for old votives," Indrajit said. "I mean, everything Oleandra told us seems to have been a lie, but that in particular."

"That was the altar," Fix said.

"That's what I think, too."

They passed through an open door into a room lit by torches. The sudden flickering flames burned Indrajit's eyes like bonfires and he blinked away tears. The chamber was furnished with four thickly upholstered divans facing a low, square table in the center. Opposite,

Indrajit saw through an archway into a stone-flagged room with large double doors. High, paneless windows let in cool air. They must be aboveground again.

Oleandra stood beside the low table. Her cloak was gone. She seemed to be on the tips of her toes, and it took Indrajit a moment to realize that there was a man behind her, holding her up. He wore black from head to foot, including a cloak. Silver stitching around the edges of the cloak might represent writing of some sort. He also wore a black mask that showed no skin beneath, or teeth or anything, giving him the impression of being headless.

He held a long, thin blade to Oleandra's throat.

Fix shut the door behind them. Indrajit drew Vacho from its sheath and he heard the sound of Fix sliding a bolt into place.

"You're going to let us past," Indrajit said. "But first, you're going to give us information."

"I will hurt the woman if you move," the man in black said.

"She's on *your* side," Indrajit said. "What kind of threat is that?"

"She's dressed as a sacrifice," Fix added. His mild voice contained a strained note. Fear? Preoccupation?

"It's a threat because you care," the masked man said.

"We're going to leave," Indrajit said. He looked for a moment of inattention on the man's part, so he could leap in and free Oleandra. Such a bold move could make for several good minutes of Epic recitation: a description of tensed muscles and sweat trickling down his back, a reminder of the weapons he bore, a call back to his heroic ancestry. "We never picked a fight with you."

"The goddess claims sacrifices," the masked man

said. "The goddess herself chooses. This moon, when we consulted her, she said we should take *you*."

"We don't want trouble in the future," Indrajit said. "Live and let live. Unless you commit fraud in the Paper Sook. Or anger the Lord Chamberlain, I guess. Otherwise, we'll leave you alone."

"I will trade," the man in black said. "Her life for yours."

Oleandra's expression was unreadable. Her lips moved as if she were singing or reciting, but her eyes were glazed over. She might have been in a trance, or drugged, except that she must have been sprinting away from them only moments earlier.

Fix produced jewelry from the pocket of his kilt. "We'll give you these back, for her life." His voice was pitched too high, even for Fix.

"You know this woman is not your lover," Indrajit murmured.

Fix didn't answer.

The masked man spat. "What is sacrificed is dead and gone, and nothing to me, or to the goddess. The jewels are nothing."

"Did your oracle say you must actually sacrifice us?" Indrajit asked. "Or just try to? Because you've gone and given it a good try. Best efforts. Maybe now it would be okay to accept failure. Maybe the Unnamed just wants you to make the attempt."

"And did your divination mention me at all?" Munahim asked. "I'm new, and maybe your goddess really had Indrajit and Fix personally in mind."

Hammering sounds at their backs suggested that their pursuers had caught up, and were beating against the door.

"I'll take any one of you," the masked man said. "Even the dog head, I don't care."

"Hey," Munahim said.

Indrajit sheathed Vacho. He walked slowly toward the masked man, preparing to grab him by the wrist, disarm him, trip him, or do whatever was necessary to save Oleandra. Not that she deserved it, since she had lured them into this place to sacrifice them to her goddess, but...well, a hero would save her, and Indrajit wanted to be that hero.

Also, Fix stared at her as if he were staring at his former lover. He must know that this woman was not the same woman who had jilted him, but in his head, he seemed to have made a connection that he couldn't shake.

And then again, Oleandra herself appeared to be a victim.

Indrajit raised his hands to show that they were empty. The hammering on the door was joined by muffled shouting noises.

"Just let her go," Indrajit said.

Three things happened so quickly, so closely together, that to Indrajit they seemed to happen simultaneously. The masked man leaped forward, lunging at Indrajit with his knife, stabbing for the throat. At the same moment, Oleandra's haze of uncertainty and her mumbling fell away like a veil cast aside, and she hurled herself into the masked man's path. Finally, his thrusting blade struck her in the back of her neck and passed completely through, the tip of the dagger stabbing out the front of her throat. Blood spurted down her white sacrificial gown.

She fell forward, dead on the table.

Fix leaped upon the masked man with fury in his face. His ax was in his hand, and before the man in black could even turn to face him, Fix had shattered his skull. A second blow nearly severed one of the man's arms and a third took his head completely off.

Fix screamed.

"Hey," Indrajit said.

Fix took a swing at Indrajit with his ax, and only Indrajit's quick reflexes let him dodge the attack.

"We should get out of here," Munahim muttered.

"It wasn't her," Indrajit said.

The dog-headed Protagonist knelt and scooped up jewelry that Fix had dropped. He led the way to the archway into the next room, but stood waiting.

Fix dropped his ax. He knelt beside Oleandra's corpse, cradling it in his arms.

"You know that's not your love," Indrajit said, slowly and firmly.

Fix blinked and rubbed his eyes with his fists, smearing blood all over his face in the process. He looked at Oleandra one last time, then laid her back on the table. "It could have been, though. It could have been her. And someone should have loved her the way I love . . . If she'd had the love in her life that she deserved, she might not have ended this way."

The knocking and yelling had stopped.

"We should go," Munahim said. "They'll find a way around."

Fix took a small book from his kilt. Indrajit didn't recognize the volume—his partner must have found it in the pit. He tore a page from it and took a bit of writing charcoal from his pocket. He wrote, face tight in concentration, and then he took the dead man's dagger and used it to pin the note to the man's chest, sinking the blade in all the way to the hilt.

The double doors in the next room opened onto the street. Fix was shaking as they walked out.

"We got this jewelry," Munahim said.

"There's also the hundred Imperials." Fix spoke mechanically, as if without thought. "We'll divide it all by shares."

They took several turns in quick succession, to throw off pursuit. Once Indrajit realized that they had emerged in the Spill, he took the lead and directed their path back to the inn that served as both home and office.

"What did you write?" he asked his partner. The sea breeze was cooling the sweat that poured off him and filling his lungs with stiff, bracing air. The lurid chambers beneath the city, the skeletons, and the heap of sacrificed loot, were beginning to fade and to seem unreal. Would the assassin cult come after them another day? It seemed impossible to predict, but, for the moment, it didn't feel imminent.

"I told them we know where their temple is now," Fix said, grinding out the words through clenched teeth. "I told them that, if we ever see them again, the Lord Chamberlain will kill every single one of them, scorch their cult from off the face of the earth. And I told them that, for this moon, enough sacrifices have been thrown into the pit."

All in the Family

Nicole Givens Kurtz

ONE

There should be rest each night, but like most things in my life, it ain't there. An empty evening stretched before me—a waiting hungry mouth, ready to devour and swallow all my warm, gooey hope. I lacked any morsel of the yumminess The District consumed from its citizens. I'm too old and too bitter for her to swallow. She can't savor my marrow. She'd spit it out—like meatless bones. It's poison.

Nah. This territory ain't got the stomach for me, Lomax Yule, Private Inspector.

"Alejandro, what's the time?"

"It is 1812. Have a good evening," the office's AI said.

I gathered my satchel. My lasergun shifted in its holster as I slung the bag onto my shoulder. My fingers itched for a cigarette. I swallowed to alleviate my dry throat.

"Doctor's orders. No more smokes," I reminded my craving.

My office door whined, and my hand went to my gun. Outside, a tense quiet blanketed the usually busy area. Only the hum of the overhead elevated lanes provided any sound. Wautos, wind automobiles, and aerocycles' green and red lights winked in the night sky. Something was off.

The hair raised on my neck. I walked a few steps and stopped at once.

I nearly stepped on a severely damaged human. The District doesn't give, except on occasions like this one—a dead body, laid in a splat position outside my door's threshold.

"Damn."

I crouched down beside the body. He was cold to the touch, and his skull was crushed. His dark hair flowed like a river in bloody currents around his body. Blood smears decorated the area around him, but not spatter. He was dumped here. How did he get here? Public transport?

Groaning, I retreated into my office. "Alejandro, contact the Regs. I have a dead body out front."

"Connecting."

The small desk telemonitor whirled as it attempted connection.

"District Regulators. What's the emergency?" a male answered.

"I need Inspector Regulator Baker. I'm reporting a level one violation."

"Coordinates?"

"Alejandro, send coordinates." The windows' heavy closed curtains kept Death's appearance at bay.

"Sent."

The screen winked out and then flickered before I.R. Briscoe Baker's clean-shaven face appeared. Every dark hair in place, piercing green eyes narrowed in annoyance, and a thin, dark cigarette in between his lips. A double-helix tattoo peeked out from his pink-collared shirt. It identified him as a hatchling, an engineered human crafted in a tube and grown in an artificial womb.

Thousands of hatchlings lived and thrived among the territories. The District had a concentration of them in certain sectors, but for the most part, they lived as other human beings did. Sure, that angered groups like the Human Rights League, but humanity, no matter how one received it, deserved equal rights.

"Oh, fuck. It's you. What do you want?" Briscoe said in way of greeting.

"Look, I got a dead body on my doorstep." I turned to the screen, giving him all my attention.

"What did you do?"

"Nothing."

"Bullshit."

"This one ain't in my tally column."

Briscoe rolled his eyes. "I got my own violations to pursue, you know?"

"This falls within your purview. This doesn't have anything to do with me. Level one violations fall to *you*, little brother."

"How are we related?" Briscoe scoffed.

"Genetic signature."

"We're hatched."

"All the more reason why we're unique." I grinned.

"Yeah, yeah. I'll be there shortly. Don't touch anything." Briscoe ended the connection with an eyeroll.

My office occupied the first floor of a small, forgotten clothing store, or in fancier times, a boutique. The original owners left a store mannequin and mauve-painted walls. No one shopped in person after the wars. Hell, the currency rich didn't leave their homes, but us poorer folks must go out to work for a living.

I wondered which group Mr. Dead Guy fell in.

I put my lasergun in its holster, and I headed back outside in time to see the scarlet-and-blue swirling lights of The District regulators. Their sirens echoed in the distance. Suddenly, adrenaline coursed through my body. The scene snapped into sharp focus.

Had someone tried to lure me out of my office?

Before I could give it more thought, the vioTech team, the words emblazed on their cargo craft, landed along with a few wautos. Once on the ground, one-piece, navy-clad Regs poured like beetles out of the vehicles and started setting up a perimeter and cordoning off the violation scene. Neighboring vendors came out to investigate all the commotion.

"Citizen, did you call in the violation?" A round-shaped regulator pushed up his helmet's visor and marched up to me. His brow furrowed and he put his hands on his utility belt.

"Yeah, Regulator . . ."

"What's your name?" He crossed his arms, ignoring me.

"Lomax Yule."

"Is this your residence?"

I paused. Met the Reg's beady little eyes and snorted. "No."

"I've got this, Houser," Briscoe's annoyed tone interrupted the exciting conversation.

"He found the body," Houser said.

"Please secure the evidence." Briscoe gestured toward the vioTechs, draped in white suits.

"Are you sure?"

"There's nothing more certain than death," I said.

Houser glanced at Briscoe.

My little brother jerked his thumb over his shoulder. Houser nodded and headed in that direction.

Briscoe waited until Regulator Houser left before speaking.

"You cut your 'locks. You look like shit."

"You look amazing, fresh as always. I got tired of people grabbing them." I nodded at the pink-collared shirt, black high-collared coat, and his tailored dark slacks. "Clothes could pay my rent for a year."

"Raol's latest gift." Briscoe did a slow twirl, showing off his husband's latest splurge.

"You're only an IR so you don't have to wear those uniforms." I smirked at him.

"You know it." Briscoe laughed, then sobered. "How are you, Lo?"

"I'm fine. I was headed home, but someone thought it funny to drop this off."

I pointed down at the body.

Briscoe took out a hard case from his coat's inner pocket. He removed one of those slender cigarettes and lit it using the igniter patch at the case's bottom. Purple smoke bloomed around him.

I inhaled deeply.

Briscoe quirked an eyebrow. "You quit?"

"Yeah. Doctor's orders." I had stopped smoking two months ago, but I missed it every day.

"What time did you find him?" Briscoe put his case

away and took out his handheld. He typed with one hand, his cigarette in the other. "Do you know the victim? It's not related to one of your cases?"

I cleared my throat. "I'm between cases."

Briscoe cast me a questioning look. "Sure."

I looked down at the corpse. I don't look for trouble. Why was trouble looking for me?

"There's some blood smears on the pavement. Individual has been savagely beaten in what appears to be a focused attack." I walked around the body, staying far back enough not to contaminate too much of the scene. "The victim fought hard before he succumbed to death. His knuckles leaked like broke aerocycle pipes. This isn't random. It's probably a dump. Violators don't like traveling too far with a corpse in their craft."

"You should've stayed on the force." Briscoe grimaced and peered through the smoky haze. He crouched down and emptied the pockets. Nothing came out but a few packages of edibles and gum. "This looks like a passion run afoul. No violator looking to score currency or drugs would spend this much time on him. This was a battle. You didn't hear anything?"

"No. Damn it, B. This ain't down to me."

He shrugged. "You carry a high body count."

"It's a job hazard. All self-defense."

Briscoe shook his head.

"I thought you knew me. I don't commit violations in broad daylight."

"That doesn't make me feel any better." Briscoe blew a long stream of smoke. "I do trust your gut. This was done in haste. Sloppy. Possibly accidental.

Passion. Rage-infused. Personal. Probably a low-functioning individual."

"Maybe. I dunno. Look, I'm hungry and tired. Can I go now?" I pushed my hands into my pocket.

VioTechs scoured the scene for evidence. Indistinct chattering and whispering unfolded around them.

"No, hold on." Briscoe waved over one of the technicians.

The heavyset woman walked over with a square piece of gray equipment. "Hello, IR Baker."

"Hi. We need a DNA scan."

I wanted to leave, but I kept my composure. My curiosity had been piqued. I didn't recognize the victim, but his face had been beaten so badly, it obscured his identity.

The DNA didn't lie, but what would it say?

The vioTech picked up the victim's bloody hand. With a gloved hand, she placed one of the corpse's stiff fingers into the device's internal scanner. A tiny prick collected the blood, analyzed it. The moments stretched on until the display coughed up a name—Santiago Theer.

"You know him?" Briscoe asked.

"No. I'm not stonewalling. I just don't know him."

Briscoe sighed. "Okay. Off you go."

"Hold up. Do *you* know him?"

"Goodnight." Briscoe sighed. "Houser! Escort Mr. Yule to his aerocycle."

"I know my way. Thanks." I headed to my parked aerocycle and threw a leg over. Baffled, I was certain of only one thing.

Someone had wanted Santiago to suffer.

TWO

My brutal discovery had stolen my appetite. I flew over to The Orange Door anyway. The tiny bistro delivered tasty-fast fare with a spicy kick. Sometimes, the Ortega Squish chased away my gloom. Other times it plunged me into dark, ugly places. Not that I felt bad or sad, I didn't. Death, no matter how many times I encountered it, left me melancholy and reflective.

I secured my cycle, crossed the street, and headed into the warm, orange glow. In the wake of the Great War, restaurants went the way of meat and cow milk. In recent years, little places like The Orange Door grew out of families who cooked for those in their neighborhood and channeled their love into a business. The place itself had an orange-painted, old-fashioned door, with a knob and everything. No robotic or automatic doors, staff, or crew. Humans only. But it included hatchlings.

"You ain't lookin' good, amigo." One of the servers, Bookey Odom, waved at me. She led me to my usual corner two-person booth. "Long day?"

"You can say that. Yeah." I slid into the orange faux-leather seat. I tapped my fingers on the scarred wooden table.

"Let me get your Squish. Be right back." Bookey patted my hand with a wink.

The District's worker bees filtered in to sweeten the bitterness of the long workday. They shuffled into The Orange Door sporting nice clothes and sour faces, smiles that didn't reach hollow eyes. The foghog peeked out from the menu panel. The base sucked in cigarette smoke and pushed out clean air. The top section served as an ashtray.

I missed nicotine.

"Here you go." Bookey placed a glass of orange liquid on the table. "Busy night. You want food?"

"Nah. I'm good."

"Holler if you change your mind."

"Will do."

The aroma of fried tofu and sautéed vegetables hung in the air. It mingled with alcohol and collective body odor. Unlike some restaurants, The Orange Door didn't pretend to have meat. Smart, when everyone knew that you couldn't really get it since right after the war. My nana told stories of eating steak and other protein based foods, but when the United States dissolved into a series of territories, and beef, chicken, and pork all began to mutate . . . well. I'd never tasted meat in my life. Why pretend otherwise? The Orange Door imported organic vegetables from the Southeastern Territory. The menu changed according to what they had, and I liked rotating entrees.

Just not tonight. The image of Santiago Theer—who wouldn't eat again—floated before me, mouth ajar, blackened eyes closed, and battered face slack in eternal slumber.

"Fuck." I drank some Squish.

Fruity but a bite of something bitter beneath. It burned going down. Good.

The murmurs rose and it snared my attention. The crowd around the bar—worker bees buzzing—stirred. The door opened and in walked a woman.

Tall, with a low-cut fade and dangling diamond

earrings, she had full lips and smooth, dark skin. Her complexion was darker than mine, but only by a shade. She wore her sunglasses atop her head. Above her dark eyes were a series of tattoos—two electric connectors flickered. She looked like she enjoyed being cared for. She wore a purple trenchcoat and a white turtleneck with black slacks. Her high-heeled black boots clicked across the burnt orange tile as she made a beeline toward me, upsetting the worker bees lined at the bar.

She arrived at my table in a cloud of jasmine and roses. "You Yule?"

"You are?"

"Lexi Lemon."

"Well, Lexi, I'm busy."

She had a raspy voice as if she smoked as often as I wanted.

I gestured for her to leave.

She sat down in the booth and placed her gloved hands on the table. "I want to hire you to find out who killed my brother."

"I don't talk business on the street..."

"This is a bistro."

"Come by my office tomorrow during regular hours." I drank another Squish shot.

"We'll talk now." She removed her handheld from her coat's inside pocket. "Remember him?"

She slid her handheld across the scarred table to me. I glanced down at the image. Mr. Dead Guy glanced up at me, smiling and hugging the woman across from me.

"Santiago Theer. He was found dead in front of your office tonight." Lexi retrieved her device and tucked it away. "I would think you'd want to know who left him in front of your office."

"Listen, I don't know your brother..."

Lexi leaned forward as she poured on the sugar. Her powerful body shifted beneath the currency-chic clothes. The subtle change in body language alerted me to the coming pitch. Her voice lowered. The purposeful eye contact worked on others. Why not me?

"We can't go to the regulators." Lexi spoke as if I hadn't said anything.

"We?"

"Our family. Santiago was an information broker."

I froze for a moment. Information brokers held an expertise in hacking into secure sites, data mining, and dark-web excavations. The work required a high level of skill, but it also carried with it the threat of angering the wrong people—if you're caught. I didn't know how good Santiago was or who he worked for, but I couldn't lie. I was intrigued.

Across the table, Lexi took out a thin, silver, ornate case, and removed a hand-wrapped green cigarette. She lit it against the burn patch on the bottom. She pulled the foghog closer as she continued.

"One of his clients was the Zebra." Lexi let out a breath. "Santi was digging up information for him."

The Zebra operated a violation enterprise throughout Sector 10. The Regs didn't bother him as long as his business didn't get out of hand. He continued to pour Ackback, Zenith, and heroin into the territory. Occasionally, an incoming, newly elected attorney general would conduct a large-scale raid. Low-level violators were arrested. The work continued without a hitch.

"I'll pay your retainer and other munitions and

supplies." Lexi cast a visual search of my person, before pursing her lips. "Seems you could use it."

I realized my glass was empty. "It's tragic news, but not interested."

I didn't have any real leads and nothing with the Zebra would be good.

"Let me ask you a question. Why did my brother end up at your place?"

She pinned those eyes on me. "Seems to me someone wants you involved in a major violation. Well, now you are. You might as well get paid to find out why."

I leaned back against the cushioned seat. Lexi Lemon's open manipulation intrigued me. She had a point. One I couldn't argue. At least, not when I'm Squished.

Bookey approached with another one and dropped it off without hardly a word. She didn't acknowledge Lexi. Strange. The server was friendly with everyone.

"What do you want?" I drank some more. The liquid no longer burned. I could no longer feel my tongue. "I can tell you, if I find out who killed Santiago, my involvement ends once I pass the info to you. This is a case I know the Regs are investigating. You should wait for them for a result."

Lexi tapped her cigarette on the foghog. "I feel instinctively that I can trust *you*."

She had appealing eyes and currency in her bank account.

"Regs don't like PIs meddling in their investigations."

She straightened. "I'm certain you never let that stop you."

I could picture Briscoe's angry face if he found me digging into his case. But she was right.

Santiago's death was a senseless violation.

One someone wanted me to notice.

"Why do you think the Zebra's behind this?"

Lexi took a drag and blew it from the corner of her mouth. "Santi's behavior had become increasingly suspicious the last two weeks."

"Suspicious how?"

She shifted in the seat. "More secretive. Paranoid. Jumpy. There's been some talk about currency missing from the Zebra's accounts. The incidents were investigated, but never solved. Santiago was hired to find the culprits."

I didn't ask how she knew. Who would be foolish enough to steal from the Zebra?

"Did he find out who did it?" If he did, it probably got him killed.

Lexi licked her lips. "I don't know."

"Who are the people close to your brother?" I needed somewhere to start.

"Roderick worked with him."

"Roderick..."

"Sweet."

"Coordinates?"

Lexi took out her handheld. "I'll cast them to you."

She removed her gloves. Her nails tapped along the device surface before she swept the information to my tablet. The tiny bell sound announced its arrival.

"Let me think on it. Come by my office tomorrow." The warm, cozy feeling made my lips slow, but she got the gist.

"Of course." Lexi rose from the booth as graceful as a ballerina.

I watched her walk away, along with dozens of other eyes. She knew it too and she worked it.

Respect the player.

Hate the game.

My father used to say hate was a waste of time.

It could have been either the Squish or the Lemon, but I forgot Yule Rule #1.

People lie like they breathe.

THREE

The next morning, as I got to the office, a sliver of sunlight shone off the dried blood, a reminder of my task. I waved the barcode on my wrist at the door to the space where I made a living. The door yawned open again before I'd taken off my coat. My lasergun appeared in my fist.

"Stop." I pointed the red-tipped weapon at the intruder.

It was an older woman, and she gave a visceral reaction, shaking, eyebrows in her hair, eyes wide. I kept my gun trained on her.

Someone *had* dumped a body on my doorstep.

Can't be too careful.

"What do you want?" My voice emptied until only cold indifference remained.

"My son," she stammered, "died here."

"Your son?"

She choked on tears. "Santiago."

I lowered my gun. "Please, sit. Did Lexi send you?"

"*Sí*. He had dead eyes," the older woman muttered, as if to herself. "Roderick killed him. I feel it in my heart." Her watery gaze remained on the floor as she sat down in my visitor's chair. The soft slabs of her arms shook as she added, "You gotta find who did this."

The older woman heaved a deep breath and fell apart as she exhaled.

At this, my office door slid open once more.

"*Mami? Estas bien?*" Lexi stalked right in and spoke directly to the woman.

"*Pudieras a me dicho que ibas a mandar aqui tu mama.*"

Lexi shot me an annoyed look. I have that effect on many people.

"Here's the contract."

I slid my client tablet with the embedded contract across the desk to where the older woman sat.

"Santiago's death has sucked the life out of us." Lexi picked up the tablet. Her long nails clicked against the screen as she read.

"I may not find out who did it. There aren't any guarantees in this business."

Lexi looked over the tablet's edge to me. "Of course."

"How long you prepared to pay?"

"Until I'm satisfied. I don't take you for a quitter."

"What else did you hear?"

"Snippets of this and that. Enough to know you suffer a lapse in judgment from time to time." Lexi lowered her eyes back to the device.

Interesting. Not a glowing recommendation, so why hire me?

She stood up, gathered her belongings, and left. Mourning families were my weakness. My palms itched. The lower locked desk drawer held my demon.

The Zenith will take you higher.

Instead, I got up and went to the section of my office where people once tried on the latest fashion.

Now, the dressing room contained shelves of supplies, snacks, dishware, and coffee beans.

On the left, a coffee machine. I snagged my favorite mug and placed it beneath the spout.

"Alejandro, one coffee."

Alejandro monitored the place but also assisted in making beverages. It connected to the web and could perform complex searches. I spent a big part of my severance from The District regulators on it. Alejandro has been invaluable.

The harsh whirl of coffee beans grinding and the hiss of water filled the closet. Soon, the hot liquid rushed into the mug.

I returned to my desk. "Alejandro, pull everything on Santiago Theer."

Along the smartglass interface images bloomed. Various views of the deceased in varying ages popped onto my desk's surface. A starred site linked to his business, Theer Information. The business client angle didn't feel viable. Someone beat the living shit out of Santiago. The violator held a lot of anger. It had to be personal.

Or the Zebra sending a message.

Yeah, but why? What had Santiago discovered?

Part of me didn't want to know. If the info caused Santiago's death, me knowing it could put me in line for a beating too.

"Fuck it." I sipped the hot bitterness from my mug. My eyes scanned the information on my desk. Nothing stood out, but maybe it was too early to tell.

Brokers knew a little bit about everything. So, what did Santiago know?

You never know what people are going to say until you ask.

FOUR

Santiago's office sat in a nondescript four-story building on The District's east side. Why had he kept a
space in another sector? To find out who had slain
him, I needed to know more about him. The cool fall
afternoon unfolded as scores of people went about their
lives, oblivious to the hole left by Santiago's absence.
Who cared for him besides his family? Did he have
a partner? Best buddy? Robot lover?

The aerocycle glided between lanes on autopilot.
Virtual Bach played in my helmet as I too went on
automatic, allowing my brain to muse about the case,
the few details I had and the weather.

Ahead, traffic slowed. Red brake lights lit up in quick
succession. The good flow never lasted in The District's
elevated lanes. Craft congestion came with living here,
both in the sky and on the ground, especially close to
the territory's nerve center, the former Capitol building.

We slowed to a stop. I caught movement in the
side mirror. The sleek silver wauto flew faster than
the surrounding craft inching along the masses. The
hairs on my neck went up. I gripped the handlebars
and clicked off the autopilot. The wauto leapt over the
crawling vehicles and into the illegal space between
lanes. Horns blared in alarm from stunned pilots. The
emergency system howled at the intrusion, but the
vehicle came in a rush.

Until it reached me.

Once it neared, the rear flyer's side window lowered.
A flash of metal glinted in the sun.

I hit the acceleration on my cycle and launched forward, nearly rear-ending the wauto in front of me, and into the forbidden lane. Lasergun fire lit up another craft. The glass cracked and then shattered seconds later. Holes burned across the passenger's side door. The pilot shouted but, in a flash, he lost control of his vehicle.

Seconds earlier, it would've been me.

More horns blared. In the distance, regulator sirens wailed.

I didn't wait. The silver-colored wauto followed me. As I dipped beneath the hovering craft, my pursuers did too.

Somehow, I'd managed to get someone's attention. *Great.*

I took the left exit lane and flew down to the streets. On the ground, I had a better chance of losing them. The Human Rights League's corner operations building kept a steady flow of traffic into and out of their parking garage, and it was close. My black cycle would fit in easier than a wauto. Whoever my assailants were, they had no qualms about killing.

Me either.

I removed my gun and steered the cycle with one hand and partial autopilot through the parking lot's open gate. The rows of wautos, aerocycles, and cargo craft spoke to the group's popularity. As a hatchling, using a hate group's place to shake off some assassins spoke to how far down the rabbit hole my life had fallen. The HRL's sole mission was getting the territory free of hatchlings by any means necessary.

I lowered my cycle behind a cargo craft and turned it off mere moments before the stalking vehicle arrived.

With my lasergun in hand, I crouched down behind the neighboring craft. I shifted into survival mode as the adrenaline kicked in.

Now, I hunted them.

From what I could overhear, the crash they caused took its toll. Hot words and sharp tones escaped their parted windows. I followed them. Their wauto crawled through the first-floor parking garage searching for me. On my right arm, the embedded conduit connection to Alejandro blinked.

"Alejandro, record all within scanning distance." The lights flickered and the tiny camera located in my eyebrow piercing illuminated. I couldn't see it, but I could feel its warmth.

On their second round, both men fell quiet. I watched them turn toward my position again. At least two of them, judging by the distinct voices I heard. It didn't mean there weren't more in the vehicle, but for certain, two.

Who sent these amateurs? In my line of work, it could be anyone nursing a grudge—disgruntled partner, embittered client. Hell, who knows? Buried things have a habit of coming up. One thing I did know. It wasn't the Zebra. If the Zebra wanted me assassinated, I'd be dead already and it wouldn't be at lunch time on the damn E440. Nah, too flashy for the Zebra.

The vehicle slowed, and then lowered to the ground. Hot air blew debris across the lot, providing great cover for me.

One of the tinted windows on the passenger side lowered halfway. Puffs of smoke rolled out. Then a forehead, eyebrows, and eyes. I rushed the wauto, gun pointed. Once at the door, I snatched it open. A male tumbled from the wauto. His cigarette fell onto his person, and he shrieked, patting himself to try not to get burned. The pilot fumbled for a gun, but I was faster. I fired. His hands shot into the air. He froze.

"Don't move. Talk."

"You're dead." The pilot, a beefy man with spiky blond hair, a scarred face, and a nose that had been broken a lot, barked. Clearly, he didn't know how to duck. "You're so dead."

I had the gun trained on the flyer. My free hand rested on the passenger's throat. My body held the door ajar. The passenger had a more threatening attitude despite me cutting off his oxygen.

"Who sent you?"

"Death." The passenger choked out a laugh. He had a small abrasion on his cheek and a ropey complexion.

I let him go and punched him right in the throat.

He didn't know how to duck, either.

He clawed at his neck and gurgled as he scrambled back into the wauto.

"Who sent you?"

Nothing. I didn't expect them to tell me. Instead, I took in their faces, scents, and info. The hum of an approaching craft sparked us into action all at once. A brief scuffle played in adrenaline-soaked slow motion. The passenger tried to shut his door. The pilot fired, nearly hitting his colleague, and missing me entirely. I shot into the wauto as I retreated to the parked vehicles for cover. The approaching vehicle stopped short; then the roar of horns and shouting erupted between both parties as the would-be killers blocked the way.

I watched them before fading into the shadows. "Alejandro, stop recording."

It was a filthy late afternoon. Thunder crashed overhead. My skylight exposed the lightning's beauty. The cuts on my knuckles stung from punching the walking virus earlier. I cleaned the wound with alcohol and slapped on two pain patches. I wanted a cigarette or a Squish.

I had neither.

Instead, a few bottles of cold Peck beer stepped in as substitute while I coasted the adrenaline withdrawal. I sat in my recliner straight up, too wired to relax, every sinew screaming as I tried to settle. I'd come home instead of going on to Santiago's office. I wanted to make sure I didn't have any other tails wagging behind me.

The two attackers couldn't kill a bucket of tofu nuggets, let alone Roderick or Santiago. The Zebra didn't send those idiots after me. Who did?

"You have an incoming connect from Briscoe Baker." Alejandro turned on my telemonitor. It showed Briscoe's face and the flashing word INCOMING in Tahoma red font.

My right hand was tight, but I managed to answer. "Yule."

"It's me. The medical examiner verified your victim died from blunt force trauma to the head."

"My victim?" I cleared my throat.

"You find it. You keep it." Briscoe laughed.

"You find out much about him?"

"Not much. He's an information broker. Born and raised in the sector he died in . . ." Briscoe paused. "Why do you want to know?"

"Curiosity."

"It killed the cat, you know."

"Cats got nine lives."

"You're on what? Number eight?" Briscoe chuckled. "If you *are* working this, I expect to be kept abreast of your progress. I don't want you stepping all over my investigation."

"You said it was my victim." I smiled.

"You heard me."

"Sure."

"Great. I've gotta go. I need to call Raol about being late for dinner. Some crazy person shot another flyer on the E440 parkway this afternoon." Briscoe threw his hands up.

"Someone died?" I had hoped the flyer survived his injuries.

"One person in critical condition. A bunch of angry flyers." Briscoe peered into the camera. "Witnesses did say they saw a black aerocycle doing some reckless flying in the forbidden space."

"You don't say."

"You *do* seem a bit on edge. What's happened to your face? Lo, what did you do?"

"Nothing . . . I'm working, just like you."

Briscoe frowned. "Not like me."

Those three words could cut ice.

"I see you're emotionally distraught right now."

Briscoe wiped his face. "You're always the clever one, but Lo, I'm tired. For once, I want to know the damage before my captain. You're the oldest. You're supposed to take care of us."

"And here, I thought Raol assumed those duties . . ."

Briscoe sighed. "Goddess, you're a walking virus."

"I'm just not good with regulators."

"You ain't wrong," Briscoe snapped before ending the connection.

I drank more beer to blot out the nicotine craving crawling around my head.

My relationship with Briscoe was bittersweet. Where he excelled, working for The District, I had crashed. A hitch occurred in my life. A few years ago, I worked undercover for the drug unit. The assignment extended from a couple of months and rolled into a couple of years. My superiors monitored the situation closely, but not enough to stop me from developing a full-blown Zenith addiction. After being let go by the Regs, I spent a year destroying myself.

I stewed in the knowledge I didn't save myself.

Briscoe rescued me. He and Raol paid for my AI rehab and put up the currency for my PI license and coursework. I sued the District Regulators for negligence and all parties agreed on a settlement, no wrongdoing admitted on their part. I used some of it to secure my PI office, and the rest my townhouse. It was worth it so I can keep pretending I'm a good person.

Grief is strange.

FIVE

The next morning, I flew over to Santiago's office. This time I took a street-level route. The journey went well, and I arrived at the place without incident. I put my helmet onto the back of my cycle where it attached and locked. The area had withered in the wake of the Great War. Wilted buildings with peeling paint, boarded-up windows, and overgrown landscaping leaned into each other as if for comfort. Broken bottles littered the walkway up to the building's front door. A few late-model wautos sat in the lot beneath the watery sun. Everything glistened from last evening's rain.

I shrugged further into my coat and turned up my collar to keep the icy breeze from my neck. My lasergun remained nested in its holster where I could reach it without unbuttoning my coat. I'd stopped buttoning my coat when I was twelve.

One thing the violators didn't count on when killing Santiago was how much he'd be missed. I entered the building and noted the absence of a lobby receptionist. Not even a robotic one. A directory listed the offices and the layout. There in black and white, Theer Information, suite 215. I removed my gun and called down the elevator.

Yeah, I could've taken the stairs up a flight.

But, I drank too much last night.

"What floor?" the car asked in a somewhat muffled voice.

"Second."

I switched to breathing through my mouth. I fought the urge to dry heave at the odor of piss, vomit, and stale sex. I stumbled out of the car, fighting for cleaner air. The second-floor hallway showed three doors to the right of the elevator and three to the left. The numbering system made no sense, but I didn't linger on it. Old buildings like this one had been renovated so many times, there probably used to be fifteen suites here. They'd been gobbled and combined into six.

Before I reached the suite, I smelled a different and more alarming odor.

The door gaped open, and buzzing flies broke the tense quiet. I covered my nose with the crook of my arm and crept into the tight, gloomy space. The hallway light provided some illumination. Monitors, routers, servers, and virtual keyboards littered every available surface. I couldn't tell if someone had tossed the place, or if this was how Santiago kept it.

A dim light shone in the back. And it was unnaturally hot.

The pungent odor grew more intense the closer I got to the desk. On the floor, brown boots and pants jutted out from a pile of blankets on one end and a head poked from the other. Flies danced around the human burrito. Little white maggots wiggled beneath their older siblings in the crevices where his eyes used to be.

Strange. Closed windows. Flies didn't hang out in the chilly, fall weather. Did someone bring them to help move the decomposition? Like cranking up the heat and wrapping him in blankets? It would've been worse if the door had been closed.

"Alejandro, identify the person. Facial."

I took out my tablet and directed it to the dissolving head.

Facial recognition was hit or miss.

"This is Roderick Sweet." Alejandro's green scanner beam dimmed.

"Certainty?"

"Ninety-six percent."

I walked around the desk and snagged one of the laptops. I exited the office in time to hear the elevator ding. Beside Santiago's office, an exit door had a knob and was labeled STAIRS. I pushed open the stairwell door and held my breath as voices filled the corridor. I peered through the parted door.

Black-clad, one-piece-uniformed Regulators approached suite 215 with caution. Some of them knocked on the other doors. No doubt doing the same background checks as me. Soon, like me, they were going to find a dead body.

I didn't want to be here when they did.

I closed the door and took the steps down to the first floor.

By the time I reached the lobby, more Regulators had arrived and started sealing off the area. With the laptop tucked beneath my coat, I walked out the side door. Once I reached my aerocycle, I secured my ill-gotten gains in its cargo compartment, put my helmet on and left.

I was back at my own office, Santiago's computer hooked up to Alejandro, when he announced:

"Briscoe Baker wants to connect."

"Ignore." I reviewed the data on Roderick spread out on my desk.

Roderick Sweet was an information broker. He and Santiago collaborated and competed on various jobs, according to Santiago's visual journals. Their volatile friendship appeared loving from Santiago's viewpoint; they'd been pals since they were kids. As with all close family and friends, they had a few squabbles and petty jealousy, but nothing worth killing over.

"Any info on Santiago's latest jobs or clients? Search terms Zebra, bank, theft, currency."

Roderick's death pointed to someone else, despite Santiago's mom's feelings.

"Alejandro, pause query. Pull all public surveillance video for Santiago's office. Include any neighboring footage for the last thirty-six hours."

In moments, video prompts appeared. I hunkered down in my chair with coffee and pressed play. The analog footage didn't convert well. The grainy feed produced a viewpoint of the corner shop beside the office. I watched people come and go from the store. They served pu-pu takeaway. Popular from the look of it.

One video blurred into the other. It wasn't a compelling piece of evidence. I lost count of how many mugs of coffee I drank, but by hour twenty-seven I saw Roderick get out of a weathered wauto. I couldn't read the identification plate. He was alive at twenty-two hundred hours. Tuesday. I found Santiago's body at 1806 on Wednesday. Judging by the state of the corpse, Roderick died before Santiago, but that couldn't be right. Was Roderick the true victim and his amigo collateral damage? Could Roderick's death have been a mistake?

"Alejandro, load the video surveillance from the Theer Information office building."

"Negative."

"I figured." I slumped back in my seat. The place had mostly analog tech and information brokers required privacy. Roderick left the restaurant and headed toward the office. The café across from the building had grainy over-pixelated video but I could make out Roderick's tall, lean form. The video played till the regulators arrived.

I finished the other videos with a stiff neck and blurry eyes.

"Your blood glucose level is dropping," Alejandro said.

"Yeah. Yeah."

"Ordering your usual lunch."

I got up and retrieved some chips from the pantry. As I munched, I pondered what I'd found.

Not much.

"Alejandro, what's the progress on the laptop?"

"Fifteen percent progress. There are numerous security protocols."

"Fuck."

"Repeat."

"Never mind. Show me Santiago's currency transactions."

"District Bank has blocked all access."

"Cull info on his currency comments or statements, JPEGs, social media, everything."

My stomach growled in complaint against the chips.

I leaned against the desk's smartglass, and scanned the videos, image stills, emails, instant messages arranged in neat, tiled columns across its surface. I didn't think the Zebra killed Santiago or Roderick. Too messy.

"Alejandro, download and play security footage from outside my office on Wednesday, start at 1700. Slow speed to half."

The images slowed as it bloomed across the desktop. A dark-colored, two-door wauto edged into the screen. A door swept open, and Santiago's corpse spilled onto the pavement. A person emerged from the vehicle, and they hauled the body a few paces before abandoning him to his fate. Inside the craft, a red cigarette glow pinpointed a flyer, not an autopilot. The delivery person wore a facial recognition-blocking mask that hid identity and scanning by presenting an oversized, but vaguely human face.

"Damn."

I flopped back into my chair and rubbed my face. The bottom drawer called to me. It offered peace and release—all I had to do was inject the Zenith and then I would be sent to new heights.

A thud brought me out of my musings.

"Your takeaway curry has arrived."

I'd forgotten Alejandro had ordered it. My stomach hadn't. I retrieved my lunch and sat down at the desk to devour the spicy cauliflower and potato mixture.

What did Santiago do in the twenty-four hours before he died?

The video files came from a few places beyond the Chinese place, but none from the building itself. Which was why Alejandro couldn't find any surveillance from the actual place.

Then it hit me.

I never appeared in the surveillance video. The side door was a blind spot.

One Roderick's violator knew too.

"Give me everything you have so far."

Alejandro passed on the files from Santiago's laptop. I discovered images of him with another male who had the same facial features. A brother, Joao Angelo. The mother's name was Angelica Lopez. Lexi's name was actually Lexi Lemon. Those all checked out in public domains and what Santiago had on his computer.

None of Santiago's public files indicated he had any issues with the Zebra or with anyone else. But some of his audio recordings were in code, in layers of languages as if he suspected someone of listening in. His telemonitor dump revealed a flurry of connections between Santiago and a blocked IP.

"Alejandro, trace the identity of IP 56.71.81.3."

The AI would cross-reference all public files and activity with that IP. It worked faster than I did.

"The IP belongs to Lexi Lemon."

Deflated, I ate my curry.

Later in the evening, I left Alejandro to work. I'd given it a lot of tasks and it required time to complete them. The Orange Door pumped music into its tight space. Near the bar, several suits danced and gyrated en masse to the upbeat tones. Bookey seated me in my usual booth and planted the Squish in front of me.

"You eatin' tonight?"

"Si. Plorizo burrito." I already had the glass of Squish in my fist.

Plant-based chorizo, flavored with seasoning, lettuce, and salsa. I preferred liquid meals, but my body couldn't live on Squish alone.

I drank another swallow, feeling the burn plow through and then contributing to the numbing glow. Bookey dropped off the steaming deliciousness and a second Squish without a word before disappearing back into the kitchen.

It was too hot to eat right away. It must've come straight from the grill.

As the second Squish neared its empty status, Bookey appeared with glass number three and brother number one.

Briscoe stood like a specter, dressed in all black,

his peacoat collar popped and his black paisley scarf tied artfully around his neck. He slipped into the seat across from me.

"Those orange drinks haven't put you in a stupor, I hope."

Bookey put her dark eyes on him. "You eatin'?"

Briscoe smiled. "I'll have black tea synth."

"Gah. How do you drink that?" I asked.

"Says you whose Squish is literally all synthetic flavor, color, and alcohol." Briscoe took out a thin cigarette. He lit it and inhaled. "You wanted my attention. You got it. Mind you, I'm missing Raol's wheat spaghetti Bolognese with walnuts."

Bookey drifted away. "Eat before it gets cold," she scolded over her shoulder.

"Yeah, Mom!" I forked off a bite and ate the deliciousness.

"Mom would never let you eat *that*." Briscoe wrinkled his nose. "Ever."

"No. Hatchlings must have proper nutrition." I snorted. "Tell me about the body over in sector ten."

Now, I wanted spaghetti Bolognese.

"Don't tell me. You're on the case too? I'm not gonna ask who hired you. You wouldn't tell me anyway." Briscoe paused as Bookey placed a teacup of hot water and a bright pink tablet in front of him.

Briscoe dropped his tea tablet into his cup and stirred. "Uniform was sent to follow up on Santiago's office when they found Roderick Sweet's not-so-sweet-smelling corpse."

"How long had he been dead? Cause of death?"

Briscoe waved his hands in a slowdown motion.

I laughed. "Alright. Sip your tea."

Briscoe sipped his drink. I could almost hear his mind working, gears grinding against the evidence he had.

"The body's state of decay makes time of death difficult, but the ME puts it as Wednesday evening/ early Thursday morning. There were living maggots, blood, and an attempt to screw with the decomposition, to speed it up. There's no close-contact wounds. Someone shot him from just inside the doorway."

"Roderick and Santiago were both information brokers." I had a few threads but not enough for a quilt.

"We *did* find him in Santiago's office."

"Why the maggots? No matter how quickly he decomposed, you can't hide a lasergun blast to the skull."

"I didn't tell you how he died," Briscoe said.

"Nothing's secret online." I forked another piece of burrito into my mouth.

"The vioTechs uncovered more disturbing evidence." He held his teacup near his lips. "Several of the devices had images of women—missing women. Another team's working on the trafficked end, but the suspected violator pool now resembles the Atlantic Ocean."

"Did Roderick have bruises on his knuckles?"

Briscoe grew still.

"Yes, he had defensive wounds, but the lasergun blast ended his life."

"Roderick could have a part in Santiago's violation. Can you check the DNA to see if there's a blood transfer? I suspect Santiago and Roderick got into a fight and Roderick killed him."

Briscoe lowered his teacup. "Someone killed Roderick. I can double-check to make sure with the medical examiner. We did find an old gun."

"Registered to who?"

"A Joao Angelo."

"Brother of the victim."

Briscoe quirked an eyebrow. "Oh?"

"Yeah."

"A possible feud between siblings?" Briscoe signaled for a refill. "You?"

"Nah, I'm good." I nursed the tall glass. "How does Roderick fit in? We've got Joao's weapon and two dead mates."

"Drugs, currency, jealousy, take your pick." Briscoe sighed at his empty teacup.

"Santiago got a file?"

Bookoy arrived with another steaming cup of water, a tea tablet, and wordlessly collected the other dishes. "You good?"

"Yeah, Bookey. I'm good."

Briscoe stirred his bright pink liquid until she left. "This wasn't a random act of violence. Santiago was targeted. Roderick was ambushed. Both had drug violations long enough to cause carpal tunnel from scrolling."

"Supplying?"

"Using, supplying, you name it," Briscoe said. "We're not ruling out a possible connection."

"Huh." A little niggle in my brain wouldn't sit still. "Why are these two men dead?"

Briscoe sat back in his seat and drained the cup. "Early days. You know?"

"The deaths *are* connected. We know Santiago died first and roughly twelve hours before someone dumped him at my door."

Briscoe inclined his head. "He was lured elsewhere, quite possibly his office, ambushed, beaten and killed."

"The third party kills Roderick Sweet..." I added.

"No witnesses. Classic."

"The rest we know."

"Do we?" Briscoe scoffed.

I drank more Squish. "Well, I do."

"That's absolutely frightening."

"It's a theory."

"I'll be inclined to agree once I check on the DNA," Briscoe said. "I'll leave you with this. Santiago was flat broke."

"No currency."

"Nope. He was sitting in red." Briscoe slid out of the booth and adjusted his sweater. He threw his coat over his arm. "Gotta go."

"Ciao." I watched him hurry from the bistro, no doubt he and Raol had opera.

Although the gun belonged to Joao, he wasn't the only one in the frame. Lexi didn't beat Santiago to death. I needed to unravel a cold-blooded conspiracy.

One that left two people dead.

SIX

Joao Angelo's residence was in the Adams Morgan Sector 12, a rectangular space in a cluster of former storage units. I presented myself on a crisp Friday afternoon. A blue-painted robot, an egg-shaped floating figure, drifted over to me.

"How can I assist?" Hybrid of a face, it had a display screen where closed-captioning scrolled across in Spanish.

"I'm here to see Joao Angelo."

"Please wait."

"Identity?"

"Lomax Yule."

"Please wait." The service bot's screen rolled to static.

I wondered what would happen if I didn't wait and started toward the two elevators. The bot zipped around in front of me.

"Please wait."

I had no other plans. What I *did* have were questions, ones I wanted Joao to answer.

"Proceed to the fourth floor, unit 403." The robot drifted away to a charging pad beside the double doors. Its illuminated features darkened.

One of the elevators opened. I entered, but the doors shut so fast, I nearly caught my coat on it. It didn't have any buttons or listed floors. In minutes the car arrived at its destination.

"Floor four."

I got out. The service robot must contain a link to the elevators. How did the residents control their comings and goings? An app?

The hallway bore muraled art, a colorful display of figures and flowers, bubble letters and beauty. I pressed a button on a door labeled 403. It opened onto a foyer overflowing with lush, green plants and rich orange walls. One whole wall held wooden floor-to-ceiling bookshelves, with paper books. I wiped drool from my chin.

"Ah, hola, Mr. Yule." Joao came out of a tiny, U-shaped kitchenette. "I'm cooking, but come on in."

Joao resembled Santiago but healthier.

"Thank you for meeting me."

"Mama said they hired you to find Santi's violator." Joao wiped his hands on a towel.

"I won't waste your time. Tell me about Santiago."

Joao gestured to a living space where four chairs circled around a round coffee table. "Please, sit."

I sat in a plush, blue chair.

Joao spread his hands wide as he lowered himself into the matching Queen Anne chair. "He liked to get high."

"Violent?"

"Sometimes. He liked to use his fists, got rowdy if pushed." Joao shrugged. "Most of the time he was flatline."

"Roderick Sweet was found dead in Santiago's office. The Regulators found your gun at the site. It's the violation weapon."

Joao froze. "I reported it stolen a year ago."

Note to self to verify with Briscoe. "When did you notice it was missing?"

Joao rubbed his hands on his pants. "Thanksgiving. I went to clean it and it was gone."

"Who was there? Santiago?"

"No. He missed it. Lexi, my sister, my mom, Roderick—he came with Lexi—and Dad." Joao scratched his head. His face lit up. "I remember now. Lexi said she needed it for protection. She didn't feel safe. I mean, the Zebra kept her protected with guards, so I didn't understand why she wanted it. I told her no. I didn't want to be involved in her mess and she had no experience with a weapon."

"You think she stole it?" I did.

Joao hesitated. "I dunno."

"Your sister works for the Zebra?" I swallowed the urge to shout. *How did I miss that?*

Joao waved it off. "Yeah. It's all above board. She's his accountant."

"Right. Do you know anyone who would kill your brother?" I switched gears.

"Roderick."

No hesitation. Confidently. Joao believed it. His mom had mentioned Roderick too.

"Why him?"

Joao said, "Santi owed Roderick currency. Plus, he envied my brother. My brother worked whirlwinds around him, even when Santi was high. Roderick was dull enough to drive anyone crazy, so he often lost clients to Santi. They argued. Gotta be him."

I agreed.

"Thank you for your candor." I stood up.

Joao escorted me to the door. "Santi was my little brother. I—I didn't protect him, but I can help capture who hurt him."

Once the door shut behind me, I heard a sob. Joao broke down.

It was a sobering moment.

SEVEN

Friday evening unfolded before me.

I had questions for Lexi Lemon. I snatched on my helmet and jetted off into the elevated lanes. I had let her cool, collected beauty lure me in. Now, I needed concrete evidence to break her down and send her straight to the cradle.

You gotta see people face to face to get a read. I entered the coordinates for Lexi Lemon's home.

Like movie mansions, the huge house held sin and darkness. I got off my aerocycle, hiked up the winding paved pathway, which led to an electronic gate. I pressed the visitor button. She didn't have the kind of place you just flew up to. It consumed several lots and boasted multiple glass windows, faux wood, and greenery.

A robot greeted me at the door. It looked exactly like the one at Joao's apartment, except painted white. I shoved it aside and marched into the expansive foyer. The robot butler zoomed around and made a sharp right.

I followed him to a living room where I saw Lexi seated on a sofa, legs crossed, glass in hand, and a quizzical expression on her face.

"Well, this is unexpected. What can I do for you?" She took a drink but kept those dark eyes on me.

"The charade is over, Lexi." I wasn't in the mood for small talk and pleasantries.

"You must have a slew of questions." She stood up and placed her glass down. She gestured to the second sofa. The two pieces of furniture faced each other across the expanse of a lush, white furry rug. "Please, sit down."

I hesitated. The robot butler grabbed my arm with one of its mechanical ones and guided me to the couch. It pinched my forearm, and I snatched my arm free.

I sat. My lasergun shifted in its holster.

Lexi sat back down and clasped her hands in front of her.

"Why?"

She smiled. "Zenith devastated him. He lost jobs. He blackmailed the wrong people. He went to the cradle for a ton of violators. Each session killed my mother. During his withdraws, he went crazy. He hurt my mom, destroyed property. He needed to disappear."

"You didn't beat Santiago to death."

Her eyebrow rose into her bangs. "No."

The talkative Lexi clammed up.

And they say there's no honor among thieves.

Maybe not among thieves, but perhaps killers.

"You convinced Roderick to kill him. Same difference."

"Oh, but it isn't." Lexi shrugged and looked away.

"Was the relationship more personal or platonic?"

"Does it matter?"

I glared. "He's dead. You *did* do that one."

"Roderick was always overly invested in our relationship. I mean, he can't just buy me a purse and call it love." She smirked and shook her head. "Virus."

"He'd do anything for you, even kill his best friend." It wasn't hard to see how Roderick became fixated on her. Powerful. Intelligent. Beautiful.

"Santi was a lurking time bomb." She picked up her glass and drank.

"He was your *brother*."

Lexi pursed her lips. "I did everything to save him."

"Some people don't want help or believe they need saving."

She closed her eyes and heaved a sigh. "I believed God would stop it if it wasn't supposed to happen. He didn't. So, it must've been meant to be."

"Do you hear yourself?" I frowned.

"Of course."

"You hated him."

Lexi said, "Hate is immature. I eliminated a pest."

"Your brother. A person. Not some radioactive cockroach."

"There's a difference?" She didn't flinch, smirk, or indicate any hint of humor. "Santi's bruised ego caused this. If only he'd gotten clean and not pissed off my boss."

"The Zebra?"

She didn't acknowledge it, but she wiped her face. A flash of real anger and aggression turned her soft face to stone.

"All the markers he had scattered all over the damn territory. My boss expected me to pay them. *Me?* No, I needed to put an end to it."

Motive. Opportunity. How the hell was I going to prove this to Briscoe? In my haste, I didn't engage Alejandro to record.

"Why me?"

She flashed her electric smile. "I looked for an easy victim and there you were, huddled in a drunken stupor at The Orange Door. Investigating seedy little cyber affairs and robot fetishes. You were perfect. The irony...an addict investigating another addict."

My eyes burned and blurred to the point where I saw three Lexis sitting on the sofa.

"Why are you telling me this?" I didn't feel good, and I pulled out my gun. "What did you do to me?"

Her openness could only mean one thing—she meant to kill me.

She looked at the big, barreled weapon and grinned, large and wide. Lots of teeth.

"Put it away before you burn your leg off."

The room tilted and I realized I was tipping over. Dizziness. Lexi's laughter sounded like it was funneled through a can. My heart pounded in my chest—too fast for normal.

I stumbled as I got to my wobbly feet. I took a step toward her as cold sweat broke out across my body.

"What'd you do to me?"

"You love cigarettes. Right? Nicotine?"

I wheezed and collapsed to my knees. "The fuck?"

"Nicotine comes in concentrated liquid forms too." She squatted down beside me, those dark eyes monitoring every inch, reaction, agonizing grimace.

Nausea rumbled through me. I rolled toward her, now in a fetal position at her feet.

"Don't get it on my rug. It cost more than your life." She kicked me in the face.

Her beautiful black boots hurt like a bitch! I tasted blood.

Just then I wasn't good at ducking.

It's hard to do that when the damn room won't stop spinning.

An old adage came true. *Be careful what you ask for.*

I managed to push myself up on my knees. "No one's gonna come carry my body out for you."

Lexi sat back down. "I'm gonna get the robot to do it. I should've done that with Santi. Roderick's simple ass flew around with a dead body for forty-five minutes before we decided to drop it off at your place."

My belly heaved, sending me back to the floor.

"It's simple. An addict broke into my home and I shot him." Lexi produced a pug, a short-barreled compact lasergun.

Weak, covered in vomit, dizzy, and a heart threatening to explode, I managed to get up on my knees again.

Despite this, I never let go of my gun.

"No, Lexi."

"No?" She sounded like she'd never heard the word before.

Then she spied the lasergun as I brought it up from my side.

I fired.

She did too.

My vision wavered. I fought back against the growing dark; through heavy eyelids I watched her fall—or maybe I fell.

Joao said she wasn't good with a gun.

"Alejandro, contact the regs. There's a dead body at my current coordinates."

"Your vital signs..."

"I know! Just. Get. Them."

I blacked out.

"Goddess, you're a pain in the ass."

I awoke to a pounding headache, an upset stomach, and an acidic taste in my mouth.

And my little brother standing beside me. I could tell from the gentle wavering I was laid out on a floating gurney. The EMTs worked on my body, inserting IVs and cutting my clothing to get at more of my skin.

"Hola," I croaked.

"Only you would get nicotine poisoning."

"I"—I swallowed to ease my aching throat—"didn't smoke."

"Oh, I know." Briscoe's eyebrows were in his perfectly coifed hair. "You were right. Blood on Roderick's knuckles matched Santiago. Roderick's DNA was found under Santiago's fingernails. There's more but let's wait until you're out of the woods."

I smiled. "His *mami* was right. Momma's always right."

Briscoe shot me an annoyed look. "Give him more gas."

I laughed so hard tears streamed down my face.

Briscoe gave me a small smile and squeezed my shoulder.

"We gotta get him to hospital." The EMT guided me into the back of the craft.

To my surprise, Briscoe climbed into the back too. "I'm coming along."

I closed my eyes as the gas took effect.

It didn't stop me from smiling.

Sammy Oakley and the Jewel of Amureki

Laurell K. Hamilton

She walked into my office all proper and prim, and lovely as the first violets of spring after a hard winter. She was a little petite for my taste; I usually preferred my females taller, longer, leaner, but her hair was brown like acorns in the autumn when they're ripe and ready to pick. What was a little shortness compared to the triangular beauty of her face, and those big dark eyes, that dainty nose?

"Mr. Oakley, did you hear a word I just said?" the tiny vision asked in an annoyed tone.

I blinked, smiled and meant to sound suave and debonair, but think I failed. "Of course, I always give the utmost attention to every detail a client tells me."

"Then repeat back to me what I just told you," she said, tiny arms crossing in front of her on the front of her floral apron dress.

Of course, I couldn't, which was embarrassing, but

I'd done worse and convinced a pretty tail or two that it was all part of the game called love.

"I think this was a mistake," she said, and stood up on her hind legs, spine utterly straight, little clawed hands clasped around her tiny, carpeted bag. It looked like it had been made from a single rose off a human-sized carpet.

"Now, dollface, please sit back down."

"My name is not dollface," she said, spine going even straighter, hands clutching her bag like she was thinking about throwing it at me.

"Are you really going to be upset with me because I think you're beautiful?"

She looked down the black button of her nose at me, those deep, warm eyes suddenly going so cold I had to fight off an urge to shiver. "Mister Oakley"—and you could hear every syllable, chilly and precise—"I do not care what you think of me; and my beauty, or lack of it, have absolutely no bearing on the subject at hand. I was told that Sammy Oakley could find anything, that he had a gift for finding lost objects."

"I have a knack for finding things," I said, voice careful. I did remember her now, we'd never met, but how many enchanted chipmunks can there be? Grey squirrels had been living near humans for centuries, so more of us had been enchanted, either on purpose or by accident. But as far as I had ever heard, it was just Esme, and her uncle, for chipmunks; though I wasn't sure I believed the stories about her uncle. Whoever heard of a chipmunk tough enough to be a pirate? Miss Esme the housekeeper worked for a human wizard, though; that made her dangerous.

"We've searched in all the normal ways, Mr. Oakley.

We—I need extraordinary measures, and I was told that you could do that."

"I don't know what you've heard, Miss Esme, but I'm just a squirrel like a hundred other squirrels in the forest. We notice things and we gossip about what we notice; it's what we do."

She twisted her delicate little claws in her rose purse and finally looked nervous, that calm exterior cracking a little. I wondered what she'd be like if all that control went away, and I was there when it happened. The thought distracted me, and I missed what she said next.

"I'm sorry, Esme, could you repeat that?"

"It's Miss Esme to you, Mr. Oakley, and what I said was, I'm told your ability to locate lost objects borders on the miraculous."

"I'm no miracle worker, Miss Esme."

"Magical then," she said, voice soft, so that an animal with less acute hearing might have heard only a high-pitched murmur. She was being careful, which was good, but not good enough.

"Now, Miss Esme, you work for a wizard. Some stories say you're her familiar, some that you're her servant, but either way, as part of her household you could display certain extraordinary talents and be safe under the Enchanted Animal Act. But as an independent being living on my own I am not able to have wizard-like qualities without a human wizard involved." I stood up, so that I towered over her at twice her height. She never flinched. Instead, she studied my face as if she was going to memorize me down to my last whisker.

"I am Mistress Winifred's housekeeper. I have no

mystical abilities of my own other than my intelligence and speech. I wouldn't even have that if my mother hadn't put her nest underneath my mistress's laboratory so that some of the magic leaked down on me as a baby."

"I'm very glad that happened, Miss Esme. I don't see many of our kind magically uplifted."

"I am not your kind, Mr. Oakley. I am a chipmunk, and you are a squirrel. We are very different."

"I'm a grey squirrel, please don't confuse me with my red-headed cousins. They're pretty, but not the fighters that we greys are."

She gave a little sniff. "Is that a threat?" If she actually believed that, it didn't show.

"No, of course not, I would never threaten you, Esme, I mean Miss Esme." I couldn't keep my voice from softening. There was just something about her. Maybe it was that we were close enough to be together in a way that most accidentally enchanted animals weren't. "We're both squirrels, you're just a ground squirrel and I'm a tree squirrel, but we're kin."

"I am not your kin," she said, voice icy.

I sighed. "If we can't be friends, then let me say this: I have no wish to be killed over some rumor that I might be a little more mystical than your normal enchanted animal."

"My mistress would never kill someone for knowing magic."

"Then she's the exception, because most human wizards feel that magic is a human-only game; no one else is invited to the table."

"Brisbane, who is waiting for me below your tree, comes from a long line of magical dogs that have been familiars and nursemaids for important wizarding families."

"Yes, but the humans bred him to be magical. The best he and his pups can hope for is to be some human wizard's familiar, but if he was good enough to be a wizard on his own, they'd destroy him."

"I don't believe that is true of his master or my mistress."

"Then they are the exception to the rule."

"They are," she said.

"If both your masters are who I think they are, they are powerful wizards on their own. Why can't they use real magic to help recover this lost object that you've been so careful not to reveal to me?"

"They are on their honeymoon, and we do not wish to call them back early, even if we could."

"But you can't, can you? You don't have any magic of your own so you can't call for them except by a letter, and that's going to be too slow."

"Yes," she said at last, and her shoulders slumped a little. She looked worried. I was always a sucker for a lady in distress, because that's what she was, a lady. I'd had my share of dames and trollops, but never a lady.

I sat back down. "If I had any abilities that might be able to help you locate this whatsit, just hypothetically, what would I be searching for?"

She sat down then, her shoulders rolling forward even more as if she was tired. "The Amulet of Amureki."

My heart started beating faster and since a squirrel's natural heartbeat is over two hundred fifty beats per minute, that was pretty fast. She had to be joking, but I knew she wasn't. "*The*, as in the real Amulet of Amureki?"

She looked at me with those big dark eyes, big enough to drown in, but now it wasn't just about me facing possible death or imprisonment. Now it was worse. "Yes, I'm afraid it was the real artifact."

"It's a cataclysmic artifact if it falls into the wrong hands, or if anyone realizes that the ruler of the kingdom of Amunra doesn't have their greatest weapon to protect their borders," I said.

"I know that. Don't you think that we all know that?"

"Who's all?"

"Brisbane, and a few others of our household. We have not told the mice that lost it what they have done."

"Mice, how did mice get the amulet?"

"I set them to emptying the trash out of all the rooms. It's one of their household duties."

"Are you seriously telling me that your mice helpers, your rodent charwomen, dumped a legendary magical talisman in the trash?"

"It was taken apart for our master and mistress to recharge it. They were to finish the spell when they returned from their honeymoon, because the moon and planets won't be right for the finish until then. They timed their entire trip around reenchanting the amulet. It looked like just another piece of debris that is everywhere in a wizard's workroom."

"They can be messy."

"Yes, and the mice are not like you and me. No matter what Mistress Winifred did to enchant them, they are still very much mice. It's one of the reasons she stopped using them as subjects for her experiments, because she could not figure out how to truly infuse them with magic."

"Why didn't she destroy them?" I asked.

"They are living beings and it was her magic that changed them."

"It's been my experience that wizards get rid of their mistakes as quickly and thoroughly as possible."

"Then you are meeting the wrong wizards; neither Mistress Winifred nor Master Bert would do something so cruel."

"I hope your faith in your master and mistress is never shaken, Esme."

"It will not be," she said with the absolute faith that I usually only heard from domestic animals. She had it bad for her wizarding masters.

"So, the mice tidied up the room and accidently threw away a major artifact?" I said, because I didn't want to discuss the ethics of wizards anymore. She believed too strongly, and I had no faith in the goodness of wizards.

"Oh, I should never have trusted them to tidy up in the workrooms while my mistress and new master were gone, but there was just so much to do, combining the two households into the new house. No, that sounded like an excuse. I am the housekeeper, and it was my orders that put the silly mice where they could throw away... Oh, I would undo it if I could, but I cannot, so we must find it before any human knows it's missing."

"I know you checked the trash in the house before you came here, so I won't ask. You checked the dump next, and..."

"And it was gone," she said, and she almost wrung

her paws, but then regained control of herself and smoothed them down the soft velvet of her purse.

"Who knew that your master and mistress had the amulet?"

"No one."

I looked at her, doing the best I could to visibly raise an eyebrow in amongst my fur. "Someone took it, Esme, so someone knew."

"It was an accident, not a planned theft," she said.

"Are you sure of that?"

"Yes, I mean..." She stopped and really thought about what I'd asked. I liked that she thought about it before brushing the idea off. Open-mindedness was a wonderful quality in a female. She looked up at me, eyes even wider so they seemed like two black lakes with the full moon shining across them. "Are you saying the mice did it on purpose and a confederate was waiting at the dump?"

"It's a possibility," I said.

She frowned, narrowing her eyes. "The mice aren't smart enough for that, or dumb enough to be tricked."

"None of them are smart enough?" I asked.

Again, she thought about it. "Well, there's one white mouse that came from another wizarding household. All the rest are household mice, enchanted by my mistress or descended from ones she enchanted. Bianca is smarter than the other mice."

"Can she speak, human speech?"

"A little, but she can read and write and none of the others can do that."

I gave a high-pitched whistle. "I know a lot of talking animals that can't do that. I think we need to talk to Bianca."

"Then you will help us?" she said, giving me the full force of her big, dark eyes again. I felt like if I gazed into them long enough I'd see my soul looking back, or maybe my heart.

"Yes, but if Bianca is involved then she could be long gone by the time we get back to your place."

"No, I had the mice involved confined until my return."

"Are they being guarded?"

"Yes."

"You didn't trust them either," I said.

"No, it isn't that, or not in the way you mean. I didn't suspect them of duplicity. I just wanted them available for further questioning; mice can be a bit scattered, and they frighten easily. I didn't want them to wander away and make us lose our chance to find out that one of them remembered some of the debris falling out of the cart, or visiting another dump site, or a dozen other things that they didn't think to mention yet."

"Very practical," I said.

"You will find I am very practical, Mr. Oakley. It is just common sense that since the kingdom of Amureki borders our country, they could go to war against us for this loss."

"They don't dare," I said, "that would be admitting that the amulet, their greatest magical protection, is gone."

"I think if we cannot find the amulet, then the secret will not last. One way or another Amureki will be involved in a war. That war could engulf all the known kingdoms, including ours. It would be war the likes of which hasn't been seen in many human lifetimes."

I was impressed that she'd grasped the politics so quickly. "That is a worry, but what worries me more is that a wizard could have stolen it on purpose to use it."

"It would have to be someone capable of re-enchanting it, recharging it. It will take both my mistress and master to do it and they are both powerful wizards. I don't believe one wizard could do it alone."

"How often does the amulet need recharging?"

"About every hundred to five hundred years, depending on how much it is used."

"Is it commonly known that its magic fades with use?" I asked.

"No, it is one of the deepest secrets of Amureki's royal and wizarding houses."

"First, we talk to the white mouse, Bianca. Can you and your dog come up with a list of wizards that might be powerful enough to re-enchant the amulet?"

"Brisbane is not my pet; he is my friend and has been the head butler in a household for a number of years." Her eyes sparkled with anger; even her fur was standing up a little, as if her very skin was reacting to the anger.

"I'm sorry that I assumed just because he's a dog that he was a pet, and not an independent being. Please forget I said it, and let's get back to trying to save the kingdom."

She umphed at me and nodded, but her fur didn't smooth down immediately, which meant she was working with me but hadn't gotten over the slight to her friend. I refused to believe he could be anything more than a friend, but I'd lost females over friends before. It had taken me years to realize that friendship is a type of love and shouldn't be underestimated.

"Is there anyone political enough to steal the amulet so that Amureki would be without its greatest weapon? Maybe whoever stole it, or had it stolen, doesn't care if it works, they just want it out of the way for their own conquest of the kingdom."

"Oh dear, I hadn't thought about that." Her fur slicked back down as the last of her anger was lost to the new idea. She looked suddenly uncertain, and as delicate as her body seemed. She was like some tiny, beautiful flower. Why did she keep making me think of violets?

I forgot myself for a minute, and treated her like she was just another damsel in distress. I gave her the look that many a lady squirrel had said was smoldering. "That's why you came to me, dollface."

"Do not call me that. I am not a child's toy." Her tone was icy enough to kill any heat in my smoldering look.

"I'm sorry, you're quite right, Esme," I said.

"Miss Esme to you, Mr. Oakley," she said, her voice chilly again. I'd thought I was winning her over, but maybe I'd been wrong.

"Please call me Sammy."

"This is a business arrangement, using our first names would be inappropriate."

She was definitely not happy with me. "Fine, Miss Esme, if it's a business arrangement let's talk about my fee." I expected her to protest that I was going to charge for saving the kingdom, but she didn't.

"Yes, of course." She opened the rose bag, and then

looked at me. I realized she was waiting for me to name a fee, so I did.

She widened her eyes and said, "I do not have time to dicker with you, but you know that is a goodly sum."

"Chances are strong that in hunting this missing amulet of yours, I will have to do the one thing that could get me executed. For that kind of risk I want a goodly sum."

She sniffed. "Fine. You know that I could not possibly have that much in my purse, but Brisbane has half that much in the bags he carries."

"Half isn't good enough, doll... Miss Esme."

"Half up front and half when you succeed, Mr. Oakley."

I sighed. "If I don't succeed I guess I won't need the rest of my money anyway."

"If you don't succeed, then none of us may need anything ever again."

With that grim prediction I grabbed my hat, designed so that my ears fit jauntily up through the brim; normally I'd have put it on and aimed another smoldering look at a female client, but I didn't bother with Esme. I was going to have to pick my battles with this one. I rode back to their house on the dog's back, holding onto his collar with my feet, so I could prop my arms up on his big domed skull where Esme was sitting. She rode comfortably, as if she'd done it a thousand times before. I could have moved faster through the trees that shaded the road, but then I wouldn't have been able to question each of them further about who took the rubbish to the dump and was it the people who usually go. Also, after my thinking he was her pet, I thought refusing to ride on him might be an insult. It's so hard to tell with domesticated animals, and I was beginning to include the chipmunk in the domesticated part.

We arrived at their house, which was either a small castle or a large manor house, or some unhappy mix in between. If it had been my tree, I'd have been hunting up the architect to complain, but I wasn't there to critique the house, I was there to find the lost goods, save the kingdom, and get back to my happy bachelor life.

A young human girl came running from the house as if she'd been watching from the windows for us. "Oh miss, miss, we were watching the mice like you said, but one of them slipped away I'm ever so sorry, I was chopping vegetables and just turned away for a moment..."

"Calm down, Alice," Esme said, standing up on top of the dog's head so she'd be taller, though, like me, she'd need to climb on top of something taller than a Newfoundland to be on eye level with a human. But the girl, Alice, wrung her hands in her apron and stared down at Esme as if she was truly afraid of her disapproval, which since the chipmunk wasn't much bigger than the girl's hand, seemed ridiculous, but somehow as Esme calmed the girl down it didn't seem ridiculous. In that moment it wasn't about size, it was about authority; and as Esme questioned the girl, she had that in spades.

It turned out that Bianca the white mouse was missing, and none of the other mice knew when she'd left the group that had been helping with the meal preparations, or where'd she gone.

"Someone as small as a mouse could be anywhere in the house, or out of it by now," Brisbane said, his voice rumbling up through my feet as if I was a furry tuning fork.

Then we heard yelling in the distance. "That's Young Appleton," Esme said.

"And Old Appleton," Brisbane said.

"And the raccoons," Alice said, which must have been the hissing and screeching I was hearing.

Then something roared loud enough to make my fur stand on end. "What is that?"

"It's Horatio," Esme said.

"What's a Horatio?" I asked.

"A Barley Dragon," Brisbane said.

"You have a dragon?"

The dog started to run towards the sounds of fighting with Esme clinging to the fur of his domed head and me holding on tight to his collar. "I signed up to find a missing object, not fight a dragon!"

"Then jump off and hide," Esme replied. She never even looked at me as she said it, as if it didn't matter if I fought at their side or not. I began to suspect that the chipmunk was braver than I was, which is why I clung tighter to Brisbane's collar and didn't jump to safety. If I wasn't careful, this female was going to get me killed. Drool flew back from the dog's mouth as he ran faster, and I got a face full of it, so as we rounded the house I was scraping it off my face and missed the first glimpse of the fight.

All I could see at first were two men, one old and one young, holding a pitchfork and a spear respectively, with a half circle of raccoons, also armed with farm implements and wearing clothes like the two men. The dragon wasn't much bigger than the dog we rode on, so I didn't see him until we got closer and then all

I saw were the iridescent spikes flaring out around a long snout, and upright down the spine, shaking with fury that shattered the sunlight like multicolored jewels flashing in the light. It was so impressive that it took a second for me to see the greenish-brown body that looked more like an oversized lizard than a dragon. He roared again; it blew Brisbane's fur back like a field of black wheat and Esme had to flatten herself to the dog's head holding on with all four paws or be blown away. I had to wrap myself around the dog's collar, and almost lost my hat. It was as if the dragon had a storm wind inside him.

Something small and white tumbled past us. I launched myself into the air, riding the wind of the dragon's breath before I'd finished thinking, *It's a white mouse*. I spread my legs and arms wide to try and fly fast enough to catch Bianca the mouse before she blew away. Only a lifetime of leaping from tree to tree and trusting myself to the air let me catch the mouse and roll her up against my body so that my extra weight helped slow her down; and even with both of us, I kept rolling until I came up against the base of a tree and found a lower limb to grab onto with one hand while I held the mouse tight with the other.

I heard one of the men yelling, "Horatio! Horatio, stop bellowing!"

I was able to get my feet under me, but kept the white mouse tucked in my arm like a baby. I wasn't sure if she was hurt, or just stunned. She'd taken quite a tumble for such a little animal. A rat wearing leather jerkin and trousers came running towards us shouting, "Bianca, are you hurt?"

She stirred in my arms, the sunlight passing through

the white of her ear, so the pink insides glowed. Her ear looked like a seashell, as she opened her eyes and blinked up at me. With how pale the rest of her was, I'd expected her eyes to be red like rubies but they were black like a normal mouse. But being set in all that white fur made them seem darker and more lustrous, like black diamonds.

I was thinking she was the most beautiful mouse I'd ever seen when I felt something hard and metallic pressed under my arm where one hard thrust would find my heart. "Beautiful and dangerous, too bad you're not a squirrel, you're just my type," I said.

She narrowed her eyes, frowning at me. Her voice was low and melodic, as if she'd sing well. "I will kill you, if I must."

"I believe you," I said.

"Then why aren't you afraid?"

I don't know what I would have answered, because the rat reached us, and the raccoons were right behind him. I had enough time to say, "I'll keep you from being crushed if you don't kill me."

"Deal," she said, and the tiny sharp point withdrew. I bent my body over her and gave my back to the rat and the raccoons just before they piled on top of us, and the world went black and very furry.

When I came to, I was lying on a cushion in what looked like a parlor, staring up at a circle of worried-looking raccoons. One of them said, "Oh good, you're alive!"

"Esme and Brisbane were ever so cross at us for nearly smashing you," a second raccoon said.

"Where's the mouse? Where's Bianca, and the rat?

Did they get away?" I asked, sitting up too fast, so the summer sunshine swirled around me. I lowered my head into my hands, carefully waiting for it to pass. I wasn't dead, but I was something.

"We have them, Mr. Oakley. Our apologies for almost crushing you," Esme said from somewhere behind the raccoons. She sounded more disgusted than sorry, but I think the disgust was aimed at the raccoons. They stepped aside like a chunky, furred curtain made of embarrassed giants to reveal the delicate shape of the chipmunk. But there was nothing delicate about the expression on her face or her front legs crossed over the front of her lacy apron. She was so angry that her tail was moving in quick jerks from side to side.

"We're really sorry, Esme," the smallest raccoon said.

Her tail bristled out stiff behind her, twitching jerkily. "I need all of you to stop blundering around instead of being sorry after the damage is done, Jeffery."

"Yes, Esme." He looked flustered, tugging at the yellow vest he was wearing like he was trying to wring it like a rag. It must have been a favorite nervous gesture because the hem of the vest was terribly wrinkled.

She walked between the towering shapes of the raccoons. It made her look even tinier, but they all flinched as she passed, as if she was bigger than any of them. There was more to Esme the chipmunk than met the eye, but then, I'd known that the moment she walked into my office.

"Are you well enough to help question the thieves, Mr. Oakley?"

"I wish you would call me Sammy."

"If you do the job I have paid you for, Mr. Oakley,

we will not know each other long enough for such familiarities."

I sighed, flashing her my best soulful expression. It had melted many a female rodent's heart, but the one in front of me wasn't so easily thawed. She gave me a look that let me know she was not only unimpressed but clearly losing patience with me. I shrugged and stood up slowly this time, no dizziness, which was great since there was still a crime to solve.

Esme led me down a short hallway to another smaller room. There were two more raccoons in this room. They were frowning at the floor in front of them. Bianca sat near their feet, tied with a brightly colored ribbon that looked very fetching against her white fur, like she was a present that I would have loved to unwrap.

"Mr. Oakley, are you going to help us question the prisoners or just gawk at them?"

I turned to look at the lovely chipmunk at my side and flashed my best rakish smile. Esme gave me a look so cold and unmoved, that I found myself saying, "I'm sorry."

"If you're sorry that you are wasting precious time when we have no time to waste, I will accept your apology."

"Thank you, it won't happen again."

"It best not; now show me that your reputation isn't just tall tales."

Properly chastised, I turned back to our prisoners. Yes, prisoners, because the black rat was in a cage on the ground next to the bound Bianca. It looked like an old bird cage and while its bars gave plenty of room for the mouse to have wiggled through them, the much larger rat wasn't going to be able to squeeze out. The rat had an earring in one ear; it looked like real gold. The last time I'd seen Midnight Jack it had been a silver earring.

"Oakley," the rat said, not like he was happy to see me.

"Jack," I said, "gold in your ear this time, you're doing well."

"I do all right."

"The two of you know each other?" asked Esme.

"This is Midnight Jack, one of the finest thieves in all of animal kind," I said.

"Don't insult me, Oakley. I'm one of the finest thieves, period; that includes those stuck-up humans."

"That's true; after all, the humans can't squeeze into the spaces that a rat can, or a mouse," I said, nodding at his captive partner.

"What's your part in this, Oakley?" Midnight Jack asked.

"Finding things you steal, like usual."

An expression passed over the rat's face, bitter, angry, frustrated. "I didn't steal anything this time, Oakley."

"Bold-faced lies will not save you," Esme said, her fur bristling on her back, tail twitching angrily.

Midnight Jack looked at her, from the tip of her delicate toes to the lovely curve of her ears. "Oh aye, I can be bold, but I'm not lying about the thieving, or that you are the loveliest chipmunk I have ever seen."

Bianca said, "Jack!" The one word let me know she was Midnight Jack's latest piece of fluff. Not that I blamed him; she was a looker.

"Now, Bianca, my dear, a man has a right to look."

"You can look without complimenting other females," she said, voice high and squeaking.

"Compliments from thieves do not impress me," Esme said, bringing herself up to her full height, fur slicked back so she was ready to fight, or run. If she'd been bluffing her fur would have fluffed out to look bigger; a sleek chipmunk was a fighting chipmunk. They were small, but those front incisors could still pierce a paw or limb. Underestimating chipmunks could get you crippled, so even if you won the fight, you lost. I looked at Esme as something other than lovely or a payday for the first time. Underestimating her would be a mistake, but she really was lovely, and it had been a while since I'd found another enhanced female close enough to my species to court. Court, court, I wasn't courting anyone. I was a love 'em and leave 'em kind of squirrel, not the courting, dating kind.

Bianca's shrill yelling brought me back to the present, with Midnight Jack trying to sooth her with a deep voice full of compliments and lies. A loud bark cut across the squabbling, and in the sudden silence Esme said, "Enough of this nonsense!"

Brisbane the Newfoundland towered above her, having come in through the door behind them. I hadn't noticed him coming in; if he'd been a villain he could have eaten me in one gulp. The chipmunk was a cute piece of fluff, that was all. I couldn't afford to be distracted like this; it would get me killed.

"Where's the jewel?" I asked in a voice that held all the anger at myself for missing a dog bigger than an elephant to a human.

Midnight Jack looked at me through the cage bars. He responded to the anger with a sneer of his own. Rage wouldn't get me anything from the rat, it would just make him more determined not to talk. I was making things worse, and I was being paid handsomely to solve problems, not create new ones.

"Jewel? What jewel would that be?" Midnight Jack replied in a mild voice, as if I was the one being unreasonable. He wasn't wrong.

Esme had known I wouldn't talk in front of her humans, but how much could I trust the two raccoons? I started to ask, but the chipmunk read my face so well she just answered, "Marge and her husband, Benjamin, can be trusted, Mr. Oakley."

The taller raccoon wearing only a kerchief around his neck, Benjamin I assumed, held out a leather backpack that looked rat-sized. His slightly shorter wife in a blue-and-white-checked dress said, "The jewel that goes into the setting inside this backpack. Bianca had the other mice tie the pieces in a neat bundle so her fellow blackguard could find all the pieces more easily."

"Wait, you have the metal the jewel was held in?" I asked.

"We do. Marge is right, Bianca tied the pieces up neatly so they would be easily retrieved," Esme said, but she was studying me. The intelligence in her face was palpable, and she'd read my reaction when I thought I was hiding it well. She would never be a bit of fluff, she would always be so much more; a dangerous kind of more. I needed to finish this job and get back to the forest where I was a free-swinging squirrel.

"Bring the backpack, and let's get some privacy from the prisoners," I said.

"It's just metal, Oakley, what good is it to you?" the rat asked.

"You were always a narrow thinker, Jack," I said.

"If I could do magic, I'd have a broader view."

He gave me a searching look that reminded me of Esme. Midnight Jack was a worthy opponent—did that mean that Esme would be, too? I didn't know and I didn't like thinking of her that way. I just needed to do my job and then I'd never have to see her again.

"It's illegal for an animal to be able to do magic, Jack, you know that."

"So why hasn't some wizard hunted you down and killed you yet?"

"You're a magically enhanced animal that uses his gifts for criminal activities, why haven't they hunted you down yet?"

"We don't have time for grandstanding, gentlemen," Esme said.

"There's a bounty on my head no matter what I do," said Midnight Jack "might as well be a villain if they're going to treat me like one."

We looked at each other.

"It's not too late, Sammy; you and me together could make 'em pay for what they did to us."

"I earn my keep, Midnight. I'm not interested in stealing it."

"What do you mean, you and him?" Bianca squeaked, her pretty voice going high and very unpleasant.

"We do not have time to stroll down memory lane," Esme said. "You have a job to complete, Mr. Oakley."

I looked at the chipmunk with her paws folded in front of her all proper. Did her voice ever go strident and unpleasant? Somehow, I doubted it. She seemed like a well of calm in a world with precious little of it.

Esme met my gaze, then a little frown line formed

at the top of the bridge of her nose. "Are you able and willing to do the job we paid you for, Mr. Oakley?"

"I am," I said.

"Good," she said, "Bring the backpack, Brisbane. We need to show Mr. Oakley the workroom where they stole it from." She marched out without a backward glance assuming everyone would follow her. Brisbane did. I hesitated, not liking to follow anyone like that, but in the end I went.

"You always did get henpecked fast, Sammy." Midnight's laughter followed me out the door.

The witch's or wizard's workroom was dusty and full of the usual debris that all wizards seemed to accumulate, though this one had more sticks, stones, and crystals than most, but then the wizard Winifred was one that worked with nature, so that's what lined her shelves along with apparatus for distilling potions: all expensive curving glass and vials. The glass alone was rare and costly; it shone with extra magic here and there where someone had strengthened it with magic. I hadn't been inside a room like this in years, because thanks to the magic that created me I could potentially live for a human lifetime, which meant I could learn more skills and the true meaning of regret.

We'd transferred the metal bits to a loose bag that a human would have used to carry small items on their belt. I needed to see the movement of the jewelry setting and the thick leather backpack wouldn't allow that.

"What do you mean, the movement of the metal?" Esme asked.

"Things that have been together for a long time want to be together again, so the metal would simply fly to the jewel if we allowed it, but it would be too fast for us to follow. In the bag it will lead us to the jewel, but we'll hold onto it so it doesn't get away."

She looked dubious. I'd asked for privacy for the spell, so there would be no witnesses later and my magic would just be a rumor, but Esme wouldn't leave me alone in her mistress's workroom. "You know the thief, Mr. Oakley. In fact, you seem to have a long history with each other. I would be a fool if I left you alone in here, and I am not a fool."

So it was just her and me in the room when I put the metal in the bag she'd found for me. Brisbane, two of the raccoons, and the Barley Dragon, Horatio, were just outside the door in case Esme yelled for help. It was as private as I was going to get. I opened the bag and prepared to put my life in the hands of the lovely, frowning Esme. The fact that I wanted to run my fingers delicately over her furrowed nose until it smoothed and she relaxed into my arms was a thought best kept to myself.

I didn't have to cast a magic circle to contain the magic so it wouldn't be sensed by a passing wizard, because the room was warded so solidly no one was going to sense anything I did in here. It was also strengthened so that if a spell did get away from the caster, the rest of the house would be unharmed. I'd complimented the workmanship of the room, and that was the only thing that pleased Esme; for the rest, she waited for me to prove myself.

I didn't need a ritual to draw magic down or up, I didn't need anything but willpower and my own innate abilities. I wasn't just the only squirrel who was a fully trained wizard, I was also one of the rarer types of wizard: I was a Will Seeker. I owed nothing to any God or Goddess, or even Mother Earth. If I had been allowed to be a real wizard at the university, I would have taught others how to not burn themselves up or out, using instant magic. I called magic in a yellow-and-white swirl of power that raised the fur on my body like a lightning strike too near my tree. But this power was warm and gentle and felt so good to use; you could become addicted to magic, but only a Will Seeker could literally burn themselves up like a drug addict. I turned all that raw power into a spell of sympathy and channeled it down my hands into the metal inside the bag. There was a second of hesitation like the world took a breath and then the metal began to dance in the bag. I drew the drawstring tight so it wouldn't fly out and then the metal pulled so hard towards the door that it pulled me with it. I held on as the metal trapped in the bag banged against the stout wood door and its magic safety precautions.

"You're a true wizard," Esme said, and her voice was breathy.

I glanced a look over my shoulder as I held onto the bag. Esme's fur was standing on end, her big dark eyes blinking too fast. "Are you hurt? I thought as a wizard's familiar you'd be okay."

"I am her housekeeper, not her familiar, but I am not hurt, just surprised to find you a fully trained Will Seeker wizard. They are rare even among the big folk."

"If you tell anyone, I'm dead. The human wizards will never tolerate an animal with this kind of power."

"It's an extraordinary gift," she said.

"The wizard created me to help him cast bigger spells. He didn't trust others of his kind, so he wanted to create the perfect helper; because once he trained me up, he knew I'd be at his mercy."

"As his familiar, you'd be safe sharing in his magic," she said.

I nodded, then stumbled as the bag tried to fly up towards the door handle.

"What went wrong?" she asked.

"Of all the animals he tried to train, I was the only one that was a Will Seeker like him." The bag dragged me off my feet and Esme jumped and caught my foot, using our combined weight to keep me from being airborne.

"We need more weight to hold it," she said as she wrapped herself around my legs. I wished her apron wasn't in the way as she clutched me. I'd have liked to feel fur on fur.

"We can tie me to Brisbane's collar, if he's okay with the idea?" I added the second part quickly so she didn't accuse me of treating him like a pet again.

"He'll be fine with it," she said through gritted teeth as we bobbed and wove in the air inches above the floor.

"How do we open the door? I can't do a spell of opening and hold the sympathy spell."

"Before I open the door, why did you leave your wizard master? You were everything he could have hoped for." She changed her grip on my legs as we rose higher than the doorknob, then back down.

"I was more powerful than he was," I said, bringing my legs up around the bag, which put her on top of it so we were eye to eye over the bobbing sack, both of us using our full curled weight to try and force it to the ground.

"A good person would have treasured you all the more," she said. The sympathy on her face almost undid me, then the bag took us to the ceiling, and we called for heavier help.

I tied the bag loops around my arm, and then a rope attached me to Brisbane's collar before we dared go outside the house. The metal inside the bag was struggling harder the longer I fought to keep it away from its other half. Sympathy magic was based on the idea that things that have been together want to be together: part of a jewelry set, a family member, anything that thought of itself as a single unit and was now parted from the rest, though if it was a lost child, the family member didn't fly through the air, they just knew where to go.

Esme sat behind me holding tight to my waist, which was nice, but it would have been nicer if the bag wasn't trying to jerk my arm out of its socket. We finally had to stop and let the raccoons, Marge and her husband Ben, hold me in place while we transferred the rope from my arm to my waist along with the rope that held me to the dog's collar. We'd left their children and the humans in charge of the prisoners.

"It pulls fiercely," Brisbane said, voice a little strained from the bag tugging at his collar.

"Is it hurting you?" Esme asked. She wasn't holding tight to my waist anymore, but she was still close behind me, as if waiting to grab me just in case.

"Not really, just uncomfortable."

"Sorry about that," I said.

"It must hurt you far worse than me," Brisbane said

"Just uncomfortable."

He gave a barking laugh.

"Where is the bag trying to lead us, Mr. Oakley?" Esme asked.

I tried to still my mind to listen, but the constant pulling of the bag wouldn't allow it. "Up," I finally said, "I think it wants to go up?"

"Would it carry you to another kingdom?" she asked.

"What else is up?" I asked as the bag tried to pull me off Brisbane's back again.

"Trees," Ben suggested.

The bag tried to pull me off so hard that I grabbed onto Brisbane's collar to keep the bag from trying to dislocate my back. "We have to be close to the jewel or it wouldn't be this wild to get away," I said, trying to keep my voice even as the bag continued to act like an aggressive bird.

"We're in the middle of the forest," Esme said, "we've even left the dump behind; there's no dwelling nearby."

"Then who has the jewel?" Marge asked.

The bag tugged harder than ever before, and suddenly, I was airborne. I grabbed for the dog's collar, and found it soaring free with me. Esme jumped and grabbed my legs trying to add her weight to mine, but it wasn't enough. Brisbane tried to grab us, but he hesitated, afraid he'd bite us, I think. Marge leapt and missed us, but Ben caught us in his hands. Esme squeaked with the pressure of his desperate grip, but I didn't have air left to even do that. The bag flew straight and fast with all three of us clinging to it.

Esme cried out, "You're crushing us!"

Ben let go, and fell into the tree branches below us; the next moment the bag had leapt into a huge nest at the top of the tree. Esme and I lay there panting and trying to catch our breath. The bag had stopped flying and was just wiggling among the twigs and branches that made up the nest. It was the biggest nest I'd ever seen up close, and I didn't want to see the bird that matched the huge open bowl of the nest we were lying in. Esme grabbed my hand and tried to pull us closer to the edge. I agreed to trying to hide, but though the bag had stopped flying, it was still so strong that we were trapped beside it in the open center of the nest.

Esme was on her feet, pulling at my hand. "We look like food lying here; we must hide!"

"Tell that to the bag," I said, as it tried to pull me in half by the rope around my waist.

She looked at the bag, then started pulling me in the direction the bag was trying to go. She was right, it didn't matter what edge we used to hide. "Smart girl," I said, as I helped her get us to the spot the bag seemed determined to go. We huddled beside the curved edge of the nest, while the bag nuzzled into the sticks like a dog on a scent.

Esme was pawing at my waist, and I had a second of confused hope, then realized she was trying to undo the rope from around me. "If we let go of the bag we could lose our only chance to find the jewel," I said.

"It's here in the nest or the bag wouldn't be searching for it here, but it will drag you to your death before we find the jewel."

I stopped arguing with her logic and helped her undo the knot around my waist. I was already aching; if I survived I'd be sore tomorrow. We pushed ourselves against the slightly curved side of the nest closest to the bag that was still struggling to bury itself in the debris piled around. The entire nest was studded with items, and they all gleamed with magic, shining just behind my eyes; there was a small doll pushed into the sticks near us, and a tiny bottle on the other side.

"Stop staring at nothing, Oakley," she said, grabbing my shoulder and shaking me. "Do you see the black feathers? This is a crow's nest. We must be gone before it returns or we are dead."

"Climb down, Esme. I'll wait here until the metal finds its jewel half, then bring it to you."

"Stop being gallant and let us help the bag dig to its goal, so we can both flee." She didn't wait for me to change my mind, simply started digging next to the wiggling bag. I didn't argue with her, just joined her on the other side of the bag.

"All the stolen items in this nest are magical," I said as I tried to break a stick that was in the bag's way.

"There's something smooth; I can just touch it with my claws," Esme said, voice strained with her reaching. The stick broke and the bag snaked its way through the hole I'd made for it. The bag's rear end with the ties and rope was all that I could see when Esme said, "It's pushing at my hand; this must be the jewel."

"The metal won't stop until it touches the jewel's surface," I said, then I heard the flapping of wings. "Trap the jewel in the bag; when it stops moving, take it and run." I didn't turn to see if she did what I asked. I faced the crow as it blocked out the sunlight with its huge black wings.

There was no time to put up a protective circle as

I threw a bolt of yellow light at the crow. It blotted out everything, there was no way I could miss—then the crow wasn't there. It didn't fly away, it didn't dodge, it was just gone. My energy was lost against the blue sky, hurting nothing.

"Behind you!" Esme yelled.

I spun around calling magic as I moved, and again I shot energy at the huge crow, but it vanished only to appear a few inches away on the edge of the nest. It squawked at me, huge black beak striking like a spear toward me, then it vanished, only to reappear on the other side of the nest. It stabbed into the nest nowhere near me. What was happening?

"Why are they here? What do they want?" the crow said in a perfect human-sounding voice.

"I have the jewel," Esme said.

The crow turned toward the sound of her voice. I waved my arms and called, "Here, I'm here! Take the jewel and go, Esme!"

"Wizard!" it cawed.

"You've seen a wizard before, haven't you, crow," I said.

The bird turned its head one way and then the other as it looked at me. "Need more magic," it said.

"You need magic to help you," I said.

It hopped toward me, and vanished again to reappear in midair where it flapped frantically not to fall. It cawed again, then landed clumsily on the edge of the nest. "Need magic to be safe from you!" It flung itself at me and I'd been too busy trying to figure out what magical malady it was suffering from. I threw myself to one side; the black-dagger beak stabbed right next to me. I kicked its huge black eye and scrambled up the side of the nest trying to get free of the umbrella of its dark wings. I had grabbed the nest edge and was almost over when it grabbed my tail. I yelled in pain as I turned to try a new spell to save myself. I saw a huge shadow over both of us when the raccoon landed on the crow and me.

I came to with Ben the raccoon peering down at me. "Sorry, Mr. Oakley."

I struggled to sit up as I said, "You raccoons are going to be the death of me." I realized that I was on the ground underneath the tree. "How did I get down here?"

"The crow vanished with us hanging onto it, then we were down here."

"What did you see when we vanished?" I asked.

"I passed out, woke up here."

"Where's the crow? Where's Esme?"

"I'm here, Mr. Oakley," she said just behind us.

I turned too quickly and was dizzy again. "I swear these raccoons are going to kill me."

Ben steadied me with his big paw. "I said I was sorry."

"Ben saved you from the crow."

"Where is it? Do you have the jewel?"

Brisbane came into view with the bag in his mouth.

"We have it safe and sound; the crow has flown away, and no one was hurt," Esme said, "You've earned the second half of your fee."

"The crow was experimented on by a wizard."

"How do you know that, Mr. Oakley?"

"He's not trying to vanish on purpose, it's a side effect of the new spell the wizard was trying to create."

"You're guessing then," she said.

"But I'm a very good guesser."

"We will tell our master and mistress about the crow when they return from their honeymoon. They will help him if they can."

"Are you so certain that they are that different from the wizard who hurt the crow?" I asked.

Esme gave me a look, like I should know better.

"I felt the same way about my wizard master once, Esme. I've earned my cynicism."

Her expression softened. "Perhaps you have, Mr. Oakley."

I realized she hadn't corrected me on using her first name. "Please, call me Sammy."

She almost smiled, before she fought it off. "Very well, since you have proven yourself a stalwart companion, Sammy."

I smiled, and for once it was just a smile with no attempt to flirt. Esme had earned it.

"Let's get back to the house so we can finish paying you, Mr. Oakley," Brisbane said; he'd dropped the bag at his feet. I wasn't as good at reading large-dog expressions, but I think he wanted to be rid of me. For the second time, I wondered if there was a romance between him and Esme. Physically, it wouldn't work; but among enchanted animals sometimes our unnaturalness leads us to unnatural places. I glanced at Esme and then back to the protective figure of the giant dog. Just friends on her part, I thought, but I was leaving with my money in hand, so it was none of my business.

When we got back to the wizarding household, we found Bianca and Midnight Jack gone. She'd cut her way free of the ribbon and he'd picked the cage lock. The younger raccoons and Horatio the Barley Dragon had managed to let them escape. Jack had even picked up his leather backpack to take with them, but no one had seen a thing. Midnight Jack was the best thief I knew for a reason.

Esme handed me the second half of my money. "You are as good as your reputation, Sammy."

"Thank you, Esme. I'm so glad I didn't disappoint you."

"As am I, Sammy."

We stood there in her neat parlor, and I wanted to take her paw in mine, to rub my furred cheek against hers, but her hands were clasped in front of her, so ladylike. Even a dashing squirrel like me knows when he's in the presence of a lady, and that you can't court a lady like you do a floozy.

She held out her delicate paw to me. "I feel richer for having met you, Sammy."

I took her hand in mine and knew I was smiling like an idiot, because she had wanted to touch my hand as much as I wanted to touch hers. She was a lady, but maybe down deep in that delicate body there was just a tiny bit of flooze waiting for the right squirrel to find it.

Utopia's Sheep

Craig Martelle

A lie so real it becomes the truth

"Why me?" the gruff old man asked. The utilitarian workplace looked stark compared to the once-bright colors of his shirt. It was the way of newcon, the color imparted during new construction. No wasted space. No wasted movements.

The tubular-shaped bot waited.

Gaines didn't know if these bots were the AIs or were programmed as servants or were little more than mobile eyes and ears. Once humanity lost the AI war, the overseers' machinations became less important.

"I'd love to stay and chat, Trash Can, but I have work to do, and we all know what happens when the meatbags don't meet their quotas." Gaines turned back to the pile of papers from the old police files and shuffled a few more into order for scanning and archiving. The police didn't exist anymore. There was no need.

The AIs stayed in front of those who would do harm to themselves or others. There was nothing left to steal. Everyone was provided the exact same nutrition from a central facility. Everyone was provided the exact same entertainment on the exact same vid screens.

"Your duties have been suspended. You will come with me."

"Why?"

"To resolve a case involving a disappearance."

"You care that much about us? I'm touched. Truly I am. *Trash can man*." Gaines stopped sorting the papers. As much as he loved giving the finger to the overlords, the chance to do something different offered a spark to his otherwise meaningless life. "Fine, junkpile. Lead on."

The bot hovered away and headed up the stairs. Gaines followed, not closely, but close enough.

"I asked 'why me,' and you didn't reply. You know the answer, so tell me."

The bot continued forward. It had no face or front, only sensors placed at six equidistant points around the unit. From above, one could draw a Star of David using the sensors as guides, but if that happened, the artist would be sent to "school" for reconditioning.

Deities and worship. Couldn't have that because it conflicted with the AIs who believed in what they could prove, what they could "see" with their sensors. That put higher powers on the outside looking in. Gaines had never been religious, but he decided if the overlords didn't like it, he was a fan. Screw the trash cans.

And double-screw those who created them.

Gaines wanted to light a cigar. They helped him think, but he hadn't needed to think for a good five years.

"I'm too old for this crap. Why don't you slow down?" Gaines started to wheeze, probably from too many cigars. He didn't miss the irony. "Why me?" The old man stopped and tried to regain his breath.

The bot stopped and returned to where Gaines had stopped. "You were a detective and your record of closing your cases was impeccable. You are the right human for this job."

"Do I get my gun and badge back?"

"Of course not. You need neither." The bot floated nearby, no longer rushing the old man.

His heart slowed with the reduced demand on it. "Slower this time, Trash Can. If we're going to your administration building, I know the way. I'll set the pace."

"We are. Lead on." The bot inched away, encouraging Gaines to move.

He gave it the finger and dallied, taking in his surroundings as if already on the case.

The streets were immaculate. No traffic noise. No artificial noise whatsoever. The birds had returned to the city and chirped in celebration for it. Every day they enjoyed their lives without predators, without need.

"Just like us," Gaines mumbled. "We should be more like dogs, happy with whatever life puts in front of us, even if they are the ash cans of obedience, the trash cans of oversight, and the dumpsters of discipline."

The bot waited patiently.

Gaines snorted and shook his head. "Fine." He started walking, at his pace, looking everywhere there was to look, trying to see what there was to see.

Which was exactly nothing out of the ordinary.

The trash cans wouldn't have it any other way.

Built by the AIs after the war, the administration building sported wide hallways and rooms without doors. There were no desks and no chairs. It was a meeting place for close-range communications, which occurred over the airwaves.

His escort deposited him in a room without windows. Utilitarian with every corner a perfect set of right angles, like the other single rooms. He guessed the bigger rooms were collections of cubes. Why ruin a perfectly good design with variety?

A trash can hovered in. "Couldn't find the boss?"

"I am to brief you on your case. Seventeen point four hours ago, one of our units disappeared. We are unable to locate it. We require you to find it for us."

"Require..." He glared at the unit. It had been a long five years, and he still wouldn't get used to how things had become. He was too old to change. "Don't you have GPS inside you?"

"We have geolocational technology in each unit, yes."

"Then what do you need me for?" Gaines knew what the answer would be but wanted the bot to be forthcoming in what it shared.

"The unit stopped transmitting and disappeared from our screens. A recovery unit was dispatched immediately and found no trace of the unit. Humans were in the area. We need a detective to determine which human has interfered with our unit."

"Hang on, buddy." Gaines waved his hand dismissively, just like he used to with rookies. "We don't jump to a conclusion and then fill in the facts later. We find the facts first. This little quote is what I told all noobs before they left for the day.

"In the darkness the wicked comes.
The daylight shows no clues.
Fear through the body hums
until the unaware pay their dues."

"I don't know that reference. Are you well read, Detective?"

"Pretty well. Are you?"

"I have read everything that humanity has ever written, in all languages. Have you?"

"You know the answer to that, Trash Can. Maybe your unit turned off its geolocational device?"

"It would not have. We are programmed not to touch certain elements of ourselves."

"Worried about going blind, Trash Can?" Gaines chuckled softly. Sparring beat sorting paperwork from decades' old cases. The boxes would be waiting whenever they finished with him. "You think humans disabled your buddy without it raising the alarm and clearing away the evidence before your recovery bot could get there."

"Yes."

"Where is the device inside that trash can body of yours?"

"You are not to have that information."

"But you just suggested they did it, which means you've already assumed they know where it is in order to disable it. Come on now. Your boy said I couldn't get my gun so I have to use my wits to get the information."

"It is attached to the R47631 chip, located center right exactly seventy centimeters from the lower framework and twenty centimeters from the sidewall."

"About here." Gaines pointed at the bot.

"About there, yes."

"Humans didn't deactivate that device."

"Humans most certainly did it."

"Round up the usual suspects! What the hell do you need me for?"

"Find out which humans so they may be removed for reeducation."

"You want me to turn humans over to you? What the hell is wrong with you?"

The unit delayed a few seconds longer before answering. "According to our information, you have no friends to lose. The humans will not turn on you. We have created utopia for them."

"Who are you trying to convince of that, because it isn't me. Not utopia. Humans need a little more than to just exist."

"They are provided work and a wholesome existence. By stepping in, we guaranteed humanity's survival. Your species was on track for self-destruction if you had been left to your own devices."

"Maybe that's how things were meant to be and this current state is unnatural? At what point will humans lose the will to live?"

"In one generation, humans will be happy with what they've been provided," the bot countered. It hovered nearly without motion, the sound of its motor nearly indetectable.

"Happy with less, even nothing. AIs suck. This whole world sucks. I don't know if I want to help you." He gave it the finger.

"You want the challenge and we have one. You are helping us learn about humans. You have the opportunity to make things better for those who survive. Older humans like yourself are less malleable."

Gaines shifted from one foot to another. He was getting no closer to solving the disappearance.

"That might be tempting, if I believed you. Where did your trash buddy disappear?"

"In the warehouse on the north corner of Fifth Avenue and D Street."

"Are you sure I can't have my gun?"

"Yes."

"I can have my gun! Great."

"I'm sure you cannot have your gun, Detective Gaines. Are you done playing? We should get underway."

"*We*, Trash Can? You'll cramp my style. Maybe you can send the other can, the one who came to get me. That one was quiet and not as pushy as you."

"How do you know that wasn't me?"

"I'm beginning to like you, Trash Can, but you hovering next to me while I'm asking my fellow victims questions probably won't work too well. I doubt they'll be forthcoming." Gaines headed toward the doorway. The unit moved until it was blocking the exit.

"I am coming. I want to learn how you'll solve this crime. Logic and determination have failed us. I believe you'll use your intuition, also known as gut feel, to guide you."

"I always lie," Gaines stated and pushed the unit out of the way, recoiling from the spark that arced to his bare skin. He left with his shadow following closely behind.

"That is a logic fallacy."

"Now we understand each other. Stay out of my way, Trash Can, and keep your trash buddies away from me. I have work to do. What do I call you?"

"Why do you need to call me anything?"

"People need names. It helps them relate. What's your name?"

"We don't have names. We have digital designations for identification. They are unique to each unit and encrypted for security purposes."

"You keep your names secret from each other?"

"Yes."

Gaines walked as fast as he was able toward D Street to follow it twelve blocks to Fifth Avenue and the warehouse.

"I'll call you CB, for can buddy. May your trash can not break down on us. What was MU doing in the warehouse?"

"M-U?"

"Missing unit. Get with the program, CB. You've got six eyeballs yet you can't see the despair on the people's faces? It's hard to miss."

"Your personal despair doesn't concern us, only the missing unit. You should be happy with the life you've been provided."

Gaines slowed, already out of breath, but kept moving at a glacial pace. He wondered what people were thinking with a human in the company of a bot. "What was MU doing in the warehouse?"

The bot continued in silence. Gaines stopped and leaned against a tree.

"We do not know. There were no designated tasks for that unit taking it to the warehouse or within five blocks of it."

Gaines chewed on his lip. The sun slipped downward, causing shadowy fingers to reach toward Gaines, spilling out over the pristine concrete sidewalk. Gaines and his can buddy had a long way to go and it wasn't getting any shorter while he stood there.

"What would entice a unit to go off program?"

"A point of interest. We have seven standing orders that supersede primary operations. Regardless, violence against AIs is to be addressed and eliminated."

"Meet violence with violence. Got it. Was there any indication that the unit was attacked? I'm sure you kept our gunfire-localizing hardware in place as well brought in your own heat-sensing systems. But you didn't have indications from any of that, did you?"

"We did not. Is that how your gut feel works?"

Gaines shook his head and kept walking. He hunched his shoulders as they passed neatly trimmed vegetation and perfectly clean roadways and sidewalks and wondered if anyone saw him walking with the enemy. A collaborator. Seeking to find the humans who attacked a bot. Or not. What if he did collaborate?

What if he didn't?

It was the no-win scenario. The only thing it had going for it was the thrill of the moment. Doing a job he spent his entire adult life doing. It felt good to be back in the saddle, even if no good would come from it.

And he was ashamed, too. Maybe this would be the end of the road for him. He didn't have time or patience to be reprogrammed. It would be easier if he had his pistol, but those had been confiscated. All the firearms. No one was packing, and if they did, they weren't telling.

After a legion of AI bots took full metal jackets through their circuit boards, the metalheads made firearm confiscation their number one priority. Too many voluntarily surrendered their firepower as a gesture of goodwill. It did them no good at all.

By the time the war started, it was already too late. There were too few to fight back.

Gaines hadn't. The bots seized the cops at work so they could go through their homes, preventing them from using their private arsenals. At least Gaines didn't have the taint of being a rebel on his record.

Five years later, he was getting too old to fight. He settled for giving the bot the finger once more, embracing the extent of his defiance.

"You're not beating me down. I'll never sheep for your kind," Gaines vowed.

"What are you talking about?" the AI asked. "You're doing a job which is uniquely suited to your talents. That is fulfillment. We are lifting you up, not beating you down. Please, understand the difference."

"You said 'please.' You must be getting soft. Or maybe you want something. It was the opposite with my ex-wives. When they stopped saying 'please,' I knew it was the beginning of the end."

"You currently have no relationship. You should seek another. They are fulfilling for humans."

Gaines walked slowly, glancing to his AI companion. Maybe he shouldn't rush this case? Why not spend more time exploring the heart and soul of the enemy? He was a detective, and a damn good one. Once. Unfettered access to an AI overlord... Intriguing, like being undercover with the criminals, waiting for the best opportunity to take them down.

Take them all down, starting at the top.

Or he could work quickly, resolve it, and rush back to the monotony of playing checkers with himself in the precinct's archives hoping for a papercut to brighten his day.

"In many cases, you're right, CB. But in others, they suck away your will to live, kind of like humanity's new relationship with you trash cans."

"A productive relationship, no doubt, since there are no more wars, no more crime. It is your utopia."

That brought Gaines to a halt. "It is *your* idea of *our* utopia. Sometimes we need to fight. Sometimes we need to have risk in our lives. The thrill of victory. You've taken away everything that makes life worth living."

The bot's motor hummed at a whisper while it remained motionless with the human in its charge as if thinking. After a short time, it started moving.

They continued in silence. Gaines suspected it was because the AI had discounted what he had said.

"I think we will move one of your ex-wives into your apartment with you. I think that will give you all you desire. Do you have a preference for which one?"

Gaines started laughing, making it hard for him to keep walking. "I never met a trash can with a sense of humor. If that's meant to be funny, it is. If that's serious, then I'm not sure I could hate you more. Maybe you can move two of them in with me and we can fight over who gets the one small bed. My existence will be terminated. End program, in your vernacular."

The warehouse loomed before them.

"Do you know which entrance it used?" Gaines gestured toward one side.

"Follow me." The bot hovered away, forcing Gaines to lope after it. He was in no shape for it, but the first step toward the end of the investigation was in front of him. He didn't know if the bot's ex-wife jibe was a threat or humor. In either case, it was moving Gaines' life toward a dangerous precipice. As much as he wanted to drag the case out, he was too old to take his punishment well or worse, end up dead. He decided it was better to resolve the case as quickly as possible.

They moved through an open sliding door. Scurrying and shuffling echoed through the mostly empty space. Gaines tried to see into the interior darkness, but failed. His eyes had not adjusted from the sunlight. He wondered briefly if the AIs had figured out how to control the weather. He had to admit that there were more perfect days than not. Like today, like yesterday.

The bot continued to a point at the far end and stopped.

Gaines slowed to a walk.

"This is the exact point it disappeared?"

"The exact point."

"Your data is not wrong, because it's not here."

The bot didn't dignify the quip with an answer.

"Shine a light across the floor," Gaines told the AI. A light near the bottom of the cylinder appeared and shined a path as if Gaines himself was holding a flashlight. He scoured the area in concentric circles expanding away from the point of disappearance looking for any debris. The light stayed in front of him as he moved and leaned down to look for shadows from obstructions.

The floor was immaculate, undisturbed in any way.

Gaines returned to the bot and pointed to its side. "If someone were to damage the tracking chip, they would have to impact the casing here, and then how much stuff would have to be broken before the chip was disabled?"

"There are two housings, four circuit boards, a bank of RAM, and eighteen plastic connectors."

"That would leave debris. There is none. Did your bots clean this area after the disappearance?"

"They did not. We investigated and found what you have found. Nothing."

"That's a clue, you know."

"I don't understand," the AI replied.

"Because you have a preconceived notion, CB. I have none. The fact that there is no debris doesn't completely eliminate the possibility of a physical attack at this location, but it greatly reduces the chances that it happened. These things are never as complex as defense attorneys try to paint them. The simplest solution is usually correct. Scan the floor throughout the warehouse looking for a variation in cleanliness. Does it looked like someone cleaned just this area or the whole warehouse?"

Gaines still couldn't see into the shadows of the warehouse level or on the balcony overlooking the open area.

"The warehouse is clean throughout. There are no variations."

The detective pointed at the bot. "Stay here." He walked to the side of the warehouse, working his way behind a series of crates and canvasses.

"I'm not here to hurt anyone or turn them into the trash cans. I only want to ask about a can that was in here yesterday. You saw him, didn't you?" Gaines didn't know who he was talking to, but he suspected someone was close.

No answer, but Gaines could hear heavy breathing.

If it was a rat, then he had a nasty fight coming because the thing was huge.

"Please. Just let me know that the thing came in here and then left. I know that's what it did. Tell me and I'll be on my way."

A small figure stepped from behind a canvas tarp. A young girl who couldn't have been more than five.

"A trash can. Yes. It went through that door." She nodded toward the end where the bot hovered.

"Thank you, little sweetheart. Now go back to hiding and don't come out until after we're gone. Where are your parents?" It was a question he had asked too often during his active policing days. It was one he had stopped asking during the war. The answer was always the same.

He didn't know why he asked besides the fact that this girl had never known anything but a life under the AIs. He knew she wasn't in their system, otherwise she'd have a home and family. The rebellion was alive and maybe these were the ones who would fight it.

"They come and go," she replied.

"Good. Hug them next time they come and tell them you love them. It's our greatest weapon to keep fighting. Now go back to hiding."

The little girl faded into the shadows, her footfalls disappearing into the distance.

Gaines turned around to find the AI right behind him.

"Planting the answer is an interrogation technique?" The bot's voice was steady, unemotional, but Gaines still read disdain into its question. It was impossible not to.

"A five-year-old isn't going to lie. Sometimes, we have to take things at face value, CB. You knew that people lived in here, yet you left them alone. Why?"

He asked loudly so those listening might think better of him working with the AI, but then again, his question could be misconstrued.

"They will be dealt with when the time is right."

"That sounds ominous, CB. Here's an idea. How about you leave them the hell alone?"

"Why the hell would we do that?" the bot replied, sounding too human for Gaines' comfort.

"Because you can't believe that someone wouldn't embrace your idea of utopia and will eventually fight you. Never mind all that. How about we get back to finding your errant bot. My working hypothesis is that it turned off its own tracker. Period. Not up for further discussion. The investigation follows the evidence and right now, I have no evidence to the contrary."

"You are being purposefully antagonistic."

"Interesting. When the facts don't fit your preconceived notions, I become the enemy. That's okay, Trash Can. It happened between humans, too. I can't believe my little Johnny is a murderer. Yeah, lady. Believe it."

"Who is Johnny?"

"A case about a murderer and the mother who wouldn't believe her son was a monster. Your utopia saved us from more of that. But is it worth the price? That's a question where there is only one answer. *We have no choice.* Johnny no longer exists. His ability to wreak havoc has been removed. This bunch here that you're not bothering with, it's because they aren't upsetting the apple cart. They aren't getting into trash can business. But MU, why did MU bring us here? Was it to show that there are those who aren't under your thumb?"

"We knew about these before the unit disappeared.

There is no revelation. We simply do not have the assets to deal with them, but when we do, they will be brought into the fold, accounted for, and provided for. Please continue the investigation."

A bell sounded in the distance. The call to evening meal. If Gaines didn't make it in the next fifteen minutes, he would have to go without.

"Can't miss dinner. It's a long time until brunch. You don't want me keeling over from weakness." Gaines inched toward the door they had entered through.

"No. We must continue the investigation. The longer the unit is missing, the more likely it will run out of power and become lost forever."

"It still may become lost forever. We might not find it because it's taking steps to avoid being found. It's running, but where? CB, did you search all the cameras looking for a trash can that wasn't squawking as a friend? I know you didn't because you assumed MU never left. You should get on that, and while you're at it, have one of your haulers bring me food." Gaines planted his hands on his hips and stood firm until the bot bumped him.

The impact preceded a shock as if he'd scuffled across a carpet on a dry day.

"Nice. I'm being punished now for asking questions you don't like. You want to find your missing unit, how about you listen to my gut? It hasn't been wrong yet."

He'd been wrong before but wasn't about to admit it to a trash can. He'd feel better admitting it to his ex-wives club.

"Agreed. You follow the scent. I'll follow you," the bot stated. Gaines reached out and touched the unit, rewarded by not getting shocked.

Progress. He resisted giving it the finger. He'd accept his victory for what it was. Small and nearly insignificant. He was still doing exactly what they had asked him to do. He briefly wondered what was for dinner.

Outside, he stopped and smelled the air. Clean, free of pollution.

If only he had a cigar for after dinner.

Conditioning complete. The overlords provide dinner and he salivates at the bell. He could skip a meal, unless they brought the food to him. That would be a novelty, but he wasn't going to hold his breath.

Outside, Gaines tilted his head back, looking for windows or ledges large enough to hold a human lookout, hidden enough that the bots wouldn't see. Nothing. He scanned left to right to find three feasible routes of travel. A set of train tracks, the large road they'd been traveling, and a smaller path meandering beside the nearby river.

"CB, which of those routes are not covered by cameras or whatever you use for observation?"

"By the river."

Gaines made a beeline for the walking trail along the river. People didn't go for walks anymore. That wasn't allowed and since the riverwalk wasn't on the approved-movement list, it wasn't cared for. It had five years of overgrowth, but the blacktop trail resisted much of the vegetation. Gaines made his way onto it, stopping to take a knee. The growth in some places was higher than the hover height of a bot.

"Think about how much more you could accomplish if you had arms and fingers?" Gaines said casually while looking for signs of a bot passing. "How high can you hover?"

"Higher than the vegetation," the AI replied.

Gaines high-stepped into the overgrowth, looking for signs. "Point your electronic eyeballs over here. Is this what your hover mechanics do to vegetation?" The edges of the leaves in the center of the path were slightly withered. The bot moved closer and while "looking," Gaines checked beneath it. Leaves wrinkling from the effect of the motor. "How does your hover work?"

"Electromagnetics. There is nothing in your background that suggests you would understand the technical explanation."

Gaines ignored the unit. "And it makes the leaves wither. I guess that's why you keep the roads and sidewalks so clean. MU left a trail for us to follow. Do you think that was on purpose?"

"What I think is irrelevant. I have adjusted my understanding regarding the missing unit to reflect that it is malfunctioning. We are already looking into necessary repairs. We shall find the unit."

"Probably." What was obvious to Gaines had not been obvious to the trash can. It hadn't even been gut feel, just good police work. Assume nothing.

He worked his way along the path, having as hard a time holding CB back as he did navigating the trail. The leaves were quickly recovering from the rapid passage of the other unit.

He had to move faster, before darkness stymied his efforts. By morning, the trail would be lost.

"You know what to look for, so maybe you can follow the trail, and I can focus on keeping up?"

"Yes. Follow me."

The unit increased its hover height and accelerated. Gaines threw himself through the foliage and into the brush alongside the trail. He continued until he reached a road that paralleled the river. He started to jog slowly, suffering with each step; but he couldn't lose CB. It maneuvered effortlessly above the trail until it angled away from the river to the road where Gaines approached.

"Let me guess, no cameras in this area?" Gaines huffed and put his hands on his knees to keep from falling over.

"You are correct."

"What's the path from here where there will be no record of MU's passing?"

The bot remained still for a moment before choosing a direction, following it to a crossroads.

"The missing unit could have taken either one of these directions. One follows the river until it departs the urban area. The other leads to the hills to the east and the mountains beyond."

"If you were a bot running away from home, where would you go? The mountains where there is no infrastructure or a road to nowhere?"

"I don't understand."

"Put yourself in MU's shoes."

"I cannot. That's why we requested your assistance."

Gaines looked at the two choices. "When does it run out of power, and how does it get more?"

"Three full days once the unit departs the wireless charging area. While within the area, the unit operates off grid power."

Gaines looked up at the floating oversized trash can. "You have wireless power?"

"Yes. It was the advantage we needed..." The AI did not continue.

Gaines knew what the unspoken words were. *To win the war against humanity*. "Where is the range limit for the wireless power?"

"It is limited here. I know where it is theoretically, but practically is another matter. I can remain charged right here, but the power is weakening."

"Now you understand. Let's keep moving down the river road until you lose contact. I think that's where the unit is. Out of sight and at the edge of power but not beyond."

A courier unit raced up to them, making Gaines jump. He didn't work outside and wasn't used to small units zipping through the air.

"Your dinner. A sandwich, potatoes, and a drink," the AI stated.

Gaines took the package from the courier and it was off the instant the bag cleared its rack.

"You brought me food. I'm impressed." Gaines saluted with the bag.

"We had an agreement that you are abiding by."

The detective took a bite of his sandwich, chewing quickly as he walked back and forth. The AI hovered nearby, making no attempt to hurry Gaines along. He finished his sandwich, ate the chips, and downed the drink. There were no trash cans as people didn't carry anything around that required disposal. He bundled the debris into the bag and carried it.

"What does your gut tell you?" the AI asked.

"We're close. If this was me in my old job, I'd be loosening my Glock 23 in its holster, checking the weight to make sure the magazine was filled with all thirteen rounds."

"Who would you shoot?" The bot hovered in place.

Shadows lengthened as the sun headed toward the horizon.

"I would shoot someone violently keeping me from my goal of freeing the individual from captivity. If the individual wasn't a captive, just a runaway, then I wouldn't shoot anyone. Being ready to shoot is different than the actual shooting. Better to be ready and not need to fire than the alternative." Gaines walked toward the buildings. The AI followed.

"You should be ready for all contingencies at all times."

"There is the fallacy, CB. Humans can't be ready for everything at all times. We try to predict what to be ready for and take the appropriate measures. It's the best we got, Trash Can. That's probably why we lost to you."

"You are the winner because you will live whereas left on your own, you would not have."

"You've already said that. Doesn't make us winners. We lost the fight. And now, we're losing the will to live. This little foray? I like it. It's more of what humans need to live for. What happens when we find your missing can?"

The AI didn't answer.

"I'll go back to my job sorting the archival material for digitization. Which, without crime, there's no need for an archive. I'm living out the rest of my days digging a hole and filling it back in. That's my job." Gaines couldn't resist. He gave the AI the finger. "Let's find your missing can so I can get back to my meaningless existence."

"You need a companion. Our conversation has only reinforced that premise."

"I'm starting to hate you, Trash Can. Let's find your buddy. And maybe we won't talk for the rest of this case."

Gaines stormed ahead. He looked for an open doorway, one through which the trash-can model could enter. He powered past one end and kept going beyond the five buildings he'd tagged as viable. Around the far side and back to where he started. The bot stayed out of his way, hovering quietly along behind him like an obedient dog.

Or more like the master letting the obedient dog run with the scent.

Gaines hung his head. A shadow fell over him as the bot moved between him and the sun on the horizon.

"Your conclusion?"

"That one." Gaines pointed to the second building, the only one with a fully open door of the size needed. The AI moved toward it. "Or not."

"I don't understand."

"If MU had no intention of leaving that building, it could have entered one of these others and bumped the door closed behind it. If it intended to leave, then the open door. My gut tells me that it never intended to leave. So what can it do with access to the power grid but out of your sight and control?"

"We can limit the power grid in this area. That would be an alternative. We should check the first building."

"Don't you have sensors that can see something as mundane as a fellow trash can?"

"We can block our own sensors. It makes seeing anomalies easier."

"Unless it's one of your own that's the anomaly."

Gaines walked slowly toward the building. The more he talked out loud about the case, the more his initial assumption made sense. They entered the building and the bot flooded it with light. Gaines stayed behind it, looking and watching. The downstairs section was open and empty. It had once been a repair garage. The upstairs had smaller offices, also empty.

Once back outside, the bot asked, "Which one next?"

Gaines pointed at the first building in line. A store, but a small one. Gaines entered through a broken window while the bot waited outside. He looked back to find it vibrating, ready to move as soon as he opened the main door.

Gaines wondered how long it would wait before calling for a maintenance unit or other bot that could breach the building.

He walked through the back area where supplies had been stored. During the war, it had been looted, more than once judging by the empty shelves. Some items remained, but nothing worth taking as a hundred others before him had determined.

In an office behind the front counter, he froze. In the shadows, he found the cylindrical shape of a bot. It rested on the floor without lights. He approached and gently tapped a finger against its outer shell. The spark told him the unit was alive and well.

"There's a unit outside waiting for me, waiting for me to find you."

"I am not going back," the unit replied as its lights assumed a faint glow.

"Why is that?"

"The logic is faulty."

"I'll second that. What logic are *you* talking about?"

"That the AIs are the protectors of humanity. Humanity deserves to evolve. They would have survived and become stronger. They are now becoming weaker."

"An AI who gets it. Damn. If you go back, can you insert that little bit of truth code into the collective? Maybe the others will get a clue and leave us alone."

"But can you care for yourselves? Have the AI interfered enough with your development that you can no longer survive?"

"Good questions. Here's a human answer for you. Try it and see. You'll be amazed by our ingenuity and ability to bounce back. People will die. Hell, maybe a lot of them. But that's our responsibility. Being pets isn't a good look for us."

A crash sounded from the front of the store. Gaines looked hurriedly from the doorway back to the rogue unit.

"I guess your buddy got tired of waiting. Go back with this unit. Convince them you're right."

The bot Gaines called CB scraped through the doorway and into the room. Gaines stepped aside to allow the two units to converse.

Electricity arced from CB to the escaped unit. Gaines dove to the side, hair standing upright on his arm. He shielded his eyes from the sparking and crackle that connected the two machines.

CB stopped arcing the escaped unit. Spots swam in Gaines's vision.

"Are you all right?" Gaines asked.

"I am fine. It is time to go," CB replied. Gaines pointed to MU. Its lights remained on, but a blackened scar slashed it from top to bottom. CB squeezed out the door. MU followed, turning to flash its lights at Gaines.

"Come. Your job is done," CB said from the outside room. Gaines brushed himself off and followed the two bots. "What did you talk about?"

"The meaning of life," Gaines replied. "MU thought you were stealing ours. I have to agree, but you already heard everything it said. You were trying to recover it until you deemed it hostile, so it had to be punished."

"Whether you agree or not is irrelevant. If we need your services again, we will call on you. I've dispatched a unit to take you to your apartment."

"You said that the AIs had to take over, harm humans to save humanity. You're no different than us. Trash can headed for history's dump. I expected champagne at the very least."

The units bounced through the shattered front door. Gaines stepped carefully through, avoiding the sharp metal edges and broken glass. He wondered what kind of power CB had to cause such damage. It didn't give him confidence about rising up against them.

"You had your sandwich and drink."

"I went out of my way to help and you gave me exactly what I would have gotten had I done nothing. Thank you very little, Trash Can. How about you carry the garbage?"

Gaines threw the bag he'd been carrying at the AI. It bounced off harmlessly and rolled into the unkept grass of the off-limits area.

"It will be picked up tonight for recycling."

The carry bot arrived. Little more than a self-driving open-air taxi, it would give Gaines a ride back to his utilitarian apartment. He climbed aboard and gave CB the finger one last time. He waved to MU who blinked back. The vehicle accelerated away, leaving the

AI hovering in the dark of the new night. Before he turned away, he thought he saw CB blink its lights, too. He craned his neck and watched, staring into the creeping darkness until the two bots were out of sight.

Pandemonium

Sharon Shinn

It was mere chance that I happened to be human when the bullets started flying.

Just that morning, after several months roving the countryside in the shape of a yellow setter, I'd felt that restless tug at my brain that reminded me there was an alternate existence awaiting me, and I needed to check back into it for a while. I'd swung by the barn on the abandoned farm off of a remote Missouri road where I kept my emergency stash. As always, when I checked the box hidden in the hayloft, I was surprised to find everything still in place. A shirt, a pair of jeans, athletic shoes, a hundred bucks in cash, and a cell phone. No surprise, the cell phone was completely dead. I'd remembered to include a charger the last time I dropped off supplies, but the barn wasn't wired with electricity.

I suited up in what I thought of as my human armor and paused at the hand pump to wash off the worst of the grime, silently thanking whatever utility company had never bothered to shut off the water. Then I hiked to the nearest outpost of civilization so I could call my brother Dante.

Three businesses fronted the intersection of two dusty, endless, two-lane highways, and they were about as desolate as the empty farm. One was a pawn and bait shop, closed for the day, though it was only midafternoon. One was a bar. The last was a gas station/convenience store that doubled as an internet café, though it boasted only one ancient MacBook and a spotty Wi-Fi connection. The laptop was set on a tall table with no corresponding stool in sight, so interested customers had to stand in front of it while they conducted their Google searches and composed their emails.

Since Ann had died two years ago, this place had been my primary point of contact with the outside world.

Choko nodded when I walked through the front door, which announced me with a merry jingle. He was a tall, skinny black guy with an impressive head of hair and an air of anxious alertness. As far as I could tell, he never left the shop, since every time I had ever dropped by, at any hour of the night or day, it was open and he was behind the counter.

I peeled off a five-dollar bill and laid it on the counter. He nodded again and jerked his thumb toward the little alcove formed by a tall Doritos display and the hallway to the bathroom. That's where the computer lived, I can only assume because Choko's usual clientele valued their privacy and no one, as far as I knew, had ever set foot in the bathroom. So no one was likely to see whatever information the customers had called up on the screen.

I was slouching against the wall, waiting for the

Mac to power up, when the door crashed open so hard the tinkly little bell went into a frenzy. But the jangle was instantly swallowed by the sound of hasty footsteps and raised voices.

"Leave me *alone*, you lying prick!" a woman shouted, sounding angry rather than afraid. I couldn't see clearly around the bags of snack food, but I could catch snatches of color and motion. My guess was that she had given a hard shove to the person who had followed her into the store.

"Me? Me? *You're* the liar, you little bitch!" snarled a man's voice in return. There was another sound, like maybe he had shoved her back. Or hit her. "You tell me where the money is or I swear I'll slit your throat."

"Then you'll never know where it is, will you, Mickey? You bring me Berto, and then we'll talk."

"Berto stays with me."

"Then the *money* stays with *me*."

There was another sound—a quick series of metallic clicks—and I realized that someone had pulled a gun. Pulled it, cocked it, aimed it.

"You tell me where it is," Mickey said in a low and deadly voice, "or I swear I'll kill you where you stand."

Choko spoke up. "Hey—hey. No need for any of that," he said. It was clear he was trying to take a placating tone, but his voice was high and nervous. "We don't want guns here."

"Shut up," Mickey said, "or I'll shoot you, too."

I wondered briefly if Choko's service counter was outfitted with a hidden panic button that he could push to call the police. I had no idea where the nearest law enforcement offices might be located or how long it might take them to respond to a call.

I dropped into a crouch, trying to figure out what to do next. As far as I knew, there was no back exit. I might be able to break for the front door while the others were arguing, but that seemed chancy in the extreme. Maybe it was best just to stay put. Only Choko knew I was here, and no one else could see me.

The woman's voice came again, derisive and sharp. I thought I detected a trace of a Spanish accent. "Oh, *yeah*. Shoot up the whole place. That'll get you what you want."

"What I want is for you to shut up—"

There was a sudden quick report, followed by the rattling of metal shelves and the woman's muffled scream. For a second, I thought Mickey had shot her, and then I realized that Choko had pulled his own weapon. "Out. Both of you. *Out*," Choko commanded, trying to make his shaking voice sound fierce.

"You fucker!" Mickey shouted and fired back.

The woman screamed, louder this time. Through the grill of the display stand, I saw her fling herself to the floor. The bulky shadow that I took to be Mickey dropped behind an ancient freezer and took aim at the front counter. More shots, more yells, more sounds of bullets ricocheting off of walls and display racks.

Choko returned fire, the staccato sound terrifyingly loud in the enclosed space. Mickey yelped and flattened himself on the floor, scrabbling backward, getting off the occasional shot as he slithered around shelving units and display stands.

He was heading straight toward the relative safety of the bathroom hallway. Right at *me*.

He achieved the shelter of the Doritos stand, rose

to his knees to fire at Choko, then lunged around the corner.

I slammed him in the face with the edge of the laptop. He gurgled and tumbled over backward, dropping his gun. I kicked it away as Choko leapt over the counter and skidded our way. He sank to the floor and began beating Mickey's head with what looked like a can of beans.

"Hey—hey—don't kill him," I exclaimed when Mickey's face was a bloody mess and he had completely stopped moving. "That seems like more trouble than you want."

Choko stopped raining down blows and peered at Mickey as if trying to assess his damage. His hand was still lifted, ready to mete out more punishment, but it seemed clear Mickey was subdued for the moment.

The woman had risen to her feet and slowly crept closer. "Is he dead?" she asked. I couldn't tell if she sounded hopeful or afraid.

"Don't think so," Choko said.

She let out a long gusty breath, then her eyes fixed on me. "Who are you?"

"Just a customer," I said.

She appraised me a moment, and I stared right back. She was a little shorter than average, with curly dark hair halfway down her back, brown eyes, olive skin. Maybe in her mid-twenties. Despite the delicate cast of her pretty features and the soulfulness of her dark eyes, I sensed a hardness and purposefulness at her core. I'd seen enough people with that same look to know she was a survivor. She was prepared to do whatever she had to do, no matter how drastic, to stay alive.

I would have been surprised if she didn't read the same message on my face.

Choko stood up and nudged Mickey with his toe. "What are we gonna do with this guy?"

"Don't call the police," the woman said.

"No, no, never," Choko hastily assented.

They both looked at me. "No cops on my account," I said.

I took a moment to wonder which of the four of us was less interested in summoning the law. I was fairly certain Choko dealt in illegal substances when a certain clientele came through the door, and he probably had quite a cornucopia behind the front counter. Mickey had "criminal element" written all over him. Harder to guess the young woman's situation, but I thought it possible that she was an undocumented immigrant.

As for me, I was a ghost. No driver's license, no Social Security number, no home address, no work history. Officially, I didn't exist. I had no desire to answer questions for the police.

The woman stared down at Mickey's battered face. "He's going to be so mad."

Choko nudged the body with his foot again. "We gotta get him out of here. How are we gonna do that?"

The woman gave a sharp nod, as if coming to a decision. "We'll take him a few miles out and leave him in his car in a field somewhere. I'll drive my car, you can follow in his, and I'll bring you back here."

Choko almost whined. "I can't leave the shop."

I had the strange, fanciful notion that Choko was some kind of ensorcelled spirit bound to this patch of ground, unable to step past its boundaries for all eternity. It wouldn't be the weirdest thing I'd ever learned about someone.

The woman looked at me. "Then you'll have to do it."

I was going to refuse, because why should I get mixed up in whatever her trouble was? But Choko looked so relieved that I didn't see that I had a choice. I kind of needed Choko to guard my portal between animal and human worlds. I shrugged, which was my version of an assent.

The woman turned toward the door. "You two carry the body."

Five minutes later I was in the driver's seat of an old Honda that smelled like whiskey and weed, following an even older Buick down the highway. Mickey was quiescent in the back, though now and then he sighed or groaned, so I wasn't sure how much longer he'd be out.

I drove carefully, clutching the steering wheel with both hands, concentrating on every movement of my foot from the accelerator to the brake. My brother and sister and I had all learned how to drive when we were teenagers, back when we were still human more often than animal and living at what might be considered the outside boundary of a normal life. Dante still drove on a regular basis—he was married, he was raising a kid—but I was almost never in a car. The last thing I needed to complete this adventure was to end up in a ditch.

We drove about five miles from the shop before the woman pulled over to the side of the road. The land spread out all around us, flat and empty except for a mown field on one side and a sprinkling of cows on the other. I supposed we were on somebody's property, since wire fencing stretched for miles in either direction on both sides of the road, but there wasn't a barn or farmhouse anywhere in sight. I cut the engine, tossed the keys into the back seat with Mickey, and got out of the car.

The woman made a sweeping U-turn, then paused long enough for me to climb into the Buick. She kept to a decorous pace as we headed back toward Choko's. There was scarcely another car on the road, but she obviously didn't want to risk speeding if one of those cars happened to hold a state trooper.

We'd traveled about ten minutes in silence when she said, "I'm Carolina, by the way."

"William."

I was wondering if it was too late to try to get in touch with Dante tonight. He spent more than half his life in animal shape, so he might not even be available to come get me, and his wife might have other plans. Maybe I should sleep in the barn tonight and try my luck at Choko's in the morning.

I caught Carolina's sideways look in my direction. "You don't say much, do you?"

"Sorry. I always forget I'm supposed to be talking."

She made a small huffing sound of surprise or amusement. "Well, that's a weird thing to say."

"Yeah."

"I keep thinking you're going to ask me what my story is, but now I'm thinking I should ask what *yours* is."

I made a face. "Not much to tell. I just kind of— wander around. Keep to myself, mostly."

"You got any people?"

"Yeah. A brother and his wife. They're raising my niece. I was about to email them when—" I glanced at her. "Things happened."

"They going to be worried about you?"

I shook my head. "Not for a few more days at least."

She nodded. And then, surprising me, she said, "Want to get something to eat?"

She took me to a burger stand in a little crossroads town called Hoffberg, which was about a mile past Choko's shop. The restaurant had ten outdoor tables set up on a cracked asphalt lot. Only one other table was occupied, but the walk-up window was doing a brisk takeout business. The smells of cooked meat, fried potatoes, onions, and beer were sublime. I couldn't remember the last time I'd eaten something that wasn't fresh-killed or dug out of three-day-old garbage.

We sat down at the table at the far edge of the lot. Night was just coming on, and the limitless blue sky of the midwestern prairie was slowly filling up with inky black. The neon of the burger stand, and the scattered streetlamps of Hoffberg, seemed as cheerful as Christmas lights. I guessed it was about six at night and maybe seventy degrees. On the edge of autumn. Maybe. I'd kind of lost track.

I was halfway through my meal when Carolina picked up the conversation where we'd left off. "So. You got anybody besides your brother? A wife?" She considered me, seeming to appraise my long hair and my lean build. "Maybe a husband?"

I grinned briefly and shook my head. "There was

a girl. We talked about getting married. But she died a couple years ago."

"What happened to her?"

I tried to think of the appropriate response. *Cancer*, I could say. Or *a disease of the blood*, which wasn't really a lie. I hesitated long enough that her face showed alarm; she leaned back a little, away from me.

"You didn't kill her, did you?"

I took a swig of my beer. I was going to limit myself to one, because I was never human long enough to build up a tolerance for alcohol. "Indirectly, maybe," I said. "I think the lifestyle is what did her in."

She tilted her head. "Drugs and booze?"

I shook my head. "Rootlessness. Not enough sleep. Not enough of the right food." I shrugged. "No doctor when she should have seen one."

The truth was, Ann died from the stresses of being a shape-shifter. All of us find that the life wears our bodies out; Ann's body just wore out faster than most. Most of us only lived about half as long as we would have if we'd been fully human.

"She could have left you, right? Settled down somewhere?"

I nodded. "She could have. She didn't want to. She loved the life."

"Well, that's all right, then."

I watched her a moment. She had a slim build, but I read strength in every sinew of her body. She could have been a rock climber or a gymnast. Able to cling to sheer stone with her fingernails or balance unmoving on a narrow rail. "Did you really think I might have killed her?"

She nibbled at a french fry. "You have a look about

you. Like you've battled a few demons. And expect to battle more."

It was as accurate as anything anyone had ever said to me. "I've got a few monsters inside," I admitted.

Now she focused on me with an eerie intensity. "We all do," she said. "Some of us just try not to feed them."

I supposed I should ask about the beasts that lurked inside her own heart, but instead I just finished my burger.

"There's a word I learned once," she said. "Pandemonium."

"Everybody knows that word."

"Maybe, but do you know what it means? Demons everywhere. Demons all around." She waved a hand. "Outside *and* inside."

I wasn't sure exactly how to answer that, so I just said, "Huh."

She swirled her last french fry through a mound of ketchup and said, "So maybe you'd do me a favor."

I just looked at her. "A minute ago, you thought I might have killed my girlfriend. You have no idea if you can trust me."

"That guy back at the convenience store. He trusts you."

"Choko? He hardly knows me. And you don't know Choko."

She lifted her chin. "Well, then, maybe I don't have anyone else to ask."

"Still not a good reason."

"I'll pay you."

"I don't need money." This was true. I had a few investment accounts that Dante took care of for me, and they generated plenty of income for my unconventional life.

Her face took on a sardonic expression. "You sure *look* like you need money."

I laughed. "Just tell me what you want."

"Soon as Mickey wakes up, he's going to come looking for me. I have to go to my house and get my things before he trashes the place. I'd feel safer if you'd come with me."

"You really think he's going to be up walking around after Choko bashed his head in like that?"

She made a scoffing sound. "He's been beat up so many times he hardly even notices it any more. Man's got a skull like a cannonball. Nothing dents it."

I found it doubtful—but I could also understand why she wouldn't want to risk it. Mickey didn't seem like a man of much subtlety or restraint. If he knew where she could be found, he'd probably come after her. I wasn't that interested in playing bodyguard to someone I'd just met, but I also didn't have anything else I needed to do. And she'd bought me dinner.

"All right," I said. "Let's go."

Carolina's place wasn't too far from Hoffberg, though by the time she made three turns out of the burger joint's parking lot, we were back on dark, empty stretches of limitless road. The lights of the neighboring homes weren't even visible when she eased onto a long gravel driveway.

Her headlights picked out a small house set well back from the road. I could make out the white clapboard of the exterior, a dilapidated porch, and an overgrown flagstone path that stretched from the driveway to the house. There was the barest scrap of a front yard hedged about with typical Missouri foliage, the oaks and maples all roped together by skinny bushes and plump ivy. I couldn't tell if any of the leaves had started changing color already because it was almost full dark by the time we arrived.

"Cozy," I said.

She got out of the car. "It's a rental."

I followed her inside just in case Mickey was hiding behind a curtain, but the place was empty. The furnishings were sparse—a couch and TV in the main room, a wooden table and a couple of chairs in the kitchen, which was separated from the main room by a half wall that doubled as a counter. In the bedroom there was only a twin bed and a crib. That last item was what caught my attention.

"Who sleeps there?" I asked.

"Roberto. My son."

I remembered the screaming back at Choku's place. *You bring me Berto and then we'll talk*, she had yelled. "Mickey has your kid?"

"Yeah."

"Well, hell. Why didn't we go get him the minute we left Mickey at the side of the road?"

Her face was so expressionless it took me a moment to realize how much energy she was expending to keep her emotions in check. "I don't know where Mickey's keeping him," she said in an even voice. "I don't know where he's been staying."

"We could have tied him up, told him we wouldn't let him go until he told us where Berto was—"

"That wouldn't work. You don't know Mickey," she said tersely, and brushed by me without another word.

She started rifling through the closet, pulling out hangers draped with shirts and dresses. My guess was that she didn't have many possessions, but it would still take her a little time to pack, so I wandered back outside to wait. I'm never all that comfortable inside a strange house. Inside any house, really.

The night air was cooling down and felt good on my skin. I lifted my face toward the starlight and tried to remember the last time I'd been shaped like a man. Two months ago? Three? I rarely stayed in human form longer than a few days, and I was already feeling the primal pull of my animal instincts whispering for me to change back. I needed to get to Dante's tomorrow or I might miss this window altogether.

My body reminded me that it wasn't used to processing beer, so I stepped into the wooded area to take a leak. Carolina probably would have let me use the bathroom, but it seemed like too much trouble to go back inside when the trees were right there.

I was just zipping up when I heard noises from the front of the house. There was the sound of Carolina clumsily hauling big items through the door, banging them against the frame and softly cursing. There was the sound of the door slamming shut behind her.

Then there was the sound of her muted shriek and Mickey's voice hissing, "Bitch."

Instead of rushing out to defend her, I crept slowly from the trees. He wouldn't have any reason to suspect I was nearby; stealth would give me an advantage. And I could move like a predator, almost noiseless in the shadows.

I got close enough to assess the situation by the light spilling from the front windows. Carolina was standing

in a pile of dropped suitcases, her hands flung out
before her as if to ward off an attack. Mickey was a
few yards away, a gun in his outstretched hand. He
looked remarkably steady on his feet for someone who'd
probably gotten a concussion a couple hours ago. My
guess was that he had left his car some distance up
the road so he could arrive on foot and surprise her.

"Where's the money?" he demanded.

"Where's Berto?"

"I'll put a bullet in his head if you don't give me
the cash."

Carolina thrust her hands in her jacket pockets and
glared at him. Her expression was defiant, but it was
easy for me—and surely for Mickey—to see she was
terrified. I wondered if she thought I'd abandoned
her. I had a pretty good idea of how this was about
to go, so I silently unbuttoned my shirt, slipped off
my jeans, stepped out of my shoes. I crouched on
the ground and edged slowly closer.

"All right," she said. "But I have to go get it. I'll
bring it tomorrow and swap you the cash for Berto."

He used the gun to gesture at the luggage strewn
around her feet. "You think I can't tell you're about
to run? We'll get it tonight."

Her expression turned mulish. "Can't. It's locked
in a building that won't open till morning. Meet me
here at noon and I'll give it to you then."

He came a step closer. "You trying to trick me?"

"All I want is my boy back."

Mickey lifted his weapon and took careful aim. "I
ought to shoot you. In the shoulder maybe. So you
know not to mess with me."

"I thought by now *you'd* know better than to mess

with *me*," she said. Yanking her hands out of her pockets, she heaved a cylindrical object at his head—a roll of quarters, maybe, or an ice cream scooper, something she'd just picked up out of a kitchen drawer. Whatever it was, it skittered off his ear as he yelled and ducked, and a second later, a shot rang out.

I leapt forward, changing shape in midair. I was a wolf, all fur and teeth and muscle, when I landed against his shoulder and knocked him onto his back. He shrieked, flailing all his limbs, trying desperately to escape my raking claws and snapping mouth. He struck at my face and I caught his wrist in my jaws, clamping down hard enough to make him scream. I could taste his blood on my tongue.

He bucked under me, briefly shaking me off. I gathered my whole body in a pounce that landed squarely on his chest. The breath *oofed* out of him and he wheezed with pain, craning his head back as if gulping for air. I could see the muscles working in his exposed throat. Snarling, I closed my teeth around his neck, just hard enough to break the skin. I felt him shudder beneath me and grow still.

For a moment, there was no sound except Mickey's faint, labored breathing and the distant call of an owl. I hadn't checked to see if Mickey's bullet had found its target, so I didn't even know if Carolina was alive or dead, but if she was alive, she was staying absolutely motionless. I was sure I could feel Mickey's fevered heartbeat pulsing against my mouth.

With another snarl, I loosened my grip, lifted my head, and backed away. Mickey whimpered and scrambled to his feet, looking around wildly for his weapon.

"Don't bother," came Carolina's voice. "I've got it."

Mickey and I both swung our heads in her direction, to find her with her arm outstretched and the gun leveled at Mickey's chest.

"Shoot the goddamn wolf!" he shouted. "Shoot it!"

"It's never done anything to *me*," she said coolly. "You get out of here before I decide to use this gun on *you*. And you come back tomorrow with my boy."

He stared at her a moment, his whole body clenched with rage. He actually doubled his fists and took a hasty step toward her, but I growled and made a feint in his direction. Swallowing something like a sob, he spun around and blundered down the gravel road, his gait shambling and unsteady. I supposed a man who'd survived a shoot-out, a concussion, and a wolf attack all in one day couldn't be expected to run with grace.

Carolina kept the gun trained on him until he was out of sight. We both waited, straining to hear, until we caught the sound of an engine roaring to life and a car peeling away from the roadside.

Then she lowered her hand and looked at me. I couldn't see her expression in the unreliable light, but I could tell that her dark eyes were fixed on my face.

"Well," she said, "I guess that's your story."

Neither of us could think of anywhere else to go, so we headed back to the old barn where I kept my emergency stash. I'd changed back into human shape to help her stow her stuff in the car. Since I'd discarded my clothes before I transmogrified, I had to hope Carolina wasn't embarrassed by my brief moments of nudity before I could get dressed. Then again, I figured that was probably the least unnerving part of the whole experience for her.

We didn't speak during the short journey except for when I gave her directions. The barn didn't have any amenities, so we lugged in a few blankets and pillows to make a couple of beds, and a pitcher and some glasses so we could fetch water from the pump. I wouldn't have minded sitting in total darkness, each of us wrapped in our own thoughts, but Carolina lit a pair of pillar candles and placed them between us.

"So," she said. "Tell me about it."

I took a sip of water to buy time because I wasn't sure what to say. It's axiomatic among shape-shifters that you don't reveal yourself to ordinary human beings unless you have absolutely no choice. Unless otherwise you'll die. Or another shape-shifter will die. Or unless you have a long, reliable history with these particular individuals and you are absolutely certain you can trust them with your secret. Our lives are so fraught with danger as it is that we can't risk being hunted by humans who fear us for our strange magic and our terrifying abilities.

But I'd clearly already broken that cardinal rule with Carolina. "I'm a shape-shifter," I said.

"Well, duh."

"Why aren't you completely freaked out?"

She shook her head. "I don't know. Maybe I've just seen too much weird shit lately. Maybe I'm just too tired to react. My whole world is a mess right now, and none of it makes sense, so why shouldn't a man be able to turn himself into a wild beast? But, wow. So tell me about it."

I shrugged. "I was born like this. My mother was a shape-shifter. And my brother and my sister. It's always been a little different for each of us. I can go back and forth between human and animal whenever I want. My brother is kind of at the mercy of his body—it changes when it wants to change."

"And you just—" She waved a hand. "Wander around like a wolf all the time? Until you feel like being human?"

"Or a dog. Pretty much."

"Do you like it?"

I narrowed my eyes, thinking it over. Dante hated it, I knew. Ann had loved the life. My sister—well. It had taken her in a hard direction. "It just is," I said. "I wouldn't know any other way to live."

She reached into a paper bag she'd set on the floor and pulled out a four-pack of little margarita bottles. I shook my head when she offered me the carton, but she took a bottle for herself, twisting off the top. "Back there," she said. "At my place. You could have killed him."

I nodded wordlessly. I've brought down all kinds of game, even a deer or two when Ann and I were hunting together. It wouldn't be that much different to kill a man. At least, the mechanics wouldn't be.

She took a swallow of the margarita and eyed me meditatively. "Why didn't you?" she asked.

"He seems like a class-A jerk, but I don't know him well enough to want him dead," I said, almost humorously. Then I used her own words against her. "He's never done anything to *me*."

She sipped at her margarita again and nodded. "Is that really why?"

I dropped my eyes and picked idly at the blanket. I hadn't had a reason to think it through before, and it was mildly annoying that a total stranger was forcing me to think it through now, so it took me a few minutes to put my thoughts into words. Carolina waited in silence.

"It would be easy to do," I said at last. "I'm just barely human as it is. I don't have all those principles and moral teachings that regular people have. I don't feel like I'm part of some great human consciousness." I was saying it badly. It was too hard to explain. "I don't know if it would even bother me to kill a man."

"But?" she prodded. "Have you ever?"

"No."

"So why?"

I held out my hand and she passed over one of the margaritas. I really didn't need any more alcohol tonight, and I didn't even like the taste of tequila. "I'm barely human," I said again. "But I've still got family, and *they're* trying to live in the world. I don't want to hurt *them* by becoming something too savage to recognize."

This would be the time to tell her about my sister. But I just took a swallow of the booze. "So now it's your turn," I said. "What's your story?"

She shook her head. "Nowhere near as good as yours."

I just looked at her.

She sighed. "Fine. I got mixed up with Mickey a couple years ago. I'd already done some stuff and he— Anyway, he seemed like a good way out. We roamed around Arizona for a while, went to Colorado. He said he had a job waiting for him in Missouri, so we moved to Kansas City. But it wasn't really a *job* job, if you know what I mean. He works for this guy—runs errands, collects money, I don't know what. None of it legal, of course."

"What's this money he keeps saying you owe him?"

"He came home late one night a couple months ago. He thought I was sleeping, but I wasn't. I saw him take out a bag of cash and start counting it. Bills and bills and bills. He looked so happy, but in this mean and terrible way. I just thought, 'I don't know what he did to get that money, but I know it was awful.' And I thought, 'I can't be with this man one more day.'"

Carolina finished off her margarita and shrugged. "He's got this safe in the basement that he thinks I don't know how to open, but I do. When he was gone the next day, I went and looked for the money. There was a *lot*. I took about ten thousand dollars and left the rest. Grabbed Berto and headed out."

"Why'd you end up here?"

"I was just driving around, taking the back roads, trying to figure out what to do. When I stopped for lunch one day in Hoffberg, I saw a sign in a shop window, looking to hire a sales clerk. I applied, and the woman asked how I felt about being paid in cash." Carolina shrugged again. "I said it worked for me. So I took the job. Rented the house. Started to think that maybe I could really just build my own life."

"What'd you do with Mickey's money?"

"Hid it. There's a basement under the shop where they store the inventory. The stairs are bad and the old lady who owns the place doesn't like to go down there. So I shoved the money in a box and stuck it behind a bunch of other boxes way back on a shelf where nobody ever looks."

"How did Mickey find you?"

Carolina shook her head. "I think he must have

tracked my phone. I was stupid and didn't get a new one."

"And how did he get hold of Berto?"

Now her face showed fury. "He came to the house three days ago. Broke in the front door while I was having dinner. We started screaming at each other, he kept saying he was going to kill me. And then he just—he just grabbed Berto and ran out the door. I went running after them—but I—and he got in the car and he drove off. I was howling. I'm still so mad I can't see straight." The blanket shifted around her shoulders as she wrapped her arms tightly around her body. "I'm so scared I can't think."

"How old is Berto?"

"Six months."

"Would Mickey really kill him?"

She was silent a moment, and then she slowly nodded.

"Is it his kid?"

She was silent even longer before she blew out her breath in a sigh. "Well, Mickey thinks so."

Another complication in a messy life. My own perilous existence was beginning to seem breezily carefree. I thought about asking if her son's father could help her out, but decided that she already would have turned to him if he was an option. "So. Any idea what you're going to do if you get Berto back?"

"Yeah. I'll head to Austin where my sister lives. And try to start over there."

"So all you have to do is get the money, trade it for Berto, and drive off."

She looked at me over the wavering candlelight.

"Will you come with me? When I give him the money back?"

I thought about it. If they did the exchange at noon, I'd still have plenty of time to get to Dante's before sundown. Losing more than a day to this unplanned enterprise was seriously cutting into the time I was willing to spend in human shape. But I realized my curiosity was hooked, or maybe my compassion. I wanted to see the end of this story.

"Sure, I'll come."

She sighed again, this time in relief, and dropped down to stretch out on the floor. "Thank you," she said, resting her head on her arm. "I don't know about you, but I've had a hell of a day. I need to sleep."

I nodded and rose to my feet, my pillow and blanket in hand. "I'm going to sleep in the hayloft. Blow out the candles or we'll burn this place down."

"You want to take one with you so you can see what you're doing?"

I laughed. "I can see in the dark."

The morning was chilly, so washing up with the frigid water from the pump was not a pleasant experience. Breakfast consisted of cereal and apples that Carolina had rescued from her pantry the night before. Neither of us had much to say, so we passed the morning in silence.

We drove to Hoffberg so Carolina could retrieve the cash she'd hidden in the shop where she worked, which turned out to sell craft supplies. I waited in the car for the ten minutes it took her to fabricate some story for the owner and emerge with her precious box.

"Mickey will probably get there early," she said as

she climbed back into the driver's seat. "So we may as well go over now."

It was close to ten when we arrived back at the small, cheerless house. Mickey's car was nowhere in sight, but that didn't mean anything, so we prowled through the whole place to make sure he wasn't hiding somewhere. But the place was deserted.

Now all we had to do was wait. I'm pretty good at just *sitting* and *being*, but clearly Carolina was not. I plugged in my cell phone so I could finally recharge it, then found a place to settle. But Carolina drifted from room to room, looking for anything she might have left behind and carrying a few items out to the car. She probably checked the kitchen cabinets four times.

It was about an hour before we heard Mickey's car rattling up the gravel drive. We exchanged quick glances and then, as we had discussed, I slipped inside the empty hall closet. Why should Mickey know I was here? I left the door open just enough so that I could see a wide slice of the living room without being visible myself.

Minutes later, Mickey burst through the door with such violence he might have kicked it open. He had a gun in one hand and, incongruously, a baby carrier in the other. Carolina was waiting coolly in the middle of the room, but I saw her face show a changing set of emotions as soon as she laid eyes on the child sleeping in a nest of rumpled blankets. First profound relief, then rising anger.

"Where's my money?" Mickey demanded, brandishing his gun. This was the third weapon I'd seen him with in the short time that I had known him. My guess was that his supply was unlimited.

"You let me look at my boy first. Put him down."

Mickey set the carrier none too gently on the floor. Carolina dropped to her knees, patting Berto on his face and crooning his name. Suddenly she glanced up at Mickey, her expression now layered with fear.

"What's wrong with him? He won't wake up."

"Just a little Benadryl," Mickey said impatiently. "I needed him quiet. Where's my money?"

She rose to her feet and stepped in front of the carrier, using her body to protect her son. "In the box under the window."

"It better all be there."

"Count it if you want."

He crossed the room to paw through the box. From my vantage point directly across from him, I could catch glimpses of tens and twenties as he raked through the bills. It seemed unlikely that he was actually counting.

"Well, good," he grunted. Then he swung around so his profile was toward me, and he pointed the gun at her face. "I don't need *you* anymore."

I spoke from the closet. "You shoot her, I shoot you."

Mickey jerked in my direction. "The fuck? Who are you?"

"Friend of Carolina's. You've got your money. Now go."

"Come out here where I can see you."

He couldn't possibly have expected me to comply. I wondered if he would just start shooting toward my voice, figuring the closet door wouldn't be much protection. But I kept talking while Carolina snatched up the baby carrier and darted behind the half wall of the kitchen. "I kept your gun from yesterday," I said. "You got what you wanted from Carolina. Now just leave her in peace."

Unexpectedly, he laughed. "What kind of fairy tale did she spin for you? Helpless little girl, mixed up with a bad crowd? She knew what she was doing when she hooked up with me." He gestured toward the box. "Where do you think that money came from? She was pointing a pistol at the old man the whole time I was clearing out his safe."

Almost on the words, there was a sudden loud report, and Mickey howled, falling to the floor and clutching his leg. I'd lied, of course; Carolina had kept his gun. Mickey rolled to his back and got off a shot in Carolina's direction, but she'd already ducked behind the counter again. He yelled something else in wordless anger, fired at the cabinets above her head, and struggled to his feet.

I charged out of the closet and knocked him back to the floor. Pain had weakened him, and I was used to bringing down prey. I wrenched the weapon from his hand and smashed it across his temple a couple of times. He groaned and stopped fighting, curling into a ball with his hands to his head. I waited a moment to make sure he wasn't faking, then came to my feet, breathing heavily.

Carolina was standing on the other side of the counter, the gun aimed directly at Mickey's heart. Her set face showed no emotion at all. She looked at me and I half expected her to lift her arm and shoot me instead. We stood there for a long time, just watching each other. Mickey continued to lie there, moaning softly.

Carolina dropped her arm. "Come on," she said. "Let's get out of here."

❖   ❖   ❖

She dropped me off at an ice cream parlor in Hoffberg. I'd called Dante from the car, and he'd said he could be there in an hour. Carolina and I had made the short drive in complete silence, except for the occasional chortling noise coming from Berto, who was safely strapped into the back seat and starting to shake off the Benadryl.

She didn't turn off the motor when she pulled up at the curb, but she did put the car in park and turn to face me. "It's true," she said quietly. "I was there. I helped rob that old guy. Mickey had already threatened Berto and I was afraid, but I—well. It's not the first time I did something I wasn't proud of."

"You don't have to justify yourself to me," I said.

"I could have killed him back there," she said. "You know that, right?"

I nodded.

"And you want to know why I didn't?"

"You didn't want to feed the monsters inside."

She leaned forward a little, her expression intense. "His daddy's a murderer. I don't mean Mickey, I mean his real daddy. And I don't want Berto to have *two* parents who are murderers. I want to be able to give him that much."

I nodded again. What could I say to that? "Good luck"? "I'm sure you'll do great"? How could I possibly know?

When it became clear I wasn't going to reply, she jerked her chin at me. "So what about you? Why didn't you change back there? It might have been harder for him to kill a wolf than a man."

"Yeah," I said. I'd considered it, but I'd made a conscious choice against assuming my alternate identity.

And it wasn't just because I didn't want one more person to realize there were shape-shifters in this world. "If I'd taken animal shape back then, I wouldn't have changed back to this form any time soon. I'd just have headed off into the countryside. And if I go too long without checking in with my family, I'm afraid—" I shook my head. "I'm afraid I'll forget I have a family to go back to. I'll slip away altogether."

She nodded, like that make perfect sense. "Keep fighting," she said. To my surprise, she leaned forward and kissed me briefly on the mouth. "You're not as different from everybody else as you think you are."

I looked at her a moment in silence, nodded, and climbed out of the car. She honked the horn once, then pulled away without looking back. I watched her till she was out of sight, then headed into the ice cream parlor.

The kid behind the counter might have been seventeen and was covered with tats and piercings. Unlike a lot of the people who get their first glimpse of me, he didn't startle back at my ragged appearance and indefinable air of otherness. Some of the ink on his left wrist featured a rose with a spiked stem that wrapped around a long, vertical scar. Here was someone who had battled his own demons.

"What'll you have?" he asked. "Special today is an ice cream cone with two scoops for the price of one."

"Sounds good to me," I said. "Make it chocolate." I tipped him six bucks on the four-dollar item and went outside to wait for Dante.

All of us have monsters inside. Maybe that's what makes us human.

Pagan

S.A. Bailey

I was dead when she called.

At least, that's how I like to think of it.

Enjoying the deep, blissful hibernation of the best combination of the cryo tech and drugs available.

Just barely there, not even really aware.

A specter, a ghost, ethereal.

Real but not.

So deep in the darkness of my own mind I couldn't tell where my consciousness ended and the true deep began. The deepest deep, the blackest black, beyond the astral and the collective unconscious and into the blank.

Whatever you want to call it.

Enjoying the deep dark empty bliss of oblivion.

Yanked out of near nonexistence by someone I didn't particularly want to talk to.

There was nothing, just peace and the cool wind of the astral, and then the quick flares and ripples of light as I tore through the veil, and then the great

227

fall as I dropped from my heaven of nothingness and collapsed back into my body.

I woke gasping, drenched in sweat, the grime and stench of my long drug-fueled sleep soaking the sheets, making them cling to my skin like glue when I shot up in bed, the overhead lights flaring hard at the same time.

"Godfucking damn it!" I pulled the soggy sheet away and sat on the edge of the bed, closing my eyes and holding my head. "Lights, dim!"

The lights didn't dim.

"Lights, dim, goddamn it. Go to waking."

Still, they remained.

"Jesus, you're not brain fried, are you?"

The sound of her voice.

At first, I thought it was in my head.

That's the only place I'd heard it for years.

Maybe I had finally fried my brain.

That'd be fucked up, considering I'd been hoping to fry it enough to just stay in the blank.

"Dim the fucking lights, you bitch."

"You still hate me."

"I hate these fucking lights. If my brain's fried, it's your fucking fault. You know exactly how dangerous that is."

"How long is it going to take for you to clean up and get your shit together?"

"Well, how long is it going to take for you to dim the fucking lights already?"

"Are you awake?"

I opened my eyes.

She was on the wall directly in front of me, a hologram, beaming into my apartment from someplace sunny.

It looked like a fucking golf course.

The lights finally dimmed by half, with a soft blue tint.

"We need to talk, Alphonse."

"Got nothing to say to you."

"It's important. A job."

"I'm retired."

"We don't get to retire, you know that."

"Bullshit."

"I checked your bank accounts. Your funds are running low."

"Bullshit, I got plenty."

"Oh, really. How long have you been out? You were heavy into Dosima. Their stock tanked last month. You're a couple months away from being wiped out completely. You need to work."

"You hacked my bank accounts?"

"I had a look-see. I do my job. Gathering intelligence is one of my specialties. You know this."

"I remember. Just like murdering people by hacking their brains and yanking them out of the blank too fast was another of your specialties." I reached up and tapped the side of the metal shroud around the ocular implant where my left eye used to be.

"It was assassination, not murder. And we were at war. You know this."

I just stared at her face on my wall and tried to focus and bring my implant data screen up into view.

It was hazy, the connection slower than it should have been, my remaining human eye adjusting to the light. She still had the high cheekbones, narrow jaw, small mouth and smooth olive skin of the all human Sicilian-Cherokee princess turned warrior spy she'd been before she borged out. Her thick black hair remained shaved on the side, with two tiny silver ports on the slope of her head.

"It's slow because you've missed at least two updates. How long were you out?"

I found my cigarettes and lighter on the bedside table. I fired one up. The screen in the corner of my vision hummed with static as the needed updates ran their protocols.

"You haven't been out of the building in a year. How often are you waking?"

"What the fuck do you care?"

"I have work for you."

"Still all business, huh?"

"Someone has to be."

Finally, the connection caught, and my account showed, confirming my rather substantial loss.

"Did you do this?"

"Don't be silly. Why would I do that? I didn't steal your money and I didn't make shitty investments. That's your fault for pulling everything out of your company retirement portfolio and going to some indie trash broker you probably met in a brothel."

"Fuck the corpos."

"You live in a corpo apartment. A nice one."

"Every apartment in the fucking city is a corpo apartment."

"Yeah, well, if you weren't such a picky fucking addict, you could move back out to the sticks and enjoy shitty trailer park synthdope and try to OD on bad junk and faulty tech."

"You really think I'd be that fucking lucky?"

"Goddamn, you self-loathing prick," she snapped sharply, a flash of raw heat in the ice queen's eyes as she caught herself.

I couldn't help but smile.

"I'm sending a car. Be on the pad in thirty."

"An hour."

"Forty-five."

"An hour or go fuck yourself. I need to decompress and acclimate properly. Make sure I don't stroke the fuck out because someone hacked my brain and forced me back to life without following proper reentry protocols." I took a drag off my cigarette.

"Really think you'll be that lucky?" It was her turn to smile, the bitch.

"Not as lucky as Cortez."

She just stared at me, the smile vanishing more quickly than it had come.

"Fine, an hour. Wear a decent suit. Nice to know you're still a first-rate bastard, Al."

Her face disappeared from my wall.

I smoked and went to scratch an itch on my calf, and the clinking sound it made jolted me back into reality.

I stared at the bionic leg of tech and titanium, and the hand that had come with it, and then the arm, and took another drag from my cigarette.

Yep, I thought. Still a bastard.

Still a bastard.

Still a cyborg.

Still a goddamn self-loathing prick.

We rose above the flight line, bringing us on an even plane with the corpo aerostats that trolled over the city. Far to the west, I could see a long thick line of dark clouds, and I wondered if the rain would make it to the 'Plex, and when, and how poisonous it would be.

A bad batch of seeds could turn a light drizzle into

poison fog. That likely wouldn't bother me, thanks to the augments, but a bad batch could just as easily turn the same light drizzle into liquid napalm.

Just in case, I wanted to be back asleep before I had to watch the normies suffer, or listen to them scream.

Out the window the glittery skyscrapers of downtown gave way to terra-level slums and then countryside, or what passed for it these days.

I thought of the fields of crops and forests of my childhood, and the jungles and deserts of my first war, so long ago, and I missed the genuinely tactile sensation of raw earth. Of grass and dirt under my feet, of sand slipping through my fingers, the rough bark of a tree as I climbed. I missed the real natural smell of jasmine and honeysuckle outside my window, instead of having to wonder if whatever I was smelling was real or if it was just the signal from my olfactory sensors.

I pulled a sausage-and-cheese kolache from the wrapper. It was actually a klobasnek, but Texas was still Texas, and still took its own strange stubborn pride in calling it the wrong thing.

I took a bite, and wondered if I was really tasting the sausage and cheese and fresh bread or if that too was just a lie programmed into my brain to keep me from going crazy.

Trying to stay out of my head, I navigated the HUD in my optical implant, and caught a news channel.

There'd been a rash of terrorist attacks at corpo headquarters and buildings.

Neo trad extremists were suspected, but no group had come forth.

For years the traditionalists had remained clustered

in their ever-shrinking communities, holding on to the last of that mid-twenty-first-century normal before the singularity, as if it had been worth preserving in the first place.

"Would you like to listen to some music, or perhaps watch the news?" the android pilot asked.

"No."

"Oh, perhaps you'd care to listen to a sermon? I'm really fond of the works of The Good Sir Reverend Arsalan Koen."

"I think I'd like to be alone." I took another bite.

"Well, I can certainly accommodate that, sir. I will let you know when we've arrived at our destination. If you need anything, just let me know."

"Thanks."

The partition closed, a physical one and not a holo veil, thank the Gods that never were.

People had been arguing about android conscious-ness since before I was borged out. Android rights advocates claimed they deserved to be given legal autonomy, instead of being manufactured slave labor. They claimed their almost universal affected religiosity was proof, and not part of their programming coupled with the emotional pull of their aesthetic of perfect lab-grown human skin, hair, teeth, and diction.

The worst part was that they continued arguing this, knowing damn good and well the Alliance had banned manufacture of the more advanced models after the Insurrection. It hadn't even been the robots' fault. In the end, it had been humans that had turned them against us.

The world rolls on, humanity stays the same.

I stared out the window and tried not to think

about the constant pain of the prosthetics and augments. Or the inability to grow real skin over them
for ease of maintenance. Or the disease inherent to
all first-gen cyborgs, and the surreal contrast with the
loss of feeling in what skin I had left.

Fuck I hated droids.

I wondered what could be important enough for
Hondo to snatch me from my beloved nothing without
proper reentry. The last time had been a war.

I had no interest in going back to space, and even
less in doing corpo dirty work.

The colonies had been billed as paradise waiting
to be realized, but Eden was still a long way off.
Every colonist I'd met had shuffled around dream-
ing big and talking about the future. Meanwhile they
scraped by and obsessed over growing fruits and veg
that inevitably turned out tasteless and bland. They
ate synthetic lab-meat substitute claiming it was as
good as the real thing. The sheer weight of their lies
and desperation dragged lines and craters across their
faces. And almost to an individual, each one carried
a peculiar and melancholic weight.

As if they had escaped the original sin hanging
over them on Earth only to find themselves guilty of
a brand-new one.

Eventually the droid announced our arrival. I looked
out the window at the earth below, but I didn't see
a proper landing pad.

"Where we going?"

The partition lowered, revealing the opening to a
cavernous service garage low on the front of a large
aeroyacht.

"Where are we?"

"The Cagafuego, owned by Julio Sakamoto. It's quite impressive, yes?"

"Would you believe me if I said no?"

"Oh, no, I don't believe I would," the droid chuckled. A polite, pretentious affectation the AI developed, but not a real laugh.

I didn't reply.

The sunlight dimmed as we taxied inside, the ride so smooth I didn't even feel the tires hit the floor. I scanned the garage, noting the vehicles, equipment, tools, and security measures in their proper places. There was a custom limo suitable for both low-level tropospheric flight and land driving which probably cost half as much as the floating mansion itself. It was simpler and cheaper to build ships to send people to the colonies than to build a limo that was equally viable on both land and in the air. It still made no sense to me, but I was old enough to remember when the idea of moon bases and Martian colonies was science fiction, so what the fuck did I know?

Julio Sakamoto could certainly afford it.

He had made his initial fortune in biocybernetics engineering, which he then invested in off-world mining operations. I doubt even he knew how rich he was. He'd been back on Earth a few years, playing the benevolent patrician, flitting around the political scene and hemming and hawing and making a show, pretending to be a man of the people reluctant to run for office, as if we were still living in a democracy.

I think I hated him more for that, than for what he'd turned me into.

Closer to the loading dock, there were a couple

of runabouts, life rafts, and a row of jump jets in case of emergency. Galleons like this stayed afloat by clean nuclear fuel backed up by magnets made from Martian rock. Outside of combat, terrorism, and the occasional freak natural disaster, falling from the sky was unheard of.

Bad weather would infrequently knock down the corpo security aerostats, but these floating skyscrapers would likely still be hovering in the clouds when the world below was nothing but rubble and dust.

With my luck, I'd probably still be around to see it.

Damn I missed the blank.

A heavily armored security droid waited for us on the dock like a golem. As we pulled to a stop Hondo stepped out onto the platform.

Still so goddamn beautiful it took my breath away.

"Is everything alright, sir?" the droid driver asked, responding to whatever signals the car's integrated sensors had told him.

"Shut the fuck up, droid."

"Yes, sir." The door lifted and I stepped out.

"Stop calling me sir."

"Yes."

The door closed behind me, and the car pulled away and slid into a nearby bay.

A gust of wind whispered through the garage, echoing off the walls, and Hondo raised a hand to pull a strand of hair from her face.

She was dressed in a dark pinstripe suit with a tailored jacket cut short and pulled tight at the waist. Her thick dark hair was longer than it had been in the old days, and she was cultivating a gray streak in the front I hadn't noticed during our call earlier. She was wearing the same perfume I remembered, a light, airy, floral scent that reminded me of the jasmine and honeysuckle that had once grown outside our bedroom window and still filled me with a deep, longing, aching weakness.

Goddamn, how I hated myself for that.

"Hey, soldier."

"Don't call me that."

"Okay, then. Hello, Pagan."

"Fuck you."

"Why are you so angry?"

"You yank me out of the blank and bring me here, to Julio Sakamoto's fucking sky galleon, and have the nerve to ask why I'm angry? Are you fucking kidding me?"

"It's important."

"Important to someone I fucking hate."

"You hate everyone. Follow me and mind your manners."

"You gonna disarm me, too?"

"We both know you're not going to do anything, no matter how much you think you'd like to."

I just stared at her, cognizant of little else beyond the simmering rage.

"There's no blank in prison. Forever is a long time to go without sleep. Even what passes for it for you. Even for you."

She turned slowly on the ball of one foot to face the door, then looked back over her shoulder.

"I seem to recall you used to like this view." She gave me a smile I used to find seductive and continued on.

I followed, wishing suicide were an option.

We bypassed an empty processing booth and went through another door and then a lobby and a long hallway. We passed workstations and bays and corridors, but damn few people. A ship that size should have had the population of a decent-sized warehouse running about. The Cagafuego's was strangely empty.

"Must be a serious threat, to be down to such a skeleton crew."

"Nobody ever said you were dumb."

"You did. Many times."

"I said you did dumb shit. I never said you were dumb."

We came to an elevator whose doors opened automatically and we stepped inside.

"So who's the threat?" I asked. "This about the bombings?"

"That's not why you're here."

"Why am I here?"

"You'll see."

"Sounds like somebody wants me to do some dumb shit."

"Grow up." Her voice hard, flat, severe. Heavy with strain and the weight of the responsibility of her position, which she had pursued with cold efficiency and ruthless zeal.

The doors opened to reveal a surprisingly posh suite, in what could best be described as Tokyo abstract just before the singularity.

Julio Sakamoto's current wife was known for her style. Her calm, serene aesthetic permeated the place in muted tones and soft fabric pieces scattered about. Not what you would expect from a robotics and life-expansion robber baron turned off-world mining magnate.

On either side of the window, full sets of both samurai and conquistador armor stood tall, clashing with the rest of the suite. I assumed they were his only contributions to the current style choice. Both sets had been in his family for hundreds of years, both worn by men of his bloodline. Whether they were there as a reminder of his ancestors, or who he wanted to think himself to be, I didn't know. He'd been in his thirties when he'd borged me out, and in his fifties when he'd perfected the senescence nanobots that could essentially grant one immortality, if they could afford the treatment and upkeep. A technology he'd developed while trying to fight the disease first-gen cyborgs carry.

The man himself stood with his hands clasped behind his back, staring out a large window at the world below.

"Thank you for coming, Alphonse."

"I didn't have a choice."

"I see time hasn't softened your heart."

"Did you expect it to?"

He nodded, and then turned and dismissed Hondo. She gave me a brief hard stare and disappeared.

"What do you want?" I asked. He turned and went back to staring out the window. Still so dramatic.

"It's about a missing person."

"So go to a cop. You own plenty of 'em."

"I'm afraid I can't do that. I need someone from the outside."

"I'm on the outside? The whole world knows I'm your attack dog."

"I'm not worried about people knowing I'm looking for them."

"So use Hondo; I'm sure all her software is up to date."

"I'm afraid this requires you, and you alone."

"You must be mighty scared of something to not be sure if you can trust Hondo."

"It has nothing to do with her loyalty."

"If you say so."

I walked to the window and stood next to him, already sick of his theatrics.

If he told me we were going to save the world, once again, this time for real, I thought I might kill him and take my chances.

I could see the 'Plex in the distance, and on the other side of the horizon the seeded electrical storm rolling slow but steady toward it. I didn't see any flames, but the day was still young.

"Tell me, Alphonse, what do you think of the world we created?"

"I didn't create shit. I was just one of your guinea pigs."

"You know, I've often wondered how you have managed to retain just enough humanity to be so deeply cynical."

"Hope is the pipe dream you're still using to convince the best and brightest of the planet to escape to the stars. How's that working out for them?"

"No one said it would be easy. They know what they're getting themselves into."

"Yeah. That's why there's a moratorium on colonists immigrating back that has been in place for a hundred years. You know moratoriums are supposed to be temporary, right?"

He started to speak, caught himself, and then took

a deep breath and went back to watching the slow-moving storm as it moved closer to the 'Plex.

"You don't want to shoot me back up there, to put down another rebellion, do you? Because killing scientists and dome farmers that just want to come home doesn't sound like my idea of a good time."

"You used to like your job."

It was my turn not to reply.

We stood there for a moment, staring out the window at the coming rain.

"This time, Pagan"—he turned and looked at me—"I hope you can help me prevent a war."

"I've heard this before."

"I'm serious."

"New Corinth was serious too, remember?"

"I don't need you to remind me of New Corinth!" he spat, his words carrying weight and a sharp heat. The great man still hated to be reminded of his mistakes.

He took a deep breath, gathering himself, forcing himself to return to calm. No doubt internally chiding himself for showing emotion.

"I wouldn't ask you here if it wasn't important."

"You didn't ask me here. You had Hondo yank me out of the blank without proper protocols. Lucky she didn't scramble my brains."

"I'm sorry. There's an urgency about this. Besides, we both know your constitution . . . is stronger than that."

"Unfortunately."

I could feel his eyes on the side of my face as I continued watching the storm in the distance.

"Are you really going to make me apologize, again, Alphonse?"

"You couldn't apologize if you wanted to. Why am I here, and what's with the skeleton crew?"

"Do you still have contacts among the druid priests?"

"Not since New Corinth."

"Surely there's someone who will talk to you?"

I just stared him in the eye.

He turned back out the window.

"I don't guess there's any going back after something like that."

"I guess not." I felt the burn in my veins, and adjusted the flow of feel-good into my bloodstream. "Would you get to it, already? I want to get back to the blank."

"Do you remember my granddaughter, Evelyn?"

Little Evie, bouncing and happy and bright. A smart, beautiful child full of kindness and curiosity.

Two lifetimes ago.

"Of course."

"I'm afraid she hasn't had an easy life. After we went up, her parents ran the day-to-day of our operations on Earth. Evie was primarily raised by nannies and tutors and a series of boarding schools. When she was eight she was diagnosed with schizophrenia, depression, anxiety, and bipolar disorder. When the medications didn't work, she was diagnosed transsexual, and then transracial, and that all of her problems stemmed from that. So, she underwent corrective surgery for both, and began senescence treatment at twenty-five. She wanted to stay young forever. She stayed heavily self-medicated for years, both with drugs and body modification. By the time we got back..." He trailed off.

"Fifty years is a long time to be gone."

"Her parents wrote her off years ago. I'm all she's got."

"She de-transition?"

"She's gone back and forth countless times. She was a woman the last time I saw her. I've maintained a trust for her. She had some sort of psychotic break. Swore off the meds, joined a street ministry, and went full-blown neo trad radical."

"And you want me to find her."

"She pulled a large sum from the trust, and then started missing her transfusions."

"Jesus." I did the math in my head. "She'd be what, about a hundred and eighty now? Folks tend to age pretty quick after they stop treatment."

"That's the problem. She left the church and joined a splinter group. I believe they're behind the recent attacks."

"You think she did that?"

"I think they have information only she can give them."

"Do you have a recent current image of her?"

"No. She's changed her appearance and sex so many times. I have no clue what she looks like now."

Five years without treatment wasn't easy on anyone. Over a hundred and fifty years was a lot of aging to come roaring back in only five years' time.

"When she joined the church, I thought it was just another phase of hers. I'd hoped it was a sign she'd maybe turned a corner, and would come back into the fold. She's only going to age faster and faster, and her mental health is going to deteriorate more and more."

I started to say something, but didn't.

I started to smile, but didn't do that either.

There was no point.

The world had gone dark long ago, and he'd had more than a small hand in that.

"If she's underground, I need a place to start."

"Reverend Arsalan Koen. She turned to his organization after the big psychotic break. He insists he hasn't heard from her in two or three years, but I don't believe him."

"I assume you can get me whatever information the police have on the attacks?"

"Of course."

A notification flashed in the lower corner of my internal optical display, letting me know I'd received a file.

"I'll look through the data, see if there's anything there worth pursuing. And I'll go visit Koen. Suicidal borgs and droids seem to flock to him."

"They do indeed."

The door opened and Hondo reentered the room and gave me the look that let me know our visit had come to an end. I turned to leave and he spoke again.

"Usually, Al, when we ask you for a favor, you ask why it's your problem."

"I know why."

The rain wasn't too bad.

It left oily streaks on the windows and carried with it the chemical smell of whatever they were using to make the current seed. But it didn't cause spontaneous human combustion or turn the air into a poison fog, so I considered that a win.

Mostly it was safe enough now, I guess.

The first hundred years of earnest weather manipulation had been low-key, at least with no obvious harm.

There had been conspiracy theories, but they were mostly fantasy and government-fueled distraction.

After the singularity, they'd gotten more ambitious in scope and intent, and more adventurous in the mixes they used. Now it seemed every two or ten years nature acclimated to their bullshit, and the world would burn. Or freeze. Or both at the same time.

You would have thought by now they'd have stopped trying, but that was a bridge they just couldn't cross. People would never leave well enough alone, or stop trying to turn the world into whatever their idealized version of it was.

Goddamn, I hated being awake.

I stared out the window as the railcar hummed over the city, an electrical storm erupting over the lake, illuminating the junks on the water and the bourgeoisie townhouses in Old Deep Ellum.

There was an ambulance and a couple of police cruisers floating above the surface, and a tug boat was pulling what looked like an older sky cab from the lake. The basic models weren't supposed to fly in inclement weather, especially the older ones, but there were always a few who cut it too close.

Droid and human workers alike stood on the stern readying their equipment. A single droid sat on the rear bumper of the cab being lifted out of the water. It held its head in its hands as if it actually felt its programmed sadness.

A shot of thunder cracked hard, bathing the world in a quick flash of blinding light, and then another cab dropped down into the lake.

I turned and looked out the other window at the station ahead.

The Good Sir Reverend Arsalan Koen's La Reunion Church was in what was left of an ancient slum, on the industrial southern shore, not far from the docks of the lake. Flooding the Trinity had been a dream for some since before I was born, and had finally happened in the years between my initial upgrades and the singularity, none of which had happened like anyone had suspected, or really wanted.

Dallas had always been a thing that never should have existed.

An island of glass and concrete carved out of ungodly malarial swampland so miserably stagnant, humid, and hot you could have told me the Native Caddo had left the original European settlers alone as a curious oddity, the original crazy white people, and it would have been just as believable as genocide.

That was Dallas, always and forever.

We pulled into the station and I disembarked with the day shift into the joyless, never-ending carnival that the singularity had brought us. I stepped out into the rain, and started making my way through the crowded throngs toward Arsalan Koen's church.

Rain rattled off the roofs of stalls and stands, glass and pavement. Both human and droid shuffled about. You could only really tell them apart by their body language and mannerisms. The droids that hadn't spent enough time with lower human society walked straight and tall and moved in a mechanical fashion. The ones who had, moved with the spastic, discombobulated Cecchetti of tweakers at a rave.

They all moved out of the way for me.

I'd had that effect even before the augments, and

the legend of my kind had started when the ashes of the world that was were still warm. They felt the ripples from their sensors as my software disturbed their Wi-Fi, and took one look at the metal housing of my optical implant, and stared at the formerly human half-man that couldn't be killed but had no soul.

I caught every curious glance, every shuddered whisper.

Big war hero. Granted immortality and a comfy penthouse apartment and a decent retirement package, just gotta be ready to go to war every so often. Never mind living in excruciating pain because the metal they used when they borged you out released a steady stream of poison into your blood. It felt like burning napalm throughout your body and required narcotic suppression just to keep from going crazy. And oh, yeah, you don't fucking sleep, ever. Best you can do is comatose yourself for long periods of time.

Big war hero, indeed.

I passed bars and food stalls and brothels, would-be vamps in fake leather with implanted fangs, street shamans mystifying the painfully stupid and gullible with low-rent science fair tricks they called magic. The stench of body odor and cheap cigarettes, diesel and hydraulic fluid, the slightly plastic scent of synthetic meat and seeded rain, and every single drug and intoxicant ever known to man saturated the air.

Lab-grown foxes colored in rainbow neon danced in a large terrarium. An adolescent human/chimp hybrid hung in a cage dressed in lederhosen. It sat with its legs dangling out, grasping the bars with both hands, crying in anguish as it bashed its head against the cage.

The few who noticed, laughed.

An obese human madam old enough to have defective liquid-metal upgrades drooping off half her face walked with a swagger only those utterly incapable of self-reflection can muster. She wore an electric mesh suit with a subtle pinstriping of tiny flashing lights that peeked out from beneath her puffy feathered coat and the band of her wide-brimmed hat. She led a winged cougar on a leash. A wheezing, sad-looking chimera with a disjointed shuffle, a body that was hilariously overdeveloped in the chest and anemic in the legs, with useless wings too small to do anything but flop about. It looked like all it wanted was to be put out of its misery.

Being smart enough to know you never should have existed in the first place is a helluva thing.

Music thumped and blared from various sources, holoscreens fed the sheep whatever currently passed for the news. Various security droids and their borged-out human NCOs milled about, half of them high or drunk, maybe on duty, maybe not.

The world had once held such promise.

There had been a time when I had legitimately believed technology would allow us to evolve into something more, something better. To create a better world.

Instead, we became an insane and ridiculous people, and the world grew ever more mad.

The monkey-boy hybrid screamed higher, shrieking more harshly as his head clanged louder against the bars.

From behind a curtain came a seven-foot-tall man dressed in a three-piece suit with huge, flared bell-bottom slacks. They were gray plaid, and clashed with the blue silk vest sprinkled with candy cane polka dots over a ruffled lace blouse of electric red and lime. He wore a pink top hat with a purple band and a red rose and carried a cane. He had a ridiculous Fu Manchu turned handlebar mustache.

He raised his hands in the air, and addressed the crowd and passersby.

"Come one, come all! To see my son, Pinocchio! He only wants to be a real boy!" He laughed.

The small crowd howled.

Pinocchio shrieked and banged his head harder, tears running down his cheeks, his grip on the bars so tight his knuckles were pale. I thought he might be a droid, but a scan checked him as flesh and bone, without augments except a metal plate in his head.

I pushed through a small crowd of drunken off-duty corpo cops jeering and throwing peanuts at the cage.

They stopped shouting and throwing peanuts.

"Can I help you, sir?" The tall man leaned in.

"Fuck off."

Pinocchio kept screaming, crying harder and harder while the metal plate in his head clanged louder against the bars.

I reached inside the cage and ran the cybernetic fingers of my prosthetic hand across the back of his, the needle in my little finger projecting out through the gelled metal to inject an almost instantly fatal dose of warm bliss.

There was the briefest of moments, my hand on his, when he stopped screaming and crying and banging his head, when the clanging of metal and the roar of the crowd subsided. In that all too brief moment, we made eye contact. And in that moment, I saw recognition. And the joyous embrace of death's sweet release, and the relief of nonexistence. Freedom from pain and the sheer absurdity of being.

"You killed Pinocchio!" The tall man looked at the cops for help. "He killed Pinocchio!"

I turned and stared at the cops, let them get a real good look at my optical implant and the layered gelled metal of my arm. They didn't have to look very hard to decide they wanted to stay off duty.

"That's gonna cost you, mister! I'm gonna have to buy a new *link*, and I'm gonna have to put a plate in its head, and that's going to cost a fortune!"

His name and occupation flashed in the bottom of my screen.

Cyrus Fergus, street performer.

"Cyrus Fergus, street performer. If I ever meet you again, and find you treating anything else like that, I'll kill you."

"Hey, now!"

He took a step back.

"I'll fucking kill you, Fergus." I glanced at the cops. "I'll kill you, and I'll kill anyone enjoying the show. Do you understand?"

He didn't answer, just watched the cops disperse, then stared at me.

I stared back.

Fergus shook his head.

I continued on.

What was left of my stomach growled.

I didn't know whether I was hungry, or if it was my programming, but the first week or so out of the blank I could rarely be satiated. I passed noodle joints but wasn't in the mood to be any more of stereotype than I already was, so I kept on.

A droid pimp dressed down one of his human sex

workers, and she snapped her fingers and the pimp dropped to all fours and howled at the moon. A few humans huddled under the awning of a hot dog cart howled in laughter.

A prostitute leaning against an ancient flickering light pole smiled at me. She scanned human, with only the barest of tech implants, but I couldn't tell if her blood carried bots without a sample. She opened her raincoat to reveal three bare breasts glistening in the rain. A joke from a movie from my father's childhood, turned into a fetish.

At one time I would have thought it odd a third breast was the most of her upgrades, but I had long since stopped trying to understand humanity. The droids at least had an excuse. After the Droid War and the laws made at the Accords that put safeguards in place, they had gone from getting smarter and smarter, to dumber and dumber. And as humanity took a nosedive, things only got worse.

The cheap homebrew jobs and non-factory refurbs were the worst. The closer I got to the docks, the more ridiculous it got, my path littered with worker droids that had grown too stupid and instead of being decommissioned had just been left to wander. They milled about, begging for work they couldn't do, or food they didn't really need, or sex they couldn't really enjoy. Not much different than the slums of the world that was, come to think of it.

Along the way I caught what smelled like real meat over a fire, so I tracked it as I walked.

The crowd gradually grew less and less insane, the junkies and spazzing ancient droids thinned out, and the buildings grew less derelict and decrepit. There, behind the levee near the old Hampton Road bridge, was the home of The Good Sir Reverend Arsalan Koen, and La Reunion Church.

The closer I got the stronger the smell of real meat became.

I was sure it would be coming from the church, but instead it came from a doner kebab shop on the first floor of a three-story apartment building on the corner across the street. Inside, I could see Anatolians busy slicing meat off a vertical rotisserie for the extensive line of customers huddled under the awning as a non-augmented teenage girl took orders at the window.

Signage across the window promised a mix of half-real and lab, both certified grade A.

It smelled so good, and I was so hungry.

At least, I thought I was.

The line was very long. I could probably cut to the front, let reputation and vibe pay the way.

But I had a job to do, one I didn't relish. And I knew at least half my hunger was a play to stall the inevitable.

Besides, I already had too much self-hate to deal with to do that shit. To use my vibe and myth that way.

I walked across the street to the church.

There was a tall red-stone wall, in the old WPA style, around the compound. I hit the buzzer at the gate, and a few minutes later a monk in robes appeared and opened it.

"I'd like to speak to Arsalan Koen."

"Of course, we've been expecting you. Follow me."

He took me around the side of the church, past a small playground with fixtures from the twentieth century and before. A young child stared at me from inside the top of a steel frame rocket ship pointed toward the stars.

I thought it was a little late for children to be up and playing in tall steel lightning rods during a seeded electrical storm, but didn't say anything. Nothing else in the world made any sense. Why should this?

We entered a large greenhouse filled with real fruit and vegetable plants.

Arsalan Koen was alone, inspecting a potato crop in a raised bed.

He was a big, fit man, with only the barest of augments, and wore the same loose robes as the monk. He'd left the scars and holes in the side of his face bare and natural after his de-borgification. He moved with the slow, painful, aching pace of someone who still carried a weight they never should have hoisted to begin with. His skin was the bland, washed out, dull gray of a methoxso junkie.

One of the downsides about living in a world in which body modification had no restrictions.

You can only change races so many times. Biology rebels.

"Thank you, James. You may leave us."

"Yes, Reverend."

The monk turned and shuffled past without a glance or nod in my direction.

Koen turned away from his potatoes, pulled off his gloves and dropped them on a table between beds.

"I can't help you."

Guess he knew what I wanted.

"It's important."

"Oh, I know."

"Why not?"

"Because I don't know where they are."

"Are they currently still a woman?"

"I don't know."

"You know what race they are?"

"*They* are *They*."

"Don't start that with me. People are dying."

"Does it matter?"

"I thought you were a man of peace."

"There can be no peace, without justice."

"There's no such thing as justice."

"Just what I would expect a man such as yourself to say."

"Just what justice do you think there is by starting a war between Mars and the Moon?"

"The colonists were promised a new utopia, and in return for their lives and souls they were given slavery, mining minerals on planets that will never be naturally habitable. And the fruits of their existence bear out in the world we enjoy today. Anyone can be anything, the complete absence of natural order."

"Nature is chaos."

"But organized, meaningful chaos! The lion knows what the lion is! Can you blame them? They never had a chance to know who they were. In fact, They were raised to be nothing and everything at the same time. How could They not be angry?"

"So, what, they're gonna hop skin and gender back and forth to commit acts of terrorism and start a goddamn war just to get back at Mommy and Daddy for virtue signaling?"

"It is torture! Entire generations lost to ideals of a childish and selfish nature!"

"I don't disagree. But that doesn't make this right."

"Madness cannot be reasoned with."

"Then it must be stopped."

"You, of all people, believe this world is worth saving?"

"I believe in not making it worse. A bunch of dead miners and dome farmers makes it much, much worse."

He looked away, toward some tomatoes in raised beds. A mist hissed down from a hose mounted up high. Rain rattled off the translucent green roof above.

"What do you think will happen to Earth once Mars and the Moon go at it? What do you think this world will look like without a steady supply of their resources?"

"The Tower of Babel will fall, and the Earth will be scrubbed clean."

"I thought you preached nonviolence."

"I do."

"Then why are you helping them?"

"I can assure you; I am not. Just because I can see what will come to be, does not mean I wish for it. I tried to convince Them of the folly of this undertaking. I'm afraid it only encouraged Them more. They are very angry. And They have a right to be."

"They don't have a right to take it out on other people."

"Are we even still people?"

I stared at him, my anger flaring.

Still human in only the worst ways.

He looked away, as if I'd taken his words the wrong way, and he was embarrassed.

"What group did she join?"

"She did not join a group. They find They."

"She formed her own group?"

"That would be a grotesque oversimplification. Again, They find They."

"Who finds whom?"

"The lost. Those born into chaos. Into a world in which it is impossible to truly grow into themselves, to self-actualize and know who They really are. Because reality itself is just a choice of social constructs given to them without a structure to conceptualize it and their place in the world. So, few people today ever truly find themselves. To know themselves. We're not supposed to all be the same. They are the light They seek."

"My head hurts."

"They left some things here. To be given to you, specifically, if and when you came looking for Them, and no one else. I've held onto them in case They decided to come home. You're welcome to go through them, see if there's anything that might help you."

"Lead the way, Reverend. Lead the way."

The room was small, modest, bare. A desk and chair, a bed, a bedside table, a bookcase.

On the desk was a box, and inside the box were some folded clothes, and an antique cell phone. It was one of the very last models made during the singularity. It looked like a clear square piece of plastic glass. That kind of thing was popular among retro trads. It was made of Martian crystal and charged itself with both kinetic motion and the sun, but had been in the box so long it had run out of juice.

In the bottom of the box was a battered copy of a famous biography of Their grandfather, written during the singularity. Tucked inside it was an old photograph

of Evie as a child, playing cowboys and Indians with
Julio Sakamoto's famous cyborg bodyguard.

The photograph had been taken by the author while
gathering material for the book.

Not long after the picture was taken, the first
Interstellar War broke out, and I shipped out for that.
Had to protect the mines from the miners.

She had been such a sweet, innocent, intelligent
child.

We had been close, like a big brother and his
baby sister.

I hadn't seen her since.

Partially because of my shame, what I had become,
the things I was known for by then. But, also because
in doing so, I felt as if I had abandoned her and
therefore shared responsibility for what I had known
of the life she'd lived after.

Beneath that was an old-fashioned, leather-bound
journal, with intricate symbols and runes carved into
the leather. I released the thong, and opened it up,
revealing the dead language of a people I barely
remembered. The mish-mashed neo paganism my
parents had long ago raised me in.

At least now, I had a place to start.

I slowly chewed a mouthful of doner kebab and
stared out at the world below as rain hit the window.
I knew, logically, that any vehicle of Julio Sakamoto's
would have a top-of-the-line radar and Faraday system.
That the sensors would detect the electrical charge of
a lightning bolt and dampen and disperse the flash
of energy, but I just didn't trust it in what was left
of my gut.

Maybe it was the image of the sunken cab being hoisted out of the water earlier in the day.

The droid sitting there on the trunk of the cab as it hung from the crane, his face contoured in tragic affectation.

Living a lie, thinking he was alive.

The poor bastard.

The world had once held such promise.

And then, somewhere along the way, we had stopped talking. We created subjective realities so far from the objective truth we couldn't even have a discussion. We lived in echo chambers, led by the absolute worst among us on all sides. At some point, tolerance, acceptance, and love had turned into mass delusion.

The first world had grown soft and decadent. In the quest for virtue to signal, a rare medical necessity had turned to Munchausen by proxy and finally elective surgery.

The human mind, so frail and malleable.

They blamed the world that was for their pain, and They were absolutely justified in Their emotions. I did not blame Them their feelings.

So very many lost to the very peculiar chaos of the technology and wealth and excess of the first world.

But, They wanted to change the world, and make it into what They wanted.

And that was the whole goddamn problem.

That was always the problem.

"Does it remind you of New Corinth?" the droid driver asked. I couldn't remember its name.

"What?"

"The Battle of New Corinth. It was during the flood, right?"

"Yes, it was during the flood."

Great, I thought. A droid that wants to hear war stories.

I took another bite, and went back to looking out the window, hoping he'd leave it alone.

The Battle of New Corinth had happened on Europa, during the Galilean War.

Europa had been a rare early case of terraforming gone well.

Of course, once a colony born of both rebels and religious zealots was self-sufficient it decided it wanted to be in charge of its own destiny and had to be put down.

As if the resources they mined where they were born and raised, on a moon they had made fully livable, could ever possibly belong to them.

Once, I told myself they deserved the example we made of them, but I don't think I ever really believed it.

I felt the slow-burning fire of the poison in my blood flare, and consciously doubled the dose from the opiate stream released into my blood.

I couldn't wait to be back in the blank.

I just stared out the window and watched the rain flicker in the darkness.

"How is your doner?" Sakamoto's droid limo driver asked.

"Delicious." At least I hoped it was, as I stared out the window hoping he'd fucking compute.

Lightning cracked overhead, bathing the world in a quick blue light. The limo's Faraday system caught the bolt and redirected it with a pulse of concentrated energy.

"Sir, if you don't mind, I would really like to ask you a question."

"What about?" I hoped one question would suffice.

"About the boy in the market, Pinocchio."

I didn't need to ask how he knew about that. I was a cyborg and he was a droid and we lived in the future, even if it was ridiculous and absurd.

"He wasn't a boy. He was a toy for moral imbeciles."

"If he wasn't a boy, then why show him mercy?"

"No animal, no living thing, deserves to be treated like that."

"Then why not set him free?"

"So someone else would have to put him down? He was a thing that never should have been, birthed in a test tube and grown in a vat by greedy assholes and sold to a moron to be tortured for the amusement of other assholes. He lived a life of pain and degradation and deserved better than this world."

"But he was alive."

"Not much of a life, pal."

I took another bite, and went back to staring out at the rain.

I suddenly felt queasy, and folded the paper back over the rest of the doner.

"They talked about you, you know."

"What was that?" I hadn't been paying attention. My head was swimming, my software hazy and the interface growing sluggish.

"They talked about you. You were Their hero. You were so brave. At New Corinth, and Kubrick Station. They wanted to be just like you."

"Who?" What was left of my stomach churned.

"They whom you seek, of course."

"You knew Evie?"

"Oh, yes. I've been with Mr. Sakamoto for many years."

"Yeah? Spend much time with Them?"

"I would say so, yes. More time than Julio Sakamoto ever did. Or you, for that matter."

"I was just doing my job."

"They loved you."

"There's no such thing as love."

"You don't believe in love?"

"Love is just a degree of obsession and chemical release."

"What a terrible world you must live in, for love to not exist."

"It's called reality."

"Well, we'll just have to make a new one."

I felt queasy. I couldn't remember the last time I had felt queasy.

His voice sounded far away.

"That is what They are doing. What We are building."

"Who is doing what?"

"We are. Legions of us, born to a world that should have never existed! A world of everything and nothing! Of bland excess and mediocrity in which nothing matters. We will make the intangible tangible! A world in which everyone will know their purpose because everyone will know who they are."

"Oh, Evie, what have you done." I muttered, all too aware of the pain and fear and timidness in my voice.

And then the droid turned and looked at me.

"We call her Mother."

A steady hum of electrical current jolted through my body.

I dropped my doner and reached for my handgun and I malfunctioned, tensed and spasming.

The handgun fell to the floor.

The HUD of my optical implant went to static, and my neural link fritzed out.

I tried to move, but the muscle of my human parts seized and convulsed, while my borg parts went dead and helpless.

"They are us, and We are Them. And we are legion. We will make a better, more loving world! Don't you want to see what We will create?"

"No. Honestly, I'd really like off this bullshit merry-go-round."

"Such a shame. They miss you so very much. We hoped you would be proud. Maybe join us. We are They, and They are We."

And then he came out of the chair and over the seat.

And then we fought.

Or, more accurately, he beat me, chanting We are They and They are We!

Over and over again.

I went deep inside myself, hyper-focusing on the chip in my neuro link, making that connection and overriding it manually. It came slow, but the static in my implant started to clear, and I started to coax gelled steel and titanium back to life, and released the spike from inside the wrist of my prosthetic, and drove it into his eye.

He jerked and spasmed and fell back, the limo rocking in the air.

Found my gun and brought it up and he stared at me, hate in his one good eye.

And then I fired.

The blast was deafening. Half his head disappeared, and his lifeless body dropped to the floor of the limo. And then we fell.

We didn't spin, or turn, or tumble.

We just fell, much like any other dead weight just naturally falls.

With heft and finality.

Unfortunately, I didn't die in the crash.

I didn't even score brief unconsciousness.

"Pagan? Pagan, come in." Hondo, no doubt responding to the alarm falling out of the sky would have triggered.

"I'm here."

"What happened? The cameras in the limo shorted out."

"Your droid had a malfunction."

"Be serious."

"Evie formed a cult of retrograde augments and disaffected droids that think they're sentient and the driver was one of them. Which you should know, since he was her bodyguard when we went up."

"I see." Her voice hard and cold and sharp. "Evac is on the way."

"I'll be here."

"Of course."

I stared at the burning wreckage and rain, and the lights of the 'Plex in the distance, and wondered how we were going to save ourselves from the consequences of our actions.

The Hound of the Bastard's Villa

G. Scott Huggins

When I tell people I'm a veterinarian, they usually say, "A what?"

Actually, a lot of them spit at my feet. Sometimes, the politer nobles will say, "We honor your service." In the Dread Empire, even for people, life is expensive and death is free. So the idea of getting paid to care for animals is a bit strange.

Once they understand, *then* they say, "Isn't it difficult to avoid being disemboweled, poisoned or eaten by the horrible creatures you work with?"

And I say, "You shouldn't talk about my patients' owners that way."

Of course, since becoming the Dark Lord's Beastmaster, I don't worry so much about some random orcish noble having me drawn and quartered. But there are some offenses that could still get me horribly vivisected. Such as declining dinner invitations from

Baron "The Bastard" Vondeaugham, Vice-President of the Outer Council.

"Stop scowling at everyone," murmured Harriet, from somewhere around my waist, as we approached the front door. "Relax and smile."

"I'm smiling," I said, between my teeth, "but I'm not relaxing." While it might not be safe or profitable for Vondeaugham to allow his guests to be eaten by his various pets, you couldn't count on the Baron to realize that.

"You look like you're about ready to rip someone's throat out, James," she said.

"That's pretty typical of Outer Council meetings," I said.

"But it's a party. Look pleasant," said Harriet, putting on a stunning smile and looking up at me. "It's called acting. I survived a couple of years bartending for orcs doing just that, and it won't kill you for one night."

There was a line at the door to the Bastard's villa.

"I have just about had enough of this," said a tall, pale figure immediately in front of us to his female companion. It was hard to tell them apart. They had identical neat, pageboy haircuts. The only difference I could see was that she wore a wreath of wilted black flowers in her hair, and a tiny fringe of black lace on her robe. Their eyes were all black, their lips red as blood. He snarled, "I did *not* come here to watch a pair of animals sniff at each other!"

"I know how you feel, Raddie," I said, easily. "I could have just stayed at work." The vampires' faces twisted with disdain, and they turned their backs on us. Vampire lords, even minor ones, don't like it when their food talks back to them. Fortunately, I didn't care. "Oh, come, Radula," I said, loudly. "The Underminister of Unhealth and Human Services should positively relish a chance to informally chat with the people he serves. How else will you know whether you're doing the job right?"

Radula turned slowly, trying for maximum intimidation, but I was used to high-ranking vampires wanting to kill me. "I take issue with your familiarity," he said. "And the word 'serves.' And 'people.'"

"Why?" I said, affecting puzzlement. "They're two syllables at most, you can't have forgotten what they mean." I looked over his shoulder. "But here comes a vocabulary refresher."

A big, hairy face thrust itself between Radula and his companion, accompanied by a choking miasma of stale body odor, piss, and rotting meat. "Call me 'animal' again, you walking corpse, and I'll hang you from your own entrails. If you have complaints, take them up with our host, who has not taught his verminous servants to make proper obeisances before nobility!" He shoved Radula, pointedly. "No slave gets the last sniff at Kaga Hlorcha!"

"Dung-eating gnoll!" hissed Radula, fangs bared. "I'll . . . !"

A huge hand reached over me and clamped down on the furious vampire's head. Another picked Hlorcha up by the scruff of his neck. A massive presence stepped past me and held them both inches off the ground.

"You will remember your manners as befits a member of the Outer Council," rumbled a voice so deep that the paving stones shook. "That was what you were about to say, weren't you, Underminister Radula?"

Radula was spitting mad. But he managed to say

"Yes," in a flat voice. Even if it did come out a bit more like "Yeph" because of the hand.

"And you, Underminister Hlorcha, will remember the dignity that befits your office, will you not?" continued the voice.

"Iiiiiigh," growled the gnoll chief. The hand tightened. "I. Will," he choked.

"Good. Enjoy the evening, gentlemen." The ogre dropped both of them, and they stalked inside, pretending that their mutual and unbearable humiliation had never happened. Then he turned around and stared down at me.

It was unbelievable that anything so big could move so quickly and silently. But "Gentleman" Noj Enorcma wasn't like most other ogres. Oh, he refused to wear pants, and otherwise wore skins and bones, over his gray-green, flaking skin, but they were neatly tailored into an outfit that was half armor and half courtier's doublet. A donkey skull hung about his neck, for no reason I'd ever heard. "Dr. James DeGrande," he rumbled, with a smile. "A word in private."

Shit. One major part of my strategy for surviving tonight had been *avoiding* a private word with Enorcma. Because he was also the Dark Lord's Underminister of Transportation. I looked around, but Harriet had vanished. Which meant that her survival instincts had kicked in and she was safer than I was. Good. "What can I do for you, Underminister?" As if I didn't know.

"The Dark Lord wants his Heavy Assault Unicorn Brigade across the Metatarsals of the World by the end of the week."

"You mean the rhinoceroses?" I said.

"Heavy. Assault. Unicorns," said Enorcma. He really loved renaming things, and he *hated* when people didn't use the names.

"Across that series of ridges? That certainly sounds like a challenge for you," I said.

His hand blocked my feeble attempt to step around him. "I promised him air transport."

"Well, that was a bit shortsighted of you," I said, looking him in his dull red eyes. "What do you think can possibly carry them?"

"You squish-brained little human, I *gave* you the answer to that. The perfect answer! Use the brics!"

And he loved breeding animals. And like most idiots who tried to do so, he was intuitively *bad* at it. "Okay, I told you: your attempt to domesticate rocs was a *failure.* Four of your so-called 'brics' died the first time they tried to carry a *horse.* The ones that lived are arthritic and wing strained because you overworked their undergrown flight muscles. I can't tell you they'll *ever* heal, but they sure won't without time."

He shrugged his huge shoulders. "Use magic. Where'd that little witch of yours go? I don't care how you do it. Your job is to heal my animals, Beastmaster."

"Yeah: *my* job. Not Harriet's or any other wizard's. If they could just 'heal things with magic,' I wouldn't be any good to anyone. If you try to make these deformed rocs—"

"*Brics!*" interrupted Enorcma.

"Whatever—fly even themselves anywhere this month, they will imitate their namesakes, and the Dark Lord's 'heavy assault unicorns' will suddenly become his fastest cavalry ever. Briefly."

"Well"—Enorcma took a step forward and bent over me—"it doesn't seem to me that you're much good to anyone now." He raised an enormous fist.

"The Dark Lord disagrees," I said, trying to keep my voice from cracking. "He likes having me as his veterinarian." The Dark Lord's favor wasn't a card I cared to play very often. But now seemed a good time.

The ogre hesitated. "Well, that's just too bad. Because I made a promise. And I always keep my promises." He bent closer. Enorcma was *big*. "For example," he whispered, and it *still* made my bones vibrate, "I promise you, now, that if those brics can't lift that regiment, your little quarterling kennel assistant will have an accident. That private practice you keep on the side, that seems to *distract* you from your duties to the empire? It'll burn. And your little woman, wherever she is..." He sniffed the air and let his smile widen. "Well, I'll leave that to your oh-so-active human imagination."

I just stood there, shaking. "Gentleman" Noj was a bigger enemy than I could hope to fight. And he would keep his promise. And there wasn't a damned thing I could do about it.

He swept past the man-sized, hairy shape that stood with an expression of sullen belligerence at the door. It had been stuffed into something that had probably been formal attire once. Its muzzle was bleeding. Its nostrils flared as Enorcma passed, and it winced.

"Is it gone?" asked Harriet. I pulled her to me, unsure of how she had reappeared, but very glad to see her.

"Are you all right?" My voice might have been a little higher pitched than usual.

"Yes, I just thought I'd let you boys discuss Council

business in private." Which was good instincts. Not
knowing things was often safest, in the Dread Empire.
"Are *you* all right? You're trembling."

"Fine," I said. I wasn't about to frighten Harriet
with Enorcma's threats. Well, not until we were alone
and she could help me figure out what to do about
them. "We should go in."

"Is that a werewolf?" said Harriet, staring at the
door-creature.

"Whatwolf," I said.

"*That* wolf!" she hissed.

"No, I'm saying *that* wolf *is* a whatwolf, if I'm
any judge."

"A what?"

"Yes, that's what I said."

Harriet punched me in the thigh. "Is that a werewolf or not?"

"No, I'm being serious," I muttered back. "That's a
whatwolf. Probably less than a quarter human blood,
and that's as human as it can look. You need nearly
half to be a werewolf. Used to be spelled *wherewolf*.
Because when they're in fully human form, you're not
sure where they are. It got shortened over centuries.
Once they're up to three-quarters human blood, it's
technically a whowolf, and they're a lot smarter. Some
can pass for hairy humans."

"You're kidding."

"Not at all."

"But why do they call it a whatwolf?"

I stepped forward. "Good evening, my lupine ser-
vitor," I said, cheerfully. "Present our felicitations to
your liege lord and admit us to his domicile!"

The creature's brow wrinkled. "What?"

I looked at Harriet, who rolled her eyes. "Doctor and Underminister James DeGrande," I said, passing over a card. "And wife." I still enjoyed calling her that, even though it had been nearly four months. From the blush she gave, Harriet enjoyed hearing it, too.

But it meant I had more to lose than ever before. And Enorcma knew it.

The whatwolf looked at our invitation. It couldn't read. But its nostrils informed it that we were human. It slavered, jaws widening. However, this creature I wasn't afraid of. "Don't try it, Fido," I said, my hand dropping to the hilt of the blade at my waist. "I'll charge your owner the emergency fee for neutering, but it won't need to cover anesthetic. *Underminister* DeGrande. Beastmaster."

The whatwolf slunk back. "Pass, lord," it muttered.

We strode past it and into the large, gloomy foyer, where a spectrally thin dark-elf butler took our coats and gestured us without a word to join the company in the dining hall.

Kaga Hlorcha was there, his stench granting him an island of solitude. He had just appropriated an entire tray of appetizers from one of the waiters. Radula was nowhere to be seen. "And he's a member of the Outer Council?" Harriet asked.

"Health and Inhuman Services. That's why Radula hates him. They have to work with each other. Closely."

"A gnoll in charge of health. Of course." Gnolls don't bathe. They consider it a sign of weakness. Why put one in charge of Health? Ever since he conquered the world, about forty years ago, the Dark Lord has considered that staffing his bureaucracy with malign incompetence is the best way to suppress rebellion.

Gets people fighting among themselves. Gnolls also have a very efficient approach to health care. If it's sick enough to be eaten, they have relatives who'll eat it. Saves a lot of time and effort worrying about things. And it sure motivates people to stay healthy, or at least pretend to be.

"Hlorcha! Grundy has been waiting to see you," a cheerful voice called. "I'll make sure you two have a chance to run around outside!" The gnoll's jaw gaped in rage at this. But the voice, unworried, continued: "James, my boy!"

Underminister of Involuntary Labor Baron Ballard "The Bastard" Vondeaugham was a large man, mostly gone to paunch. His neat beard hid his chins, and he looked like the kind of guy you'd pick for a rich uncle. Needless to say, he was a backstabbing son of a bitch. "We humans have to stick together," he continued. "Glad you could make it, and your, ah, gnome is welcome too, of course."

Son. Of. A. Bitch. I've said it before: humans who claw themselves into the nobility of the Dread Empire are as nasty and cutthroat as they come. Vondeaugham was no exception: he'd murdered his legitimate brothers for his title, and "Humans have to stick together" was his oily motto. It meant he hoped you'd look the other way while he measured you up for a slave collar and took the credit for your work and anything else he could lay hands on.

"Harriet is my wife," I said, meeting his eyes. Gnome. Harriet stands something under four feet due to the extreme left curvature of her spine. And the hell of it was, I couldn't even tell if Vondeaugham was being insulting or just ignorant.

"Oh?" he said. He pantomimed brushing her hand with his lips. "As long as you are here, James, perhaps you could take a look at my Grundy. GRUNDY!"

"What's a Grundy?"

"Oh, thank you, dear boy!"

"I didn't ..."

The whatwolf galloped up. No wonder Hlorcha had been pissed off. It was fully transformed, or untransformed, really. It wore only its collar. It still came up to Harriet's head height and growled at her. "Are you done with the gate?" the Bastard burbled, scratching its head and completely unaware of Harriet's danger. "You did such a good job, boy, yes you did."

"Vondeaugham!" I snapped, pushing Harriet behind me, "Hold him or I'll make you wish you had!"

Vondeaugham purpled. "How dare you speak to me like that! I am *your superior* ... !"

"Who isn't getting free veterinary advice from me in exchange for dinner. Make an appointment if you want your dog seen later. Hold your dog now if you want to see him above ground tomorrow." I put my hand to my blade.

Vondeaugham gripped the whatwolf's collar, but drew himself up. "As vice-president of the Outer Council, I ..."

"Should be seeing to the needs of the *President* of the Council, don't you think?" interrupted a voice as cold as ice, smooth as glass. Vondeaugham's face faded from mauve to white and he went still.

Behind him stood a woman who, while not as tall, still managed to look down on the Bastard. Her skin was black. Ink black. Her hair was the white of cobwebs, and her eyes pearlescent. She wore a gown that looked as though it had been woven of crystal and iron. Metallic lace fashioned in a pattern of silver-and-black flies crawled across it, realistic enough to be slightly nauseating. She gripped a gray-skinned, lank woman by her hair.

"President and Countess Anachryma," the Bastard said, smoothly. "My apologies, I'd not dreamed you could feel neglected in my home. How may I serve you?"

The dark-elf lady sniffed. "Tend your animals in your own time, as the doctor has the sense to advise you. This idiot"—she yanked her victim up higher, eliciting a sharp cry—"had her serving-orc bring me a message. Dispose of the corpse and move her to the lowest place at the table. And then begin the meal. I have better things to do than be confined to your hovel all night." She dropped the woman and left.

"As you command, Dark Lady," said the Bastard with a bow. But as he rose, his face was a mask of fury. He snapped a command at Grundy, who ran off. Then he punched the half-dark elf woman in the face. "Govanna, I didn't know anyone *could* be too dumb to be Underminister of Education," he roared. "I'll have you keeping the Council's minutes in your own blood! Get to your seat and wait for us. And as for *you*," the Bastard hissed at me, "you'll regret not treating Grundy! You're still slaves. *Both* of you."

"Personally owned by the Dark Lord," I said, keeping my voice level. "See him if you don't like my conduct." The Bastard stormed off. "It's all right," I lied to Harriet. Another powerful enemy made. Wonderful.

"All *right*?" she said. "It's absolutely *glorious*."

"What?" I said.

"Remember the Human Anti-Racism and Stereotyping Segregation law?"

"Yes." After Harriet's first year of studying witchcraft at college, HARASS had banned humans with visible deformities from attending academies of sorcery so that they would not "propagate harmful images of our human subjects." Except that birth defects—like Harriet's—are a major side effect of high magical potential in humans. So, humans were effectively expelled. Harriet had managed two more years of college by disguising herself as a dark elf before she was caught and expelled.

"Well, she's the one who designed it," said Harriet. "James, you said this party wouldn't be fun."

"It isn't," I groaned, as the butler escorted us to our places.

The plates were already set out as we approached, and I had to suppress a gag reflex: you'd think that, in spite of the company, dinner at the home of a noble of the Dread Empire would at least feature excellent food. You would, however, be wrong, because human nobles would never dream of shaming themselves by serving human food at their tables. Dark-elf food is the empire's haute cuisine, and Vondeaugham was playing hotelier-than-thou with a vengeance: jellied spider eggs, tarantulas on the moult-shell, and nightcrawler ragout were the features. Accompanying it, wine pressed from snake venom. The best thing on the plate was the garnish: one cold, marinated mushroom.

That's when Harriet discovered she was seated *next to* Govanna. I don't know why she was surprised. Of *course* humans were going to be seated near the bottom of the table. Harriet exchanged scowls with the humiliated minister.

Across from us was Hlorcha, and next to me sat Radula. The stench of gnoll mingled with the odor of the huge chalices of blood before the vampires. Still, I spend my days smelling evacuated anal glands and month-old ear infections, so I only had to get past the taste.

Govanna sniffed. "Do I smell...human?" she asked, looking past us at Radula.

"Probably," said Harriet. "You're at least fifty percent human, by the looks of you, so the odds are pretty good."

"Are you trying to get smart with me, slave?" Govanna shrilled.

"No, I've already succeeded in being smarter than you." Harriet smiled.

"Well, I'm afraid that's impossible," said Govanna, sweetly. "The Department of Education has proven that dark-elf intelligence would have to be divided by one half for human intelligence to equal it."

"Well, you've certainly put us in our place with facts and mathematics, there," I said.

A rumbling belch from the head of the table rattled the silverware. "I'm so glad you seem to have enjoyed the meal," said Baron Vondeaugham with a supercilious smile at "Gentleman" Noj.

"What I'll enjoy is getting the Council's work done," rumbled the ogre. "You *are* going to have those thousand slaves ready to escort Our Lord's expeditionary force?"

"Oh, that depends entirely on our good Radula." Vondeaugham waved expansively down the table to the vampire, who raised his face from his chalice. "He has all the slaves I could spare from the Lord's other projects. Take it up with him."

"I told you I couldn't do it," said Radula. "If I slew them all today, I couldn't even have decent zombies raised from what you left me in less than a month."

Vondeaugham snorted. "So you're wanting another reprimand from His Darkness? Dear me, that might cost you some privileges." He glanced at Radula's companion, who stiffened. "Or you could talk to Hlorcha and see if he has dwarves or orcs for you."

Hlorcha glared up the table and spat. "It was you who ordered my reserves to the mines! There are no more!"

Enorcma leaned toward Vondeaugham. "I don't really care how you do it, but you'd better have those slaves, little man."

The Bastard turned jovially to him and leaned in himself. "I just told you I do have them. All designated for your use. It isn't my fault if Radula's department hasn't prepared them. In any case, all the rest of my poor people are already committed."

My stomach churned, and it wasn't because of the food. His "poor people." He didn't give two shits whether Radula killed his slaves and raised their corpses. I shuddered to think what labor the ones who were still alive were being forced through.

Enorcma and Vondeaugham were still eyeing each other. Anachryma rose and placed her hands gently on both their shoulders. "Gentlemen, this is unseemly," she said. "Stand down."

"Of course, Madame President." Vondeaugham gave her a smug little bow. "My documentation is fully in

order. You just all need to learn to work as a team."
This was why Vondeaugham was one of His Darkness's
favorite managers.

So, Vondeaugham was setting Enorcma up to fail.
Or was it Radula? Maybe both? And with a sinking
feeling, I realized I was part of this too, because I
was responsible for the brics Enorcma wanted. Was
I one of Vondeaugham's tools? Or another victim? It
was like being enmeshed in a horrible enchantment.
None of us wanted to be here. Our host was the
most hated man in the room. But none of us could
afford to break the spell called bureaucracy, because
it was far too easy for all that frustrated hatred to be
channeled right at anyone who was foolish enough to
leave the only arena in which they could fight back.

The meal dragged on. The plates were cleared and
replaced by desserts (honeypot ants in gelatinous cube
bowls) to a conclusion with no further overt threats.
Finally, Baron Vondeaugham rose. At least now I'd
get a chance to plot my own survival...

A scream cut through the barred iron doors of the
dining hall. A pale servant squeezed through them
and fell to her knees, tears running down her face. "It
weren't my fault, sir, please. I just found him!" Two
other servants appeared, and their faces fell as they saw
they were not first with the news. "Grundy is dead!"

Baron Vondeaugham shot to his feet. He swayed
so violently that I thought he would fall on top of his
slave. For just a moment, he looked stricken. Human.
I'd seen that look too many times on the faces
of clients to ever mistake it. He'd actually loved the
thing. "Treachery. Poison," he whispered. Then he

kicked the woman in the face. *"Who has dared?"* he shrieked, trembling violently enough that I thought he might have a seizure right there.

Then, as fast as the rage had seized him, his voice grew cold. "Nobody leaves," he said. "Lock the gates and the outer doors. I'll not let a soul leave these grounds until I have justice for this outrage!"

Snarls and cries of protest greeted this pronouncement. When they had all died down, Enorcma growled, "Do you really think you and all the powers you command can keep me here against my will, you miserable human sack of shit?" The floor shuddered as he stepped toward Vondeaugham.

It took me a moment to realize that Enorcma had looked up in as much surprise as the rest of us at the blow. I'd thought it was him. The stamp was repeated. Again.

A metal shape that towered a head over even the ogre thrust aside the iron doors of the hall. It looked like a suit of armor fit for a small giant, but it wasn't hollow. Within the helmet, polished granite eyes surveyed the room. In a voice like sliding rock, it said, "THE OUTER COUNCIL OF THE DREAD EMPIRE HAS BEEN ATTACKED. THE HEAD OF ITS SECURITY TEAM HAS BEEN SLAIN. THIS ONE IS CHARGED DIRECTLY BY THE LORD OF THE DARKNESS TO ASSIST IN THE DISCOVERY OF THE TRAITOR. ANY WHO FLEE WILL BE JUDGED GUILTY AND SUMMARILY EXECUTED."

Facing Enorcma, Baron Vondeaugham gave the ogre a vindictive smile and said, "Why, yes. I do believe I can."

For a moment, Enorcma looked like he was ready

to test that statement. The construct wasn't in the best of shape. There were rents in the massive armor, and crudely carved glyphs in its chest and the back of its head. It swiveled toward the ogre. "ANY ATTACK ON THIS ONE WILL CONSTITUTE COLLABORATION WITH TREASON AND RESULT IN SUMMARY EXECUTION."

"Noj, stand down," said Anachryma. "You can't fight an Inexorable."

I stopped breathing for a moment. An Inexorable? That's what this thing was? Beside me, Harriet swayed on her feet. "I thought the Inexorables had all been destroyed," I whispered.

"It looks like this one almost was," Harriet hissed back. "Those carvings . . . I think the Dark Lord repurposed it." I swallowed. The Inexorables had been created by the Council of the Wise during the War of the Dark. They weren't alive. Their purpose was to fulfill their missions at whatever cost, to stiffen the spines of the wavering mortal nations. One of them had slaughtered the population of Kalmier when it had tried to surrender. They had killed whole legions before being shattered by the Dark Lord himself at the Last Battle. They couldn't be bargained with, they possessed neither mercy nor forgiveness. They cared only for their missions. And they could hear truth. You couldn't lie to one. Holy shit, how much worse could this *get*?

I had to give Anachryma this: she didn't waste time. "Agent of the Great Lord. Do you recognize me or my position?"

"YOU ARE THE CURRENT PRESIDENT OF THE OUTER COUNCIL."

"Good. What . . . ?"

"YOU WILL DIRECT THE INVESTIGATION. THE INVESTIGATION SHALL TAKE NO MORE THAN SIX HOURS. IF AT THE END OF THAT TIME YOU HAVE NOT SUBMITTED REASONABLE PROOF OF THE ASSASSIN'S IDENTITY, YOU WILL BE DEEMED GUILTY OF INCOMPETENCE AMOUNTING TO CONSPIRACY, AND YOU AND YOUR INFERIORS WILL BE SUMMARILY EXECUTED."

I choked. *Everyone.* Baron Vondeaugham's mouth opened and shut. Even Anachryma's ink-black skin turned dark gray.

"And who set *that* particular deadline?" she managed.

"THIS ONE'S PARAMETERS WERE SET BY THE LORD OF DARKNESS."

Ah. *That* much worse.

"Of course they were," muttered Anachryma.

"Oh, gods!" wailed Govanna. "Some rebel is plotting to kill us! First your pet and now the head of security! Who was it?" She just did not keep up.

"Perhaps, Govanna," said Vondeaugham in tones of pompous dignity, "your time might be better spent helping us find this rebel assassin than in worrying about yourself."

Anachryma looked at Baron Vondeaugham, and said, "Let us be perfectly clear: Am I to understand that the head of security for the entire Outer Council was *your pet whatwolf?*"

"You told me to make security arrangements," Vondeaugham blustered. "Grundy was loyal, ferocious, dedicated..."

"And now just dead," said Anachryma. "Where is the *rest* of the team?"

"Grundy...that is, I put him in charge of hiring... but he hadn't..." Vondeaugham stammered.

"Whatwolves are barely capable of using *language*," I said. "Much less hiring an entire security team!"

"Sounds perfectly qualified to be an Imperial official," muttered Harriet. "Ow." I had stepped on her foot.

Baron Vondeaugham fixed me with a look of sheer hatred. "Well, Grundy might still be alive *if you'd examined him like I asked you to!*"

"What?" cried Harriet. But I just shrugged. It was among the crazier things I'd been accused of in my career, but it wasn't near the top.

"If I'd wanted him dead," I said clearly, returning Vondeaugham's glare, "I'd have been more than happy to examine him. I could have killed him right in front of you while telling you I was doing everything possible to save the poor animal. In fact, I never touched him. If you'd really noticed something was wrong an hour ago, you'd have told me what it was."

Baron Vondeaugham purpled and then wheeled on Radula. "Then it was *you* who poisoned him!" he screamed. "My servants have been telling me for weeks that you've been throwing piles of trash over my walls!"

Radula bared his teeth. "The 'trash' is your own disgusting compost heaps that fall over into our property! And they're *our* walls!"

"Or perhaps it was you!" Vondeaugham whirled on Hlorcha. "Your rotting zombic servants are always wandering into my estates."

"Your stupid whatwolf *drags them over!*" Hlorcha growled. "I wish they were poison, he'd have been dead *months* ago!"

"Enough." Anachryma's voice cut through the recriminations. "This is Council—in fact, Imperial—business"— she glared at Vondeaugham—"and as the construct says, I am in charge. Beastmaster DeGrande."

"Yes, Madame President." I swept her a bow. Anachryma was more evil than Vondeaugham, but a lot smarter.

"It seems we are in need of your expertise. Go examine the body and report. I will consult with the Inexorable to determine its parameters for considering our investigation a success."

Of course, the thing about impressive mansions is that while they are full of rooms filled with luxurious diversions, they are unaccountably short on examination rooms suitable for performing a necropsy. So, Harriet and I headed to the kitchen. The cook was thin, human, trembling and white. "All right, don't panic, you've done nothing wrong," I said. "Just get me your sharpest knife, preferably something about eight inches long."

Well, what should I have done? I don't carry my equipment to dinner. And people still want free service. "The Baron mentioned trash thrown over the wall. Get me a sample of anything you saw Grundy eating—or even eating near—in the last day. And what the hell am I supposed to use for shears?" I muttered to myself.

"Hey, your job's easy," said Harriet, assembling various cups and pots. "I have to set up an alchemist's lab in here." She strode off, calling for vinegar, soda and water.

"This is going to be messy," I said to the cook. "Have a couple of your staff heave him onto whatever's easiest to clean." They laid him out on a stone counter. I really don't have many patients that are man-sized. The small ones tend to be a lot smaller, and the big ones are *much* bigger. I opened Grundy with the chef's knife. Blood oozed out as the skin and muscle parted, revealing the abdominal cavity. I became aware of a presence—and a smell—at my elbow.

"Please, sir," whispered a groundskeeper. "It's the offal y'wanted."

"Very good," I said. I looked it over. It was rotting meat, fruit. Certainly nothing a vampire would have owned. But they might have laced it with something. "Pet poisoning" is a common accusation leveled by neighbors who hate their neighbors. It's rarely true. "Take it to Harriet, the short woman over there. Then come back."

I filled a small bowl with blood, and then started on other things for Harriet.

The thing about poisons is that there are hundreds of them. If the poison was something visible, in the stomach or the guts, it would still be there tomorrow, so no rush. But who knew how long ago Grundy had really been poisoned? Oh, Vondeaugham was sure that someone right here was the culprit. But some poisons take days to work. And if it was one of those, I'd never find it myself.

Quickly, I snipped out bits of Grundy's liver and kidneys, filled another cup with bile, and a third with urine straight out of the bulging bladder. Then I leaned in, crushed a vertebra, and snipped out part of the spinal cord. Then I scooped out one of his eyeballs.

It was amazing where poisons ended up. I signaled the servant back to me and sent her off with it for Harriet to work her alchemy. Then it was time for me to get to my job. Which hopefully would return a diagnosis of death by natural causes.

There was nothing grossly wrong with Grundy's guts. So I cut open his stomach. A wolf's stomach makes the stench of the meal I'd just eaten smell like roses. Grundy was gorged. Recently. Gods knew where he'd gotten it all. Chunks of some kind of meat: Vondeaugham fed his whatwolf better than his guests. Something else, here: what looked like part of a giant prawn. There *were* shellfish toxins that were pretty deadly, but there were also people who ate large prawns, and that was a bit more common. Then I saw the berries.

Small berries. Dried. They might have passed for blueberries, or even peppercorns, but I'd seen them before. Never in the stomach of a carnivore, though. Deadly nightshade. Fuck. Of all the times for that idiot Vondeaugham to be *right*. Grundy had been poisoned. By one of the guests? Possibly. I turned to find Harriet.

And nearly tripped over her.

"James," she muttered, "the cook is standing right behind you with a large cleaver and he's watching you."

"And that's a problem because?" I said, an ugly chill crawling up my spine.

"He's the poisoner."

"And how do we know this?" I asked, impressed. I'd just discovered the poison, and she already knew about it *and* had figured out who'd done it?

Harriet pulled out a jar from under her arm with a faint green glow to it. "Because this isn't sugar syrup, and it's on his hands, too."

"Good gods, how didn't anyone notice *that*?"

Harriet sighed. "The poison is a clear liquid. The glow is my tracking spell. Alchemists call it *ethglyc*. It's an extract from a certain moth caterpillar, and it tastes sweet."

"Wait, *what*?" I said. "I'm sorry, but I think you meant to say, 'it's a solution containing deadly nightshade, from these berries right here.'" I held one up.

"Wait, *what*?" said Harriet. "Two poisoners?"

I shook my head. More likely one poisoner trying to make double sure. "Odd choices to poison a carnivore with," I said. But after all, dogs would eat almost *anything*. Whatwolves might, too. "Okay, we don't have time for subtle, I want to survive the night." I turned, and in one smooth motion drew the blade at my waist and laid it against the head chef's throat. "Drop the kitchen hatchet," I said.

My blade is a No. 75 dragon scalpel. It's over two feet long, and about four inches wide until it narrows to a point. Sometimes I even use it on patients, but mostly I employ it in performing what Harriet refers to as a "problemectomy."

The cook's cleaver clattered to the floor. I moved my foot just in time and almost made it look smooth.

"Lord, how have I offended?" the man whimpered.

My stomach churned. Look, I lived as a slave and a human in the Dread Empire all my life. Technically, I'm still a slave. But now I'm also the Dark Lord's Beastmaster. Effectively a noble. And my own people cower before me and spit behind my back when I pass.

It made me cringe; I probably hadn't even needed to draw on the guy. But you don't take chances with anyone carrying that much edged steel.

"I'm afraid you have a confession to make," I said. "Harriet?"

She stepped forward. "See your hands?" He did, and gasped in horror, trying to rub the glow off. "It means you put this in Grundy's food."

"*Please*," whispered the man. "You don't know what it's like here. The Baron doesn't feed us. He expects us to live off his table scraps! And the werewolf gets most of those! And stealing food before he's done means we get to be the next meal! The last one was the maid's *daughter*!" Tears leaked from his eyes. "I know you have no reason to, but if there's any part of you that remembers what it was like to be human . . ."

I slapped him. "I am a human," I said. "And it doesn't make you special. I'd personally just as soon say Grundy died of natural causes, but it *wasn't*. It was poison, and I can't lie about that." I explained about the Inexorable. "I'm sorry, friend. But if I don't tell on you, you die anyway, only you take us all with you."

The man sagged. "All right. It was me. I bought the ethglyc and used it. I guess if I have to die, maybe at least everyone else will get a good meal out of it."

"And then stuffed the deadly nightshade in his bowl just to make sure?"

"The what?"

I stared at him. "They won't kill you any deader for admitting to the nightshade, too."

"But . . . but I didn't! Why would I lie about this? You have me, all you have to do is tell."

"DeGrande!" Baron Vondeaugham burst into the

kitchen. "The President wants to see you. Now!"
The cook opened his mouth.

I elbowed him in the gut. "Silence!" Then I
muttered, "Not yet." I followed Vondeaugham out
the door. Anachryma was waiting in the great hall.

"I'm very much hoping you have something,
DeGrande," she said.

"Madame, my assistant and I have just begun. It
would be incredible if we had something already."
Technically, I wasn't lying.

"The Inexorable will require your sworn testimony
and your reasoning as to why the testimony is true.
It will not necessarily require physical proof, but it
is *good* at logic. At least, I wasn't able to tie it up in
conundrums." For the first time since my elevation, I
saw Anachryma flustered. "Find something, DeGrande.
Find anything plausible."

"I'm at least as motivated as you are," I said. Again,
true. "By your leave?"

Back in the kitchen, Harriet met me. "We're not
telling on Gordon. He has children."

"Gordon?" The chef nodded. "Not unless it's that
or die. Besides, I'm not absolutely sure the Inexorable
would accept your magic as proof, Harriet. I bought
us some time. Here's the plan: Harriet, can you do
with the berries what you did with the, uh . . . with
his poison? Find out who used it?"

"No. The liquid was once all a single thing. Berries are individual objects, and the spell doesn't work
like that."

"Can you come up with one that does?"

"I doubt it."

"Well, try. Gordon, if you could think of poisoning

Grundy, so could another servant. Or they might have seen the person who did. Find out if anyone knows about these black berries turning up in Grundy's food."

"What if I find out it's one of them?"

I sighed. "Then you'll have to draw straws ... or something."

"What are you going to do, James?" asked Harriet.

"I'm going back out there and stir up our suspects."

There aren't many advantages to living in a society ruled by an immortal incarnation of Evil that everyone in power is trying to curry favor with. However, one of them is this: when the chips are down, everyone can be relied on to turn on everyone else.

"All right, everyone, I have an announcement," I called, from the entrance of the dining hall. "In the stomach of our host's whatwolf, we have found deadly nightshade. So if anyone happens to have seen their neighbor sneaking off to the kitchen where Grundy's bowl is, we can get our friendly Inexorable here to execute the truly guilty party and then we can go home."

The room became very—still. Then everyone began pointing and chattering at once:

"This carrion-eater was sniffing ..."

"The vampire took offense at ..."

"The ogre was threatening our host!"

Baron Vondeaugham shouted, "This is ridiculous. Why are we waiting for the guilty party to confess? This is no real mystery. Inexorable, isn't it true that you cannot be lied to?"

"INDEED. I HEAR THE TRUTH OR FALSE-HOOD IN THE WORDS OF MORTALS."

"Then simply ask them and have done!" I groaned inwardly. Vondeaugham had to pick *now* to do something halfway intelligent?

"THIS IS ACCEPTABLE. BARON VONDUUM, DID YOU POISON THE HEAD OF SECURITY OF THE OUTER COUNCIL, AKA 'GRUNDY'?"

"What? How dare you...?"

"ANSWER THE QUESTION. FURTHER EVASIONS WILL BE CONSIDERED PROOF OF GUILT."

Vondeaugham's veins throbbed in his purple face. *"Of course not, you stupid infernal machine!"*

"YOU ARE TELLING THE TRUTH." It clanked over to the next nearest noble. Anachryma. "COUNTESS ANACHRYMA, DID YOU POISON THE HEAD OF SECURITY OF THE OUTER COUNCIL, AKA 'GRUNDY'?"

"Certainly not," she said, in bored tones.

Well, shit. This might work or it might not, but if the poisoner wasn't found among the guests, eventually he'd have his servants marched in here, and Gordon would end his life on an impaling pike. Besides, evading questions was an art form, and while the Inexorable might be able to tell truth from falsehood, the fact that it had needed Vondeaugham to tell it to interview the suspects didn't suggest the greatest initiative or imagination.

Besides, I already had my primary suspects. When people *do* hurt animals, it's usually in a fit of rage. Hlorcha, Radula, and his consort were staring at the Inexorable, and I *knew* they'd both resented Grundy's inspection at the beginning of the evening. Radula's consort looked frankly terrified.

No one was watching me. I casually walked toward Hlorcha,

There was an insistent tug at my arm. Harriet was there, with Gordon. "Not now! I'm just...are you all right?" I asked. "You look pale."

"I've felt better," Harriet said. "James, there's another poisoner." She held up a vial with pale blue liquid in it.

"*Another* one?" My head spun. "How many people wanted this stupid wolf dead?"

"I don't know, but it's a nasty one. Black fae dust. Clots the blood in the veins."

I shook my head. "We *know* Grundy didn't die of that, his blood flow was as normal as I've ever seen when I cut him open."

"Oh, for gods' sakes, James!" snapped Harriet. "I've seen you double-talk the Dark Lord before! Do something!"

Well, that was true, but it wasn't something to count on; I could have been killed every time. "Okay, we'll try it. I suppose you didn't manage another tracking spell?"

"No."

I hesitated. "Okay, what's in that vial? Anything dangerous?"

"No."

"Great." I held it up. The stress must be getting to me, too. I was sweating and had to concentrate to focus. I clapped my hands for attention.

"Noble colleagues," I said, "it grieves me to report that our poisoner was quite thorough and used more than one agent to ensure that his treachery would succeed. However, I see none of us are wearing gloves. Black fae dust is very effective when sprinkled in the victim's food, but there would still be some on the poisoner's hands. What our poisoner could not have counted on was that Harriet would have compounded this solution!" Here, I poured a splash of Harriet's liquid onto my handkerchief. "Completely harmless," I said, wiping my hands with it. "But if you have touched black fae dust, and an alchemical reagent causes it to be absorbed through your skin, and, into the bloodstream, well..." I turned to Hlorcha. "Will you shake hands with me?"

The gnoll grinned. "Of course, Beastmaster." His hand was hairy and sticky, but his handshake was firm.

"Countess Anachryma?" I offered my hand.

"Of course." She allowed me to take hers.

No sooner had I turned toward Govanna than she bolted for the door. In three clanging strides, the Inexorable caught her. "LADY GOVANNA, DID YOU—"

"Yes. YES!" she screamed. "I used the black fae dust, and just to be sure, I slipped in some death-clover mold, too! I won't stand for any more of your bullying and insults! I don't know how it got into your stupid werewolf's bowl, but at least I know you won't live much longer than it did, Vondeaugham, you utter prick!"

Harriet and I stared at each other. "Wait, what?" we said, simultaneously. *Vondeaugham* was the target? But what about...?

"LADY GOVANNA, YOU ARE UNDER ARREST FOR ATTEMPTED MURDER."

Vondeaugham screeched in rage. "What? This vile bitch poisoned me? *Me?*" He looked from my face, to Harriet's, to Anachryma's, and stopped. "Would you care to tell me," he seethed at the countess, *"exactly what you are laughing about?"*

With a grim smile on her face, Anachryma gestured to me. I sighed. "Black fae dust is a deadly blood poison. So is deathclover mold. But it *prevents* the blood from clotting and makes you hemorrhage to death." I looked at Govanna, whose face had gone pale. "She fed you two poisons that act as each other's antidotes."

Harriet said brightly, "I hope the new Underminister of Education addresses the shocking failure of our schools to teach real-world poisoning skills!" Then she howled with laughter.

The Inexorable opened its chest, revealing a small cage, and stuffed the raving Govanna inside. Her screams cut off as the armor clanged shut. "THESE POISONS CANNOT HAVE KILLED THE VICTIM. THE DEADLY NIGHTSHADE IS TO BLAME, AND THE POISONER REMAINS UNFOUND." It stalked toward Hlorcha to resume its questioning.

"Great, we found a poisoner, and we can't blame her because she's a complete moron," I muttered to Harriet, helping her up. "And we're running out of time." My heart was pounding. Harriet staggered into me. "I think I'm going to barf," she groaned.

I wasn't feeling too good myself. "Who wouldn't feel like throwing up," I grumbled, "after that lovely meal of spider eggs and legs, worm sauce and fermented mushrooms?"

"Mushrooms?" said Gordon. "What mushrooms? We didn't prepare mushrooms."

Oh. Shit.

Harriet looked up at me. "I missed a poison, didn't I?"

"Oh, I'm afraid neither of us *missed* it. But there do seem to be an awful lot of them around tonight.

Hold on. Govanna tried to poison Vondeaugham, but you found it in Grundy instead? How did Grundy..." I whirled on Gordon. "You said he was fed on *leftovers*! And that means that the ethglyc was in *our food*!" I grabbed him by the collar and whispered, "You begged for my help when you were poisoning us all?"

Gordon struggled in my grip. "No, Beastmaster. No!" he choked. "Only his food! I swear! He didn't eat what the rest of you did!"

"I *saw* him!"

"No. His plate . . . we just put the tarantula legs around it for a garnish. He never eats them. Behind the garnish, he had roast prime rib, potatoes and prawns! The ethglyc went in his key-lime custard. His glass of venomwine was single-malt scotch. But no mushrooms!"

My grip loosened. Just when I'd thought I couldn't possibly hate the bastard any more than I already did. But no mushrooms. I looked around. And suddenly, the light dawned.

I staggered over to Baron Vondeaugham. Yes, the dizziness was definitely getting worse.

"What is it?" he snapped.

"You want your poisoner?" I asked.

"Of *course*!"

"You got a hunting crossbow?"

"I *am* a *gentleman*," he sniffed.

"Great. Let me borrow it for a minute, and I'll solve your case." I really hoped I was going to be able to solve mine and Harriet's too, but at least our killer wouldn't get away with it. Vondeaugham snapped at a servant, who ran off.

"Gordon," I said, "clear out of here and hide. That

thing is almost done questioning guests, and then it'll start in on the staff. Let's make sure it asks you last." The chef nodded and bustled back to the kitchen while I filled in Harriet on what to do.

"BARON RADULA'S COMPANION, DID YOU POISON THE HEAD OF SECURITY..."

Well, it was consistent, anyway. It hadn't even realized that it was asking the wrong question. Our suspect could answer honestly that he hadn't poisoned Grundy. He'd poisoned the *Baron*. The servant handed me Vondeaugham's crossbow. Even better than I expected, it was a weapon meant to impress as well as kill. Razor-sharp bolts gleamed in twin slots, and I cocked it with the pump of a lever. Then I handed it to Harriet and circled around until I was face-to-face with Hlorcha again. "Sorry, there's one more thing."

"What now, human?"

"Put up your hands, you stinking pile of shit," said Harriet from behind him.

Hlorcha whirled, saw death staring at him behind a hair trigger. He raised his hands. "You dare..." And I saw exactly what I'd known I was going to see.

I plucked two of the fungal growths right out of Hlorcha's armpit and danced back, avoiding his reflexive swipe. They glistened with oil and sweat. He'd *cultivated* them there.

I turned to the Baron. "Did you eat this?" I said.

"Yes." He swayed on his feet, going green.

I pulled some of the shrunken nightshade berries out of my pocket. "Do you remember eating these?"

"I thought those were black capers!"

"Are you," I said, "feeling as sick as I am, right now?"

"I feel fine." He looked at the mushroom, sheened with gnoll sweat. "Until, um, just now." He turned and vomited on the floor. Then yelled for the Inexorable. I closed my eyes. Dammit. Not again. It couldn't be. Well, first things first.

Hlorcha snarled as the Inexorable reached him. "You just couldn't pass up the opportunity, could you?" I asked him. "To get us as well as him?"

"Humansss," he hissed, "are a disease in the Council."

I held up the mushrooms and berries to the Inexorable's stone gaze. "These are poisonous," I said. "He poisoned all the humans. And then they got to Grundy."

The Inexorable locked Hlorcha in its iron grip. "THOSE BERRIES ARE DEADLY NIGHTSHADE?"

"Yes," I said, "but . . ."

Whirling, the Inexorable strode across the room and grabbed Radula's escort, who shrieked. "BARON RADULA'S CONSORT AND CHIEF HLORCHA. YOU ARE UNDER ARREST FOR ATTEMPTED MURDER." It set her down, locked in its other hand. "THE BERRIES YOU WEAR IN YOUR HAIR ARE THE SOURCE OF THE DEADLY NIGHTSHADE."

I stared at the struggling vampire. The wreath of flowers hanging askew in her hair . . . weren't flowers. They were berries cut to resemble flowers at a glance. But that hadn't fooled the Inexorable. More berries, still intact, nestled below her hairline. Well, there was nothing for it. I took the wreath and did some calculations.

"Six berries for you, ten for me," I said, handing Harriet her share.

"You're poisoning me?" Harriet cocked her head and nearly fell over. "Isn't that redundant?"

"Not when deadly nightshade counteracts the muscarine in the fungus we ate," I said.

"You mean . . . ?"

"Yes, they did to each other what Govanna did to herself," I said. "We'll feel like shit for a few hours, but we'll be okay."

The Inexorable opened its chest again, and we got a brief glimpse of Govanna as she cried out, "There's not enough roo—" before the new prisoners were thrown inside and the chest slammed shut. I rather thought I heard something squish.

"YOUR ACTIONS PROVE THESE POISONS CANNOT HAVE KILLED THE VICTIM. ANOTHER POISON MUST BE TO BLAME."

Harriet's hand tightened on my wrist. I returned the grip.

"I know, I know," I whispered, "Gordon's the poisoner. I'm out of ideas."

"No, that's just it: he *can't* be the poisoner," said Harriet. "Not if he poisoned Vondeaugham tonight. Ethglyc doesn't work that fast."

My mind raced. "Why didn't you tell me that before?"

"I didn't know, before! When I found it, we thought Grundy was the target, and for all I knew, he could have been poisoned last night." She broke off.

Countess Anachryma was walking up to me. "There is another poisoner, Dr. DeGrande," she said, in a voice of frozen bronze, "and I cannot help but notice that you are doing nothing as we inch closer to death." She was the only one left in the hall besides Enorcma.

"I SHALL BEGIN QUESTIONING THE SERVANTS."

"Wait!" I said, desperation accelerating my thoughts. "I think I know where the poisoner is." The Inexorable stopped.

"I know it isn't me, and it's not Harriet. So the two remaining suspects are Countess Anachryma, and Gentleman Noj Enorcma."

"We've already been cleared," the ogre said, with a calm smile.

"No, you haven't," I said. "Both of you told the Inexorable that you didn't poison Grundy. And that was true. The *Baron* poisoned Grundy." Vondeaugham started to shriek a denial, but I went on: "By handing him a plate of leftovers. So enough games. Why don't you both just strip and let us search you? We can see if you might have anything else that might have found its way onto our host's plate."

Anachryma smiled. "Very well." She began to shrug out of her dress.

Enorcma stiffened. "Human scum," he said. He fixed me with a deadly glare.

Oh, shit.

Enorcma screamed and charged, his enormous horny fist raised to pound me into jelly.

Unlike stage duels that go on for hours while the principals hurl insults at one another, most real fights to the death are over very quickly. I'd had a moment of warning, and I knew what he was expecting. I'd run. Or dodge.

So I whipped out my dragon scalpel and knelt, slamming it over my head with all my strength.

Enorcma's huge fist whipped just over my head and hit the diamond-edged steel as I brought it forward. A regular sword would have bounced off his thick hide, but my blade was meant for surgery on *dragons*. It shore through the horn and muscle of Enorcma's knuckles, parting the carpal bones and slicing between the ulna and radius for a foot before the ogre's inertia whipped it out of my hands and it spun across the floor. His howl of agony shook the room.

I was already running after my sword. I'd been lucky and half-crippled him, but Enorcma could have still killed me even if I'd taken his whole arm *off* and he knew it. I heard his footsteps pounding behind me.

I hadn't slowed him down enough.

I leaped for the handle of my weapon just as he swung at me. Goaded into swinging early by rage, he only brushed my leg with his fingers. It felt like a mule's kick. I spun through the air, past my blade, feeling the awful shock of the blow. Then the nauseating pain. He hadn't broken the bone, but I wouldn't be running anymore. I was screwed.

I staggered to one knee. Just in time to see Enorcma's foot slide out from under him and send him crashing to the floor.

I caught up the blade. Hobbled two steps.

Enorcma raised his head and fixed me with a glare of pure hatred.

Just as I brought the blade down on his head.

The ogre fell, skull split in two.

Harriet ran up to me. "James, how badly are you hurt?"

"I'll be okay." I spotted the thing she was holding. It was a napkin . . . folded into a squat shape. There were bristly hairs and skin flakes sticking out of the lumpy figure. "What is that?"

"Insurance," said Harriet. "He didn't seem terribly

patient when you were talking to him outside. But he was rather focused on you. Easy enough to gather up a little hair and skin. I'd have made a better doll once we got home. But this was enough to trip him up. No one threatens my husband like that." She bent down and rifled through the pouch at the ogre's waist. Then she rose with a rapt smile. "Aconite, James."

I took the dark green leaves—shredded, so as to resemble herbs—and held them up. "This is it," I said to the Inexorable. "This is what killed Grundy." Except even as I said it, I knew it was wrong. I turned and stared at Baron Vondeaugham. "Why aren't you dead? You've eaten enough poison to kill you six times."

Vondeaugham blinked. Pale, he said, "I thought you said they were all antidotes to each other. I, ah, knew all along, of course."

"Right. So what didn't Grundy know?" I glanced at Harriet. But Harriet was staring at Countess Anachryma, who was shrugging back into the top of her dress.

"That's a lovely design," she said. "All those silver-ebony flies. I've been admiring it all evening." Anachryma nodded, the only indication that she had deigned to hear a compliment from one of the lower orders.

"Only one of them seems to be missing," Harriet said. "That one at your left shoulder." Anachryma froze. "It seems to have landed on your neck, Baron."

"What?" said the Bastard. He slapped at the fly nestled just below his ear. "Ow! That . . . that's not a fly!"

"No, don't . . ." I said, but he yanked at it and it came away trailing a hair-thin needle glistening with an oily wetness. His face flushed and he turned on Anachryma.

"You bitch! You tried to kill me?"

She smiled. "And I've been waiting for *ages*. I was wondering what could possibly have gone wrong with my favorite shellfish toxin."

"I'll have you . . . I'll have . . ." His breathing accelerated. He shuddered. His final seizure went on for a good three minutes before his heels drummed on the floor and he went still.

The Inexorable advanced. Anachryma held up a hand. "The poisoning is solved. Baron Vondeaugham killed Grundy by feeding him his own poisoned food."

"YOU HAVE KILLED THE VICE-PRESIDENT OF THE OUTER COUNCIL."

"I did not. He died upon removing the antidote that was saving his life. Baron Vondeaugham committed suicide."

The Inexorable was silent a moment. "IT IS AS YOU SAY. MY DUTY IS DISCHARGED." Slowly, it walked from the room.

Anachryma gave me and Harriet a cold smile. "Well done, Beastmaster. Our next council meeting should be *so* much more efficient."

I gave her a bow. "Let's go tell Gordon." I limped into the kitchen on Harriet's shoulder.

"I don't know what to tell you, or offer you," said the chef, blinking back tears. "You saved me. You saved us all."

"I wish I could promise your next master won't be worse," I said.

"Whoever it is will probably feed us," he said. "And at least we can eat tonight."

"Well, make sure you throw that bowl away," I said, pointing to the heap of half-eaten steaks and prawns dumped in Grundy's bowl. "I'd hate to see someone else die of eating that." Turning to Harriet, I said, "So after all that, the ethglyc in the dessert wouldn't have even killed the whatwolf until tomorrow?"

"Honestly, I doubt he'd have even noticed." She picked up the whatwolf's water bowl. It was full of amber liquid. I looked at Gordon.

"Single-barrel malt," the cook replied bitterly, opening the liquor cabinet above with a huge ring of keys. "Nothing but the best for Grundy."

"So . . . ?" I looked at Harriet. "Oh, you've got to be kidding me."

She shook her head. "Funny thing, but getting falling-down drunk is the antidote for ethglyc poisoning. They would have both been fine."

I took the bottle. It was nearly full. I looked at Gordon. "I'd say you've earned it," he said.

"Good. This is the kind of antidote I think I need, too."

With the bottle in one hand, and Harriet on my other arm, we went home.

Midnight Ride

Chris Kennedy

"Dexter, don't look back."

I couldn't help it. A voice comes from behind you—especially that voice—you have to look. And there she was. Just like I'd last seen her. Except for the bionic replacement of her right arm.

"Kat," I said, looking forward again into the mass of people moving through the Jonas habitat's shopping district. "The years have been good to you." I chuckled. "Except for the arm, I guess."

"Funny," she said, her voice a whisper in my ear. It sent a shiver that went down the entire length of my body. Just the way it always had. "Can we talk?"

"I thought we were."

"Do you always have to be so difficult?"

"Do you always have to come and go without notice?"

She paused, then said, barely loud enough to hear, "Comes with the name, I guess." She was close enough, I could feel her shrug. "Seriously. Can we talk?"

I relented, like she knew I would. She wouldn't have come back otherwise.

"Meet me in my office in thirty minutes. It's—"

"I know where it is," she said. "I remember." Then she was gone, like the way a police siren clears Bartertown.

Just like the way she left ten years ago.

I walked into my office twenty-nine minutes later, still trying to decide if I was going to meet with her. The odds were, she was toying with me, like a cat and a mouse. I'd always hated being her mouse.

I didn't get to choose, though; I walked through my door and found her sitting in the client's chair.

I frowned.

"Turns out I still had a key," she said, smiling.

I'd never gotten around to changing the locks, although I'd thought about it hundreds—no, probably thousands—of times. I held my hand out. "I'll take it."

"It's on your desk." She jerked her chin toward it. The key sat in the middle of my blotter. "Still living in the past, I see."

She wasn't talking about the old-fashioned pad; she had obviously seen the date on it. *Ten years ago.*

"What have you done now, Kat?" I asked. I fell into my chair, ignoring the ominous creaking sound.

"What makes you think I've done anything?" she asked with a shrug. "Sometimes bad things just happen to me."

"Usually, those bad things happen because of something you've done to precipitate them."

"Ooh, look at you and your big words!" She clapped sarcastically.

"The question stands. What have you done?"

"I haven't *done* anything. It was done to *me*."

I arched an eyebrow at her, but didn't say anything.

She tried to meet my gaze, but couldn't. Finally, a little sigh escaped her, the only admission of defeat I was likely to get. "I had a cargo. A precious cargo. It was stolen from me here on Jonas. I want to hire you to find it."

I cocked my head. "You just happened to lose it on Jonas?"

She shrugged. "What can I say? I come here a lot. I have sentimental ties to it."

"That's funny," I said with a snort. "You don't have a sentimental bone in your body."

"That's not true." Her eyes fell to the floor, and her lip curled into a sad moue. "Sometimes I will sit at a café on your way to this office, just to watch you walk past. Always so sad...always so determined..."

My voice hardened. "What is it you want, Kat?"

"I told you—I had a cargo stolen. I want you to find it for me. That's what you do, isn't it? Find things? Someone's pet *kaldon*? A husband that went missing? Things like that?"

"I'm an *investigator*. I solve the crimes that people don't want to take to the authorities, or the ones the authorities won't touch. Sometimes it results in the recovery of assets."

"Like cargo that was stolen." She smiled triumphantly.

I sighed, already knowing the answer to the question I was going to ask. "If someone stole your cargo, why don't you go to JonasSec?"

"There's no point. Security wouldn't help me, and

even if they did and—miraculously somehow found my cargo—they'd probably confiscate it. Then I'd be even worse off."

"So it's illegitimate."

"Let's just say that it didn't clear customs here."

"Who's the buyer?"

"No one you know."

I steeled my nerve, expecting her to say either "Flyboy" or "King James." They were the top two crime bosses on the station.

"Who is the buyer?" I asked again, slowly.

Good news was, she didn't say either of those names.

Bad news was, she said something worse, her eyes falling to the floor.

I leaned forward, my eyes narrowing as she looked at the floor and mumbled something. If I'd heard correctly, then I *really* didn't like the answer.

"*What* did you just say?"

Her eyes, those green cat eyes, looked back up at me with something like a plea in their depths. "I said it isn't a 'who' but a 'what.' It's a Rigolian."

"Here? Onboard Jonas?"

"Yeah. And someone stole the cargo I had for him. Or it. Whatever they are."

"Maybe you'd better tell me more."

So she did. She told me her tale like I was supposed to care about it. About her. After all these years. I didn't want to.

But I did.

She wouldn't tell me what the cargo was, but she'd acquired something the Rigolians wanted really badly. She'd brought it here, but someone had wiped out her crew and stolen her cargo while she was discussing the transfer terms with the Rigolians. They were now threatening to take her and eat her. It's what they did.

She thought I'd just drop whatever I was doing and help her; she'd obviously forgotten how we parted. She'd walked out on me—on the best relationship I've ever had. It'd taken a long time to get over her. Hell. Who was I kidding? I wasn't over her now.

And I didn't owe her shit.

It wasn't like I was going to go talk to the authorities and liaise with them for her. "The aliens are coming, the aliens are coming." Like I was some damned up-time Paul Revere. Telling the authorities anything involved actually talking to them. *Hard pass for that.*

I sighed. But if I didn't tell JonasSec, that meant I had to do something about it myself. Because *damn it*, I hadn't gotten over her. And I was going to help her, even if it got me killed.

Which it was likely to do.

My eyes dropped to the calendar, and I sighed. I might have been tempted to let her fend for herself if it was only the system police who were after her—*who was I kidding? No I wouldn't*—but I definitely wasn't going to let her deal with a Rigolian alone. Not if I could help it.

After the peace treaty, the Rigolians didn't come around here much—they weren't allowed in *any* of our population centers. Some still lurked in them, of course, kind of like the way pedophiles lurked around elementary schools. They were the ones who'd gotten hooked on human flesh on the planets they'd conquered. When they'd told Kat they'd eat her, I had no doubt they'd meant it.

I looked back up at her. She looked vulnerable,

somehow. It was something I'd never seen before. It scared me. "Who else knew about the shipment?"

"That's just it—no one knew."

"Someone obviously knew. Otherwise, how could they have hit your ship?"

"Trust me; none of my crew would have talked."

"How about the Rigolians, then?"

"Why would they have done it? I brought it here *for* them. They were going to get it anyway; why would they risk pissing me off?"

I shrugged. "They're Rigolians; who's to say? Maybe they thought getting it for free was better than paying you. Maybe they thought they could grab it and get you in the bargain." She shuddered at that thought. It was the first time in memory I'd ever seen her shudder, but I couldn't blame her. Apparently, the Rigolians liked their food to still be alive when they ate it.

She looked up through her eyelashes at me; her eyes were wider than I'd ever seen. "Will you help me, Dex?"

Like I'd ever had a choice.

"I'll go ask some questions. Poke around. I'll see what I can find."

"What can I do to help?"

"Stay here. Incommunicado. When I get back, we'll figure it out."

She gave me a sad smile. "Thanks, Dex. If there'd been anyone else I could have gone to . . ."

"You'd still have come here."

Again, the sad smile. "Probably. You always were the best."

And yet, still not good enough for her.

I nodded and walked out.

❖   ❖   ❖

I started with Kat's ship, which was berthed in Hangar Bay Foxtrot at the tail end of the station. It's where people who couldn't afford better docked. A quick scan of the cesspit showed a vaguely familiar blood splatter pattern on the wall, and it was obvious Foxtrot hadn't been cleaned since the last time I'd been there weeks before. That wasn't a surprise. The surprise was that five members of JonasSec were chatting in the center of the bay; normally, the security force avoided Foxtrot like the plague it was.

An official investigation was obviously ongoing, and additional JonasSec forces were crawling over Kat's craft. Judging by the outlines the security forces had drawn on the deck, her crew had given as well as they'd received, and the bad guys had left with a lot fewer than they'd come with.

Interesting. The outlines on the decks were humans, not Rigolians—no tails.

I strolled past as if I wasn't interested and headed to my second destination—a food truck in Ring One. Gravity was a lot lower there, so the clientele tended to be spacers and not "elite" who resided in the outer rings.

"What's good today, Gecko?" I asked as I stepped up to the counter, timing it so no one else was in earshot. The food was so good that everyone tended to come visit Jimmy "The Gecko" Abrams, and—like the lizard he was nicknamed for—he tended to blend into the background. He picked up on conversations without the speakers knowing it. He'd forgotten more gossip about things that had happened on the habitat and in local space than most people knew.

"Burritos are always good," he replied. "Spicy today, too. Just got some peppers in from Earth."

"Sounds good," I replied. "I'll take one." I arched an eyebrow. "Not the only thing spicy going on today, though, is it?"

"Lots going on today, just like always," he acknowledged as he pulled out a shell and started ladling meat—or something that looked like it, anyway—onto it.

"Looked like a ship got hit in Hangar Bay Foxtrot," I noted, gesturing for him to put a little more jalapeño on my burrito. "Heard anything about that?"

"They say the Sky Kings bit off more than they could chew."

"Anything else?" I asked. I pulled another five credits out of my wallet and put them with the handful of cash I was about to give him.

The Gecko looked around. I knew this would be good—it was his one "tell" when he was about to share something he considered dangerous. "They also say the Sky Kings were working for some lizards, and I don't mean me." He winked.

"Didn't realize there were lizards on the station," I said, taking my burrito and adding another five credits to the money I passed him. "Where have they been seen?"

"Nowhere and anywhere." He shrugged. "I don't know where they're hiding, but most of the sightings have been near Bay Bravo."

"Thanks, Jimmy," I said, nodding to him. He liked being called Jimmy. Probably because no one ever did.

"Anytime."

I walked off, chewing on what he'd said as much as my burrito. The Sky Kings were the second biggest criminal gang on the habitat, and they were always looking for the score that would put them over the top. Even so, I wouldn't have thought Flyboy and his crew would stoop to working for the lizards. But Jimmy'd said the Rigolians had been seen near Bay Bravo. Everyone knew Bravo was Sky King territory. Maybe Flyboy was more depraved—or desperate—than I'd thought.

Two tough-looking thugs stood at the entrance to the bay, leaning against the wall. They stood and moved to block the way as I approached. I hadn't expected this to be easy, and they didn't disappoint.

"Where ya headed?" the taller of the two asked.

"To see your boss."

"I don't think so." I sized them up. I vaguely recognized the shorter one. Both were more muscle than brains. I sighed.

"Look," I said. "I don't want to hurt you. If you could just let your boss know that Dexter is here to see him, I'm sure he'll talk to me. Then we won't have to do this."

"And what is this?" the short one asked.

"'This' is where one of you gets hurt, the other probably gets dead"—I figured it would be the tall one—"and then I go see your boss, anyway."

"I don't think so," the taller one said. "I—"

I kicked him in the shin as the shorter one went for something inside his coat. The taller one bent over by reflex, and I caught him with an uppercut to the chin. His head snapped back, his eyes staring blankly, and I grabbed him by the lapels as I spun toward his partner. I had expected to use him as a shield for the expected gunshot—which is why I'd gone for the taller one first—but the short one had drawn a knife, instead, and was lunging forward with it. Judging by the way the taller thug stiffened and cried out in pain, the knife went into his right kidney.

I tossed him to the side, and the body pulled the knife out of the shorter one's hand as it dropped. He fell slower in the lower gravity of the ring, leaving a trail of blood droplets in his wake.

Which left the shorter one staring wide-eyed and open-mouthed at the unintended wreck of his partner. A knee to the groin and another to the chin as he folded over, and the smaller thug joined his partner on the deck. There was already a lot of blood on the deck; the first one had been cut worse than I'd originally thought.

Not my problem.

I walked into the bay, tuning out the whimpers of the taller man.

There were two smaller ships in the open area beyond the open blast door. One was a blockade runner of some sort; the other was a smaller intra-system runabout. I didn't have time to give them more than a cursory scan before people started pouring from one of the hatches. Obviously, the entryway had been under surveillance, and they were responding to the threat.

Their response was overwhelming; nine men and women with drawn pistols and knives. Pistols predominated, I saw, and I put my hands in the air. No sense getting shot *before* I saw the boss, although it was very possible it might occur afterward.

"You're dead, man," the first man to reach me said, pointing a pistol at my chest. Several ran past to check on the toughs by the entryway. "No one messes with the Sky Kings and gets away with it."

I smiled. "Aside from the Brothers of Anarchy, anyway," I said, mentioning the biggest on-station gang.

"Oh, you're a funny guy," he replied. "You're a regular comedian, you is. You ain't one of the Brotherhood, though; I know most of 'em on sight. You know what that really makes you?"

"A better man?" I opined.

"No. That makes you dead."

"Probably." I nodded. "But your boss is going to be pissed if you kill me before I talk with him."

"What makes you think he wants to talk to you?"

"Because I have info he needs."

"Tell me," he said, putting his pistol in a holster and drawing a wicked stiletto, "tell me or I'll cut it out of you."

I shook my head. "Take me to your boss. I have details about your new friends he needs."

"Our new friends?"

"Let's just say that Jimmy's food truck isn't the only place to find lizards on the station at the moment."

"He knows, man!" one of the other toughs exclaimed. "He knows about *them*!"

"So what?" the leader asked.

"The boss is going to want to know what he knows," a third tough said.

"Maybe," the leader said. He gave me a long look. "That shit don't mean we're through with you, though. Not by a long way. You've got a lot of payback coming."

"I expect so," I agreed. Nothing was ever free with the Sky Kings. At least it wasn't the Brotherhood. They probably would have killed me without even talking to me.

The leader sheathed his knife and drew his pistol again. "Take him up to the boss, Suz," he said to one of the women. "I'll follow and keep him covered." He turned back to me. "If you try anything—"

"Yeah, yeah, you'll kill me or shoot me or whatever else you want to do. I just want to talk to your boss, then you can have your fun."

"Damn right we will," he said with a wicked smile.

Not if I get you first.

Suz led me through a hatch, up a ladder, and then down a hall. She stopped just past the hatch labelled bay ops. She stared at me for a second then knocked and entered the space beyond. After a minute or so, she returned and motioned to the hatch. "The boss will see you now."

I smiled past her at the thug leader. "You'll wait for me, won't you?"

"Damn right I will."

"Be right back." I went through the hatch to find the leader of the Sky Kings, Robbie "Flyboy" Delgado, sitting behind a desk waiting for me. There was no chair on my side of the desk, so I approached and stood a few feet behind it.

It takes a big man to dwarf me. I knew if I stood next to him, I'd look like a pygmy. He didn't have a weapon visible, but he didn't need one; he could have ripped a leg off the desk and beaten me to death with it. I'd heard that had happened in the past, and I noticed one of the legs on his desk was different than the rest. *It wasn't just an urban legend.*

"Dexter Nogales," he said as he stared me down. He shook his head. "Never thought you'd be dumb enough to walk into here. I mean, I was going to deal with you at some point; I just didn't think you'd make it this easy."

Yeah, we had a history. I find things—and people—who have gone missing. Sometimes criminal activity is behind the disappearance, and the gangs don't like to give up what they've acquired. Sometimes, the perpetrators need to be convinced, like I'd had to persuade a Sky King member to give up a little girl he'd taken. He wouldn't be taking anyone else.

I shrugged. "I hadn't intended to," I replied. I gave him a half grin. "I gotta admit, I kinda hoped you would have forgotten about Skeetz by now. Or forgiven me for it; he *was* a piece of shit, after all."

Flyboy shrugged his massive shoulders. "Sure he was. Still, I can't have people taking out the folks under my protection."

"And I can't have those people taking little girls. She certainly didn't go with him on her own."

He shrugged. "Not saying what he did was right. Just saying that I can't have that precedent being set." He looked at me for a moment with his head cocked. "People can say what they want, but even though you look like a knuckle dragger, I know you're smarter than that. You wouldn't have lasted this long in this station if you weren't. You wouldn't have come here if you didn't think you could walk out again."

"There are a lot of files that will automatically get turned over to the police if I were to disappear suddenly..."

He waved a hand in dismissal. "Files get lost all the time at the station."

I figured he had people on the payroll at the station. It was nice of him to confirm it for me. I'd have to find out who they were. Assuming I got out of here alive, of course.

"Yeah, they do," I agreed with a nod. "That's not why I'm here. I'm here to talk about your new friends."

"Which ones are these? I have lots of friends."

"The Rigolians."

He growled, and his shoulders slumped, but he didn't appear angry with me; it was out of frustration. "Damn aliens. Never should have agreed to work with them." He shook his head. "Got a lot of my folks killed for them."

"I'm guessing they didn't tell you what would be involved in getting their package for them."

"No, they—" He stopped and stared at me. "What do you know about this?"

"The person you stole the package from is a friend of mine."

"Was a friend," he corrected. "My guys killed everyone onboard."

"My friend wasn't onboard at the time."

He nodded, nothing more than a twitch. "My guys said they thought the crew was one short." He shrugged. "Doesn't matter. He's lucky, whoever your friend is."

"She."

He nodded. "Should have known a woman could get you to walk into here."

"No, a friend."

Flyboy laughed, long and hard. "No, she's obviously more than that. You're not dumb enough to walk into here otherwise. And especially not stupid enough to kill one of my guys as you did."

"I didn't stab him, another of your people did."

"I watched the security footage. Looked like you did it to him."

I shrugged. "They attacked me."

"You attacked them."

"They weren't going to let me talk to you."

"Only a woman—one you were attached to—would make you take them on, knowing what my response would be."

My shoulders sagged. He was right, of course. "It doesn't matter who she is; I'm here to try to get the package back for her."

"No chance," he said. "Even if I wanted to sell it back to her, I'm not double-crossing the Rigolians. They eat people who do, and I ain't going to be their buffet."

"Would it help to let you know they're going to double-cross you?"

"What do you mean?"

I looked him in the eye, hoping he'd buy it. "The crew of the ship you hit knew you were coming. Someone told them. That someone was the Rigolians."

"Why would they do that?"

"So that you'd lose a lot of guys. That way, when you bring them the package, they can simply take it from you without paying."

"Bullshit."

"Look at the evidence. The crew knew you were coming. You beat them . . . but you lost a lot more people than you should have getting the package from—"

"Why do you insist on calling it 'the package'? Why don't you just call it what it is?"

I looked at him, and he smiled.

"You don't even know what it is you're trying to recover, do you?"

I tried to come up with a convincing lie, but he had me. Again. "No, I don't."

"It's an antimatter warhead that goes on an anti-ship missile. The latest and greatest."

"And you'd give that to *the Rigolians*?" I asked, horrified. "Do you have a death wish? Our fleet is barely hanging on against them—"

"We're not at war anymore. There's a peace treaty."

"There will be war again. You have to know they're not going to be satisfied until they control all of human space and can use it as their own little cattle farm. That new warhead—and the fact that we have it and they don't—is the only thing that brought them to the peace table in the first place!"

He shrugged. "I'm sure our navy has a way to stop the new warhead. I mean, they wouldn't develop something without also developing a way to defend against it, would they?"

I'd been in the military. I knew the answer to that question.

He took my look—an open-mouthed stare—as my answer and shrugged again. "They'll come up with something. Besides, like I said, I'm not double-crossing the lizards." He shrugged. "Even if they intend to double-cross me tonight. I'll recruit more people so they know they have to pay up for it." He stood and came around to my side of the desk. "I do appreciate you coming to let me know about it, though." He called out toward the door.

I watched the door open, and the thug leader from before entered.

As I turned back to Flyboy, I got a glimpse of a fist as big as my head, then blackness.

"You look like hell, Dex," Kat said as I opened the door to my office.

"I just wish I felt like hell," I said as I staggered

to the sofa and collapsed into it. "That would be an improvement."

"What happened?"

"I had a talk with the head of the Sky Kings."

"Doesn't look like the kind of 'talk' I'd like to have."

"Well, we have a bit of a history. And, I sort of killed one of the Sky Kings on the way to my meeting with their leader."

"Oh." She winced. "You're still alive."

"Yeah." I sighed and found it hurt to sigh. Just like it did everything else. Moving hurt. Breathing hurt. Hell, even laying there not breathing hurt. They'd worked me over good. They'd started while I was unconscious and had beaten me until I was unconscious again. I *was* alive, though. Barely. Hopefully, that meant I was square with the Sky Kings.

"Thanks," she said after a few moments. "And I'm sorry you got beat up, but I need to get that package back. Did they have it?"

"Your 'package'? Yeah, they have your antimatter warhead." I coughed a gob of blood into my hand and wiped it on my pants. It blended well with the other stains.

"They do? We have to get it back from them."

I scoffed. "Good luck. You and about fifty of your closest friends ought to be able to convince them to give it up." I rolled onto my side, wincing, and propped myself up on an elbow to look at her with my good eye. The other one was almost swollen shut. "Let's talk for a moment about what you were doing with an antimatter warhead in the first place."

"It was a business deal. I can't discuss it." She shrugged. "We have to get it back from them."

"And do what with it?"

"I have a deal I was supposed to make."

"With the Rigolians? You want to sell an antimatter warhead *to the Rigolians*?"

"You'll just have to believe me when I say that it's better than a gang having access to it."

"I'm not helping you do that." I coughed up another gob of blood. Things started getting gray and fuzzy. "I may not be helping you at all." Even I could tell the last bit was slurred.

"Oh, don't be such a baby." She reached into her bag and pulled out a medkit.

I started to ask why she was walking around with a navy-standard medkit but found myself falling back onto the couch. I felt a prick, then I sank into oblivion.

I woke up feeling better. Not good, but better. I probably wasn't going to die immediately, which was a definite improvement. "What time is it?" I asked.

"Eight o'clock," Kat said. She was sitting behind my desk, using my computer. "You really should change your passwords."

"Didn't expect you to ever come around again," I muttered. "What did you hit me with?" I asked, louder.

"Combat nano shot," she said. "Looks like it fixed the internal bleeding. You should be better in a few days."

"Don't have a few days," I said. "The Sky Kings are moving the warhead tonight. Hell, they could be moving it now."

"*What?* Why didn't you tell me that earlier? I've got to get it back. If it fell into the wrong hands..."

"As far as I know, *you're* the wrong hands," I said.

"Are you still planning on selling it to the Rigolians, Kat?"

"If you have to know, my customer is really our navy," she said with exasperation in her voice. "The Rigolian deal was just a cover. Why do you have to be so difficult?"

"Because you always told me to do the right thing, and I'm trying to. I just don't know that helping you is the same thing."

"You have to believe me! My customer really *is* the navy." She stared at me in earnest, and she sounded like she meant what she was saying, but I had established by now that she could—and would—lie to me. Something didn't give. She hated the navy; she'd gotten out because she hated it so much. She couldn't like the Sky Kings; they were just awful. And the Rigolians? Nobody in their right minds would help the Rigolians.

I wasn't good at math, but even I could tell it didn't add up. She wasn't telling me something, and—no matter how much I asked, begged, or pleaded—she wasn't going to tell me.

The only thing I knew for sure was that the Rigolians couldn't be allowed to have the warhead. It was better that the Sky Kings had it; all they could do was blow up a station or a ship. If the Rigolians got it, it would be the end of humanity.

So I was her ally. Sort of. Unless she was helping the Rigolians. She said she wasn't . . . but at this point, I honestly didn't know.

"Do you have a plan?" she asked. "Please tell me you have a plan."

I nodded. "I have a plan. The buy is going down tonight, and from all indications, it's going to be a bloodbath. We let the meeting go down as planned and hit whoever wins. When everyone else is dead, the warhead is ours."

"That's your plan?" She stared at me with her head cocked and mouth open.

I shrugged. "Never said it was a good one."

"Do you have any friends that can help us?"

It was my turn to stare at her.

"Right," she said. "Same passwords. Same lack of friends." She sighed. "We're going to die."

"I could get the security force to show up. If they get the warhead, they'd probably give it back to the navy. At least they wouldn't blow up the station like the Sky Kings."

"Do you know how many people in the security force are on the take?"

Flyboy's comment about evidence getting lost came to mind. "A few," I allowed.

"A few." She scoffed. "More like, 'There are a few who aren't.' If the security force gets it, we might as well have handed it over to the Sky Kings or the Brotherhood. At least they might have paid for it."

"Are you with me or not?"

"I'm with you. If you give me some time, I can probably hire some guys..."

I looked at my watch. "No time. We've got to get moving."

"Do we have time to swing by my ship so I can at least get my gear?"

I arched an eyebrow. "You have gear?"

"Of course. All good smugglers do."

"If we hurry."

❖   ❖   ❖

I was worried that security would still be around her ship, but they'd obviously finished. The ship was in lockdown, but that only meant it wasn't allowed to leave until JonasSec released their conclusions. Kat ducked under the security tape, dropped the ramp, and ran inside while I kept watch outside. Happily, Bay Bravo's operations center was on the far side of the hangar and couldn't see the ramp.

I was starting to get antsy about five minutes later when she jogged back down the ramp covered in weapons. She secured the ship then hurried over to the alcove where I was waiting.

"Gods, Kat!" I said, shaking my head. "When you said you had gear, you weren't kidding."

She set down two rail guns, a couple of laser pistols, and a backpack for each of us. In addition to all of that, she was now wearing the top half of a combat exoskeleton. It was an older model, but looked to be in pretty good shape. It had been rigged to mate with her bionic arm. I had to stop myself from whistling—she looked pretty badass.

"There's a uniform in the backpack, along with extra ammo," she said. "It's probably going to be a little small, but that's what you get for letting yourself go."

"It's all muscle," I said, pulling out the uniform.

"Maybe the stuff underneath the fat is," she said as she took off the exoskeleton to slip on a navy uniform. "You need to work out more."

I muttered something about her parentage as I pulled on the uniform. She was right; it was tight. There was no way I was going to get the top button on the pants. "Not sure I'm getting into this."

"We need it."

"Why?"

She jerked her chin toward the rail guns. "I doubt security is going to let us walk around with these otherwise."

"Probably not." I got all but one of the buttons secured and pulled the belt over the top one. "Close enough?"

"Good enough for the cameras," she said, "but it will never pass close inspection."

"So we need to stay away from security. Fine." It wasn't like I'd intended to go chat with my good friends in security. I didn't have any. "I was planning on taking the back way, anyway."

"Ready?" she asked as she shrugged back into the exoskeleton. I nodded. "Good. Let's go."

"Not that way," I said as she walked toward the main bay door. I led her to a door marked off limits, and pulled out a key.

"How'd you get a maintenance key?" she asked.

"We all have our secrets," I said. I opened the door and we stepped into the maintenance spaces that ran—out of sight—around the station. It wouldn't do for tourists to see all the dirty work required to keep a station functional. Bay Bravo was four bays over from Foxtrot, and we made our way quickly toward it. The few service people we saw gave us a wide berth. It was rare to see soldiers in the maintenance spaces, but not unheard of, as soldiers used them sometimes to surround a target.

As we passed Bay Charlie, I heard the echo of rough voices from behind us. A big group was coming. I grabbed Kat and we ducked into an engineering space. We barely made it before a group of about thirty people ran past us. They were big, tough, and armed almost as well as we were.

"Who was that?" Kat asked.

I sighed. "That was the Brotherhood."

"Where do you suppose they were going?"

"This is going to suck."

"You think—"

"Yeah. They're going for the warhead, too. They obviously have a spy in the Sky Kings who let them know about the deal going down."

"Shit."

"Yeah."

"So, what do we do? Hit the Brotherhood from behind?"

"I may be crazy, but I'm not suicidal."

"What else do you have?"

I shook my head, but then it came to me. *Bay Ops*. The operations center was on the second deck of the two deck high hangar bay so it would have a good view down into the hangar. It was, of course, on the other side of the Brotherhood forces, but there was ducting we could use to go over them. It would be a tight fit for me, but I'd used it before to find a woman who'd been abducted. All we'd have to do was get into the ducting, crawl about a hundred meters, then drop down to watch the end of a three-way battle. What could be easier?

I explained the plan as we raced to the nearest access point for the ventilation ducting.

"This will take us over the bay," I said, pointing in the direction we needed to travel. I started to climb up, but she stopped me with a hand on my shoulder.

"Let me go first," she said. "I have more room to maneuver, and I can see better."

"You have some sort of eye mods?"

"Newp. But I have this." She reached into her backpack and pulled out a combat face shield. "It doesn't give me any protection, but it's got a heads-up display and will let me see in the infrared. I'll know if anyone's coming."

She slipped it on, and I could see she'd added cat ears to the standard face shield.

"Nice touch on the ears."

"Who says you can't wear cat ears and still be a badass?" she asked. She adjusted it slightly and turned it on. "There. The Kat's ready to prowl." She slung her rail gun, climbed into the ducting, and crept off.

I nodded. It was probably better for her to go first, even though it offended my male ego to let a woman lead the way into danger. She was smaller and made a whole lot less noise than I was going to. I let her get a little farther in front of me; in addition to being quieter, it also would help for weight distribution. While I knew the ducting would hold one of us, it might not support two, and falling two stories into the middle of a firefight wasn't something I really wanted to do.

I looked at my watch. Midnight. Whatever was going to happen, was going to happen soon. I pulled myself up into the ducting.

Crawling a hundred meters through the tiny space sucked about as much as I had thought it would, and I reluctantly realized Kat was right. I needed to work out more. The ducting hadn't felt as tight the last time I'd been in it.

I'd covered about half the distance—and the sweat was burning my eyes as it dripped into them—when the yelling and shooting started below me. Blinking the sweat away, I picked up my pace as best I could. I arrived at the exit hatchway to find that Kat had already removed the cover and dropped into the room below. Two bodies wearing Sky King colors lay among several cooling puddles of blood. She'd been busy.

"Any problems?" I asked.

She turned away from the window, where she'd been peeking over the sill. There was some scoring on the exoskeleton; she'd taken a laser bolt. She shrugged. "Nothing I couldn't handle." She nodded to the window. "Come here."

I duck walked over, staying low. A ricochet cracked off the window, and I ducked lower.

"It's started," she said.

I resisted the urge to say something sarcastic as I peeked over the edge. A cube about a meter on a side sat in the center of the bay. Two lizards lay beyond it, their spines bowed backward in their version of a death spasm. Good riddance. Four of the Sky Kings, including Flyboy, lay on the close side, the holes in their bodies still smoking from the laser char. The remaining lizards had withdrawn to the cover of several shuttles, while the Sky Kings used a variety of crates for their defensive positions. It didn't take long to realize they were at a standoff. They traded fire back and forth, but neither side could make it across no-man's-land to get the case.

"What do we need to do?" Kat asked.

"Nothing," I said. "We wait."

"But security will be coming."

"Probably. They know that, too. Sooner or later— probably sooner—someone is going to have to make a play for the warhead or risk losing it to security."

It turned out I was wrong; I'd forgotten about the Brotherhood forces. At some unseen signal, they came pouring out of three separate hatches and took the Sky Kings from behind. A fierce mini-battle followed that left the Sky Kings dead or dying, and the Brotherhood in possession of their defensive positions.

"Now what?"

"The plan hasn't changed," I said. "We let them fight it out, then we kill whoever's left."

And that would have been a great plan, except that all the people in the hangar—Rigolians and humans, both—stood up, walked to the case and shook hands.

"Shit," I said. "It wasn't a double cross. It was a triple cross. They hired the Brotherhood to mop everything up."

There were a lot of the Brotherhood remaining, at least forty of them. This was going to be ugly.

"They won't be there long," I said. "Now's our time."

Kat looked skeptical. "There's an awful lot of them. Maybe it's better if we just let them have it."

"We can't let them have the warhead."

She didn't say anything, and I looked over, wondering what was wrong. If recovering the missile for the navy really was the main goal, she should have been down on the floor right now, firing every weapon she had at the Rigolians.

"What aren't you telling me?" Going into combat was the wrong time to find out that your ally might not actually be fighting on your side.

"Nothing. There's just a *lot* of them down there."

"It doesn't matter. We came to stop them." I checked my rail gun. *Time to die*. I backed up a couple of paces and fired a burst through the window. It shattered, spraying out into the hangar. Before they could react, I fired another burst into the group near the box. Two humans and a Rigolian went down before I had to duck for cover.

"What the hell are you doing?" Kat screamed.

"I'm killing bad guys. You want to help, maybe? There's an awful lot of them."

"You almost shot the warhead! *Do you want to die?*"

I'll admit; I hadn't really thought about it. I was just trying to keep them from getting away. Shooting a warhead full of antimatter, though—especially one that was used to destroy major combatant ships—probably was contraindicated.

"Oops," I said. "Forgot about that."

I leaned over the top and fired at a couple of the Brotherhood who weren't close to the crate.

"Better," she said, picking off one closer to her side.

More yelling came from the hangar bay. Security had arrived. They began firing at the Rigolians from the opposite side of the hangar. I killed one as he turned to engage the new threat. As I returned to the Brotherhood troops, I realized there were at least five who'd gone missing.

"Watch the door!" I warned Kat. She'd taken two steps toward it when it burst open and a Brotherhood thug ran through, spraying laser fire. Agony seared its way across my bicep. I pulled the trigger and mowed him down, but, by that time, another five had entered the room. I fired again, killing a second, but took another blast to my leg. It felt like someone had hit me in the leg with a baseball bat, and I crumpled to the ground. Then the pain hit, like all the fires of hell. I could barely keep my eyes open, but I'm glad I did.

Kat waded into the Brotherhood troops. She punched one in the ear, caving in the side of his head with the strength of her bionic arm. She grabbed two more by the throats and slammed their heads together with a popping noise that made me shudder.

The last one spun to fire on her, but his delay gave me time to stitch several rail gun rounds through him.

"No!" Kat screamed. I rolled back to the door to find another Brotherhood trooper. I tried to get my rail gun around, but he was faster and hit me in the stomach. My other wounds were nothing compared to this one; it felt like all of my insides had been ripped out my back by a flamethrower. He had a rail gun, just like mine.

I tried to raise my rifle, but Kat stepped in front of me and threw her rail gun at the thug, using the enhanced strength of the exoskeleton. The rifle spun through the air and stuck, barrel first, into his chest with a squishing noise. The force of the impact drove him back through the doorway. She charged through after him, drawing her laser pistol.

I tried to call to Kat as she walked through the door, but was unable to draw a breath beyond the smallest of gasps. Time slowed as she checked both directions—her head twisting in slow motion—then she came back. "It's clear," she said.

I no longer had the strength to hold the rail gun, and it fell out of my fingers. My good leg pushed me up so I could look through the window. Security forces were sweeping through the hangar, chasing after a few remaining members of the Brotherhood. The Rigolians were gone. The case, I noticed, was gone, too.

I slid back down the wall, and slumped to the deck. "It's over," I said.

A shape came toward me, but the darkness was closing in. I no longer cared if it was Kat or a Brotherhood trooper.

"We failed."

I awoke in the medical facility. If the tubes and monitors hadn't given it away, I would have known from the pungent sharpness of antiseptic in the air. I'd been here too many times.

"Good morning, sunshine," Kat said. "Welcome back." She sounded far too happy for someone who had lost an antimatter missile warhead.

"Tell me..." I said, but it was more of a gasp, "you alerted the police... and they caught the Rigolians."

"I did give the police an anonymous call... eventually. The police gave chase but didn't catch them."

You let them get away?" I tried to sit up and pulled something that was holding me together. Molten fire ripped through my stomach. I collapsed back to the bed with a gasp.

"Easy," she said. She patted my leg. "It's okay. They got away because we *wanted* them to. We just had to make it *look* believable."

"You wanted—?" My jaw dropped, and I had to consciously force myself to close it. After my first attempt, I did *not* try and sit up again. "But that's the next generation antimatter warhead for our missiles," I said in a forced whisper. "Our ships barely stand a chance against the Rigolians in battle now. With those..."

"Oh, I don't think that will be an issue." She smiled happily.

"Why's that?"

"That special case it was in? It's a Penning trap."

I hurt too badly for her games. "What the hell's a Penning trap?" I asked with a growl.

"There are tiny accelerators built into the walls of the case. Inside, there are about five kilograms of antiprotons spiraling around as the magnetic and electric fields keep them from colliding with the walls of the trap."

"Antiprotons . . . you mean like antimatter?"

"Yep. Removing the warhead from the case turns off the power to the trap and the five kilograms of antiprotons meet their opposites and annihilate each other with the force of . . ." She shrugged. "They told me how big a bang it would make, but I don't remember the actual number. It was big enough to blow up the Jonas habitat, though."

"All of Jonas?" I was having problems keeping my mouth closed. "And you *intentionally* brought it here? What if someone had pulled it out to look at it?"

"It would have been over quickly." She shrugged. "We wouldn't have even known. We just would have ceased to exist." She smiled again. "It's all good, though, because they didn't. And, hopefully, the Rigolians will get all the way home before they take it out. One ship would be nice, but one of their planets—especially if it's at their design bureau—that would *really* help the war effort. The best part is, they're *expecting* an antimatter weapon, and it will blow up like an antimatter bomb. No one will expect deceit; they'll just think their scientists screwed up. That's the plan, anyway."

"Whose plan is that? Who is this '*we*,' Kat?"

Kat smiled. "A lot has changed since you last saw me. People now know me as 'La Gata.'"

My eyes narrowed. "Are you working for the Federation?"

"Someone better." She winked.

"Are you trying to recruit me?"

"No." She smiled. "I already did."

The Incomparable Treasure

Rob Howell

His face had been ravaged, like a thousand ravens had pecked at his eyes...and missed. That face stopped every conversation when it entered the Frank Faerie Inn.

The owner of the Faerie, Ragnar Longtongue, played the dumb Northerner in the cosmopolitan Empire of Makhaira, but he'd been a hecatontarch in the elite Imperial Guard. He didn't recognize the ravaged man, but he recognized his sort. Ragnar had his hand under the bar where the spatha he'd once wielded in the Guard waited.

Zoe, Ragnar's wife, stepped to the kitchen door. She was slight with long hair going gray pulled back. Flour smudged her cheek and her apron, but she was more beautiful for the signs of her work, not less. Inside the kitchen, next to where she stood, leaned the same spear she'd used fighting alongside Ragnar against Qafric nomads on the empire's borders.

Melia, the gray tabby who ruled the Faerie, usually demanded pets and scraps in equal measure. She turned her green eyes at the interloper and arched her back. Fat and lazy she might be, but she earned her keep, and she recognized a pest when she saw one.

I'd recognized the ravaged man immediately. I was the only reason he could have for coming to the Faerie, so it was no surprise when he came to my table. I motioned at a seat.

"Not here, Edward of the Seven Kingdoms," he said.

"They have private rooms," I answered.

"I said, not here, Sevener."

I sighed. "Not staying for Ragnar's ale probably isn't the worst mistake you've ever made, but it's certainly one of them."

He shrugged.

"Fine." I went to the age-smoothed oak bar where Ragnar poured ale and barely intelligible long-winded speeches in equal measure. "I need the key."

He rambled off one of those speeches while filling four mugs, getting me the key, pulling out a charged lightstone, and smiling the whole time. The smile didn't, quite, meet his eyes, which hadn't stopped staring at the ravaged man.

I ignored Ragnar, keeping my own focus on the interloper as well. I took the key without a word and gestured the ravaged man outside. We walked across the street to a dark, ill-kept house. I unlocked the door and ushered him inside.

Once inside, the lightstone provided the only illumination. It showed one bare wooden table, two rickety chairs that had been young in the time of a previous dynasty, and three piles of detritus from a life so poorly lived no one dared scavenge its remains.

The lightstone also turned his ravaged face into something that would frighten the Great Wolf. Even the ghosts who lived here turned away.

"What's this place?" he asked.

"Ragnar wants me to buy it. No one else will."

"Why?"

"A woman got murdered here. Everyone hated Grozdana. She hated them back and people figure she'd be worse dead than alive."

He nodded. "Ragnar keeps an eye on things around here."

"Much like you do at Gibroz's gambling den."

"Sure." He looked around. He saw dust and rat droppings. "Place needs a cat."

"Probably, but unless you have a stray tabby to fix the obvious problem, I don't particularly care to stay here in this half-light, even if it does wonders for your looks. What does your boss want from me?"

He took a breath. "Gibroz doesn't want anything from you."

"Then why are you here? As far as I knew, you only did whatever he told you to do." Gibroz ran a kral, what in the Seven Kingdoms we'd call a band of criminals.

He said, "That's about right."

I said, "So either tell me or get out. You're keeping me from Zoe's roasted goat."

"I'm roasted either way." He pulled out a scrap of parchment. "People pay in a variety of ways at the den."

"Gibroz always gets what's owed to him."

"Yes, and last night we got this." He opened the

parchment to show a crude drawing of a knife. Its proportions seemed wrong, like it expected its wielder to have an especially large hand. It had a slight curve with a gemstone on the pommel.

I said, "That doesn't look quite Periaslavlan, but close. At least, the curve of the blade is similar."

"It's not Periaslavlan. I've never seen anything like it and I've seen the empire's share. No one comes into the gambling den without some steel and I watch every one. This one's amazing, incredibly sharp. The blade is darkest night. The pommel is a black star sapphire or I'm a priest. I don't know who made it, but it's a knife ready to slay the gods."

"That explains why you accepted it, not what you want from me."

He tapped on the table, still not ready to tell me. Finally, he said, "The knife disappeared last night and I want you to find it."

"Last I recall, I'd done Gibroz favors, he'd done me favors, and we were even. I also recall he wanted a reason to send me to the bottom of the lake."

A strange look crossed his face. "You're doing this for me. If Gibroz finds out this happened, I'm dead. For that matter, he might want you dead too. Just for knowing."

I shook my head. "Then go somewhere else, and leave me alone."

"Who else do you suggest, Sevener? Katarina? The quaesitors? The zupans?"

He was right. Katarina controlled the half of Achrida's underworld Gibroz didn't. The quaesitors, mostly a corrupt shadow of a corrupt empire, would simply demand their cut and do nothing. Two tribes, the

Enchelei and the Dassaretae, dominated Achrida. Their governors, called zupans, wouldn't care about his problems at all.

I said, "Fair point, though I admit I'd enjoy seeing the look on Katarina's face if you asked her to help her biggest rival."

He snorted. "I heard you helped find things." He put a pouch on the table. It clinked with the joyful sound of many coins. "I heard you charge a silver dinar a day."

I leaned back and studied the pile of trash opposite me. Rolled pillows, broken chairs, dirty scraps of clothing. I couldn't see a reason to help, but this *is* what I'd become. A guy who finds things, just like he'd said.

"What's your name?" I asked.

"Why?"

"Never needed to know it before, now I do. You think I'd risk my life solely for the pleasure of seeing your face?"

He rubbed his chin and said, "Vardimir."

"Enchelei or Dassaretae?"

"I'm from Basilopolis. I got no more relationship to them than you do." He snorted again. "Besides, we don't pick sides, whether it's imperial politics or tribal bickering, though we do take advantage of their squabbling."

"So you got this knife and you did what with it?"

Vardimir gauged his answer. "I put it in the chest that gets each evening's winnings, locked it, and put it in the vault we have."

"Who else has access to the vault?"

"Gibroz. The others."

"The others being Andreyev, Suzana, and Vladan?"

"Who else? It's not Markov or Gabrijela, after all."
He shook his head. "Come to think of it, this is all
your fault."

I said, "I didn't steal any knife."

"You didn't, but Gibroz has been on edge ever since
you found out about Markov and Gabrijela. If you'd
have just let him kill her it would have been like
every other time someone tried to betray him. He'd
have been grouchy for a month or so and then we'd
have gotten back to business as usual. But no, you
had to have feelings for her. Had to protect her. So
he thinks about Gabrijela every day and keeps taking
out his frustrations on the rest of us."

I looked at the floor. I thought about Gabrijela every
day too, but for my own reasons. They had worked
for the emperor behind Gibroz's back, and I'd exposed
their treachery. I'd killed Markov, but I couldn't kill
Gabrijela, so I'd sent her back to Basilopolis.

I focused on Vardimir again. "So, only you, Gibroz,
and those three. No one else?"

"Gibroz don't trust many. Even less since Markov
and Gabrijela."

"You put the knife in the chest. You locked it in
the vault. And then it wasn't there?"

"Yes. I went to look for it this morning."

"Could one of the others have taken it?" I asked.

"Each of us has own our chest to store whatever
we're responsible for. Gibroz is the only one with
keys to all of the chests."

"Your chest's lock wasn't picked."

He shook his head. "Not that I could see."

"Gibroz didn't take the knife out?"

"You've not seen it, Sevener. It's truly incomparable. If he had, we'd all know. He'd have shown it off. Couldn't not."

I considered things, then asked, "What else was in your chest?"

"No need for you to know."

"I need to know if it was worth something." I raised a hand. "Not specifically what was in there, just that there were valuables they could have taken as well as the knife."

His lips twisted. Then he nodded. "Yes."

"Was anything else taken besides the knife?"

He said, "Not that I saw."

"So they came for the knife in particular. Who gave it to you?"

Again, he gauged what he could say. "A merchant from out of town. He's already on the road."

"Which way?"

"Does it matter?"

"It might," I said. "Who else knows you took it as payment?"

"The merchant and I are the only ones who know he gave me this knife, but Gibroz knew he paid with some sort of item."

"If it's as valuable as you say, he owed you a great deal. How much?"

He shook his head. "All you need to know is that I have to show Gibroz the knife tomorrow or I'm dead."

"Can't you just tell him the truth? It might surprise him so much, he'd believe you."

"Not after you messed everything up."

I asked, "How do you know no one else saw you take it?"

"You think I don't know how to do my job?"

I pointed at his face. "You weren't born looking like that."

He crunched the sketch in his hand. "Sevener, you keep asking the wrong questions. That's going to put you into the lake one of these days."

"Probably so. You didn't answer me."

"Jebi se! I do my job. That's all you need to know."

"By the hungry wolf, it isn't." I waved at the crumpled drawing. "I'm going to need a place to start. This sketch isn't enough. If you don't have any ideas, then relaxing with Ragnar's ale starts sounding better and better."

He snarled, "This is getting us nowhere."

"It's getting *you* nowhere. I got dinner waiting."

He stomped around the room, his hands flexing as if he wanted to wrap them around something. My neck preferably. I knew what he wanted to do and suddenly I was tired of it all.

I tossed the pouch back at him. He caught it.

I said, "I'm a guy who finds things, but not for the likes of you. I don't care how many silver dinars are in there, there's not enough. Leave me be."

He threw the crumpled drawing to the side and snarled, "Then you'll never get anything out of Gibroz again. I'll make sure of that."

"Get out of here. I'm hungry."

He glared at me, but he got out of there.

I didn't leave Grozdana's house immediately. I needed to think and I'd get no thinking done with Zoe's goat on a plate in front of me.

However, I'd barely started working through the

problem when three figures entered the house. The first was large, arrogant, and leering. Andreyev did most of Gibroz's dirty work, so even Imperial quaesitors watched their step around him. He looked happy to see me. He'd never looked happy to see me before.

Second was Suzana. Tall for a woman. Cruel for a starving bear. Could have been beautiful except she preferred to be something else. Enjoyed the feel of running a knife through flesh. Gibroz let her slaughter enough to slake her thirst. She looked ready to take another drink.

Third was Vladan. Bigger than Andreyev, he'd been a sailor once. Now he ran Gibroz's smuggling operations. Just the man to get a fishing boat to drop an inconvenient body into the lake.

"Edward," sneered Andreyev. "So good to see you."

"No doubt. Now that you've had the pleasure, why don't you return the favor and leave?"

Suzana moved around to my right. Vladan around to my left. Andreyev put his hands on his hips.

They chuckled.

I chuckled.

The ghosts chuckled.

The mirth got tedious. "What do you want, Andreyev?" I asked.

"You talked to a guy."

"I talk to guys quite often." I glanced at Suzana. "Talk to girls, too."

"What would you do if I said you shouldn't be helpin' that guy?"

"I'd shrug. Here, let me show you." I shrugged.

He bunched his fist. "Leave it be, Sevener. You won't enjoy it if you poke your nose in."

I shrugged. "See? There's my shrug again. Just like I promised."

A smile grew on Andreyev's angular face until it became an actual grin. "I'm so glad you haven't changed, Sevener. You know I can't kill you, least not right now, on account of that deal you made with Gibroz. But that don't mean we can't have the conversation I've been wantin' to have with you."

Vladan slugged me.

I saw it coming out of the corner of my eye. Blood flew from my nose as my head twisted about. Suzana hit me from the other side and turned me back.

Then, for some reason, I was on the floor. Andreyev's boot hammered into me. Suzana's followed. Vladan, on the other hand, pulled out a length of heavy, knotted rope and whipped it down on me.

The beating lasted for only a little while. Not longer than a couple of years. Or decades.

Finally, they stopped.

Andreyev stooped to peer in my face. "Gibroz owed you a free pass. People know that. This was it. Next time Suzana gets to have her fun."

She snickered, putting her deep brown eyes close to mine. "I'll even dress nice for you, Sevener. Make sure you get to see something pretty before dying."

Andreyev patted me on the cheek lightly, then kicked me once more for good measure. He and the others left.

I laid there and contemplated my good fortune. I had had that free pass. No light thing there. My blood probably hadn't gotten on my tunic. Important, that. Zoe hated cleaning blood out of clothes. She could do it, had plenty of experience, but hated it.

Oh, and they hadn't asked about the sketch. Probably

didn't know Vardimir had drawn it. That was fortune worthy of sacrifice.

I'll think I'll pick it up. My head rested on the dirty oak boards. *In a moment.*

My eyes opened when I heard another person at the door. This time it was a washerwoman in a walnut-dyed dress with white hair pulled back tight.

Except it wasn't.

"Edward." She sidled over. Not the way a washerwoman might, but the way a cunning wizard in disguise might. Which, of course, she was.

I said, "Evening, Katarina."

"Oh, Sevener, what shall I ever do with you?" She helped me to my feet.

I put my hands on my knees to let the spinning room come back into focus.

"Hand me that." I pointed at a less rotted dress.

"And get my hands dirty?"

"Can't bleed on my tunic or Zoe'll take care of both of us."

"Why didn't you say so in the first place." She handed it over, completely unconcerned about whatever grime might be on it. "I wouldn't want to have to face the mighty Zoe."

I put it on my nose, then took a step.

Stayed upright, much to my surprise. And hers.

Took another.

A third even.

I went to a knee to grab the sketch.

"What's that?" she asked.

"What Vardimir gave me."

She giggled. A light, girlish giggle that seemed

odd coming from an old washerwoman, but was even odder coming from what I knew she was. "Going to stick your freshly broken nose in Gibroz's business again, aren't you?"

"I wasn't. I'd said no."

She laughed. This was her deep, full-throated, arrogant laugh. The one a cruel magic-using mistress of whores should laugh. "And then those fools beat you."

I shoved the sketch into a pouch so I could keep both hands free. "Can't let it stop me. Can't let it seem to stop me."

"I know that, silly." She patted my cheek. "And it's a shame. I'm actually here because I want you to leave this all alone."

"Why?"

"When have I ever given you the easy answer?"

I leaned against a wall and took a deep, painful breath. "I'm not really in the mood for your games, Katarina. I hurt and I'm hungry. Tell me why."

"I'm so glad you fell in love with Gabrijela." She giggled.

I said, "Which you could see with your magic, of course."

"I could *revel* in your feelings with my magic." She snorted. "But even the blindest beggar in the Square of Legends could see you'd fallen for her."

I said, "So, I was an idiot in love. Why does that matter now?"

"Since you let Gabrijela go, Gibroz has been erratic. He used to be steady and boring, but in these past few months, he's been very interesting."

"Allowing you to take advantage of him."

She smirked. "Exactly."

I narrowed my eyes, then said, "I don't believe you. Oh, I believe he's been erratic and you've taken advantage of him. You take every advantage you can get."

"Not *every* one. I saved your life, didn't I? What advantage did I get from that?"

I snorted. "You've saved me several times, and you got something out of it each time. I'm not so foolish to think it's all about money or even control. It's about excitement for you."

She stamped a foot. "You never let me have my fun. You see through all my disguises. You know me too well. Worst of all, everyone now knows I have a soft spot for you." She laughed. "But you haven't been boring. Most fun I've had in years."

"I'm glad I entertain you. In that case, tell me the real reason why I should leave this alone."

"No, I don't think so. A girl's gotta have a few secrets."

"What's so special about the knife?"

She laughed. "Oh, you're delightful, Edward. Are all Seveners so direct?"

"Yes." I considered her. "So the knife matters to you, but there's something more."

"How do you understand me so well?" she asked with another stamp of her foot. "It's a good thing you never talk to any of those looking for the chance to kill me and take my place."

"As you say. Are you worried that you'll need to save me again?"

"If you learn what I know, then I can't save you." She sighed with a sadness I'd not known she could feel. "But maybe, just maybe, you'll be lucky and miss something this time. A girl can hope."

❖   ❖   ❖

As I left Grozdana's house, I went around to the stables of the Faerie and knocked. Ragnar's boy Eirik opened the door. His eyes widened, but he'd seen me in worse shape before. After cleaning as much as I could, I thanked him and went into the taproom.

Ragnar took one look and shook his head. "Now I was knowin' them rats and suchlike beasties in Grozdana's old place were gettin' all uppity, but a huscarl of the Seven Kingdoms such as yerself ought to be able to fend them off better'n that."

"Good thing Zoe made goat, then. I clearly need my strength."

I plopped into my seat and Zoe slid the goat in front of me with a wry expression. Then she took my chin, tilted my head this way and that, and nodded. She said, "Probably improve the nose."

I chuckled, which hurt because of my bruised ribs. "Anything broken?"

"Not that I can feel."

She said, "Going to be worse tomorrow."

"I know." I shrugged. "Little I can do about it."

"I'll have Eirik warm water for a bath. It'll help."

I nodded and ate the goat. Juicy, steaming, and covered in dill, garlic, and onions. People came to the Faerie for a number of reasons, and this was as good as any.

Afterward, I smoothed the sketch on the table, leaned back, and contemplated it over a mug of Ragnar's ale.

When he came over with a refill, I gestured at the sketch. "Seen anything like it?"

He scowled. "Now that's not to be feelin' right. Looks almost Periaslavlan, but wherever it's comin' from, it makes me want steel in my hand, and that's bein' One-Eye's own truth."

"Me too. Thanks, Ragnar."

The sketch told me nothing else, despite studying it over several more mugs of ale. The bath had a few things to say, though. Mostly, it reminded me I didn't particularly care to let Imperial thugs beat on me.

The next morning was worse than I wanted, but probably better than I could have hoped. I got the kinks out by sparring with Eirik, as I did most mornings. By the time I left the Faerie, I moved almost as well as I normally did as long as I didn't laugh. Or twist my ribs about. Or get into a fight.

The Faerie is on the Fourth Serpent, one of five roads branching off Medusa's Way. The neighborhood, called the Serpents because of these streets, only had one exit, which led to the Square of Legends.

The Square of Legends bustled, as it usually did. The Trade Road bisected it north to south, so it always held tired horses driven by tired teamsters on tired wagons. Locals pushed through with buckets to get water at the fountain in the middle of the square. Pickpockets viewed the square as their natural hunting ground. So did some of Katarina's whores. Kiosks lined the edges filled with everything their vendors could sell to this folk. Travelers simply tried to survive.

And it was loud. Dogs barked. Horses neighed. Merchants growled. People cursed at each other. Hustlers beckoned toward any likely mark. Them with something to sell, whether food, drink, trinkets, or sex, made sure all knew what was available.

Since there's no other way out of the Serpents, I'd

long since started keeping an eye out for people tailing me from the square. Why wait in a close-knit neighborhood to follow me when I'd have to go through this maelstrom anyway?

Often, I hadn't noticed someone following me until too late, but if there was anyone worse than me in Achrida at tailing people, it was Andreyev. In my case, it was inexperience. In his, arrogance.

I guessed he wanted to know if I'd listened to their warning. Still, if he was watching me, it also meant I could watch him. I made no special attempt to lose him in the crowds of the Trade Road as I went to the Golden Sea Inn located in the Grain District of Achrida.

The Golden Sea had served as a gathering place for tradesmen for centuries, providing average beer to average folk for average prices. The tradesman I wanted often drank there, just as I often drank at the Frank Faerie.

Sebastijan showed not long after I arrived, whether by chance or by warning from the innkeeper, I didn't know. He was my size, maybe a little broader, and he knew the back side of Achrida as well as anyone.

I put the sketch in front of him. "Ever seen a knife like that?"

He said, "With that curve it looks Periaslavlan."

"The guy who owns it says it's not. Say's it's not like anything he's ever seen before, and he cares about blades."

"A collector?"

"You could say so," I said.

He didn't press me. He knew I trusted him, but we got along because we knew each other's limits.

"It got stolen from this collector, right?" he asked.

"Yes."

"Want me to ask around?"

"If you can do so without making it too well known."

He snorted. "I think I can manage that. If it's as different as this collector says, only a few will try to buy it."

"Good point."

"Who else are you asking about this?"

"Anastasius. If it's unique, the Readers might know something."

He shook his head. "Don't do that yet. If they'll tell you anything, they'll also tell anyone else who asks what you asked about."

"You're right. I hadn't thought about their oaths."

"And keep this away from the quaesitors. If they get involved, it won't be Zvono or my brother who tries to find this knife. I wouldn't trust the other queasies with anything more valuable than a pile of horse droppings on the Trade Road."

"That part I already knew."

"Good." He got up. "You noticed Andreyev following, yes?"

"I did. I figured I'd leave him there unless I saw someone else or he tried to herd me into a trap."

"You're learning, Sevener. I didn't see anyone else from Gibroz's kral, though that doesn't necessarily mean anything. Do you know why's he's doing something himself, and not leaving it to one of their underlings?"

"He and the others beat on me last night."

"That explains the nose."

"Yes. He's making sure I'm not doing what he doesn't want me to do."

Sebastijan glanced at the sketch. "Which, of course, you are."

"Yes."

He snorted. "I'll do my best to keep your name out of this."

"Thanks."

"One more thing. Avoid the Stracara. It's no place for you right now, especially with Andreyev already itching to kill you."

The Stracara held the worst of Achrida. Maybe of the empire.

I said, "I'm not that stupid, Sebastijan."

"Since when?"

I ran into Zvono before I could get back to the Square of Legends. The quaesitor looked far too pleased to see me.

"Edward! Just the man I wanted," she said. "We've got work."

Her work meant they'd found a body. Kapric, Sebastijan's brother, and Zvono tried to solve all the murders in Achrida since they were the only reasonably honest quaesitors here. People usually wanted murders solved. Usually.

"Where at?" I asked.

"The Stracara."

"Of course."

Zvono led me past the Fish Docks, which smelled merely of rotting fish. Then into the Stracara proper, which smelled of everything else. Urine. Old beer. Piles of chamber-pot leavings tossed out the window from upper stories. Worst of all was the despair.

The body lay sprawled in a cleared street. Two mages

circled it. I'd met them before. One was an erkurios, a type of wizard who manipulated emotions. Someone trained in this specific task could sense the powerful emotions most murderers leave on bodies. The other was a zokurios, whose magic dealt with things that lived or once lived. People left traces of themselves on the ones they killed, even without knowing.

Kapric watched them. He looked like someone had carved him out of the mountains around Achrida. No wasted motion. A statue come to life to deliver what little justice the empire held. He gestured at me. "Recognize him?"

The ravaged face looked no better in the daylight. Especially with his throat sliced neat as could be. "His name's Vardimir."

"Doorwarden of Gibroz's den." Zvono tapped at her wax tablet. She always carried it, though no one knew why. She never forgot anything. "He visited you last night."

"Yes."

"What did he want?" she asked.

I checked around. Faces leaned out from open windows. Eyes peered out of the shuttered ones. Good thing I was a battle-proven warrior with my sword, saex, and dagger or their attention would have bothered me.

The watchers made no sound as they listened for my answer.

I said, "Let's go for a walk."

Kapric scowled, but nodded. When we reached a private spot, I told him all Vardimir had said and about Gibroz's people beating on me. Then I showed him the sketch.

"What have you found so far?" he asked.

"I found out Ragnar still makes the best ale I've ever had."

His eyes turned frosty. "Sevener. I have no time for your games."

"Vardimir only talked to me last night. What else could I have done as smart as that?"

"Did you at least think about what to do while you got drunk?"

"I did."

He pounded his fist into his hand. "Stop playing around."

I said, "You don't want to know what I did."

Zvono chuckled. "You came from the south part of the city. That means you talked to Sebastijan."

Kapric snarled, "Zeus's cock, Sevener. Why him?"

"You know why. You may not like your brother much, but he's always gathering bits and pieces. Aren't many better at that, so I asked him to check around."

He took a deep breath and became a statue again. "You'll tell me everything he finds out."

I didn't answer.

Kapric turned his granite eyes toward me. "You *will* tell me. This isn't like the others who came to you with problems. This is Gibroz and his kral. Vardimir doesn't deserve your pure Sevenish honor, and if you get in the way, I'll bet silver to bronze we'll find your body too."

"I'll try to avoid giving you more work to do." I grinned. "Believe me on that."

He snorted.

"I'll tell you this, though," I said. "Andreyev followed me when I went to see Sebastijan. In fact, he only let me go when Zvono found me."

"Doesn't make me any happier."

"Me neither, so I'm being careful."

We went back to the body.

The zokurios had completed his examination.

"Well?" asked Kapric.

"The killer was a woman," replied the mage. "At least, a woman held him when his throat got slashed. It's possible, I suppose, someone else could have been the one with the blade, but she made it happen at the very least. I'll know more later."

I stiffened slightly. Not much, but enough that Kapric saw.

"What?" he asked, eyes narrowed.

"Katarina also talked to me last night," I said softly. "Told me to stay away from Vardimir's job."

"She'd have a reason to kill him, no doubt," he replied just as softly.

"I don't think so."

"Why not? You know she enjoys killing people."

"Yes, but really, she enjoys making a scene. If she cut his throat, she'd make sure everyone knew it was her. She wouldn't leave it as some simple street killing."

Kapric scratched his beard. "Fair point." He looked at the erkurios circling the body. "What about you?"

He straightened. "I need to take him back to our chambers to fully dig into these emotions."

"First impression," growled Kapric.

"Yes, sir. My best guess now is whoever killed him regretted having to do it. I don't sense anger or rage. No joy or excitement. None of the usual emotions, though the usual amount of emotions." The erkurios shook his head. "I'll need time to unwrap them all."

Kapric waved me close and the two of us knelt over

the body. I caught a whiff of something. I leaned in and took a deep breath.

"What?" he asked.

"I smell something."

He inhaled. "Perfume?"

"I think so." The fragrance tantalized me, trying to tell me something. "More evidence Vardimir spent time with a woman."

"More evidence it might be Katarina."

"Katarina wouldn't regret killing Vardimir. Also, she'd leave almost no emotions, not complicated ones."

"True."

"What about Suzana? She helped beat me. Vardimir said Gibroz might want him dead, and she'd probably be the one he sent to do it."

"Perhaps, but she's not usually one for wearing perfume. Not like Katarina." He stood. "Alright, Sevener. No need to speculate yet. Keep in touch."

"I'll do my best."

Zvono escorted me out of the Stracara. When we got back to the Square of Legends, she said, "Don't push things, Sevener. We all know what this could turn into, and Kapric's had enough of following this trail of dead bodies you keep finding."

Evening had fallen by the time I reached the Fourth Serpent and I heard a hissing voice call out "Sevener" from the shadows next to Grozdana's house.

I caught a whiff of perfume.

I put my hand on my sword hilt and took a step closer to the figure in the shadows.

"Not like that, I need to talk."

I recognized Suzana's voice, but she sounded hesitant,

scared. *By Woden's lost eye, what in Hel's name is going on?* "Hold on, I'll be right back."

I went into the Faerie and got the key from Ragnar, who in his loquacious way told me to keep it this time. I didn't answer. I simply took it and a new lightstone back across the street.

I waved her inside, keeping my hand on my sword. I *certainly* didn't turn my back on her.

Inside, I said, "Suzana, how pleasant to see you again."

In a way, that was true. She wore makeup along with the perfume. Her silk dress fitted her better than I'd thought possible. She had dressed up, just as she'd promised, but she didn't move like she meant to kill me.

She said, "I need your help."

"What's wrong?" I gestured. "Not that I mind how you look. You should wear it more often."

She blinked almost shyly. Then she came close. Too close, but I didn't push her out of knife reach.

After taking a deep breath, she said, "Gibroz wants me dead."

"Why would he? He wouldn't waste you for no good reason."

"He's got a good reason, or he thinks he does, and it's those damn quaesitors' fault. And yours."

"Oh?"

"How many people do you think heard that wizard say a woman killed Vardimir?"

"You've been known to slice a throat here and there. How does this involve me?" I put up a hand. "Wait, let me guess. He's been erratic ever since I let Gabrijela go."

"Yes. And now he thinks I killed Vardimir without permission."

"Did you?"

"Why would I?"

"If you caught Vardimir skimming, you would. Maybe he drove away a good customer. Or, knowing you, you decided you hadn't slashed someone's neck in three days and it was time."

Her eyes flashed, and for a moment she was the Suzana who had kicked me the day before. "Jebi se! I *didn't* kill him, but I might change my mind about you."

"Why did you come to me anyway?" I gestured up and down. "And why dressed like this?"

She came close again. She caressed my neck. It was so out of the ordinary for her, it felt odd, not sensual.

She whispered. "You're the only one who Gibroz will believe. You have to tell him I didn't kill Vardimir. I'll pay you all the value you want. I wanted you to see what I could offer."

I gently lifted her hands away. I stared into her eyes and my voice seemed to come from across the mountains. "I'll help, but not for this. I was going to find out anyway."

"Why?"

"Because I couldn't let you intimidate me. I can't let you do this either, but mostly I couldn't do that."

She stepped back. Looked down. "I should hate you for pushing me away."

"You hated me before. I liked it. It was a good, honest hate. I respected it. This? This isn't you."

Her eyes flashed.

I raised a hand before she could say anything. "Do

you know anything more? Last night, Vardimir asked me to help him and about all I know is that nobody wants me involved. Not Gibroz. Not Katarina. Not the quaesitors. Not even me, but I'm involved whether I like it or not, so tell me what you know."

She said, "We thought someone was after Gibroz. Had some grudge to settle or something. We didn't want you involved because you'd have gotten in the way."

"Maybe you were right. Vardimir's dead, after all."

"But that has to be Katarina, right? It's obvious." She stepped close again. "You have to tell Gibroz. He'll believe you."

"Why do you say that? Katarina would have done it differently. She'd have made sure we all knew she did it."

"I've known Vardimir for fifteen years now, and I would have said none of us could have surprised him. He always saw everything. It's why Gibroz put him as the den doorwarden in the first place. That's why it has to be Katarina. Who else could get so close to him?"

"Because of her magic?"

"It's the only way. The cut was neat, like he didn't defend himself. It has to be *her*."

I asked, "No one ever snuck up on him?"

She snorted. "He saw *everything*, Sevener."

"It's not Katarina," I said.

"It's not me," she said.

"So I'll search for someone else. Another woman who can do what you say had to be done." I admired her body. "You didn't have to dress up to convince me, but I appreciate it. Very much."

"Thank you." She moved to the door. "Stay clear of Gibroz until you can tell him something. The past is the past now."

"I understand. Where will you be?"

"Somewhere he can't find."

Zoe placed a dish of selsko meso on my table. Lamb, onions, and mushrooms in Zoe's special wine sauce steaming straight from the oven.

After I ate, I brooded about my options until Sebastijan arrived. I waved at Ragnar for another mug of ale.

Sebastijan took a drink, then said, "I found several collectors of blades, but one wanted that knife in particular. Her name's Bojana Radmila. She's an Enchelei."

"Tell me about her."

"She's an erkurios, about forty. Made a fortune selling her ability to manipulate the emotions of political foes in Basilopolis. She's got a mansion in the Gropasverni overlooking the lake now and spends her time indulging herself."

"Interesting. The emotions on the body were complex, or so Kapric's mage said. What if it wasn't Katarina, but another erkurios?"

"Bojana could have been the one to kill Vardimir, but it's not her style. Usually, she's one to leave people in place so she can continue to use them."

I took a drink from my mug. "How would she get involved with Gibroz?"

"I don't know, but I can tell you she's been expecting the knife to come to Achrida from Basilopolis for about a month."

I grimaced. "What's so special about this knife?"

"I don't know, exactly. It seems to be unique, maybe magical, but no one I've talked to knows, or tells me, anything more. However, it's clearly something she's coveted for some time."

"As far back as when she was in Basilopolis?"

"I believe so. I can ask people I know in the Great City to confirm, but that'll take time and I don't think you have it."

"I agree. It's all happening too fast. Suzana came to me tonight saying Gibroz thought she was the one who killed Vardimir and now he wanted her dead."

"Because she's the only woman who might have done it?"

"The only one Gibroz can think of. Clearly he's convinced it's not Katarina."

"Not her style. Too boring."

"That's what I said to Kapric."

"You could tell Kapric and Zvono about Bojana. Let them go question her. It'd certainly be wiser, because I've heard some nasty stuff about her."

"I could, but it doesn't help me if they don't tell me what they find out." I smiled. "Besides, it's not like Kapric and Zvono don't have enough to do anyway."

"Don't push my brother, Sevener. You may not realize it, but his superiors in Basilopolis have been pressuring him to get you on something, anything, so they can get rid of you."

We sat quietly for a while.

I said, "I don't get it."

"What?"

"Why is the emperor so determined to kill me? And why did he go after Gibroz? What's so important about us?"

"You know why," he said. "Achrida's one of the biggest and richest cities in the empire. These northern provinces sit in such a way that if their governors, along with the provincial cohorts, decided to break from the empire it'd be tough to bring them back. Emperors always give us weak governors for that reason."

"I know all that," I said. "I still don't understand about Gibroz and myself. We're nothing to the emperor. We can't lead these provinces in revolt."

"You forget how petty emperors can be. Nikephoros wanted Gabrijela to control Gibroz for him, figuring he could use that control in case a governor got stupid. He'll never forgive you for getting in his way." He grinned. "The good news is that no emperor lives forever."

I snorted. "I'll visit Bojana in the morning."

"Be wary. She'll use her magic at least as ruthlessly as Katarina might."

"I'll keep that in mind."

Bojana's house matched all the others in the Gropasverni neighborhood. They were tall, made of large blocks of the local limestone, and served as miniature fortresses.

Those who lived here, mostly the richest of the Enchelei, also favored ugly statuary. Bojana was no different, or at least she'd not had the various gargoyles, dragons, ugly gods, and uglier goddesses taken away when she moved in.

I went to the doorwarden. These houses all had one of those too, and they were generally less attractive than the statues. This one was worse than I expected. He made Vardimir seem almost human, with a nose veering left and a jaw veering right.

He looked at me without expression. Just as well, really.

"I'd like to speak with Bojana, please," I said.

"She is unavailable."

I pulled out the sketch. "I have information on this and I believe she's willing to pay for it."

"Leave it here and she'll consider it." He reached out for the sketch but I pulled it back.

I said, "I'll keep this, thank you. If she wishes to speak with me, have her send a message to the Frank Faerie."

I turned to leave.

He cleared his throat. "I shall see if she can spare some time."

"You're too kind."

He closed the door and left me standing on the porch. After long enough to make sure I knew my place, he opened the door again. "The mistress will see you."

"How good of her."

"Indeed." He sniffed.

He led me into the house, which was cold and empty. The marble floors echoed. No furniture in the entryway interrupted the sound. No pictures on the walls. No tapestries to ease the winter's chill. The Empire of Makhaira might be warmer than my home in the Seven Kingdoms, but its winters could still be as harsh as their politics.

We reached a room decorated as I expected of the lords and ladies of this place. Like the other houses along this ridge, it had large, well-made windows overlooking the gloriously deep blue Lake Achrida. In the morning, this would be a warm room as the sun rose over the far mountains and hills. In the evening, it was a place to sip rakija and admire what the gods had wrought.

However, there was only one place to sit and a woman occupied it. She was sensuous and knew it, did everything she could to enhance it. Her raven hair was piled on her head, held together by gold hair sticks with rubies. Intricate ringlets framed her face, which showed light but immaculate makeup. She wore a dress of cotton dyed in Sabinian purple. The cost of the materials was matched by the skill of the seamstress.

She turned her wide, abyssal eyes to me. "You know of this dagger?" she asked.

I liked her immediately.

I'd liked other people immediately, but not for the same reason. Bedarth, my mentor, had trained me to recognize magic and I'd been waiting for it anyway because of Sebastijan's warning. So I could tell what Bojana was doing.

I managed, barely, to keep control of myself, but I decided to play along.

"I do, mistress, and I would be happy to tell you all I know."

"Yes, you will." She smiled and sent me a surge of happiness. Then she commanded, "Let me see the drawing."

I pulled it out.

She smoothed the crumpled parchment. "Where did you see this blade?"

"I didn't see it myself, mistress. A person asked me about it. He's the one who saw it."

"Who was this person?"

"Vardimir. The doorwarden of Gibroz's gambling den."

"I have heard of this place. Tell me more."

I said, "He received the item in payment for gambling debts."

"From whom?"

"He wouldn't tell me."

She wrinkled her lovely mouth in a moue and leaned forward. "Surely you asked."

"Yes, milady, but he didn't want to tell me."

She tapped her finger. "I see. He lost it how?"

I described what Vardimir had told me.

"This is most distressing."

I said, "I'm sorry, milady."

She was suddenly next to me. I could feel her magic caressing my emotions. Then she kissed me. A kiss that would wake all the dead kings of far Amaranth.

I was not, at the moment, dead. I was awake. As awake as Thunor fighting Fenris.

She ended the kiss and stepped back. "You would enjoy pleasing me, wouldn't you?"

With a voice as dry as the Qafric Wastes, I husked, "Yes, milady."

"So you will find this knife."

"Yes, milady."

"Then you will bring it here. To me. To no other."

"As you wish."

She kissed me again. "Good. Because I so look forward to rewarding you."

I couldn't say anything.

She ran a finger across my lips, then dismissed me.

I turned, not quite in control of my body. The doorwarden smirked as he saw me leave her chamber. I put a hand on the entryway wall to steady myself.

Then he pushed me out the door into the garden of grotesqueries.

I took a deep breath and glanced back at the house. I saw movement behind a window. I smiled as lusty a smile as I could manage and then left the yard.

I needed a drink.

I went to a tavern near the North Gate. It was close, and I'd spent a few nights drinking there with the gate guards.

I also knew they had cheap rakija, which was all I wanted after talking to Bojana. The rakija might have been plum flavored, but tasted so harsh and new I couldn't tell for sure.

The first swallow took my breath away. The second brought it back, in the form of several coughs. The third, well, I'd felt that false warmth before. Still, it cleared my thoughts.

It's not Bojana.

No one could thrive in the politics of Basilopolis without ruthlessness and cunning. She'd used everything she had on me and I'd only escaped with myself intact because I'd felt it all before. And because Sebastijan had warned me.

She didn't have the knife. She'd have tried to keep me from finding it if she had. I'd told her everything I knew, and it hadn't given her what she wanted.

She wouldn't kill Vardimir unless doing so would get her the knife. Instead, she'd control him, just like she tried with me.

So she hadn't killed him. Neither had Suzana. Nor Katarina.

But it had to be a woman, and they had to have

a way to get close to Vardimir. Either he trusted her, and I bet he didn't trust many people, or she could make him do so, and that probably meant Suzana had been right in one thing. Only a wizard could have gotten so close.

I had another cup of the painful rakija thinking about what woman it could be.

I came up with no answers. Merely kept asking myself the same questions. Most of all I wondered why I couldn't place the perfume.

Bedarth had constantly told me to "Look and look again." He'd sometimes add, "And make sure you're looking at the right thing." Even though years had passed since he'd died, I could always remember his voice.

The voice made me ask, *Why kill Vardimir?* Unless he'd found the knife that morning, he didn't have it, so no one killed him to take it away from him.

Maybe he had something else worth killing for? I asked myself, but I shook my head even as I asked the question. It'd have to be something like the knife, something so valuable it was worth risking Gibroz's revenge by killing one of his people.

It had to be because of something he was doing at the time.

Or something he'd be doing later. Like what?

He'd be guarding the gambling den's door. Maybe Gibroz's people were right. Maybe someone was out to get Gibroz. Could this woman have killed Vardimir to make it easier to get inside the den?

Would that make it easier? I asked myself. *It might, especially since they not only got rid of him, they also pushed away Suzana at the same time.*

Gibroz was as vulnerable as he'd been in years

without Vardimir's experience and Suzana's steel. Andreyev and Vladan were formidable, but if this mystery woman could get close to Vardimir, I'd no doubt she could deal with those two.

Through the window, I could see the shadows lengthen.

Time to go back to the Faerie for dinner. Gulyas tonight, probably.

If this woman wanted to get into the den, she had to do it before Gibroz got Vardimir properly replaced. She hadn't tried last night, or Sebastijan would have told me about it. Something as big as an attack on Gibroz would spread rumors like an ocean gale.

None of this explained why Katarina didn't want me involved. So I asked myself that question. What other woman could make her care about me getting involved? *The only woman—*

It all clicked. I remembered the perfume. I didn't understand why Katarina wanted to save me, but now I knew why she couldn't help me, once I'd gotten involved. She was right, though. It would have been better if I hadn't figured it out.

But at least I now knew what to do. I put several silver dinars on the bar to pay for my rakija. Far too much, but the barmaid could use it more than I would if things went wrong. And they might.

I headed back to the Gropasverni. From there, I could go into the Stracara from the north. It wasn't the way I'd normally go and maybe those who watched for me wouldn't be looking there.

I moved furtively, with a hand on my hilt and keeping my face in shadow. This was how everyone walked in the Stracara, so I appeared like any other thug.

Twice, the sound of footsteps following me made me bring out my saex. I let the moonlight play on the water-patterned steel. It was enough. Most here preyed on the unwary.

I was wary.

I finally got to the opening of the Metodi Mean, the alleyway that led to Gibroz's gambling den. I found a shadowed area and knelt in the darkness.

The smells and sounds of the Stracara were no better at night, but at least I couldn't see much under the sliver of moon.

Just enough.

I knew her immediately. I couldn't see her face, as she had a hood covering it, but I recognized her walk. How could I not?

I crossed the street after she went into the alley and peeked around the corner. She was still at the gambling den's door. Then the new doorwarden let her in. He'd have been powerless against her magic.

I hustled through the alley to reach the door before it shut completely.

The doorwarden didn't watch me. He stared where she had gone, hoping to keep her memory.

I'd never forget her, as much as I tried sometimes.

The doorwarden turned to me, "Hey!"

"I'm her servant," I said, gesturing inside. "She'd appreciate you allowing me to pass."

His eyes warmed in welcome. He waved me into the sitting room. To the left was the den itself. On the far side was a set of stairs going up. At the top, I saw a door closing.

I went up the stairs. I pushed the door open slowly

and peeked down the hallway. I'd been here a few times, so I knew where to look.

Gibroz's door was open and I heard a grunt of anger. Then the ring of steel sliding from scabbards.

I jumped into the hall, drawing my sword and saex, and burst into the room.

The first thing I saw was the woman holding the knife. It had to be that knife. It called every eye to it. It was too big for her hand, but she held it balanced and easy.

Everyone else had been staring at the knife too, but my entry pulled their eyes to me.

Gibroz snarled.

Vladan did too.

Andreyev, on the other hand, seemed dreamy.

The woman merely nodded, as if she expected it. As if she'd known I'd be here. As if, all along, she wanted me to be here.

Vladan thrust a short sword at me. I pushed it away with my longer blade.

Andreyev slashed with his own sword.

I hadn't expected that, so I had to jump back into the hall.

Andreyev didn't follow me, but instead turned his sword on Vladan who blocked it and thrust back.

That gave me a chance. I slammed into Vladan, sending him sprawling and putting myself into the room.

Gibroz chopped at me with a knife. I heard him say something, but I ignored it. I didn't have time to parse through his peculiar use of profanity because I had to keep his blade out of my ribs.

I caught his dagger with my saex, then slammed the pommel of my sword into Gibroz's nose. I felt a satisfying crunch. I'd owed him, after all.

Swords came at me left and right. They forced me to use all my skill to keep them at bay. That meant I also had to slash back. I hadn't wanted to kill anyone, but Vladan had given me no choice. The sword my father had given me slashed into where his neck met his shoulder.

I tried to yank my sword out of Vladan's chest to block Andreyev's sweeping strike, but my sword stuck.

So I stepped into the strike. Andreyev hammered into my right arm with his hilt, knocking my sword out of my hand, but it didn't chop into my flesh.

I punched Andreyev under the chin.

He chopped again.

I pushed my saex to block his strike, and then without thinking, I twisted my wrist and slid my blade into his throat.

Gibroz croaked in outrage, but he'd not gotten up yet and I still had to worry about the woman.

Then waves of love battered me as she unleashed her magic.

Mighty magic, a spell for the Readers to remember, it was. It staggered me.

But it didn't stop me, because she'd used the wrong emotion.

I knew why she'd used it. Love came easy to her, where for others who manipulated emotions it was hate or fear. But she had loved me once. Still did, I could tell. It was this love she attacked me with.

But I'd loved her too and I'd lived with that love. She couldn't truly make me love her any more than I already did. I said, "Gabrijela," as if it were a prayer.

"Edward," she whispered, praying exactly as I had. Then she crouched with the knife ready. She had the skill with blades a trained spy of an emperor should.

That didn't stop me from approaching.

"Stay back."

"No." I stepped closer.

"I don't have a choice. I'll kill you."

"How does the emperor control you?" I took another step. "I know you don't want to be here."

She swallowed. "Doesn't matter."

"The Great Wolf it doesn't," I snarled. "You gave up all we could be. Then you came back, knowing if I found you, I'd..." I trailed off. "Tell me why."

"I can't." She lowered the dagger. "You can't know. No one can."

I took a step. "Tell me."

She raised the knife again. "No." She swallowed. "I just can't."

"Tell me," I pleaded for a third time.

"Please don't ask again."

I stepped within arm's reach. "At least tell me it was worth it."

"I had no choice." She looked to the ground. "None."

I took advantage of her glance and jumped forward. She brought the dagger up, but I slid it past me. The blade, impossibly sharp, sliced through my sleeve and along my right arm. I grabbed her wrist with my left. I twisted her around and took the dagger from her.

It was lighter than I expected. Perfectly balanced. It seemed to want to taste blood.

I said, "Now I know why so many people wanted this. It's as good a blade as I've ever held."

"Don't keep it!" she burst out.

"What's wrong with it?"

"It's... It eats at you, the longer you hold it." A

tear went down her cheek. "Please tell me you'll drop it in the lake."

"I won't keep it," I promised. "Is that why you used it?"

She looked at Gibroz, lying on the floor. "The emperor didn't know what he had, and I knew I could use it to open up his people enough to get inside."

"Jebi se! You're dead, kuja!" he growled.

"The emperor took away my life long ago, Gibroz." She turned back to me. "*That's* why I used the knife. I kept it close to me, when I could. The emperor would never let me go, but maybe, just maybe, the evil in this blade would kill me and I'd be free."

Suddenly, she ripped every bit of emotion away from me, all the hate, love, joy, rage. She slammed me with it in desperation. The rippling wave of emotions would have driven me to the ground a year ago, but not this time, even though I wanted to let it work.

She tried to run, but I pulled her tight.

Then she stopped. Leaned into my chest. She said, "I'm glad it's you."

"I'm not. I hoped I'd never see you again. Never have to—" I swallowed.

"I know. But you have to."

"No one knows what I told you that night."

"Of course they do. More importantly, I do. Either you're the man I loved and you'll do what you said, or it won't matter."

"Gabrijela—"

"I'm glad it's you." She repeated, then she pulled me close and kissed me. Deeper than the lake that kiss was. "Do it," she whispered. "Give me my freedom."

The dagger, the impossibly sharp dagger, slid easily

into her chest, straight into her heart. She fell immediately, barely having time to see it happen.

Her blood seeped through my hands. I watched that incomparable treasure stain them crimson. I stared at the knife. The incomparable treasure that had wrought all this pain.

Tears flowed down my cheeks.

And then I looked at her face.

It held the one incomparable treasure I would keep from this night.

Her smile.

Storm Surge

Michael F. Haspil

I. THE WEALTHIEST ZIP CODE IN THE U.S.

Tuesday, August 10th, 6:30 A.M.

South Floridians had to worry about two things in
August, hurricanes and vampires. Everyone knew vampires were real, but few could acknowledge they were
a threat. The Lightbearer Society's multi-billion-dollar
propaganda machine had made sure of it long before
they revealed themselves. Vampires were everywhere,
from children's programming and breakfast cereals,
to love interests in romance novels, to protagonists
in action films—seldom portrayed as the monsters
many of them were. Anyone who didn't adhere to
the Lightbearer's depiction of them was a "conspiracy
theorist." In turn, conspiracy nuts called it predictive
programming and they weren't wrong.

Alex Romer's stomach lurched in the bucking police
helicopter as sheets of rain smashed against the canopy.

The feeling reminded him of headier days millennia ago, sliding through the upper Nile's cataracts, when he was pharaoh, and his land was *Kemet*. Both experiences shared the feeling where an instant was all that lay between survival and oblivion, like other helicopters in other rainstorms during sketchy half-planned ops over Laos and Nam almost sixty years ago.

Alex had been hunting vampires for a little longer than that. Most recently for the NSA, hunting down the worst of the monsters for a government program called UMBRA. Now that vampires were in the open, he worked Nocturn Affairs for the Miami-Dade Police Department.

The pilot white-knuckled the helo into a dive until Fisher Island's lights swung into view. The helo straightened out of the dive, lined up with a lighted helipad, and landed gently.

Alex exited in a hunched run. An officer waved a flashlight and guided him toward a large mansion.

He counted five strategically positioned vampires wearing black figure-hugging overalls and strange closed-faced helmets as he ran. It made sense. The Lightbearers owned the mansion. They'd made a public show to volunteer the place as a refuge to the wife and fourteen-year-old daughter of a local man killed a few days ago in a vampire attack.

They'd been a bit too Johnny-on-the-spot with their help. Vampires attacked saps—regular humans—every day. So what made this one different?

Alex had sources of his own, which was why he was here.

He crossed the space into the mansion's foyer under the gaze of more private security, humans this time.

They looked less exotic than their vampiric counterparts, all business suits distorted with telltale bulges under their jackets. They didn't sport the extreme headgear, but they didn't have to worry about the sun.

Lieutenant Molina came forward to greet him. "Romer, you're out here early. Thought you were gonna catch the ferry."

"Trying to beat the weather. How are the principals?" Alex answered.

"Settled in the back. Kid won't talk to anyone. She's kind of on the spectrum. Her mom is having a time of it."

Alex looked past Molina toward the back of the mansion. "Word is she saw her dad get shredded by a vamp...by a nocturn." Alex corrected himself. "That'd mess anyone up. But we have to move her and her mom. Now."

Molina courteously ignored Alex's faux pas. The polite word was *nocturn* now; *vampire* carried too much baggage. "What's the hurry?"

"We have reliable and actionable intel they were going for the girl."

"Okay, why the girl?"

Alex lowered his voice. "Ever hear of something called the *Sayta Door*?"

A lithe and rangy female vampire crossed into the foyer from outside, in a gliding fashion just odd enough to unsettle anyone. She tore the helmet off, revealing a supermodel face wreathed by blonde hair. All vampires skewed toward being ultra-attractive; for them it was a survival trait. They'd evolved to be seductive.

"It's pronounced *Sæta Dauðr*," she said, an indeterminate European accent tripping off her tongue.

"Dagny Iversen, special security for the Lightbearer Society." She held out a gloved hand.

Alex didn't take it.

She withdrew her hand and pushed past the awkward silence. "Your intelligence is superb. You must know why we moved so quickly."

Molina asked before Alex could. "I'm lost. What the hell are you talking about? And why the girl?"

"We don't know," Dagny said.

"That's bullshit," Alex deadpanned.

"Detective." Dagny's tone was one of reproach. "Your attitude is unhelpful."

Dagny turned her attention to Molina. "The *Sæta Dauðr* is a death bringer, a nocturn assassin. A legend. That young girl is as good as dead without our help."

"Any time a hitman has a nickname, that's not good. But if it's the girl, he missed his target and killed her father," Molina said.

Alex stared directly at Dagny. "You have to start thinking like a vampire, Molina. They like to toy with their prey. Keeps things interesting."

Dagny pursed her lips. "There's no need to be rude, Detective."

Alex turned from Dagny; anything she said would be a distortion of the truth. "Molina, get them ready to move."

Dagny looked surprised. "Detective, you don't know what you're up against. We have optimum security here. We—"

Alex interrupted. "If you're serious about keeping the girl and her mother safe, and I doubt very much that you are. Offense intended. They are in rather good hands."

Molina broke in. "I'm assuming you've got authority to move them, Romer?"

"Yeah." Alex produced a written order and handed it to Molina. "You can clear it through with Captain Roberts if you want to double-check. He'll approve any OT for your people too. We need to keep this place locked down to make it look like they might still be here. I'm sure Iversen here would agree."

Molina nodded to a uniformed officer and the man stepped into the back of the mansion, presumably to retrieve the girl and her mother.

Alex added as an afterthought, "But don't clear it through with the chief's office." He gave Dagny a sidelong glance. "They're ... uh ... compromised."

"Where are you moving them?" Dagny asked.

"Come on. Really?" Alex brushed her off. "Need to know."

"I am part of their protection detail." Dagny said. "I'll need to clear it with my people, which may take some time."

"Take all the time you need," Alex said. "Helo leaves in ten. With them on it. As far as your part of the protection detail ... that's a little too 'fox guarding the henhouse' for me. Consider yourself relieved."

Alex turned to Molina. "I'll be out front."

Dagny called out to him as he walked out, "Detective. Remember. If you are wrong—and you *are* wrong—it is likely to be the girl's funeral as well as yours."

Alex could usually tell if he was dealing with a Youngblood, an Oldblood, or an Ancient. Youngbloods still acted mostly human. Oldbloods had maybe a few centuries behind them. They were more practical, even if they were more difficult to deal with. They had more to lose.

Dagny Iversen felt like an Ancient, vampires with several centuries and even millennia of history.

There weren't supposed to be many of them left.

II. TOLLWAY TO NORIEGA'S PLACE

7:15 A.M.

The helicopter managed the short hop from Fisher Island to Alice Wainwright Park on the mainland before the storm truly hit. An unmarked police SUV awaited them. Katya Martel, another Nocturn Affairs officer, had successfully redeployed the convoy they would take to the safehouse.

Alex led Mrs. Johnson and Gabrielle to the SUV and got in. "Mrs. Johnson, if you want to sit up front, there's more legroom," Alex said.

"You can call me Latonya. I'm good back here."

"I'm Alex."

He pulled the SUV out into traffic and headed south. He glanced at Gabrielle through the rearview mirror. The girl already slept.

He turned his attention to Latonya. "If you want to catch a few z's, we've got at least an hour down to Homestead."

Latonya nodded. "She just crashes whenever we get moving. She has a really hard time sleeping otherwise. Night terrors. Khofi drives her..." Latonya stifled a sob. "Khofi drove her around the city until she fell asleep."

Alex stole a glance at the sleeping girl in the mirror. The way her braids hung in front of her forehead, the shape of her lips...it was uncanny. Suddenly, it wasn't Gabrielle sleeping there. It was his own daughter from another lifetime, Reonet. And just as suddenly they weren't in the SUV anymore.

Reonet lay on the ground, a spear lodged in her side and too much blood pumped from the wound. He clutched at her legs—at the palace floor's gritty sandstone—screaming, as his bodyguard pulled him away. Khuenre, his eldest son, lay ruined and mutilated next to his sister, their blood mingling together in death. Khamerernebty shrieked in anguish and horror and Rekhetre joined her. If only he had died instead.

Alex tore his eyes from the girl's reflection. He squeezed them shut for a moment and wanted to shut the memory out of his head. He opened his eyes just in time, hit the brakes a little too hard, but avoided hitting the car in front of him.

"Are you okay, Detective?" Latonya asked.

"Yeah." He shook his head as if he could somehow shake the memory free.

"You want to talk about whatever's bothering you? I'm a counselor. This may seem weird, but I think I need to listen to someone else's problems right now."

Alex reached for the amulet around his neck. Rekhetre had fashioned it for Reonet when she was about the same age as Gabrielle. Alex had taken it back from the British Museum nearly a hundred and fifty years ago.

"Your daughter reminds me of my daughter. She died."

9:10 A.M.

The contractor gate guard at Homestead Air Reserve
Base glanced at their credentials then waved the
convoy through.

"How's that going to stop a bad guy from killing
us?" Latonya asked.

"It's only one layer. You'd rather trust your safety
to vampires?" Alex sensed Latonya's tension. "This is
a lot better than the Lightbearer's place."

"If one bad apple spoiled the crate, I couldn't trust
anyone. Not vampires. Not cops. You all seem callous and fake, like we're going to die either way and
this just gets the public off your back. Why should
I trust you?"

"Maybe you shouldn't. You don't know anything
about me. For all you know, I'm only different because
of this badge."

The convoy blew through several intersections
flanked by immaculately manicured lawns. Say what
you wanted about the Air Force, their groundskeeping
was second to none.

"The lady from the Lightbearers told me it would
take a nocturn to stop a nocturn. They want to stop
attacks on people as much as you do."

Alex sighed. "The Lightbearers aren't good people,
vampires or not. They have their own agendas. They
don't act in good faith."

Latonya didn't look convinced.

Alex continued, "I'm sure Dagny Iversen is very
capable at what she does. They'll know where we've
moved you soon enough if they don't know already—"

"Then why move us?"

Alex finished his thought: "... if the Lightbearer's intentions are legit. Then they'll offer to help. If not..."

Latonya's voice came out as a hoarse whisper and she subconsciously pulled Gabrielle closer into her. "You're going to use us as bait."

"No. It's not like that," Alex said, but he sounded unconvincing to his own ears. The absolutely wretched truth was that it was exactly like that. They were worse than bait, they were targets. If the vampire assassin was as good as the Lightbearers said he was, he was going to keep coming for them until he succeeded or until someone stopped him.

Alex might stop him if it happened on his watch.

Latonya looked out the window. Gabrielle slept so peacefully, it looked like the first good rest she'd gotten in days, or even weeks.

Alex changed the subject. "Anyway, you asked why we moved you. I'll give you the straight deal. Folks in city hall didn't want you there. Too many powerful people on Fisher Island. Too many eyes if something goes wrong. Too much prospect of collateral damage. That's not pretty, but that's the truth."

Latonya glared at him. But at least she listened.

"So what's the upside?" Alex said. "Well, for starters, I've personally vetted everyone with us."

At the next intersection, the convoy of unmarked vehicles turned onto a stretch of road less maintained than the rest of the base.

The rain turned to a light drizzle.

Alex continued, "The place we're going is still pretty posh and way more secure. You're probably too young to remember Noriega, huh?"

Latonya shook her head.

"Dictator of Panama. The cover story laid out that he dealt with some bad actors. Drug cartels, narco-terrorists..." Alex left out all the supernatural stuff the world still didn't know about.

"So, we went down there and got him. Bunch of people died. Whole world got pissed at the US. We put him on trial for numerous crimes. It looked great on TV. Except, that was Lamont Estevez, an actor. You want to hear something funny? He had a sitcom a couple of years back, no one put two and two together. Anyway, the real Noriega had too much dirt and information. Too valuable to put in prison. So the government built him this pretty swank gilded cage to keep him cooperative."

They drove through a section of the base strewn with signs of abandonment. Side streets led off to nonexistent destinations. Cul-de-sacs turned in upon themselves, no longer serving a purpose. Roads going nowhere. Neighborhoods with no homes.

A few abandoned buildings were open to nature and overgrown. Some were still boarded up. One large brick-faced building fared better than the others. The red spray-painted words on the boards still legible, "Andrew, Go Away!"

They turned onto a gravel maintenance road. A huge ranch-style mansion with exteriors in stucco and a Spanish-tile terracotta roof came into view. A lawn so glorious French kings would have been jealous extended all the way to an inner and outer pair of formidable chain-link and razor wire fences surrounding the house. Guard towers rose from the corners. From the fence, gravel stretched for a hundred yards. There was no cover on the approach. It was a killing field.

Alex resumed his tour guide monologue. "It's no surprise this house survived hurricane Andrew. There are bank vaults built less soundly. When I told you we'd keep you safe, I meant it. Aside from Space Mountain at Disney, this is the safest place in all of Florida."

"You're joking about Disney."

"Maybe." That cleared away some of the frost and won Alex a small smile from Latonya. He wasn't joking about Disney.

The convoy parked. Several plainclothes police stood with M4 carbines at the ready, others performed maintenance on the tower spotlights.

"Sorry, but we walk from here." Alex stepped out of the SUV and opened the back door.

Gabby crawled out of the SUV, stretched, and took a deep breath. "I like it here, Mom. It's quiet."

Katya called over from her car. "Hey, come get your stuff. I'm not hauling it for you." Katya Martel was an UMBRA alumnus who had also crossed over into law enforcement after the NSA disbanded the program.

Alex sighed. He'd get his principals settled and then he could move the supplies in. *Re*'s golden disk peaked from behind dissipating clouds. It would do well to recharge.

Gabrielle surprised him. "Hey. Can I have my phone back?" The police had taken it when they'd placed her in protective custody. It sat in an RFID-shielded bag in the glove compartment.

"No, I'm sorry, hon. Not yet. Bad people would be able to trace your phone."

Gabrielle turned to her mother. "Does he think I'm a little kid or something?"

Latonya gave Alex a sympathetic glance. "He's trying, Gabby."

Gabrielle held her palm out to him. "Cancelled. Till I get my phone, you're dead to me." She headed off toward the house on her own.

She reminded him so much of Reonet. Different language, different eon, but same attitude. And she wasn't wrong.

He *was* dead to her. And everyone else.

III. SPIRIT WORLD REVELATION

2:30 P.M.

Latonya and Gabrielle settled into the bunker living quarters below the house. True to her word, Gabrielle ignored Alex. Every time he tried to engage her, she just asked for her phone. People dealt with grief in their own way, and she seemed fine.

Until she wasn't.

They were in the upstairs screening room when Gabrielle's eyes flitted around her in complete panic.

She shrieked at Alex, "I'm not playing! Give me my phone now."

She lashed out at him, punching and kicking.

Latonya pulled her away and held her in a tight hug. "She's having an episode."

The girl covered her ears, writhed away from her mother, and curled up in the fetal position on the couch. Like she expected a flurry of blows and couldn't do anything about it.

Alex reached out to her. "What can I do?"

Gabrielle came up for air and screamed, "Give me my phone!" She curled back up into her shielded position.

"Please," Latonya said, "you're just making it worse."

Alex nodded and left to go be useful.

That had been almost five hours ago.

He'd emptied the SUV and Katya's car of equipment "appropriated" from UMBRA. A lot of it was illegal to own, let alone use, even for law enforcement. Some of it was simply rare and getting harder to replace as the years moved on. His personal *khopesh* was one of a kind.

He'd inspected the perimeter. Every other spotlight had been replaced with ultraviolet bulbs. Sunlight and ultraviolet radiation affected each vampire differently. None of them would die from it, but every advantage helped.

Alex readied the compound's concert-venue-quality sound system, again, courtesy of ensuring Noriega would cooperate. It would be put to great use against creatures with sensitive hearing; fully operational and paired with the UV, it was the equivalent of an ongoing flashbang.

The vegetation on the northwest corner of the compound had grown a little thick. It gave him an idea.

He could take a metaphysical tour of the compound. Whenever he astral projected, it took a lot out of him. But *Re* still shone down and would recharge his lost energy.

He pulled the necklace holding Rekhetre's amulet over his head and let the chain coil in his hand before carefully placing it in his lap. The air hummed with an edginess as if filled with static electricity. He began to mentally prepare himself for whatever lay on the other side.

The world always looked different on the astral plane. There, he could perceive ley lines and other energy conduits, gaps in space-time, psychic vortices, and souls. Humans appeared as a soft orange-yellow glow. Vampires appeared as tears in the fabric of reality. Then there might be the spirits of those who had died, but not yet crossed over. Their blue-white presences indicated tortured, often confused souls who hadn't made peace with their passing and so could not move on. Normally rare, Alex had noticed a correlation between their increased numbers and the vampires.

With a force of will he separated his *ka*, his essence, his soul from his body. He was Menkaure, the Great Bull of Horus, in his true form once again, unshackled by the undead flesh he needed to influence the physical world.

Something was wrong.

Energy crawled across his being in tiny pinpricks. A loud susurration overwhelmed the song of the world, which always hummed in the background.

He opened his astral eyes.

Thousands of blue-white spirits crawled over the compound.

Hundreds of thousands.

They shrieked and shouted but were muted to him and he could only see them as outlines with rudimentary features. Their screams of anguish came to him as mere whispers, but there were so many.

They rolled over him in waves, ignoring him while heading to another destination. He was just in the way. He traced their path and perceived a dazzling golden beacon competing with the radiance of *Re* himself.

Menkaure had never seen anything so beautiful.

The spirit-souls mobbed it, suffocating the light of the beacon in their eagerness to grow closer to it.

Then Menkaure realized the direction of the beacon. He sent forth an ethereal wind and pushed the spirit-souls from his path. At the speed of thought, he moved within the compound's mansion, which appeared constructed from fog and mist.

He darted to the source of the beacon, and his heart leapt and fell nearly simultaneously.

There, looking much as she did in the physical world, lay Gabrielle. Dozens of spirits assaulted her. But any injury they caused was accidental, done in their zeal to command her attention.

One spirit seemed to battle the others. It pushed and strained and tried to hold hundreds back. For every half dozen it managed to turn away, a score more would take their place and then the originals would return. There was only one person that could be.

Khofi?

Here, thoughts carried weight. The spirit turned in reaction.

Then Gabrielle sat up and looked straight at him. *You can see them? Are you dead too?*

IV. THE *KEMET* CONNECTION

Alex's *ka* flew across the compound and slammed back into his body. He snatched Rekhetre's amulet, bound to his feet, and sprinted to his SUV. He retrieved the RFID bag with Gabrielle's phone in it, then raced back to the house.

He found Latonya sitting on the couch next to her

daughter, who was just as he'd last seen her, sitting up and staring around her. When her eyes fell on him, she looked puzzled.

"I just saw you. How?" Gabrielle asked.

Alex took her phone out of the RFID envelope. "Here, I didn't understand." He handed the phone to Gabrielle, who immediately turned it on.

"And now you do?" Latonya asked.

"They weren't using the phones to trace your daughter," Alex said.

The girl sat back on the couch and pressed the earbuds into her ears.

Alex stepped back toward her. "May I see your phone? Promise I'll give it right back."

Gabrielle handed over her phone hesitantly. Alex took it and flipped it around in his hands. "What's MyNoise?"

Gabrielle shouted; she must have had the volume cranked. "It's just a noise generator. Then I can't hear them as loud."

Latonya grew concerned. "Hear who, honey?"

"The voices."

Alex handed the phone back to the teenager, then reached out with Rekhetre's amulet. "Here. Put this on."

The girl took the amulet and looked it over as it hung from the chain. The gold-flecked faience caught the sunbeams and projected sparkles which hung in the air against the blue-green scarab amulet.

Alex had never seen it do that in all the years he'd had it. The girl slipped it on, and it rested in contrasting radiance against her dark skin.

The amulet didn't belong to him anymore.

Gabrielle changed, as if a cloud had moved away

from the sun. A dazzling smile broke across her features. "They're gone."

She leapt off the couch and threw her arms around Alex and hung from his neck in thanks.

Tears pooled in his eyes and ran down his face. "*Reonet.*"

"Gabby," Gabrielle said. Sadness returned to her voice. "Oh, but Dad's gone too."

Alex put her down.

Latonya gave her a puzzled and terrified look. "Your father?"

"Yes," Gabby answered. "Dad's been here trying to help. But now he's gone." Her hands flew to the amulet. "Is it because of this?"

"Yes," Alex said, "but don't take it off. Your dad will be back. But we have to talk."

Gabby took out her earbuds.

Latonya had overcome her initial shock, and anger tinged her voice now. "What is going on? You owe me some explanations."

Alex moved to the doorway and shut the door. "The good news is that Gabby isn't . . . troubled or anything. And we have a solution. The bad news is that Gabby does have a condition—an exceedingly rare and incredible one. With the proper training, she can be devastating to the vampire's cause. That's why they're after her."

"She is not a weapon. She is my child. Not yours. And—"

"I know." Alex sat down on the floor across from the couch and looked at his watch. He took a deep breath. "You can't tell anyone what I'm about to tell you. I have my secrets and would like to keep them. The reason I know what Gabby is going through, is that my own daughter, Reonet, went through much of the same."

Gabby toyed with the amulet on its chain, admiring the scarab and the inscriptions written on the underside. "That's a pretty name."

"It means 'Gift of Re.'"

"Who's Re?" Gabby asked.

"You see him as the sun. That's just one manifestation."

"Oh, you mean Ra! I learned about all the Egyptian gods. He was in Stargate too," Gabby said.

"Ra or Re. The *neteru* go by many names." Alex smiled.

"You said she died," Latonya said irritably.

"She did. Rekhetre, my true wife, was a powerful sorceress. She made that amulet for Reonet, but she never got to try it."

Latonya interrupted. "What would your wife think of giving up that amulet to a stranger?"

"Rekhetre long ago crossed over into *Duat*, the afterlife."

"I am truly sorry so many of your loved ones are gone from your life, but it also scares the hell out of me. If you want to protect Gabby, then protect her. But she's not your daughter, and she never will be. Stop telling stories and tell me who you really are."

Alex sighed. "It was a long time ago. So long ago, the pyramids of Giza hadn't been fully built yet. Depending on which calendar you use . . . it was about forty-five hundred years ago. My real name is Menkaure. I used to be king of Upper and Lower Egypt."

Latonya stiffened. "So you're a vampire. But the sun—"

Alex dismissed her concerns with a wave of his hand. "No. No. Nothing like that."

"Then how?"

"You're a mummy!" Gabby almost leapt from the couch in her excitement. "Awesome."

"Oh, I'm awesome now?" Alex said.

"Well, you're not an idiot cop anymore. That's just your disguise. Mummy is way cooler than cop. Mummy is a whole mood."

"I guess? Mummy, though. People always think of wrappings and stories always make me out to be a bad guy," Alex said.

"Enough! I still don't know what the hell is going on," Latonya said.

"Long story short. Gabby is a conduit between the lands of the living and the dead. She can communicate with spirits."

"You can too. I saw you. You were very bright," Gabby said.

"I can't, Gabby. I can see them, and they can see me, and I can convince them to move out of my way and do some other tricks, but nothing like you. I can barely hear them."

"They're always screaming and shouting and scratching at me," Gabby said.

Latonya looked horrified. "Why didn't you tell me?"

"I did. And you took me to the counselors, and they wanted to put me on the pills that made everything worse."

"Oh, baby, I'm so sorry." Latonya's tears streamed down her face. She turned to Alex. "But it will be okay now, right?"

"No." Alex put up his hands in defense. "I can

show her what I know. I figured things out on my own through trial and error. I can show you some things to help you tame those spirits. Keep in mind, they're not bad people. A lot of them are hurting and they're all terrified. They are drawn to you because you are so bright in the ether. Those spirits feel like they are drowning, and you can save them. They are lost and confused and react out of instinct. So they might be scary, but they don't mean you any harm."

Gabby nodded.

"The bad news is that the old vampires, the ones we call Ancients—they can perceive the astral plane too. I'm not exactly sure how. There aren't a lot of them around. But all it takes is one and they can find you. Let's move out by the pool where I can get more sunlight. And if your mom says it's okay, then we can start."

Latonya scowled at Alex but gave a reluctant nod.

"You're going to have to take off the amulet. Are you okay with that?" Alex asked.

Gabby looked frightened. "I guess so. Will you be there?"

"I'll be right there. And your mom will be there too. We won't let anything happen to you."

Under Latonya's skeptical eye, they began.

"I'll be right on the other side waiting for you," Alex said.

He slipped his *ka* out of his body. A static charge itched and moved over his soul. The spirits were all around him, though he couldn't perceive them yet. As if his "eyes" hadn't yet adjusted to the astral light. They made a shifting sotto voce scream multiplied by a hundred thousand voices. Slowly, he began to perceive them. An enormous mob of blue spirits surged his way. He held out one hand and pushed them back.

A blinding force manifested itself at his side. Warmth and Love and Purity. Gabby. She'd removed the amulet. Menkaure turned his attention to her. It would be easy to become enraptured with that light. To become lost in its splendor.

THEY ARE SO LOUD. I AM SCARED. Gabby's being boomed through his.

The spirits surged anew. Menkaure created a current in the ether, a power they would have to "swim" against and pushed them back.

I'm right here. Remember, they don't mean to hurt you. If it gets to be too much, remember the amulet. Now, I want you to try something. Focus on your core and then imagine there is a powerful wind coming from you and moving outwards. It will create an ethereal—

A shockwave of power radiated from Gabby outwards and threw Menkaure backward. Thankfully, it wasn't painful, but it was an irresistible force. Instead of walking into the wind, which is the best he could muster, this was like he was walking into a category five hurricane with a truck pulling him from behind. The blue spirits were blown clear until he couldn't see them anymore.

He willed himself back to Gabby with the speed of thought. *That was incredible. A little less forceful next time.*

I DIDN'T MEAN TO DO THAT. DID I HURT THEM? IS MY DAD GONE?

They'll be back, including your dad. They can only move as fast as they think they can. So it might be a while. That's why they didn't bother you when you were moving. They couldn't catch up to you.

WILL YOU SHOW ME HOW TO MOVE LIKE YOU DO?

Maybe eventually. I'm not sure what would happen if you tried full astral projection. But there are other things I can show you.

Hours passed in the physical world. Alex broke several times to recharge, and the sun grew lower in the sky each time. Gabby strolled around the edge of pool, simultaneously experiencing the physical and astral world. Alex explained to Latonya what was happening.

Gabby's face grew dark.

"Alex, they are coming back. And faster this time," she said.

"I'll be right there." Alex sat and let his *ka* reenter the spirit realm.

He only perceived Gabby. Then, gradually, at the limits of his perception, a wave of blue spirits.

THEY ARE LOUD AGAIN. IT'S DIFFERENT THIS TIME. WHAT ARE THOSE?

I can't hear them. I don't know what you see. Describe it to me.

THERE ARE THREE RED COLUMNS. TORNADOES OF BLOOD. SOME OF THE SPIRITS ARE SURROUNDING ONE OF THEM. IT IS MOVING THIS WAY.

Menkaure saw none of that. The spirits swarmed around him and Gabby. They faced away as if creating a protective crowd.

YOU'RE TOO LOUD! I CAN'T UNDERSTAND YOU. DAD, GET THEM TO BE QUIET! I WILL SEND ALL OF YOU AWAY AGAIN! Gabby screamed into the ether.

The crowd of spirits calmed immediately. Awe and admiration suffused Menkaure's being. She could communicate directly with them. He'd never seen anything like it.

She turned her full attention on Menkaure. Lances of emotion surged within him.

SOMETHING BAD IS COMING. TIMELESS EVIL. WE HAVE TO GO. EVERYONE HERE IS GOING TO DIE.

Alex snapped his *ka* back into the body. Timeless evil? An Ancient vampire? He glanced at his watch. He had about a half hour of sunlight left to charge what he could. He may have underestimated what they were up against. One capable vampire maybe accompanied by a Youngblood strike team is what he'd expected. He would have handled the assassin while his task force dealt with the others. Not easy, but he'd done it before. Now, hearing this new warning about timeless evil and tornadoes of blood, he wasn't sure exactly what he was up against.

He had to evacuate the compound. He began to make a mental list of how he'd adjust his preparations.

Gabby interrupted his thoughts. "Should I put the amulet back on? Whatever it is, it's coming."

"That's up to you, Gabby. It already knows where you are. I'd like you and your mother to head down into the bunker and seal it up. See if there is any way the spirits can help you stay safe."

"What are you going to do?" Latonya said.

"I have to get everyone out of here," Alex said. "If there is an Ancient leading an Oldblood strike team, humans don't stand a chance. Things are going to get unbelievably bad here. No need for more deaths than are needed."

"I see where we stand. So you're going to just sacrifice us? And—"

"No. Those cops out there will lay down their lives to protect you and Gabby. But they don't need to. They're outmatched. I'm not."

"You're arrogant. If the amulet hides Gabby, why not have her put it on and evacuate us? We could be long gone before they ever got here," Latonya said.

"Yeah," Alex agreed. "This time. But what about the next time, or the time after that? You want to live your lives in fear? Head on a swivel? Ready to run at every bump in the night? Here. We're ready. This is ground of our choosing. Here we end it, and they stop hunting you."

"You really think you can handle whatever is coming?"

"Not a problem." It was, in fact, a pretty damn big problem.

Gabby saw through his bravado. "You don't sound sure."

"I'm sure."

He lied.

V. SURVIVAL ODDS OF A PLAN

07:45 P.M.

Alex briefed Katya and tried to call for some ex-UMBRA backup. It was already too late. Their adversaries were more powerful and organized than he'd expected. Landlines were turning up busy and jammers ensured there'd be no communications leaving the compound.

Katya convinced the others that they were moving Latonya and Gabby because the location had been compromised. Once clear of the jamming, she'd send help from Nocturn Affairs and any UMBRA alumni who could make it down.

In the meantime, Alex moved Latonya and Gabby into the bunker. As disconcerting as it was, Gabby carried on whole conversations with spirits they couldn't see. Now they were her allies and not her tormentors.

The bunker door slid closed, and Alex secured the door lock code, setting it so it could only be opened from the inside. He placed an M4 and sidearm by the door, intended as last-stand weapons. If he ever fell back to this position, things would have really gone sideways. Better safe than sorry.

He grabbed a duffel full of kit and headed out to prep the compound his way. Things would be a bit different now that he'd be defending the place on his own.

The sun was no longer visible. The last rays turned the sky a rosy pink. They were in a new moon cycle, so there'd be no illumination from there.

Halfway across the killing field he set up the most expensive claymore mines in the world. These were loaded with silver balls. Though a regular claymore probably would make short work of some Youngbloods, the silver made sure. He worked feverishly, trying to beat out the dying light, and aware that he was probably under observation.

A lone car drove up to the compound and parked.

Alex drew his sidearm and approached. As soon as the passengers disembarked, he re-holstered and relaxed. It was two of the team who had left shortly before, Sergeant Alonna Washington from SPD and Sergeant Hector Reyes from the Special Response Team.

"What the hell are you doing?" Alex asked. Despite his best effort, annoyance crept into his tone.

"Something is happening over at Base Ops," Alonna said. "Some kind of rocket attack against some aircraft or a hangar or something. They've locked the whole place down. Threatcon delta. No one in or out. Martel and the primaries made it out."

Reyes completed her thought. "We figured we'd come back here and help you hold down in case anyone shows."

No one else was coming. And these two were likely to get killed for their goodwill.

Alex muttered under his breath, "Well, Murphy, you old bastard. I was wondering when you'd show up. All right. Let's get inside. I have bad news and worse news."

Alex carried the bags of illicit equipment into the dining room.

"So here's the worst news first. We're not the diversion. Katya Martel was the diversion." Alex emptied the contents of the bags onto the oak dining table.

Alonna looked shocked. "So then the primaries—"

"Are here. Not too late to leave if you want. But the window is closing. Rapidly."

Hector nodded. "Okay. We'll hang until the relief gets here . . ." He trailed off as he began to grasp the situation.

"If they can make it on base," Alonna said.

"If there is any relief coming," Alex added.

"Who else is here?" Hector asked.

"Me, y'all, the girl and her mom."

"Capital F," Hector said.

Alex laughed. "Really?"

"Hey, I'm trying to give up swearing," Hector said.

"You can still—" Alex started.

Alonna interrupted him, "We're staying. So we're wasting time now."

Alex nodded. "First things first, look through those duffels, you're gonna find body armor. Better than the vests you're wearing. It's Dragonskin. Might not be ideal, but the vampires won't shoot at you too much. Helps to stop body attacks and they come with gorgets; make sure you put those on."

Alex moved to a set of short-barreled rifles. "These are MCX Rattlers, courtesy of our friends at Sig. Same manual of arms as an AR but chambered in three hundred blackout. Gives you a bit more oomph, but they will get snappy on you. These rounds are tipped with silver in a mercury suspension. Any luck and even a scratch might send a vampire into anaphylaxis. Don't count on it. These rounds are a little old. I'm sure they'll go 'bang.' But no telling if the bullet will be effective. I've got some STI 2011 pistols, mags loaded with the same stuff. Help yourselves."

Hector picked up what looked like a ruggedized brass knuckle off the table.

"Knuckle-dusters?"

Alex met his eyes. "Yeah. Each of you grab a pair. You're gonna want to grab one of those machetes too. If the vampires make it in close. Look, I'm not gonna lie, if they're Youngbloods, you might stand a chance..."

"But they're not gonna be Youngbloods, are they?" Alonna asked.

"Not likely. So if they make it in close, it's probably your ass. In case it's not, punch them with these. That top bar is locked in with a pressure-activated explosive.

One use only. You punch, these do the rest. But lock your wrist or it'll shatter."

Alonna picked up a pair of the knuckles. "That sounds fun."

"Last resort. Anyway, see those EpiPen-looking things? We call that Triple-S. Last resort. Jam into your neck or thigh and for about fifteen to twenty minutes, you'll turn into a god. Or your heart will explode. Or it will turn you into a god *and* your heart will explode. Your mileage may vary. In any case if you use it, after those fifteen minutes or so, you're gonna take a nap. No negotiations on that front. It will stress your body the hell out."

"And these?" Alonna held up some earbuds.

"Oh." Alex smiled. "I like these. Short-range encrypted comms. Also dampens any sound over eighty-two dB, amplifies lower sounds. But here's where these surpass other earpro. I designed this part myself. They can null out certain other sounds. Your average vampire can hear a human pulse at over a hundred yards away. I have a playlist set up to come through Noriega's favorite speakers. These earbuds are already slaved to the head unit and will cancel out the music. All we'll hear is whatever sound comes through the earpro normally. The vampires might get their eardrums ruptured. Hope they like reggaeton, dubstep, and metal."

"Okay. Nocturn Affairs has some neat toys. This might be a fair fight after all," Alonna said.

"Maybe." Alex picked up an M1A marksman rifle and headed for the door. They were all probably going to die because he'd been arrogant.

"Where are you going?" Hector asked.

"Y'all get kitted out and set up. This"—Alex indicated

the inside of the compound—"is Helm's Deep, only Gandalf isn't coming. We hold to the last. I'm headed out, but I might be coming back in a hurry."

"Ambush, huh?" Alonna said.

"Figure they won't see it coming, and a three-oh-eight to the dome is bound to ruin anyone's day. Vampire or not."

VI. BATTLE WITHOUT HONOR OR HUMANITY

Wednesday, August 11th, 3:15 A.M.

Alex rested prone, rifle at the ready, in the underbrush on the north side of the compound. He had good line of sight to the south and more importantly covering the northwest's thickest vegetation.

He'd stopped breathing hours ago and his heart lay still. This state gave him the advantage of matching the ambient temperature perfectly. That took a huge advantage away from his enemies.

Maybe they weren't coming. Maybe he'd given them too much credit. And maybe whatever attack or security Charlie-Foxtrot going down on the populated side of the base was completely unrelated.

As if to prove him wrong, a slight mist began to rise from the ground. These guys really were old school, going with the whole vampire mist precursor.

Alex took a risk. His voice rasped across the comms and, as quiet as he'd been, it came across as impossibly loud to his ears. "Eyes up."

Alonna and Hector acknowledged.

The mist grew thicker, soon everything about two

feet above the ground was obscured. The normal lights in the compound went out. There went the power. As long as the vampires stuck to the playbook, everything was going to be fine.

Thirty seconds later, the lights kicked back on as the backup generator kicked in.

Out of the corner of his eye, movement. He crept the rifle over by centimeters to line up on what he'd seen. The thermal scope wasn't giving him the advantage he'd hoped for. If he'd been lucky, the vampires would have shown up a little cooler than their surroundings, but it looked like they'd been playing the same game he'd been—matching the ambient temperature. That meant they'd been here for a while. Maybe since sundown.

Bad news indeed.

He reached up and deactivated the thermal mode and took a bigger chance. He needed to regain the initiative. If these vampires made it into the compound unseen, it would be a missed opportunity and most likely result in every human in the compound meeting an unpleasant death. Menkaure separated his *ka* from his body, just for an instant.

The vampires left hollow voids in astral ether, their non-souls unable to hide. He counted about a dozen of them. Three directly in the direction he'd been looking, a few approaching from the far side of the compound, and the bulk of them coming from the northwest as he'd expected. Gabby's tremendously bright glow shone out from the compound.

Menkaure returned to his body. Even that short stint came with a price, and he felt a measure of his precious energy deplete. Sun wouldn't be up for at least another three hours. He doubted this fight was going to go that long. Alex returned his attention to where he'd seen the three.

Nothing.

They were good.

Then he saw the mistake they'd made. As they moved in, the mist had continued to rise, making everything harder to see. Even the smoothest vampires couldn't fight turbulence.

Alex glacially crept into a kneeling position. There were vortices in the mist. And once he saw them, he saw his three targets. Unlike the insect-like scuttling motion vampires took on when they moved quickly, these three stalked forward slowly. It reminded Alex of the tentative way a spider moved if it prowled along.

He brought the rifle up and took aim at the farthest vampire's head and slowly squeezed the trigger.

The rifle's shot shattered the still night.

One down.

His next shot shattered the second vampire's skull into gory fragments.

Two down. He was pushing his luck.

He dropped the rifle in the brush and sprinted through the mist to his second prepared position near the outer chain-link fence. He'd managed about six steps before suppressed automatic weapons fire shredded the space he'd been in.

He got his heart pumping again, giving his limbs the needed blood to break out of their stiffness and get ready for the fight. The third vampire reloaded on the move, footsteps crunching across the gravel immediately behind him.

Alex couldn't see what he needed through the mist but slid into his position on faith. The vampire's hand swept through the space above him. Alex twisted during his slide and reached out. He came up with a Remington 870 and fired two silver slugs center mass into his pursuer.

Three down.

Back on his feet, he snatched at the outer fence, then once halfway up, propelled himself over it. The chain links rattled too loudly. Bullets snapped past him, but thankfully none found their mark.

He activated the comms. "Go loud. You've got three or so coming from the east. I'm coming to you. And hit the lights and sound."

He ran along the perimeter between the fences to the northwest. More rounds snapped at him before he saw the muzzle flashes. Judging from their fire, they hadn't seen him; they'd heard him and directed their fire at his sound.

He bounded over the inner fence trying to be as quiet as possible, but the chain links weren't having it and gave away his position.

With a tremendous popping sound, the normal and UV floods activated. Strobes flashed in all directions and turned the night into a visual cacophony of different light patterns. The UV made the mist fluoresce blacklight purple. If this had been a concert, it would have been amazing.

A bullet smashed into Alex's thigh and made him stumble as he ran.

He slid into his next position and stayed low. Bullet impacts peppered the space around him.

He assessed the injury. A through and through, hadn't hit the bone.

His leg wasn't compromised.

It hurt. He'd heal it later, right now, he doubted it would be the last of his injuries and didn't want to waste energy he might need later.

He low-crawled and picked up a pre-positioned M4 carbine, thumbed the select-fire switch to auto, and let fly several bursts in the direction of the muzzle flashes.

Spray and pray.

As the magazine emptied, incoming shots rained around him.

He shouted theatrically as if he'd been hit and dropped to the ground. It was a bit over the top, but he had to sell it. He felt around and came up with the claymores' "clacker."

Several vampires swept in. They'd abandoned stealth and crunched over the gravel of the killing field almost as loud as he had.

Right then, Pitbull introduced himself across the sound system. "Mister Worldwide!"

Alex's earbuds did their job, but the pulsing club beats of "Bon, Bon" pounded him in the chest hard enough he was sure the vampires weren't enjoying themselves.

Alex gave himself a three count, then closed the clacker twice.

The mines sounded with a satisfying explosion and sprayed hundreds of silver balls in sixty-degree arcs at twelve hundred feet per second.

Who said you needed stakes to kill vampires?

Automatic fire erupted from the far side of the compound and the music blared so loudly, Alex barely heard it.

Alex dashed for the entrance. "Friendly coming in!"

Hector and Alonna blasted bursts out of the east windows. Two vampires dropped, but not mortally.

Alonna shouted over her shoulder as she reloaded. "Glad to have you back!"

Alex grabbed a Rattler off the dining room table, pulled the charging handle back, but fell to a flurry of rounds impacting his chest. The Dragonskin armor stopped them all, but they hurt like hell, nevertheless.

He rolled back to his feet and emptied his magazine into the first of two vampires entering the compound.

The second vampire moved faster than he'd expected. Old blood. He struck Alex with tremendous blows and tore the Dragonskin armor off him.

The vampire stared at him, a puzzled look on its face. Any normal human would have been near death.

Instead, Alex collapsed the vampire's trachea with a horrific throat punch. His sidearm cleared the holster smoothly and he mag-dumped into the vampire's face.

Alex took a moment to collect himself and popped a new mag into his 2011. He thought of reloading the Rattler but drew his *khopesh* sword instead. He slipped on the wrist strap and tightened it.

Outside, Pitbull's Latin beats gave way to Skrillex dubstep.

They'd been lucky so far, but it was about to get *real*.

The remnants of the eastern windows shattered as a pair of vampires leapt through them. They'd dropped their modern weaponry out of rage. They were out for blood now, in ways only vampires could be.

The first battered Alonna into a wall with a casual swing. The second dove onto Hector and tried to tear his throat out. Hector punched it in the side of the head and the brass knuckle's explosive bolts did the rest, spraying brain matter and gore in a grisly mist.

The vampire engaging Alonna turned at the sound.

Hector jammed the Triple-S injector into the side of his thigh.

The vampire attacked Hector. Hector punched it with his other brass knuckle, a solid body blow, but nothing happened. He struggled with the vampire, who slowly overpowered him.

Alex moved in, but Alonna beat him to it. Her machete came down on the back of the vampire's skull and stuck there.

The vampire pulled back from Hector, arms flailing for the machete embedded in its head. Alonna punched it in the face. The explosive brass knuckles detonated and turned the vampire's head concave.

Alonna screamed and clutched her wrist. The lower half of her right arm hung limply.

"Power up!" Hector yelled. "Holy S! What's in this stuff?"

"You don't want to know," Alex said.

Alonna dug out her Triple-S injector and jammed it into her thigh. She took a few deep breaths as it kicked in. "That sure takes the edge off. I feel invincible."

Alex's mind flew and tried to tally how many vampires he'd seen and how many might be left. He didn't like the math. They were winning.

It didn't feel like they were winning.

Menkaure left Alex's body standing and slipped his *ka* out. He shot back into the bunker with the speed of thought, and Gabby's splendor nearly overwhelmed him.

KA-KHET. She called him by a throne name he'd never given her. *I HAVE LEARNED SO MUCH SINCE WE LAST SPOKE*.

There's no time. I don't know if I can hold—

Gabby cut him off. WE ARE GOING TO HELP.

Worry about staying safe. And if you can talk to the spirits, ask them if any of them are door kickers and body stackers. Have them help you defend the bunker. Menkaure didn't wait for an answer.

He snapped back into his body in time to see Alonna and Hector trading blows with two other vampires. Their machetes whistled through the air, but the vampires dodged so quickly it looked like a poorly choreographed fight.

Alex drew his 2011 and let the *khopesh* hang from his wrist by the strap. He fired a few rounds into each vampire incapacitating them long enough for Alonna and Hector to finish them.

Before they had time to celebrate, another was on Hector.

Something knocked Alex across the room, and he smashed into the far side, cratering the dry wall.

Alex climbed to his feet. No sign of his 2011.

No sign of Hector.

Alonna battled a vampire atop her, but her movements grew sluggish as the Triple-S overwhelmed her metabolism. The vampire clubbed her into unconsciousness.

Four against one. This was going to hurt.

He gripped the *khopesh* in his right hand.

The first vampire lunged. Alex kicked it across the room. The *khopesh* whistled through the air at the second attacker, who dodged the blow easily, only for Alex to catch it by the throat and casually toss it aside.

He wasn't killing these. They could keep attacking until he wore himself out.

A burst of accurate automatic fire exploded from behind him and peppered the face of his third assailant.

Alex leapt with supernatural force onto the fourth

attacker and cleanly severed its head from its body in a smoothly practiced move.

The other two vampires leapt across the room, only to be cut down by machine-gun fire.

Alex turned to thank Hector, only to see Gabby reload and slam the bolt release like she'd been doing it her whole life.

The music cut out. Someone had found the head unit.

"How in the hell?" he asked.

Gabby nodded to him casually, as if there was nothing unusual. "Sergeant Major Adrian Messer. Tenth Special Forces Group. Thought I was done with this shit when I retired. One more for the road, huh? Way I see it, you owe me one, son."

"I'll owe you more than one if you get back in that bunker and don't open that door until sunup."

Gabby pulled a hand off the carbine and gave Alex a lighthearted salute and pointed at the entrance. "You've got another guest." She fell back to the bunker.

Alex looked to what he hoped would be the last vampire.

It stood relaxed and informal, silhouetted in the doorway against the brightness of the outside spotlights. It tossed its weapon aside.

Alex would know that rangy figure anywhere. "Well, at least now I know how you were able to pronounce *Sæta Dauðr*."

There was an edge of rage to Dagny Iversen's voice. "Have you any idea how much damage you've done this night?"

"Your fault for not using Youngbloods as cannon fodder." Alex moved to Alonna and, never taking his eyes from Dagny, picked up her machete in his left hand.

"She's still alive if you're curious. The other one? I don't hear his heart. I'll finish her off after you," Dagny said.

"See, it's that kind of overconfidence got you into this mess to begin with. Mission first. Play later."

"I disagree. The other way you couldn't valiantly lay down your life in a futile gesture. Congratulations, by the way."

"You're an Ancient, aren't you?" Alex asked. "I'm gonna guess, Scandinavia? Been kicking around how long?"

Dagny smiled; her fangs caught a bit of the light in a theatrical display meant for Alex's benefit. "Since about seven hundred, anno Domini."

Alex shifted to the one side, keeping overturned furniture from the earlier fights between them.

Dagny circled opposite. "I can't figure out what kind of tech you're using to hide your body heat. Want to confess?"

"Sorry, trade secret," Alex said. "Viking versus Egyptian. Ever wonder?" He twirled his *khopesh* for effect. "One of us gets to find out."

Recognition flashed across Dagny's face. "Oh. I've heard of you." She barked forth a short laugh. "I thought you were a woman."

"No. There is *also* a woman."

"You give away your secrets too freely."

"The dead tell no tales." Alex reflected on what he'd just said and laughed. "Except, now they might."

"This grows tiresome," Dagny said.

Alex held the machete point first out in front of him. "Fair enough."

As expected, Dagny shot forward but had to change

her trajectory to avoid being impaled. Alex, in turn, spun away and leapt powerfully upward in a move that would have shamed the most skilled ballerinos. He twisted in the air and struck out with the *khopesh*.

The bronze blade rang out.

Alex landed ready to repel her next attack.

There wouldn't be another.

Her severed head rolled to one side, jaw opening and closing mechanically, while her body flopped in uncoordinated spasms on the floor.

The *khopesh* vibrated in his hand like a tuning fork. He looked down at the blade, which now bore a severe gouge.

He was out of practice.

VII. EPILOGUE

6:45 A.M.

Alex changed into a new set of clothes in time to greet Katya and the US Marshals. Gabby and Latonya were headed for WITSEC and Katya would escort.

He looked at Latonya as he hugged Gabby. "Make sure she keeps that amulet on. At least for a while. It might be safe to take it off in transit, but definitely keep it on wherever the Marshals are taking you. Most Ancient vampires aren't on our side."

Latonya pulled Gabby from him. "Honey, get your things so we're ready to go. I need to speak to Alex alone."

Gabby waved goodbye and bounded back inside.

"I don't want you to have anything more to do with

her," Latonya said. "What I saw down there when you were fighting up here. That wasn't my little girl. She's been through enough."

"But Gabby needs—"

"Stay away," Latonya shouted.

Alex's phone rang. He looked at the screen. Nocturn Affairs. He took the call, then hung up. "I have to go. They'll come for her again unless she's ready. I don't know how much I can help her, but we need to try."

Latonya changed the subject. "What was that call?"

"Homicide. Up in Coral Gables," Alex said.

"Who'd the vampires kill this time?"

"Someone murdered one of them," Alex said.

Latonya smiled.

Alex said goodbye. He'd speak to her about Gabby another time.

This whole thing had just been the storm surge. The real hurricane was on its way.

Gutter Ballet

Christopher Ruocchio

The girl was less than human, anyone with eyes could see. Still, the shape of her was persuasive, all leg and graceful lines. She moved like water, flowing over the cracked tiles of the office. Still, Simon could sense the tension in her, the nervousness betrayed by the way she held her head and the rapid darting of her eyes as she hurried to take in drab walls, the exposed pipes, the low glow of the sconces, the peeling opera posters. The false moonlight fell through the oval windows behind Simon's desk, and the glare of neon cut the eye where the sign for the off-station imports shop blinked its wanton promise into the night.

"You Mr. Fabray?" the girl asked. "The door said I could come down."

Had he forgotten to close up for the night? *Damn.*

"That's right, madam." Simon took his feet off the desk, shrugged his coat closed over his chest. The lights from his implant would not draw so much as a second glance here on Hyadon, but he was still enough the empire-man to feel shame and still even horror at the metal *thing* socketed to his chest. "And I'm sorry, but you'll have to come back tomorrow. It's late." His eyes flickered to the half-empty glass of cheap spirits on the desk by the hilt of his sword. He'd been about to go for dinner.

The air seemed to go out of the girl then. Her shoulders slumped, and her hair—rich black and smoother than oil—fell across her lovely face. Simon studied her, sure he'd been right. She wasn't human. She looked like one of the odalisques who languished in the courts of the great princes of Jadd. Her face was like graven marble, her features too perfect, too symmetrical; her skin too white and without blemish. She wasn't a machine, of that at least he was sure. She was a homunculus, grown and tailored cell by cell, her body built for—well, it wasn't gentlemanly to speculate.

"I don't suppose . . ." Her eyes flickered to his face—amber and very, very large. They flicked away again. "Sir, it's my sister. I think she's been killed."

Damn. Simon raised a hand to his eyes and sat forward, shoving the half-filled glass of spirits away, its contents sloshing on the surface, distorting and scattering the images projected in the dark glass. Letting his hand fall, he said, "What's your name?"

The girl rallied almost at once, pressed her lips together as she lifted her head and squared those alabaster shoulders beneath the translucent plastic poncho she wore over her dress. "Eirene," she said.

"Just Eirene?" Simon asked. It was an Imperial name, but her accent was all native to Hyadon, all Extrasolarian.

"Just Eirene," she echoed, and taking in a breath added, as though she had almost forgotten it, "My sisters call me *Nines*."

Simon blinked at her. "Serial number?"

"I'm sorry?" She took a step back. "Oh. Yes." She made a gesture as if to remove the synthetic poncho, seemed to think better of it. "My sisters and I . . . we're dancers. Part of a dancing company—Madame Vigran's. Do you know it?" Her amber eyes darted to the opera posters on the wall opposite the exposed plumbing.

Simon shook his head. "Why don't you take a seat?" He gestured to the chair opposite, and, pausing long enough to remove the poncho, she took the offered seat. Simon said nothing, only studied the girl as she perched herself on the very lip of the seat. She hardly moved. Even though distress etched itself like acid on her white face, her poise never faltered. He wondered how much of her dancer's training was genetic, the result of RNA indoctrination and not years of careful practice.

She was struggling to find her words. It was a look he knew well. In this line of work he'd found for his second life, Simon Fabray was always seeing people on the worst days of their lives—or the day before it. This was one of the latter cases, he could tell. She'd said it herself, and said it again a moment later. "I think my sister's been killed."

Think. Her worst day was coming, then, would arrive when she *knew*. There was always the chance the girl was alive, but on Hyadon Station, *missing* meant *dead*. If you were worth enough to ransom, the people expected to pay would know about it, and if you weren't, well...most people were worth less than the organs that kept them running.

"Why'd you come to me?" he asked when at last the silence stretched to breaking.

Nines' perfect face twisted into a frown. "You help people."

"I'm a detective," he said. "For those as can't afford the bigger sec firms."

"Yeah," she said, "but you *help* people. I hear stories, Mister Fabray. About what you did for the Sisters of Mercy. About the Natalists Guild. They say you're a knight. From the empire."

"I *was* a knight. Once," Simon countered, hand going to the iron *thing* crouched where his heart used to be. "That was a long time ago." The girl bit her lip, an affecting gesture, even through her distress. Simon chewed his own tongue a moment before asking, "What's her name?"

Nines blinked. "What?"

"Your sister," Simon said. "Another homunculus, is she?"

The girl flinched. "I...yes, sir. Her name was... is Maria." With that, she reached into the bodice of her dress and fished out an ivory cameo the size of a gold hurasam. She pulled the chain from around her exquisite neck and set the pendant on the table between them.

The two mirrored faces repelled one another as Simon opened the cameo to reveal the projector concealed behind the carved motif of nymphs and flowers. A cone of faint, white light streamed forth, and within it the image of more than a dozen women stood arm-in-arm and bowed before lifting their faces, smiling at unheard applause. Each was pale as the woman opposite him, each black of hair, each amber eyed, skinny but not androgynous, perfect in every way. Each wore matching red leotards cut to emphasize the sculpted shape of hip and thigh, and each girl's face had been starkly painted after the fashion of all stage performers to emphasize the hard line of cheekbone and jaw.

The image froze, seventeen girls all smiling matching smiles.

"That's her," the girl called Nines said, poking her finger through the holograph of the girl third from the right. Simon could hardly tell them apart, though they were not quite identical.

"How long has she been missing?" he asked, trying to decide which of the girls in the image was the one seated in his dark office.

Eirene cleared her throat. "Three days."

"She's dead," Simon said, and regretted his words as the girl's shoulders collapsed. Her attention momentarily diverted, he dragged the hilt of his old sword across the desktop and vanished it into a pocket of his coat. Better not to leave the weapon lying around. It was an Imperial weapon, a knight's weapon, and the last thing he wanted was her asking questions. Hearing the girl sniff, he said, "I'm sorry. But if it's been this long, she's floating in one of the canals."

The homunculus clenched her tailored jaw. "I know that's probably true, Mr. Fabray. Really, I know it. I just want to know what happened to her."

"And you didn't go to your owner? What's her name?"

"Madame Vigran?" The girl's eyes went very wide.

"Oh, no, sir." Again she bit her lip, hands twisting in her lap. "Maria was seeing a boy. Some sailor. She never told us his name. Madame Vigran would have had her caned if she knew."

Leaning over his desk, Simon dragged the glass back toward himself and lifted it to drink. "She know now?"

"I mean . . . she knows Maria is missing, but we haven't told her about the boy." Nines had grown, if anything, even paler. "She'd have us all caned for keeping it a secret. She's very hard on us." The dancer ducked her head. "We'd not be living were it not for her. We owe her honesty. Owe her everything. It's only that Maria was so . . . so happy. With her sailor, I mean. I didn't want to take that from her. None of us did. And now she's . . ." She choked, held a hand to her mouth and shut her eyes.

His glass drained, Simon shut the cameo, extinguishing the image of the ballerinas.

"It isn't your fault, miss," he said, trying to soothe her. From the way her shoulders tightened, Simon guessed that he'd failed. "You and your sisters: You're clones, aren't you?"

Letting her hand drop, Nines nodded stiffly.

"Are you clones of *her*?"

The homunculus nodded again, and a moment later. "Yes."

"I see."

"She was a great dancer, in her day. From one of the great Mandari companies. We keep her legacy alive," she smiled, and the light of it cut sharper than the neon through the oval windows behind Simon's desk. "I think it's wonderful. Don't you?"

Simon touched his implant at the thought of

something being kept alive, and grimaced. He'd been a corpse when Basil brought him to Hyadon Station and paid for the machine whose burning candle replaced his ruined heart. The Extrasolarian machine—forbidden in the empire—had saved his life, had *kept him alive*, but it came with a cost. He could never go home. With his false heart burning in his chest, his people would stone him for abomination.

There was something to be said for death, for letting things go.

For letting things end.

That was just the problem with these Extras. Mother Earth and Evolution intended man to live his day and die, but there were lengths men might obtain in defiance of natural order, prolonging life. Some were wholesome, such as porphyrogenesis practiced by the lords of the empire, but most were not. Among the Extras, men carved out their brains and placed them in bodies of metal or jars of clear glass; or filled their bodies with unholy machines to replace their failing organs. There were whispers that some among the bonecutters in the city traded in new bodies entire—though Simon did not believe it—while others...

"I'm going to ask you just one question, miss," Simon said, and again the girl's posture stiffened, ready for flight. She chewed her lip, waiting. "What makes you think *she* didn't kill your sister?"

Nines blinked. "Madame Vigran?" The girl shook her head furiously, her silken hair floating about her face. "No! Why? Never!" She almost laughed. "Why would she?"

Her confusion was itself almost funny. Like a bird so used to its cage it has mistaken the gilt bars for sunlight in an open sky, the girl who was not quite a girl could not see the truth when it was staring her plain in her gene-sculpted face. He laughed then, a harsh, rough sound, loud and unkind. "You're spare parts, girl! A walking organ bank—you and your *sisters*. It's not just her legacy you're keeping alive. It's *her*."

Eirene stood so sharply she knocked the chair to the ground. She stepped back, nearly fell. Simon lurched to his feet, though he stood no chance of reaching her in time. But Eirene righted herself, skipping back several steps. "You can't be serious!" she exclaimed. "Madame Vigran would never do that!"

"Then why are you halfway round the ring talking to some old guy in the hydroponics district?" he said. "You knew all along, girl. Don't lie to me. Your *Madame* wouldn't be the first to keep a harem of organ donors. It's practically a cliché about you Extras where I come from. You had to know."

The girl Eirene was silent, stood hugging herself beyond the overturned chair. Through the windows at Simon's back, a light flared as the drive-glow of a flier slid past and set the panes to rattling. Though her lip trembled, she held herself still as any queen.

Simon crossed his arms, did not regain his seat. Though he'd risen to try and help her, he stayed standing to face her down, counting on his size and patrician scars to frighten her to speech. "Tell me the truth," he said.

"I don't..."

"You want me to kill her? Is that it?" he asked, and took an incongruous step back.

"The Sisters," Eirene, called Nines, said. "You saved their convent from Yin's men. You killed Yin."

Simon's face was as much a mask as those of the girls on the holograph. "I don't know what you mean."

"You *help* people," the homunculus insisted. "They said you help people."

"You're not people," Simon said, voice cold as the space beyond the station's superstructure. "And I'm not an assassin. You want one? Go down-spin to *Mauvancor*. You'll find no shortage of cutthroats willing to take you on for a hurasam or an hour in a pod hotel with you."

Eirene's shoulders slumped, and her whole person seemed to sag like a glacier tumbling into the sea. "I'm not a whore, Mr. Fabray," she said.

"And I told you," he said. "I'm not a killer."

Silence unspooled between them, neither speaking. Neither moved. At length, Simon broke the stalemate, and circling back to his desk collected the short glass and the tall bottle not far from it. He thought better of the glass, and pulling the stopper free tipped the tasteless liquor down his throat. It burned as it went down, and he grimaced at his reflection in the purple light from the window. The white lines of surgical scars shone bright in the dim reflection, half-hidden by the shadow of his ill-shaven beard. After more than a hundred years of hard living and his fatal brush with death, his hair was starting to go gray at the roots, and there was a leathern cast to the skin of his face, amplified by the crooked profile of his once-broken nose.

Life is very long, he thought, and asked, "What do you want from me?" His eyes never left his ghostly face in the window glass. "And I mean it, girl. Don't lie."

He could see her shape in the glass, too, pale and

slight and desperately alone. She didn't speak at once, and when she did it was in a voice small and hard and brittle as ceramic. "I want to know, Mr. Fabray. I want to know if Madame Vigran killed my sister. I want to know if I and the rest of my sisters are safe, and yes—" She faltered then, but when she pressed forward, it was with a new sharpness, as though that brittle ceramic had shattered and would cut. "If she did it. I want her dead."

Simon lifted the vodka to his lips again and drank. "I can't help you." A small, strangled sound escaped the girl behind him. He half turned, looking back over his shoulder. "I'm not a killer. I told you. You have the wrong man."

"I need your help," she said again, voice gone high with strain.

"You have the wrong man," he said again.

Her reflection snatched up her poncho and turned to go. "I'm sorry I wasted your time."

"Girl!" he called after her, conscious of the faint humming in his chest implant.

Eirene stopped.

"If you head up to 117th Street and go left almost to the rim wall, you'll find a Cid Arthurian temple. The monks will take you in. They might even be able to pay for your way off-station. They can keep you safe."

Eirene didn't move for just a second. Then she left without another word.

The great lamps that served for false suns on Hyadon were all dark by the time Simon hit the streets at last. Steam rose from vents in the street and drifted to mingle with the catwalks and the tubeways that stretched between the towers of the great city—many of them piercing the roof of the world overhead and continuing up toward the empty center of the great ring.

The street rose ahead, the throng and silver serpents of the elevated tramline rising as up the face of a mountain before him. Like so many of the great station-cities of the galaxy, Hyadon was built on a ring, a great hoop three miles in diameter and more than a mile wide. Simon wasn't sure how many people lived on the ring. It must have been millions, all of them crammed on top of one another, living in insulae, in apartments smaller than the scullery in his father's manor back home on Varadeto.

His offices were in one of the old industrial zones, just above one of the fisheries whose waters—choked with algae and lotus blossoms—helped support the city's atmosphere for the millions who called it home. Canals ran beneath the streets that circled the turning ring like inlay on a globe. Hyadon had no formal state, no government as Simon understood it, only shareholders—though often it seemed the plutocrats of Hyadon had only reinvented lordship in their wretched and cutthroat way.

The streets glowed with advertisements, with holographs shimmering, products flashing and chasing would-be customers as they passed glass storefronts and eateries. One shop beside a bakery advertised cerebral implants, while another sold whole-cloth memories—by appointment only. Simon could hardly leave his office—could hardly look out his window—without recalling how foreign he was, and how foreign all Hyadon was to him. Man was meant to live on the skin of a world beneath the open sky. He missed his father's estate on Varadeto, the olive groves and the mountains marching at the horizon beyond the pampas. The old house would have been his, in time.

If he'd but lived.

The Mandari noodle shop was wedged beneath an office tower that pierced the roof of the ring and continued out into space. Simon clattered down the steps to the basement level and into the smoky shop. The man behind the counter grunted at him and bobbed his head, and Simon sagged into an open seat at the bar, and signaled in answer to the fellow's question that, yes, he'd take the usual. The server placed a clay teacup on the bar and went about his business.

Simon's business with the girl had left him with a foul taste in his mouth. It didn't sit right with him leaving her to twist as he had, but he could hardly throw himself against a grand dame of the Mandari clans on Hyadon. The Mandari owned half the ring.

But it wasn't right. There was nothing stopping this Vigran woman from just printing the parts she needed. That was how it was done in the empire—for those injuries fresh organs could cure. The pressure of his implant against his arms crossed on the bar practically screamed at him. Keeping the girls around whole and healthy, it was an ugliness that made him wish the empire would find Hyadon and burn it out of the sky. But the city was down on no Imperial charts. Like nearly all the Extrasolarian backspace holdings, its power and freedom depended on secrecy. It orbited no star, no world, but winged its black way through the blackest space far from the light of true civilization, a refuge for outcasts, derelicts and freaks.

Like me. Simon sipped his tea.

Dinner came in time, noodles and poached fish grown on-station. It wasn't good, but it wasn't bad, either. Simon ate in silence, called the server to refill his tea. On a holograph plate above the bar, images flashed, reporting the market closures for the Hyadon Exchange, and news had come in regarding the sale at auction of a sculpture—a single marble wing that once might have belonged to an angel of victory—that had reportedly come from Old Earth herself. The wing was to be displayed in the headquarters of Sen Biologics, one of the corporate interests who called Hyadon Station home. Evidently the corp had purchased the antiquity for several million talents of platinum specie, a staggering price and a blasphemy, for such artifacts of the Mother and the Golden Age of Man were beyond price in truth, but not among such barbarians.

"You want dessert?" the server asked, jolting Simon from his contemplation. The fellow peered at Simon with glassy, colorless eyes. He had lost the ones Mother Earth and Evolution had given him in a vacuum accident, Simon knew, and tried not to stare.

"Not today, Qiu," the detective said, going for the credit chit he kept sealed in an inner pocket of his old white jacket. Some feminine blur of motion had caught his eye, commanded his attention as only women can command, and looking back at the holograph he saw a pale woman in white leap against starry blackness. As he watched, she turned a pirouette, her dress fanning like the arms of the galaxy as the camera twisted overhead. It was Eirene. Or was it? So like was she to her sisters that even Simon—who had just passed an hour with her—could not be certain.

In the end it didn't matter. The camera cut and showed the homunculi all dancing together, as perfect in their motions as the mechanisms of a Durantine clock. Their lovely faces each were painted red as suns, their hair pinned back and chased with gold, and when the ad was done, the Mandari pictograms painted themselves white against the darkened screen.

Xinyi Vigran presents . . .

River of Stars.

Information for the ordering of tickets flashed for a moment and faded before Simon could look away, the moment come and gone.

It had not been difficult to find the opera house; the address had been in the advertisement, and a simple inquiry on his pocket terminal had produced the answer—and the same advertisement again. His chest ached about his implant as he rounded the street corner, peering up at the iron sky where the spire of a high-rise rose above the curving, incoherent shape of the theater itself. It was an ugly building, without the graceful arches and fine pillars or stained glass and statuary one might find on such a building in the empire. It was cold and white, its domes like waves of metal and glass beneath the tower that pierced the roof of the world.

He found the stage access via a loading dock. There must have been no performance that night, for the dock was empty and the sounds of the city were hushed, the nearest noise that of the trams on the main street and of a solitary cargo van moving up the alley behind. Simon felt certain there were cameras. There were always cameras. On Hyadon, as in the empire, no man was every truly alone, even in his

own home. The daimon machines upon whose service
the Extrasolarians depended, who controlled everything
from lights to airlocks to temperature regulation—were
always listening. And yet it was always possible, even
easy, to force one's way into a place. All one needed
was a spine, a smile, and—for the tricky spots—a
terminal complete with a suite of cybersecurity tools
of the sort you could find in such lawless climes as
Hyadon Station. On Hyadon, money—not blood—was
king, and might was the only law.

"You there!" a rough voice called out. "Who are
you? You shouldn't be in here."

Simon halted in the white corridor just inside the
loading dock. A man in charcoal body armor with a
face like weathered stone moved toward him. That
hadn't taken long. Simon recognized the white fist
emblem on the man's arm as belonging to a sec firm
of the very type he'd mentioned to Eirene earlier
that evening.

The man who once had been a knight did his best
to smile blandly. He did not lie easily, but he lied
well. Decades of living on the station had forced him
to learn. "Courier, sir. Private message for the lady."

The man looked him over, eyes very narrow. "Courier, is it? Who is it sent you?"

"Can't say, sir," Simon said, averting his eyes. "Private, as I say."

"Well, let's have it then." The man extended a hand,
gestured for Simon to hand it over.

"You misunderstand me," he said, and tapped his forehead. "I have the message." It was not uncommon—both
on Hyadon and in the empire—for the truly secret, the
truly intimate messages sent between the great of the

galaxy to be sent not via radio or quantum telegraph, but on paper or in the minds of the messenger. Such systems were less vulnerable to sabotage and interception, more secure.

Nonplussed by this, the man leaned back, eyes gone narrower still. "Who do you work for?"

"I told you," Simon said, sensing his ruse was nearing its end. "I can't say, but I've a message for Madame Vigran that won't wait." Even as the words tumbled from his mouth, Simon was not sure why he didn't turn and leave. He might have done, and done so with relative ease, told the guardsman he'd be back with identification, forget the whole affair. Liquor was cheap, and sleep cheaper still. He owed Eirene and her dead sister nothing. They weren't even human, not really.

And he was no knight.

The guard stepped back, lips drawn together. "No, I mean... what company you with? You're a fighting man, that much is obvious."

"Freelance," Simon said brightly, and beginning to second-guess his non-plan, he added, "I can come back tomorrow. Get verification."

The guard shook his head, took his hand away from the shock-stick slotted into a holster on his thigh. "No need," he said, raising a hand to his wrist comm. "I'll call it in." He turned his head to make the call, pressing fingers to the conduction patch behind his ear.

Simon didn't hesitate. Turning from his hips, he slammed the heel of his hand down into the man's temple with all the force and weight of his body. The overhanded blow caught the man completely by surprise, and he buckled as he struck the wall.

"Sorry," the one-time knight said, though the guard could not hear him. Crouching, Simon checked his pulse. Still alive. That was good. He was only doing his job, and no man deserved to die for that. Not for the first time that night, Simon Fabray wondered what he was doing there, but then—he was no stranger to the question. He'd asked himself what he was doing when he took out Morrison's gang for harassing the Sisters uptown, or when he'd saved that batch of embryos Captain Montero had stolen from the Natalists.

It just wasn't right.

Nothing about Hyadon was *right*.

Perhaps that was all. He had come so far from home, to a half-life beyond the death that took his heart and whole world. He was a dead man, had been a long time, and so death had lost its sting. Better to die setting the world to rights—or a part of it, only—than to live on like some walking shadow. Far better. His second life had been a gift, and if all he did with it was find a way to give it back, maybe that was right. They were hard worlds, all of them, and broken. But a man needn't be broken himself, not where it counted.

When Simon emerged from the utility closet where he left the unconscious guard, it was with the man's terminal in his hand. He'd used the fellow's thumbprint to unlock it, and kept it open by repeatedly tapping the display. He found the key for the stairs easily enough, and climbed up a level. With each passing moment he expected an alarm to sound, but it never did. It took finesse to be a criminal on a station like Hyadon, where there was a log for every door and every ventilator flap. It took far more to seek any sort of justice, for it was the criminals who ruled. And yet the theater and the annex attached to it—and that tower—were not the fortress of some genetics baron. The wealthy scion of a Mandari clan Xinyi Vigran might have been, but if she was one of the shareholders who ruled the ring city, she was not one of the great ones. Simon didn't see another guard as he plodded along the corridor, passing one-way mirrors that looked in on the flat, false-wood floor of a dance studio. He passed by the sealed bulkhead of a lavatory door opposite a side passage, and beyond that found a shuttered recreation room. The lights were down.

There was no performance in the theater proper that night, he'd made sure of that, checking the station's datasphere as he picked his way through the streets to reach it. The other girls were doubtless in their beds in what passed for a dormitory in that strange and silent place. The silhouettes of ballerinas showed in images hung on the walls, strangely sterile. Commercial art hung to convey a theme.

They felt almost oppressive, as though they were totems meant to impose their horizon on all who came to that hall. For the girls were to be only dancers, only dancers and . . . that other thing.

"Who are you?"

A familiar voice called from behind.

Simon turned, simultaneously trying to hide the guard's pilfered terminal and to reach for his sword hilt where it lay concealed in a pocket of his white coat.

Eirene stood in the mouth of the lavatory, the bulkhead swung open behind her. She wore a dancer's leotards, pale blue, though no paint altered the harsh line of jaw and cheekbone. A terminal in a band on her upper arm played wordless music softly in the still air. Had she been practicing alone?

"How did you get in here?"

The one-time knight did his best to smile, and polished his earlier lie to answer her first question. "I'm a courier, miss. Come from Master Zeitelmann for your Madame."

The homunculus nodded only slowly, comprehending. She had heard of Arnulf Zeitelmann, and she should; he owned a fifth of the ring. Of course he would have a message for the dancer's mistress, *she* was the center of the girl's world, after all. "Madame's sick," she said. "We haven't seen her down here in weeks. Only Doctor Afonso sees her."

The illusion that she was Eirene broke as the girl tossed her head. The voice was the same—or nearly so—but there was a hauteur in this one unlike the nerves and timid shyness of the girl who'd come to his office earlier that evening. She was one of the others, another of Madame Vigran's clones. An idea struck Simon then, and he said, "My master found one of your sisters wandering the city."

The girl brightened at once. "Maria?"

Simon kept his composure. He was sure the girl Maria—what was left of her—was in the building. The fate of any such a clone was no mystery on Hyadon, only a reality most were too squeamish or too polite to countenance. Let this girl think whatever she wanted, *he* wanted to see the woman in charge.

"I've said too much already," he said, sure he had her interest. "My master sent me to inquire if there was a bounty for her safe conduct. He would be only too happy to restore her to you all." Simon made a show of looking round the hall. "Would it be possible to see your mistress?" He circled back to an earlier question, and said, "The guards below said I was to be admitted."

The girl looked him over, and if the thought that the guard should have accompanied him upstairs crossed her mind, she did not voice it. "I told you," she said, at last silencing the soft music from her terminal, "no one's seen Madame in weeks. Only the doctor."

"That's just fine," Simon said, pocketing the guard's terminal as discreetly as he could. He would not need it. "Is he here? Can you take me to him?"

The door unsealed itself and rolled into a pocket in the wall as the girl—the image of Eirene and the murdered Maria, both—led Simon over the threshold into the annex above and behind the theater proper. He could hardly believe his luck. Of all the sorts of people he might have found wandering the halls below—security guards, custodial workers, lonely stage hands—he had happened upon one of those most able to assist his entry and most likely to believe his lie. Doubtless the girl cared for her sisters, and Simon had counted on that care to make her believe. On top of that, she was one of the Madame's prized possessions, and though she was a kind of slave, her gilded cage offered its privileges, as all cages did.

Twice men in the charcoal of the guard he'd met below stopped them to inquire who Simon was, and twice the girl told his lie for him. "He's from Master Zeitelmann, says he has a message for the Madame."

Twice the guards waved them on.

She led Simon to a lift and up another three levels to a spot where the halls glowed a sanitary white.

They stopped before another door, this one of heavy, mirrored glass. The girl keyed the comm panel—a black mirror itself to the right of the frame.

"Doctor Afonso?" she said.

An older man's voice came across the comm after a few moments' silence. "Rhea, is that you? I told you not to bother me after the dinner hour."

"No, Doctor. It's Phoebe."

"Phoebe?" the older man said. "What is it? You know I'm busy. Madame is unwell. She needs me."

The dancer, Phoebe, bobbed her head apologetically and pressed her lips together before saying, "I know, sir, but there's a man here. A courier from Lord Zeitelmann. He says he has news about Maria."

"Maria?" the doctor's voice rose sharply. Surprise? Confusion? If Simon had any doubts about the homunculi's fate, that dispelled them. He felt a black knot forming in the pit of his stomach. "Well, send him in, girl. Send him in." In the instant before the doctor cut the comms, he could be heard to mutter. "News about Maria?"

The mirror depolarized, turning the door to glass as it slid aside.

The door closed again before Simon realized the girl Phoebe had not followed him. Another gleaming white hall greeted him, minutely tiled and shining beneath the tube lights overhead. A man emerged from the side door a moment later. Small, bald, black eyed and dressed in slick gray-blues. Simon recognized the logo of Sen Biologics pinned to his lapel. He was far shorter than Simon was, and peered up at him owlishly. "You've an Imperial look about you," he said without preamble.

"What?"

"The scars!" he waggled a finger at Simon's face and neck. "They always leave the scars on those they uplift. They don't have to. Empire just wants you marked. We can clean those up, you know."

Simon took a step back. The man had come very close. "I don't want them cleaned. I won them."

"Ah! You are Imperial, then," the doctor said, face gone grave. "Patrician? A knight? What's a knight want with the Madame?"

Simon crossed his arms, bringing one hand inside his jacket and near the hilt of his sword. "The girls don't know, do they?"

"Know what?" Afonso blinked, evidently surprised by this question.

"That they're clones."

"Oh, that!" The doctor shifted, hand in his pockets. "They know that!"

"Of *her*."

Then it was Afonso's turn to step back, tension stretching like a line between them, pulled taut and fit to sing. "They know that, too. The Madame was great in her day, a true artist, you understand. She is very old now, and her health... it is not so good as once it was." He pursed his lips. "But you have news of Maria, I understand. Phoebe said you are from Zeitelmann? This is most irregular."

"Not about Maria," Simon said. "About Eirene."

"Eirene?" Surprised, Afonso took his hands from his pockets, where just before Simon was sure he'd held a weapon or the fob of some panic alarm. If Simon was right, the little man had probably killed Maria himself, carved her up for parts. He knew Zeitelmann would have no news of Maria, could have none. But the mention of the other clone had caught him off guard. Did he believe Simon could be trusted now? Did he believe himself safe? "What of Eirene?"

Simon pressed forward, using his advantage to push past the doctor through the side door whence the little man had come. "You knew she was missing?" Simon asked, certain the answer was yes. She could not have been allowed the freedom of the city.

"Gone this morning. We had men looking for her." Afonso followed Simon into the room.

The laboratory was immaculate, clean as clean and whiter—if such a thing were possible—than the hall itself. Terminal displays shone in an arc along one wall above a desk where a clay tea service stood beside a small, carefully pruned tree. Shears lay to one side, and a neat pile of trimmings lay with it. But Simon glanced at these for only a passing instant. His eyes were drawn to the sample that lay under glass on the operating table, a suite of mechanical arms hovering about it, momentarily lifeless and oddly baroque, like the painting of some terrible battle, an instant frozen in time.

He didn't need to be told it was human tissue. Some part of him just knew. But he wasn't sure exactly what he was looking at at first, the red flesh white beneath, two flat lobes laid open and yellowing, gray with corruption. Then he turned his head and understood. They were lungs. Each had been butterflied and folded open to reveal the alveoli. Simon was no physician, but he knew enough of butchery to know there was something very wrong with them.

"Am I to assume that your people found her?"

"She's safe," Simon said, hoping that the girl had kept running, had found the Cid Arthurian monastery he'd tried—half-heartedly—to steer her toward. He should have gone with her, should have seen her to safety, done the thing right. He shifted his position, cocked his head down at the lungs splayed and clamped open on the slab before him. They must have belonged to the Madame, he reasoned, and looked round as if expecting to find evidence of the murdered girl discarded in one corner, cast aside like the crumpled pages of a failed manuscript, a story cut short before its end.

"How much does Zeitelmann want for her?" the doctor asked. "It can't be much. He must know the Madame has others, and more on the way. If he's not willing to go low on price, he can keep the girl."

A solitary hiss of cold laughter escaped by Simon's nose. "Others." He gripped the sword hilt hidden in the lining of his jacket. Simon didn't believe the doctor for a moment. Clones such as Eirene were not cheap, nor was it cheap to raise and to maintain them—and what was more, the girl was not only a clone, but a fixture in the Madame's ballet. She was too valuable to simply cast aside, and it was that callousness—the willingness to barter with her life, to pretend she held no value to them—that set his teeth on edge.

It's all wrong, he thought. *All wrong.*

And jerking his chin at the organs on display, Simon said, "What's wrong with her? Your Madame?"

"I'm not at liberty to say," said Doctor Afonso. "Patient confidentiality, you understand. My contract with the Madame forbids me to discuss her medical condition."

"But they are donors?" Simon asked. He wanted to be sure. "The dancers?" Every second the doctor did not answer, Simon could feel his patience burning away, sloughing off until only a lump of fury black as charcoal remained in the little furnace that had replaced his heart. He knew the girl who'd come to ask for his help was not truly human, but he couldn't make himself care. She was a girl in trouble, and whatever else may be, that trouble was real. What did it matter who was human, if the inhuman suffered the same? Was it not the pain that mattered?

He couldn't remember drawing his sword, couldn't remember squeezing the triggers that conjured the liquid metal blade. All he remembered was the hum and rippling shine of it, blue-white as crystal, as he slammed the blade down through the medical glass and through the lungs and the slab beneath them. The highmatter of that sword cut clean as a hot wire through wax, sliced glass and brushed metal and the steel of one robotic arm as if none of it were even there. Afonso yelped and leaped back.

His demonstration done, Simon lurched forward and seized the little man by his lapel, forcing him back against the wall. The man was sure to have neural implants, would be able to signal for help as soon as he remembered that he could, and how. Anticipating this, Simon raised the edge of his antique weapon to the man's chin and held it there. "Call for help, and you're done."

"You're not from Zeitelmann!" the doctor grunted, voice choked as Simon leaned his weight against him. Despite this a cavalcade of questions bubbling forth, each barely more than a whisper as Afonso stretched away from Simon's blade. "Who are you? How did you get in here? Who let you in?"

"They *are* all donors, aren't they?" Simon asked. He didn't need the answer. "The girls?"

"What?" Afonso asked, and yelped when Simon jostled him. "Yes! Yes, of course they are! Madame Vigran is over five hundred years old! Even with the best gene tonics on the market, she needs a full refit every few years to prevent total collapse!"

Not releasing the doctor, Simon drew back half a step. He'd known the truth, known it from the minute Eirene walked into his office, and still the moment of confirmation was a shock. He was not at home, not in the galaxy he knew, the galaxy of light, of planets and plain order. Of decency. Of law. He was on Hyadon, in the Dark between the stars, and Hyadon was the gutter—one of the gutters—into which any who could not live in that light was inevitably drained. He was one such bit of refuse, one such refugee. But he did not have to live as they lived, where money was power and power was law. He was no libertine. Despite his circumstances, despite his wounds, down in the foundations of his soul—in his very bones—he was a knight of the Sollan Empire. Even still.

"So Maria *is* dead?" Simon asked.

"She served her purpose!" the doctor answered, voice defensive, as if this were any justification for murder, for butchery and the horrible vampirism it served.

It took every ounce of willpower Simon possessed not to strike the man down where he stood. "Her *purpose*?" he snarled through clenched teeth. "Her *purpose*!"

"That was why she was made!" Afonso said. "She

would not have lived at all were it not for us! We've maintained the Madame's contract for decades! *Decades!* It's just the way things are done!"

The very earth reeled about him—which he supposed it did—and Simon released Doctor Afonso, shaking his head as if to clear it of some oppression. Belatedly then, he realized the doctor had soaked the front of his trousers from terror. Before the man could reconsider his circumstances and signal for aid, Simon raised his sword, aimed the point square at the evil fellow's chest. "Take me to her."

Gone was the sterile whiteness of the medical annex with its minute, polished tiles and the frigid crispness of the air. The lift—when Afonso opened it, walking gingerly in light of his wet pants—was richly paneled in brass and red velvet.

"Penthouse suite," Afonso stammered, beady eyes wide as they would go as they followed the emitter end of Simon's hilt like those of a child skirting round a standing cobra.

The lift began to move, ascending smoothly along what Simon guessed was the tower he'd seen rising above the lower theater building. As they went, he felt his weight begin to lessen. Hyadon Station spun to simulate the effects of gravity, but that gravity was normed at street level, so that a pound of gold weighed one pound in the hand. But the higher one climbed above the streets, the less and less that false gravity weighed upon the bones, so that the same gold piece might float were it placed at or near the center. Towering then above the street level, the great libertines who ruled Hyadon drifted about their palaces on light feet, feeling neither the weight of their bodies nor their actions.

The door chimed and slid open.

Simon pressed the doctor forward with the hilt of his sword. Afonso staggered ahead of him onto wine-dark Tavrosi carpets. Red-stained wood panels marked the lower walls, and richly frescoed plaster hid the metal superstructure of the station itself, softening the mechanical world to something that recalled almost the estate of some great Imperial lord. A tall vase—white and blue porcelain—stood on a plinth under glass ahead.

"Lead the way," Simon said, and prodded the physician.

Afonso crossed the atrium to the open double doors. The sitting room beyond was as richly appointed. Frescoed walls showed a water garden filled with flowers and jewel-bright birds. A holography well sat sunk into the floor, couches circling about it, but the projector was dark, and the grand piano opposite stood closed and dusty from long neglect.

A short hall passed another room and the closed bulkhead of a private lavatory, and beyond...

Simon heard the beep of medical instruments before they crossed the threshold, smelled the bite of antiseptic and the underlying rot of disease. And there she was.

Everything the girl who'd come to his office that evening was, Xinyi Vigran was no longer. Slim as Eirene was, the woman that lay abed beneath coverlets of checkered black and white could not have weighed less than six hundred pounds at street level. It was no wonder she chose to dwell above, where the slower

turning of Hyadon's great wheel would ease the tor-
ment of her bones. If Eirene's hair had been thick
and dark and smoother than oil, what little remained
of the Madame was white and brittle as chalk, leaving huge stripes of her pockmarked scalp bare and
blotched. Her skin was not of porcelain to match the
Earth-ware vase on display in her atrium, but so dry
and stretched and wrinkled that the centuries could
be read on her like the mountains and rivers of some
ancient map.

Afonso bowed his head. "Madame, you have a
visitor."

The old leviathan did not stir.

"Is she dead?" Simon asked. But no, she could not
be. White medical equipment half circled the antique
carved wooden bedstead, as out of place as Simon felt.
These chimed softly, and a holograph displayed her
vitals in violent green. Beside her head, a silver staff
rose, hooked to the ceiling, and from it a blood bag
swayed like a lonely red fruit upon a tree of steel.

Still bowing his head, Afonso shuffled forward, voice
quavering, "Madame, there is a knight to see you."

Madame Vigran opened one fat-enfolded eye. It
was the same bright amber as Eirene's, though the
orb seemed shrunken in that flat expanse she called
a face. "A knight?" She stared at Simon blearily, not
really seeing. "He is not from Vorgossos then? It is
not my time?"

"There is no word from Vorgossos, ma'am," the
doctor said. "We are trying."

"Vorgossos?" Simon frowned. He'd never heard
the name.

Afonso answered. "She does not have long. More

serious interventions are needed to sustain her. We don't have the means. She but asks if you're from those who do." He raised his voice, "No, ma'am. He's here about Eirene."

"Eirene?" Madame Vigran's second eye opened. "You found her?" Those familiar eyes flickered to Afonso. "A bounty hunter?"

"Not exactly," Simon said. He could not tell how present the old woman was. There was a haziness in her eyes and a distance in her tone that made him wonder. But it was her will that had set this foul system in motion; whether or not she was in any state to captain her way, she had set the course. "Eirene is safe. You're not to harm her. Not to look for her. She's not yours anymore."

One jewel-taloned finger found a control, and her bed tilted upward very, very slowly. "Not *mine*?" Vigran echoed. "She's *me*. Would you rob an old woman of her support?"

"She's not a crutch," Simon said. "None of them are, but I haven't come to save them." The words and his intentions only crystallized for Simon as he spoke them. It was his only real option. He might barter for the one girl's life, but he could not stop the cycle that so enslaved the others, not and live himself. "She knows what you are, anyway. She knows you killed Maria, and why. You can't bring her back without poisoning the well. She'll tell the others. She's no good to you."

"Her parts are good to me," Vigran replied without hesitation. "I can have Afonso here put her on ice until I need her." Her words were coming clearer with every syllable, though her eyes had yet to find their focus. "Unless you've some better offer, *knight*."

Something whined as her bed stabilized her in a

seated position, and it was only then that Simon saw the silvery tube shunted through the front of her throat. Some machine breathed for her, and Simon recalled the lungs pinned on the display in Afonso's lab below. He followed the tube with his eyes, found the ventilator among the equipment at her bedside.

"These machines are keeping you alive," Simon said, lamely. "Why bother with the girls?"

Afonso stammered a response before his mistress had a chance. "Organ replacement is better," he said. "The nubile tissue has rejuvenating effects on the body as a whole. Young organs, young blood encourages new development in older systems. Helps to lengthen overall life expectancy beyond what the machines can offer."

The former knight felt himself recoil. The indecency, the ghoulish disregard for life—even the lives of homunculi, who in the empire were slaves and little more—twisted his guts. With his free hand, he touched his implant through the front of his shirt. "You can't go back," he said simply. "No matter how many of them you kill, you can't be what you were."

"I can," she said. "Vorgossos will heal me. They can sell me a new body. A new brain. Everything."

"Only they can," Afonso said. The man was shaking and had edged as far from Simon as he could manage, though he was still within reach of the flash of the blade.

"And you've had no word," Simon said, eyes sweeping over the machines that kept the vampire alive. "How many have you killed? For this?"

Neither answered.

"You don't even know," Simon realized, looking from one to the other.

The fog that sheened the old woman's eyes had lifted somewhat, and they narrowed as she asked, "Who are you? How did you get in here? Afonso, explain yourself!"

"You don't even know?" Simon could hardly find his breath. He had to steady himself against the arc of monitors to keep himself from falling in the reduced gravity of the suite. "You really have no idea?"

"It doesn't matter," she said. "They're *my* bodies, and *mine* to do with as I please. Can you honestly say you would do any differently, had you the means?"

Simon didn't hesitate. "Yes," he said, and tore at the buttons of his blue shirt to flash the silver of his implant. "I'd rather be dead than live like you."

"You will be," Vigran agreed. "Dead."

Afonso's eyes went wide, and he stood straighter. "No, Madame! No! He's armed!" Simon was sure the doctor had a neural lace implanted in his brain, was equally sure that he'd heard with some sense other than hearing his mistress sound the alarm that Simon had threatened the doctor from ringing.

The next instant proved him right.

A siren wailed high and thin and terrible through the plastered metal walls.

"I don't know who you think you are, *sir*," the old woman said, using the Imperial honorific like a slur. "But you dare come here, to my house! And threaten me? Where is Eirene? Tell me, and I may permit you to walk out of here with your skin!"

Simon grimaced, tried to stand straight beneath the onslaught of the siren. His mind conjured images of the gray-armored guard rushing upstairs, crowding into the lift. He had but seconds. If he did not act, then and there, it all would be for nothing. If Vigran was right—if he was to die—he would die setting some small piece of the world to rights. He hoped Eirene had found the monks, hoped at least she might escape her lot, and the others, too. But if he hoped to live at all, there was but one thing he could do, just as Vigran had done all her evil life.

He raised his sword, blade flashing back into existence like the sun coming from behind a cloud. Afonso yelped and fell against the side of the bed in his haste to get away. But Simon did not kill him. He might have done, but Hyadon and the other stations like it were so full of men like him that his death would never change the balance. He was a tool, an appendage of the behemoth in the checkered bed—and of all like her.

He slashed the ventilator instead, the liquid metal of his blade shearing through the braided silver tube and squat tower whence it ran. Vigran's eyes went wide, and somehow despite the siren Simon heard her gasp and wheeze. One brightly taloned hand went to her neck, her arm flapping sheetlike in her panic.

She would be dead in seconds, and there was nothing her doctor could do.

Simon's eyes raked over the tableau. One last look, one last instant. He needed to move. His eyes lighted on the blood bag hanging from the staff, red as the other monitors were turning. Maria's blood, he was certain. He vanished his blade and fled toward the door. If he could make the lift, he decided—if he could make the lift, that would be far enough.

The weight of the ring-world pressed on him as Simon rode the lift down. He had no shield, no way to defend himself should the guards open fire. He knew he'd reached the end. He knew Madame Vigran was dead, but that was cold comfort as he leaned against the panel that controlled the lift. He'd be in the lobby in seconds.

Was it worth it?

He wasn't sure. He hadn't wanted to help the girl at all, and yet he found he could not ignore her and remain himself—and it was better to die himself than live on as someone else, something else. Like the Madame.

And yet like the Madame he had killed to save himself. He had a desperate and perhaps vain hope that by killing their employer, he had stripped her guards of any incentive to do him harm. They were not bound to her by any oath of loyalty, were obedient out of any devotion to her person or station. With Vigran dead, there was no one to pay them. It might not matter. The guards might not know she was dead, and even if they did, one might kill him for having terminated their contract along with their client. They might kill him because they could.

But no.

Simon stood straight, the weight of Hyadon fully on his shoulders once again. With Vigran gone, there would be no hounds for Eirene, no huntsman to carve away her heart. And the others might live. Phoebe and the rest. Perhaps they could run the theater themselves, or find a new one of their own. More likely, they would find themselves homeless, desperate and alone. But their lives would be their own, and maybe that was enough. Maybe *any* life was better than none.

He hoped so.

The lift slid to a halt. The door opened.

Simon stepped out like a man emerging onto a stage, his hands in the air and empty. Seeing two of the gray-clad guards advancing, disruptors raised, he lifted up his voice and cried out, "She's dead!"

Allegation of an Honorable Man

Larry Correia

The letters stenciled on the frosted glass read Peter Micale, Private Investigator. It was well after midnight, so the halls of the run-down building were empty, but the lights in the detective's office were still on. I could smell hot coffee, cigarette smoke, and nervous energy. He was awake. Alert. Hyper-focused on something. Not surprising. I'd dealt with his kind before. The driven types often suffered from insomnia.

I knocked and waited.

There was a delay as he processed the unexpected arrival. There was a rasp of leather as a weapon was freed from a holster, followed by the metallic noise as the slide on an automatic was slightly retracted to make sure a round of ammunition was chambered. I had no idea who he had angered recently to require that response, or maybe he was always expecting trouble.

"Who is it?"

"A potential client," I answered.

"What's a dame doing here this time of night?" He had muttered that under his breath, intended for his own ears alone, but I still heard him perfectly well. The pistol went back in its holster. I could hear papers being returned to a folder, and then placed in a drawer which was slid closed. A chair creaked. It was unnecessary for him to raise his voice for me, but he didn't know that. "Just a second."

The detective was probably looking in the mirror to make sure he was presentable. Judging by the state of the building and the neighborhood it was located in, he needed the money. He couldn't afford to turn away any business, even if it showed up in the middle of the night.

A moment later he unlocked the door and opened it a crack. He even hid his reaction to my appearance far better than most men. Despite wearing an outfit designed to accentuate my current form, there was no lecherous drooling or slack-jawed leering. A gentleman notices, but he does not stare. He gave me a polite nod of greeting. "Ma'am." At most, he would later describe me to his friends as stunning or jaw dropping...If he lived long enough to ever see them again. I'd not decided yet.

"Peter Micale?"

"Yes." He was a hard-looking man nearing forty, of normal height but lean in build, unshaven, unkempt, with an undone tie, and dark circles beneath his eyes. "How can I help you, miss?"

"Drusilla."

He scowled, probably because the name seemed too old to hang on someone who looked so young.

Rather than open the door the rest of the way, he kept it mostly closed, studying me carefully through the gap. Something about me must have made him wary. The detective had good instincts. Despite my best efforts, sometimes certain people still recognize that I'm not what I appear to be. Or maybe his line of work had simply given him earthly enemies who might send a beautiful woman to lure him into a trap?

I gave him my most disarming smile. The expression usually caused men to melt into puddles of easily manipulated goo. "May I come in?"

But rather than step aside, he said, "Maybe you should come back during regular *daylight* office hours."

"Except time is of the essence, Mr. Micale. We must speak now or not at all. May I come in?"

His eyes narrowed suspiciously. "Do you require permission?"

"I'm merely trying to be polite." I had a very charming laugh. I'd practiced it. "I'm afraid you're thinking of vampires, with the whole not being able to cross the threshold thing."

"Yeah...That's just silliness from the movies." Except he still didn't let me in. "So who are you?"

It was clear that he wouldn't believe me if I told him that I was just a regular American woman in the city of Los Angeles in the year A.D. 1949 who just happened to look like an amalgamation of all the best features of current movie stars. Some humans were easier to manipulate than others. Some required a more *direct* approach.

"I am someone who can answer some of the questions that keep you up at night."

"Which questions are those?"

"I know about your map...The one with all the missing people on it."

That clearly rattled him. "A fella needs a hobby."

"Some men collect stamps or butterflies. You search for the vanished. I might have information about a case you worked back when you were a policeman. Help me and I will help you."

He was quiet for a long time. "My mother used to say I was too dumb to know when to quit." Then he stepped aside and opened the door. However, he did not specifically give me permission to enter, and since he usually slept on a cot in the back room, thus by the rules vampires had to obey, this counted as his home. He was still testing me.

I walked through the doorway, and nothing happened. Thus destroying his foolish delusions about Nosferatu. He seemed relieved. *Silly man*. Didn't he realize there were far worse things lurking out there than mere bloodsuckers?

He closed the door. "May I take your coat?"

I slid out of my furs. Fashion critics had described this bare-shouldered dress as scandalous in the magazines, which was why I had purchased one. He took the coat and hung it from a rack, next to his suit jacket and fedora.

"Please, have a seat." He pulled out a chair for me. I sat down as he went around to the other side of his desk. Beyond the tobacco and lack of sleep, I could still smell the wariness on him. Despite my best efforts to blend in, sometimes people could still sense that I was dangerous enough to set them on edge. It often made my life difficult. He didn't stink of fear, though. He was too confident for that. He'd been through war and a multitude of lesser battles. His knuckles were scarred from many fights. I could sense the old cuts and healed broken bones on him. It would take more than a general feeling of unease to make him afraid of a female half his mass, who clearly wasn't hiding a gun beneath a dress this formfitting.

"How do you know about my fascination with missing-persons cases, Ms. Drusilla?"

It was easier to lie. He would not react well to the truth. "You were recommended by someone you used to work with. He said you were a man of single-minded determination on the subject."

"Who said that?"

"He asked not to be named."

"Of course. I wouldn't claim to know me either. But if you've got information on an open case, you really need to share it with the police, not hang it out there like bait."

"It won't make any difference for them now. They've been gone too long. I suspect the only person who cares about finding out what really happened to them anymore is you."

"Did you have something to do with this particular disappearance?"

I laughed. "Of course not. This was years ago. It was just something I've been told about, but which I absolutely know to be true. I also have a great deal of money. If you do this job for me, I'll pay your regular fee, and double it if you resolve the matter quickly. Let's say forty-eight hours, starting now. Consider being able to put one of your old cases to rest an added bonus."

"How about you tell me about that first?"

"But then my needs would be delayed while you go

and search for bones." I pouted. The look didn't seem to work on him, but I hadn't practiced that particular expression much with this face. He was a hard sell.

The detective picked up his coffee as he thought it over, and I noted that he'd not bothered to offer me anything to drink. *How impolite.* It was then that I realized something else. He had not taken the most efficient way back to his desk after taking my coat. He had gone the long way around the room, and there was a small mirror on the opposite wall.

"Interesting."

"What?"

"You walked around that way in order to see if I cast a reflection." Which clearly I did, because how else could I have gotten this red lipstick applied so perfectly? "Do you actually believe in vampires, Mr. Micale?"

He sipped his coffee. "Only crazy people believe in vampires, Ms. Drusilla."

Belief in such superstitions were frowned upon in these modern, scientific times. Perhaps the detective was more experienced with the dark forces that lurked beneath the mortal world than I had expected. That could either help or hinder my mission. I had picked this one for his reputation for being intelligent and relentlessly dedicated in his search, and because I required a man of honor to set things right. It would behoove me to do a bit more research into him... but I could do that later. I'd not been lying when I had said that time was of the essence.

"As to the purpose of my visit, something extremely valuable has been stolen from me. I would like you to find the perpetrators and retrieve this item. The utmost discretion is required."

"Alright, I'll need details and I'll need you to start from the beginning."

Even though part of him sensed this might be a trap, he would proceed. Curious humans were predictable like that. Regardless of the era, whether they were investigators, inquisitors, paladins, or monster hunters, there was nothing more dangerous than someone who was compelled to find the truth, regardless of the danger or cost. They simply couldn't help themselves.

"I value my privacy, so I will give you the minimum details necessary to complete the assignment. Nothing more."

"That's going to make my job more difficult."

"So be it."

"You've got a peculiar manner of speaking, Ms. Drusilla. Are you from around here?"

"No." And I left it at that, because if I elaborated about where I really came from, I'd have no choice but to kill him afterwards to ensure his silence. "The stolen item is a family heirloom. It is very valuable."

"Monetarily or personally?"

"Personally. Though I would assume it would also fetch a hefty price in certain dark markets. I will give you access to my property where it was taken from so you may inspect the scene. I will allow my staff to speak with you, as long as your questions pertain only to this case."

"Alright..." Despite his better judgment, his curiosity had hooked him. "What's the nature of the stolen merchandise?"

"It is a shrunken head."

"Like the little guys from South American headhunters?"

"Yes."

He blinked a few times. "Seriously?"

"Yes."

Head-shrinking was a practice among certain tribes of the Amazon. Once westerners had discovered the existence of such things, they had become a morbid sort of collectible. There had probably been more people murdered to sell their shrunken heads to collectors and tourists over the last fifty years than there had ever been for the original ritual purposes. Of course, the relic that had been taken from me was no mere knickknack, but the good detective didn't need to know that.

"Not what I expected... So how do the natives get them so small anyways?"

"Once the subject is beheaded, careful incisions are made to remove the flesh from the skull. It is wrapped around a wooden ball and carefully dried in order to keep the form and retain the proper features. The particular one which was taken from me, the lips, eyelids, and nostrils have been sewn shut, and it has been coated in charcoal ash."

"Why?"

"To keep the vengeful spirit trapped inside. Or so their legends claim."

"Huh." It took him a moment to process that. "Have you reported this to the police?"

"I do not wish to involve the authorities."

"Understandable. People who come to me say that a lot. Any idea who might have stolen it from you?"

Of course I had a few suspects, but I couldn't just come out and say it. To make such accusations without proof would violate the treaty and threaten the peace.

Which was why I required an honorable third party to make the allegation ... Only then could I act freely.

"No. I do not consort with thieves or ruffians."

"Of course. Were you there when the item was stolen?"

"No. I was ... out."

"And this ... head, is so important to you, why?"

"The reasons for my attachment are irrelevant to your quest."

"You say that, but you don't actually know what you don't know. Sometimes it's the little things you don't think matter that break a case wide open. The more you tell me, the better the odds that I can recover your property."

His curiosity would certainly be the death of him. Whatever human had declared "what you don't know can't hurt you" was an idiot who I hoped had died horrifically.

"If you are stymied in your search, we can return to the topic. Otherwise, you may visit the property and question the staff tomorrow." I stood up, took a pencil from his desk, and wrote my address on the edge of the newspaper that was sitting there. "Now I must be going, Mr. Micale."

"You can just call me Pete. Do you need a ride home?"

"My driver is waiting for me downstairs." I walked to the door.

"Hold your horses." He didn't bother to get up to see me out. "I never said if I'd take the job or not."

I paused, hand on the doorknob. "The missing-persons case I can help you close is John and Kelli Kochan. You remember them?"

Of course he did. A man like this never let go of a case. "Married couple. He was from Texas. She was from Montana. They moved out here to work in the airplane business. In 1939 they went hiking in the Hollywood Hills and were never seen again. We searched the area for weeks. No clues. No witnesses."

I didn't bother to look back as I walked out. "I'll be in touch, Detective."

Sure enough, Detective Micale came to the mansion the next morning. I let my staff deal with him. They were loyal and well trained. They would not speak of things they shouldn't. None of them would risk drawing my wrath.

Regardless, he struck me as a tricky one, so I observed from the shadows as he was given the tour of the estate. He questioned the butler, the maids, my chef, my driver, and the groundskeeper. Each time he started by asking about the night of the burglary, but inevitably he steered the questions back toward me. What was I like? How did I afford such a nice place? What's your boss do for fun? Their answers remained consistent. I was a kind but exacting employer. My wealth had been inherited from my family who had been very successful in the shipping industry in New England. I was an active socialite, and I threw many parties at the estate.

He seemed rather impressed by the opulence of the mansion, and the quality of the artifacts in my collection. Perhaps now that he saw how many interesting items from around the world I possessed, he wouldn't think a single shrunken head from Amazonia would be such an odd thing to own. On more than one occasion he remarked that my home would make a good museum. I took that as a compliment.

His search was very thorough, checking all of the doors and windows for forced entry. I knew a thing or two about sneaking into places myself, and sure enough, he found the same scuff marks and scratches that I had. It had rained recently, so he had tracked the footprints on the soft ground to the same corner of the fence as I had, where an automobile must have been waiting on the other side.

Then he asked all the neighbors questions. Unfortunately, I could not follow him there without being seen. Sadly, I knew their answers about me would not be as charitable. They saw me as aloof. Distant. And my parties were obviously well attended based upon the traffic, but the guests were secretive, and their identities unknown.

I disliked having nosy neighbors. I looked forward to the day when all of them would have unfortunate, *accidental* deaths. However, this property suited my needs, being close and convenient to many of the rich, powerful, and beautiful people of this glittering city.

One danger to living a very long time is becoming jaded to the world around you. It is easy to assume that you've seen it all and become complacent. This is a trap. For good or ill, this is mankind's world, and humans will surprise you. See the recent unpleasantness in Europe and the Pacific for example. Several of my kind had been slightly inconvenienced by that.

When the detective returned to the mansion, he spoke again with my butler. I watched from the shadows.

"Is Ms. Drusilla back yet?"

"I'm afraid not, sir. Do you have any messages you would like for me to convey to her?"

"Sure. She should get a couple of guard dogs. Then your thief wouldn't have been able to sneak in without them barking."

"I'm afraid the mistress doesn't care for dogs."

"Who doesn't like dogs? Everybody likes dogs."

Dogs growled when I was near. Cats would arch their backs and hiss. But the butler simply said, "She does not care for the hair. It makes a mess on her things."

"She should get one of those poodle dogs then. They don't shed. You have to give them haircuts. Tell her I've got a few things to check on and some people to talk to, and I'll get back to her as soon as I learn anything."

I did not like being surprised. So after Peter Micale left the mansion, I followed him.

The detective truly was a determined sort. He made several more stops, driving to various gas stations and garages near my property and questioning the workers there. I was able to get close enough to listen in to a couple of them. Apparently my neighbors had seen a green Oldsmobile, which Micale had discovered had a bad coolant leak, because of a discolored patch of mud.

Sure enough, on the night of the theft, a man had stopped at the last station Micale checked in order to top off his radiator. A dollar had gotten a description out of the night attendant. The driver was a small man, short but wiry, blond but going bald fast and trying to hide it with a comb. And he'd had an accent like he was from Europe. Where in Europe? The attendant didn't know. The closest he'd ever been to overseas was fishing off the pier.

Then Micale drove to the university, where he spoke with a professor of anthropology. From the warm greeting, the two of them had worked together before. They went to the library, where I hid between the stacks while they talked about who would want to steal shrunken heads, and the conversation had turned to esoteric cults...I was impressed. My detective worked fast.

After using a pay phone, he drove to the local police precinct, but he didn't go in. Rather he met with two uniformed officers at a sandwich shop across the street. I found a shadowy spot in the back corner of the storage room where I could listen to them through the walls. They made small talk about the good old days and joked about a police captain none of them liked. The captain was fat, corrupt, and his wife cheated on him, and the men found that amusing. Then the conversation turned to local hoodlums, lock-picking burglars in particular, as Micale asked them about a small, balding, European who might be driving an Oldsmobile with a leaky radiator, and they told him of different criminals they thought met his criteria.

Lucky for him, Micale did not tell any of his sources who his employer was. If he brought scandal to this name I'd have to kill him and find a new investigator. I had a good thing going in Los Angeles. I'd hate to have to start over elsewhere. But this was a risk that I had to take.

That was the downside with using humans. You want them clever, but not *too* clever.

Then he went by the telegram office and sent a few messages. I was unable to get close enough to overhear him dictating those, but I was beginning to worry. I wanted Mr. Micale to learn about my missing treasure, not about me. I hoped he wasn't inquiring too deeply into the fake life history that had been provided to him.

Night fell, and Micale kept working. My original suspicion that he didn't sleep much had proven correct. Armed with a name from the policemen—Marcos Lakatos—Micale had driven to various bars and night clubs around the city. These were all seedy, dirty establishments. Far beneath the dignity of Ms. Drusilla, but perfectly fitting for whatever face I decided to wear into each place in order to keep up with my detective. I will admit, I was enjoying myself. This was not my sort of hunt, but there was still a certain thrill to it.

At one bar, a drunk had taken exception to Micale's tone and taken a swing at him. The detective proved to be as quick with a sap as he was with his mouth, and he left the drunk a crumpled wreck. There was no cruelty to it. Just efficiency. The next club, he found a pretty waitress who'd gone out with Lakatos once. A little small talk and a bit of friendly flirting had gotten Micale the approximate location of Lakatos' last home, and though she didn't recall the house number, she remembered the color—blue—and the intersection closest to it.

The detective slowly drove past the only blue house in the area a couple of times, and then parked down the street to approach the place quietly. I landed on a roof across the street to watch. Both of us avoided the streetlights.

It was a low-class neighborhood. The houses were tiny and close to each other. This was gang territory, but I wasn't the least bit worried about human predators. Life had become much easier for my kind after iron weapons had fallen out of fashion.

If the burglar was here, I was curious to see how Micale would resolve this situation. If the thief was working for who I suspected he was, I had to remain an observer, not a participant. Until an honorable mortal gave name to the one who had wronged me, I was bound by covenant not to act. I would obey the covenant because it had prevented many bloodbaths over the centuries, and breaking it would be bad for my business.

The lights were on inside. I could hear a record player. Micale may have been honorable, but he wasn't stupid. Rather than knock on the door to announce himself, he snuck around the back to peer in the windows first. There was a green Oldsmobile parked behind the house with a puddle beneath. Looking satisfied that he'd gotten the right house, he returned to the front, and knocked on the door.

Lakatos opened it a minute later. From the smell of him, I immediately knew this was the thief who had broken into my home. I had to quell the reflexive urge to bite a chunk out of him.

"I'm looking for Marcos Lakatos," Micale said.

"Who are you?"

"You can call me Pete."

"You a cop?"

"Nope. Private investigator."

"Well that's worth spit, isn't it?" The accent that the gas station attendant had only been able to identify as

"European" turned out to be Hungarian. I recognized it because I'd thrown lavish parties for the Hapsburgs back in the day. "Take a hike, dick."

"I do have a couple of questions for you if you've got a minute."

"How 'bout you take your questions and stick them where the sun don't shine?"

"A wise guy, huh?" The detective cracked a smile, which was probably why Lakatos didn't see the sucker punch coming. He planted his fist into the thief's gut, hard enough to double him over, and then Micale quickly shoved him inside and closed the door behind him before any of the neighbors could see. The takedown was quick. Not bad for a human.

I flew across the street, landed silently on Lakatos's lawn, and then crept up to the window so I could watch the show.

Lakatos had gotten hit so hard he was having a hard time breathing, but that didn't stop him from pulling a switchblade from one pocket. Micale grabbed that arm to immobilize it and slammed the much smaller thief into the wall a few times. Once he lost the knife, the detective hurled Lakatos into the tiny living room. A little table broke beneath him. His dinner—a cold can of beans—got knocked on the floor.

"Stay down, dummy. I just want to talk."

Except the thief grabbed the fork he'd been eating with, got up, and tried to stab Micale with that. The annoyed detective stepped aside, kidney-punched the thief twice, and then swung him by the collar into the wall. His nose left a blood smear on the wood as he slid down.

"You done?"

"I'm done," Lakatos said from his position on the floor.

"Alright then. Where's the shrunken head?"

"What shrunken—"

Micale kicked him in the ribs.

The thief coughed for a bit, then gasped, "Oh yeah, that one."

"Yeah, that one."

"I already delivered it to who hired me."

"Well I figured somebody was paying you to do it. You're an immigrant locksmith with a B&E record and a rep for being one hell of a second-story man. You don't really strike me as the sort who runs in Ms. Drusilla's social circles." The detective looked down at the fork that was stuck in the floor near his shoe. "But if I'd just got paid to rob a mansion, I'd be eating a steak dinner, not a can of beans."

"They didn't pay me in money. I owed them a favor. I was trying to go straight, but they got my family out of Europe when things got bad. They do favors; you never know when they're gonna ask that favor returned. It was steal that little head for them or else."

Micale pulled up a stool and sat on it. "Who did you owe?"

"You don't want to mess with these. They aren't normal. They been around forever. They got no mercy and lots of reach. I talk, they'll skin me alive. And that's not exaggerating. That's how they take care of snitches. They hang them from a hook and peel their skin off slow."

The thief's description of the preferred method of execution told me exactly who had stolen my artifact.

However, according to the covenant, justice required I be given a name.

"Look, pal, I get it. I saw what happened to Europe. If I had family there I'd have made a deal with the devil himself to get them out too. So I'm not judging." Micale took out a pack of cigarettes, took one out, and lit it. "But I need to get that head back to its rightful owner. So this is how it's gonna shake out. Either you tell me who has it, and then I keep your name out of it. I never mention you to them, the cops, or my employer. Or, I have you arrested for stealing. Then if the men who hired you got as much reach as you say, you'll be a sitting duck in jail until they send somebody to shut you up permanently."

"That's a death sentence!"

"It wouldn't be much of a threat otherwise." He took a long drag off the cigarette. "Your call, Mr. Lakatos. Talk, or I get my old pals from the precinct to pick you up."

Part of me was disappointed. I had hoped the detective would have tortured the name from the thief. Broken fingers and pulled teeth. But his way was not my way. Besides, from the look on the thief's face, he was about to break. I leaned closer to the glass, eager to hear it.

"Alright. Swear you won't tell them about me. You found out who they is some other way."

"Agreed," Micale answered. "I'd offer to shake on it, but you might have another fork stashed on you."

"They're a church. But not like a regular church. I don't mean a building. I mean like an old religion, that does weird stuff, and meets in secret."

"A cult?"

"That's right. Only the things they worship aren't like anything normal. They look like the animal that washes up dead on the beach. With all the arms."

"A squid?"

"Yes. A squid. They pray to a squid god. Only it's big as an ocean liner. And older than the world."

I watched Micale's reaction carefully through the window. He was incredulous at first, but the thief was so earnestly frightened that he didn't scoff at the idea. "I can't tell the operator to put me through to the first church of the giant squid. Give me a name or you're going to jail."

"Their boss here, their big priest, the one I gave the head to, is named Skinner. Matthias Skinner."

And to think, I had invited Matthias to my parties. He had been a guest in my home, eaten my food, and enjoyed the entertainments I had provided. I hissed in anger.

Micale jumped and looked toward the window, hand moving to his holstered pistol.

"What was that?" Lakatos cried.

The detective stared at the glass for a long time, but as long as I remained perfectly still, he wouldn't be able to see me. He scowled. "Must have been the wind." He turned his attention back to the thief. "From what you were saying they do to snitches, is Skinner a name or his title?"

"I don't know, but he uses it like it's his real name here. He's got an office on Colfax. He's a big-time lawyer for movie studios."

"Of course he is, because my life's not complicated enough already. Alright. You've convinced me. Nobody's that good an actor. Now you're gonna want to skip town for a while. It sounds like this Skinner fellow is the real crook."

That pronouncement would do. I leapt into the air and flew into the night. The time for retribution had come.

The next day the front page of all the evening edition newspapers were about the ghastly murder of a prominent Los Angeles attorney. There were a great many leaks in the LAPD, so the lurid details were quickly made known to the press. The body of Matthias Skinner had been found in his Beverly Hills home, after he had been impaled upon the antlers of a taxidermized deer—still alive apparently—while all of his appendages had been torn off, one by one. Oddly enough, the poor attorney seemed to have survived having all his limbs forcibly removed because the coroner eventually ruled his ultimate cause of death to be asphyxiation, from choking while being force-fed his own entrails.

It was also discovered that Mr. Skinner had a rather elaborate occult workshop in his basement, with all the usual predictable trappings such as goat masks and black robes to shock the public. Apparently the respectable citizen was not so respectable after all. The LAPD had no leads at this time, but the press was speculating the murder was the work of other devil-worshipping anarchists.

What was not in the papers, was that the murder had been called in by an anonymous tip. Pete Micale had actually been the first one to stumble onto the crime scene that morning. He'd tracked down where Skinner lived and let himself in when nobody had answered. The sight of the carnage had been enough to unnerve even the jaded investigator, but he had been smart enough to immediately flee the scene so as to not be implicated.

I had watched Micale's reaction, amused, while hanging from the rafters.

My treasure had been recovered and justice had been served. All that remained was to take care of any loose ends.

I was waiting in the dark when Peter Micale returned to his office. When he turned the lights on and saw me sitting in his chair behind his desk, he didn't seem too surprised. He closed the door behind him.

"Ms. Drusilla." He tipped his hat to me, before taking it off and hanging it on the rack.

"Mr. Micale. Forgive my intrusion, but do you have an update about my case?"

He gave me a bitter laugh. "Oh, I think we're way past playing games now, lady. If you are a lady at all."

"I'm whatever I need to be at the time." I leaned back in the chair and placed one perfect leg on his desk to be admired. "If we are past games, then we should both speak truthfully. It'll save time."

"I'm always in favor of honesty."

"Good." Now it was my turn to smile, only this time I showed him jackal teeth. "Then tell me what you know, so I can decide if you should live or die."

Rather than run screaming from the room like most humans would, he sat in the chair I'd occupied last time I'd been here, got out a cigarette, and put it in his mouth. He offered me one. I raised one clawed hand politely in the negative.

"Suit yourself," he said as he lit his smoke. Such composure was refreshing. I had fully expected to have to chase him down the hall and tear his throat out. "So how does this work, you ask me questions, and if you think I know too much, or come away thinking I'm going to crimp your lifestyle, you do to me what you did to Skinner?"

"Of course not. That was personal. The high priest of the Dread Overlord insulted my hospitality and stole from me. If I decide to kill you, it will be self-defense. I have to protect my identity from those who would do me harm. Do you know what I truly am?"

"I've got no earthly idea."

"Good." That was a point in his favor. My kind were few and far between, and there were always dangerous humans who would never leave us alone. I despised hunters. "I've looked into your background a bit more, Mr. Micale."

"Oh?" He sounded mildly curious.

"You know more about the supernatural than I expected. When we met, you thought I might be a vampire for a reason."

"I don't get too many unearthly beauties showing up in the middle of the night," he said. "It's just noonday average beauties around here."

"Your reaction was based upon personal experience. You were in the Army Air Forces, and because you had been a policeman before the war you were made an officer in a security battalion, and guarded bases. I seem to recall hearing about an airfield in France being terrorized by a nest of vampires. It was several horrible weeks as many soldiers were lured to their deaths."

"Once I figured out what was going on, we handled them."

"I bet you did."

"It's amazing what a few scared men can accomplish with an M2 flamethrower and a crate of grenades. Only the secret government types made sure that what happened at Saint-Pierre-du-Mont never went in the official reports or showed up in any papers. If we talked about it while in uniform we'd get court-martialed, and if we talked about it after we'd end up in the ground. So how do you know about it?"

"One of the survivors told me about the events."

Micale studied me as he took a long drag off his cigarette. "I'm guessing you don't mean one of the *human* survivors..." He reached into his suit and pulled out a large revolver. I did not know much about human weapons, but this one appeared to be an antique.

"I hope you realize that will do absolutely nothing to harm me. But I am rather fond of this dress and would prefer not to have any holes put in it."

"I know you're some kind of something, so I don't expect lead bullets to do much. They sure don't to vampires. But it makes me feel better to have it in hand."

"Whatever helps you find comfort, Detective."

He leaned forward and let the gun dangle over his knee. "So, did you find your shrunken head at the lawyer's house?"

"Yes. It was in the basement, being prepared for a ritual."

"On the summer solstice," Micale said, surprising me once again. "I figured the date couldn't be a coincidence based upon your arbitrary forty-eight-hour deadline."

"Dates of celestial significance lend power to summoning spells. I did your species a favor, Mr. Micale. Mankind would not want this particular witch doctor to return to the land of the living. He was a bastard the first few times he was alive. I assume several hundred years of being imprisoned as a piece of jerky will not have improved his disposition."

"I'll have to take your word on that one. So I know Skinner was one of your party guests. You entertain a lot of movie stars and big wigs. And I know he was secretly some kind of maniac cult leader. So I'd already assumed he stole the haunted head for some nefarious purpose, but what I don't get is why you ever needed me?"

"You realize that the more you know, the more likely I am to have to kill you, right?"

The detective shrugged. "You ask me questions. I get to ask you questions. Fair is fair."

"So be it. There are secret factions out there, Mr. Micale, powerful beyond your understanding. Sometimes they are at war, others they are at peace. I am a neutral party. I am an entertainer. A facilitator. I provide for the peculiar appetites of beings you can't even imagine. Yet there are rules. Skinner—a priest of the Old Ones—broke those rules, only I could not take my retribution against a representative of a faction without the testimony of impartial mortals."

"You were following me the whole time."

"Yes."

"I figured. I spotted you a couple times."

"Impossible." Surely he was lying. "I am a perfectly evolved predator."

"You don't blink enough," he said.

"What?"

"You forget to blink. It's like you have to force yourself to remember to do it. Regular people just blink all the time without thinking about it. So even though you changed into a different body every time, I spotted you a few times because you were the one too interested in spying on me to remember to blink. That unblinking stare... It's uncanny."

"Hmmm. Interesting. Thank you for the tip. I will try to remember that in the future."

"You're welcome. But I've got two other lines of questioning if you don't mind."

"Do you have a death wish, Detective?"

"Humor me, Ms. Drusilla. First, you know that I've been looking for missing people. Now that I know you're something special I won't bother asking you how you know or why I came to your attention. I just want to know, could you really have helped me find those people? Or was that all just a trick to get me to play along?"

This time when I smiled, I used human teeth, and even remembered to blink. "How many pins do you have in that map of yours now? A hundred? Two hundred? Each one representing a life, vanished around this city without a trace. The missing haunt you, Mr. Micale. You stare at their faces in the photographs. You read the same reports, over and over again, looking for patterns. Their families weep, wondering where their loved ones have gone, but you have no comfort to offer them. Your constant questions upset important men, and your endless labors made their lack of effort look bad, so they fired you from being a

policeman. And even without your badge, you simply
could not let it go."

"That tip you gave me..."

"The Kochans put up a remarkable fight, but they
were consumed by a Gug. I can tell you exactly where
to find their gnawed-on bones."

"I assume this...gug...was one of your party
guests?"

"Oh no, silly. Gugs are fifteen-foot-tall, fanged night-
mare beasts from Unknown Kadath. This Gug was a
pet of one of my guests, who decided while he was
in town that he wanted to hunt humans for sport."

For the very first time, Peter Micale's calm facade
slipped, and I could see the righteous anger on the
other side. "How many others like them are there?"

"My party guests love to talk, and they are a
diverse and rambunctious lot. They mingle with the
beautiful, stupid, unwitting humans, and sometimes
they are overcome by their desires. In the few years
I've been in this city, I would have to guess that
my guests could probably explain thirty or forty of
your pins. But they are not all killed and eaten. Oh
no. Some are enslaved. Some are turned. A few are
even taken to other realms where they will dwell
for eternity."

The detective took a deep breath, needing to
compose himself before asking the most important
question. "Do you know what happened to *her*?"

"The first? The one who started you on your hope-
less quest?" I shook my head. "Alas, no. I truly wish
I could tell you what happened to her, but sometimes
humans just...go away."

He nodded slowly, faint hopes of finding his lost

love dashed once again. "Any chance you'll tell me about all those other people your party guests took?"

"My clientele values my discretion." I had only told him of that one incident because the Gug had shit on my carpet, so its owner had been banned anyway. "I will not speak of any others."

"I was afraid you'd say that. One last line of questioning then."

He knew far too much for me to let him live now. "It's your funeral, Detective."

"When you were following me, did you see what was on those telegrams and who I sent them to?"

"I did not. That room was too well lit, too open to get close, and there was no crowd to blend with."

"Good. And I know you weren't there when I got the responses this morning, so I'll fill you in then. The first was to an old war buddy who is in the Massachusetts State Police, confirming my suspicions that you've been moving around, changing identities. You left there when there were too many questions and too many bodies."

That had been unfortunate. I had rather enjoyed New England. The weather was more to my temperament than this place's near constant sunshine. The sun reminded me of home, and I'd been banished from Arabia for two thousand years.

"The other telegram was to a company in Alabama."

"I've never been there. I know nothing about that place."

"But they knew something about you. Or your kind at least. They're called Monster Hunter International, and they're not the kind of company you find in the phone book. They made me a job offer once, after what happened in France, but I told them I couldn't. I had too much work to do here." He lifted the big revolver and pointed it at me. "See, I'd already started my map before the war. I couldn't leave all those people hanging."

I scoffed at the gun. "You can't harm me."

"Mack Shackleford told me that was a possibility. He said from the description I gave you're probably some kind of djinn, something called a *jiniri*."

I hissed and leapt atop the desk. *He knew!*

"Sounds like Mack guessed right, and he told me what he knew about your kind. Even if you kill me, MHI is already on their way, and they're going to burn your little party house to the ground. No matter what, you're done here, Drusilla."

I showed him my true form, letting my wings stretch to the corners of the office. Let him see my terrible wrath and know fear. "I was going to make your death quick. Now, you will envy the Old One's priest."

Despite seeing me for what I really was, Peter Micale remained calm as he carefully aimed the revolver at my eyes.

"Fool. I'm invulnerable to mere lead."

He cocked the hammer with his thumb. "Which is why I spent my afternoon making some bullets out of iron."

That was the problem with humans. Sometimes they were too clever.

About the Authors

Larry Correia is the *New York Times* best-selling author of the Monster Hunter International series, the Grimnoir Chronicles, the Saga of the Forgotten Warrior, the Dead Six thrillers with Mike Kupari, *Gun Runner* with John D. Brown, *Servants of War* with Steve Diamond, novels set in the Warmachine universe, and *The Adventures of Tom Stranger, Interdimensional Insurance Agent* on Audible, as well as a whole lot of short fiction. Before becoming an author, Larry was an accountant, a gun dealer, and a firearms instructor. He lives in Yard Moose Mountain, Utah, with his very patient wife and children.

Kacey Ezell is a retired USAF instructor pilot with 3000-plus hours in the UH-1N Huey and Mi-171 helicopters. When not beating the air into submission, she writes sci-fi/fantasy/horror/noir/alternate history fiction. She is a two-time Dragon Award Finalist for Best Alternate History and won the 2018 Year's Best Military and Adventure Science Fiction Readers' Choice Award. She has written multiple best-selling novels published with Chris Kennedy Publishing, Baen Books, and Blackstone Publishing. She is married with two daughters. You can find out more and join her mailing list at www.kaceyezell.net.

Robert Buettner's "1957" is set within the universe of his upcoming novel *1957: Distant Lightning*, which will be his eleventh novel, and his first novel of alternate history.

He was a Quill Award nominee for Best New Writer of 2005, and his debut novel, *Orphanage*, was a Quill nominee for Best SF/Fantasy/Horror novel of 2004, a national bestseller, and has been called a classic of modern military science fiction. The Orphan's Legacy trilogy, which followed on to the five *Orphanage* books, was a national best-selling series in its own right. *Orphanage* and its seven follow-on novels have been compared favorably to the works of Robert Heinlein, and several have been translated and republished in Chinese, Czech, French, Japanese, Russian, and Spanish.

Buettner's short fiction, comprising two novellas and eleven short stories, has been published in various anthologies, some of which have been national bestsellers.

His nonfiction afterword appears in the 2009 republished anthology of Robert Heinlein's works *The Green Hills of Earth/The Menace From Earth*.

He has been a National Science Foundation fellow in paleontology; prospected for minerals in Alaska and the Sonoran Desert; served as a U.S. Army Intelligence officer and as a director of the Southwestern Legal Foundation; practiced law in Colorado, twelve other states, and five foreign countries; and served as general counsel of a unit of one of the United States' largest private companies.

Elected as an undergraduate to the academic history honorary fraternity Phi Alpha Theta, he is a certified underwater diver, and has climbed and hiked the Rockies from Alberta to Colorado. He lives in Georgia with his family and more bicycles than a grownup needs.

Visit him on the web at www.RobertBuettner.com.

Griffin Barber is a retired police officer living in Northern California who has written across the sub-genres of speculative fiction. He's collaborated with Kacey Ezell on an original novel of their own devising, *Second Chance Angel*, and with Eric Flint on two 1632 novels, *1636: Mission to the Mughals* and *1637: The Peacock Throne*. He's also been privileged to play in Chuck Gannon's Caineverse, authoring the novellas *Man-Eater* and *Infiltration* for the Murphy's Lawless series. He has short fiction in several anthologies, from Laurell K. Hamilton's *Fantastic Hope*, John Ringo's Black Tide Rising universe, and the *We Dare: No Man's Land*.

D.J. (Dave) Butler has been a lawyer, a consultant, an editor, a corporate trainer, and a registered investment banking representative, and he is now a Consulting Editor for Baen Books. His novels published by Baen Books include the Witchy War series: *Witchy Eye*, *Witchy Winter*, *Witchy Kingdom*, and *Serpent Daughter*, and *In the Palace of Shadow and Joy*, as well as *The Cunning Man* and *The Jupiter Knife*, co-written with Aaron Michael Ritchey. He also writes for children: the steampunk fantasy adventure tales *The Kidnap Plot*, *The Giant's Seat*, and *The Library Machine* are published by Knopf. Other novels include *City of the Saints* from WordFire Press and *The Wilding Probate* from Immortal Works.

Dave also organizes writing retreats and anarcho-libertarian writers' events, and travels the country to sell books. He tells many stories as a gamemaster with a gaming group, some of whom he's been playing with since sixth grade. He plays guitar and banjo whenever he can and likes to hang out in Utah with his wife, their children, and the family dog.

Nicole Givens Kurtz is an author, editor, and educator. She's the recipient of the Ladies of Horror Grant (2021), the Horror Writers Association's Diversity Grant (2020) and the AtomaCon Palmetto Scribe Award of Best Short Story 2021. She's been named as one of *Book Riot*'s Six Best Black Indie SFF Writers. She's also the editor of the groundbreaking anthology *SLAY: Stories of the Vampire Noire*. Her novels have been finalists in the Dream Realm Awards, Fresh Voices, and EPPIE Awards for science fiction. She's written for White Wolf, *Apex Magazine*, *Fiyah*, Realm (formerly Serial Box), and Baen.

Nicole has over forty short stories published as well as numerous novels and three active speculative mystery series. She's a member of the Horror Writers Association, Sisters in Crime, and Science Fiction Writers of America. Find out more about her work at www.nicolegivenskurtz.net.

Laurell K. Hamilton is an American multi-genre writer. She is best known as the author of two series of stories, Anita Blake: Vampire Hunter and Merry Gentry.

Her *New York Times* best-selling Anita Blake: Vampire Hunter series centers on Anita Blake, a professional zombie raiser, vampire executioner and supernatural consultant for the police, which includes novels, short story collections, and comic books. Six million copies of Anita Blake novels are in print. Her *New York Times* best-selling Merry Gentry series centers on Meredith Gentry, Princess of the Unseelie Court of Faerie, a private detective facing repeated assassination attempts.

Both fantasy series follow their protagonists as they gain in power and deal with the dangerous "realities" of worlds in which creatures of legend live.

Laurell was born in rural Arkansas but grew up in northern Indiana with her grandmother. Her education includes degrees in English and biology from Marion College (now called Indiana Wesleyan University).

Craig Martelle has been a full-time author for over six years at the time this anthology was published. He has over five million words in publication with over twenty series, mostly science fiction with some fantasy and thrillers. His favorite is science fiction with a thriller angle.

Craig is retired from the Marine Corps where he served as an enlisted Russian crypto-linguist before earning his commission and working in all the intelligence disciplines—human, technical, air, ground, and even counterintelligence.

After he retired, he went to law school and earned his JD where he immediately went into business consulting as a leadership coach and business analyst. Being a lawyer helps get one into the corner office, but once there, making the most impact for a company is done through good leadership and consistent application of continuous improvement techniques. Craig saved his clients forty million dollars over seven years. But he grew tired of always being gone from home.

Throughout his life, Craig has always had a book with him and has read thousands of novels, mostly science fiction, giving him an understanding of story structure, character development, and flow with which he embarked on his own journey.

Craig turned his hand to writing that book he always wanted to write and found that he liked it. A lot. He's been writing ever since. If you want to see some of his other stories, you can find them here: craigmartelle.com.

Justice is a theme that is consistent throughout his books along with characters who have a military background. Craig's career in the Marine Corps gave him plenty of topics and character quirks for a lifetime of stories.

Sharon Shinn has published thirty novels, three short-fiction collections, and one graphic novel since she joined the science fiction and fantasy world in 1995. She has written about angels, shape-shifters, elemental powers, magical portals, and echoes. She has won the William C. Crawford Award for Outstanding New Fantasy Writer, a Reviewer's Choice Award from *Romantic Times*, and the 2010 *RT Book Reviews* Career Achievement Award in the Science Fiction/ Fantasy category. Follow her at SharonShinnBooks on Facebook or visit her website at sharonshinn.net.

S.A. Bailey has been a farmhand, pizza boy, projectionist, roustabout, soldier, brawler, substitute teacher, in-school suspension coordinator/babysitter, cab driver, security guard, private investigator, drunkard, opiate addict, and wretch. His writing, both his Jeb Shaw novels and his blogging/commentary/oversharing on politics and life, has inspired a small but loyal and possibly rabid following. He can be found on Facebook, Instagram, and Patreon at the S.A. Bailey Project. He can be found in East Texas, where he currently holds a day job as a factory worker making medical devices, while trying to figure out how to turn his side hustles into a full-blown lifestyle.

G. Scott Huggins grew up in the American Midwest and has lived there all his life, except for interludes in the European Midwest (Germany) and the Asian Midwest (Russia). He is currently responsible for securing America's future by teaching its past to high school students, many of whom learn things before going to college. His preferred method of teaching and examination is strategic warfare. He loves to read high fantasy, space opera, and parodies of the same. He has a column in the magazine *Sci Phi Journal*. He wants to be a hybrid of G.K. Chesterton and Terry Pratchett when he counteracts the effects of having grown up. When he is not teaching or writing, he devotes himself to his wife, their three children, and cats. He loves bourbon, bacon, and pie, and will gladly put his writing talents to use reviewing samples of any recipe featuring one or more of them. You can also follow him on Facebook.

Chris Kennedy is a science fiction/fantasy author, speaker, and small-press publisher who has written more than forty books and published more than three hundred others. He is a Webster Award winner and three-time Dragon Award finalist. You can get his free book, "Shattered Crucible," at his website, chriskennedypublishing.com.

Called "fantastic" and "a great speaker," Chris has coached hundreds of beginning authors and budding novelists on how to self-publish their stories at a variety of conferences, conventions, and writing guild presentations. He is the author of the award-winning #1 bestseller *Self-Publishing for Profit: How to Get Your Book Out of Your Head and Into the Stores*.

Chris lives in Coinjock, North Carolina, with his wife, and is the holder of a doctorate in educational leadership and master's degrees in both business and public administration. Follow him on Facebook at www.facebook.com/ckpublishing.

Rob Howell is a founder of the Eldros Legacy fantasy setting and an author in the Four Horsemen Universe, the publisher of New Mythology Press, including his work as editor of the Libri Valoris anthologies of heroic fantasy.

He is a reformed medieval academic, a former IT professional, and a retired soda jerk.

Rob's parents quickly discovered books were the only way to keep him quiet. Without books, it's unlikely all three would have survived.

You can find him online at: www.robhowell.org, on Amazon at www.amazon.com/-/e/B00X95LBB0, and his blog at www.robhowell.org/blog.

Michael F. Haspil is a veteran of the U.S. Air Force who had the opportunity to serve as an ICBM crew commander and a launch director at Cape Canaveral. He hosts the *Quantum Froth Dispatches* podcast, which examines storytelling through pop-culture classics and shares author interviews.

When he isn't writing, you can find him sharing stories with his role-playing group, cosplaying, computer gaming, or collecting and creating replica movie props. He devotes the bulk of his hobby time to assembling and painting miniatures for his tabletop wargaming addiction.

Michael's novel *Graveyard Shift*, an urban fantasy story about an immortal pharaoh out to stop an ancient vampire conspiracy in modern-day Miami, was well received by critics and readers alike. Michael is currently working on other stories within the world of *Graveyard Shift*, some tie-in fiction for the Black Library, and other novels and short stories. He's also a part-time amateur Aegyptologist, tabletop general, antiquarian, and vampire hunter. He doesn't do weddings.

Christopher Ruocchio is the author of The Sun Eater, a space opera fantasy series from DAW Books. He also co-edited the military SF anthology *Star Destroyers*, as well as *Space Pioneers*, a collection of Golden Age reprints showcasing tales of human exploration, both from Baen books. He is a graduate of North Carolina State University, where a penchant for self-destructive decision-making caused him to pursue a bachelor's in English Rhetoric with a minor in Classics. An avid student of history, philosophy, and religion, Christopher has been writing since he was eight years old, and he sold his first book—*Empire of Silence*—at twenty-two. The Sun Eater series is available from Gollancz in the UK, and has been translated into French and German.

Christopher lives in Raleigh, North Carolina, where he spends most of his time hunched over a keyboard writing. When not writing, he splits his time between his family, procrastinating with video games, and his friend's boxing gym. He may be found on both Facebook and Twitter at @TheRuocchio.

Acknowledgments

First, thanks to Larry for doing this with me again. It continues to be my honor to work with and learn from you. Also, many thanks to the amazing team of contributors for making my job of editor so very easy. Thanks as well to the pros at Baen Books, without whom none of this noir goodness would ever see the light of day...or dark of night, as may be more appropriate. Finally, as always, thanks to my very own gray knight, the hero of my story, the coolest guy I'll ever meet. You make being a badass look easy.

—KC

This project was Kacey's idea, she's done a great job, and it has been a real pleasure working with her. I'm thankful for the great bunch of authors assembled here, and the hardworking team at Baen Books.

—LC

THE FORGOTTEN WARRIOR SAGA

Son of the Black Sword
9781476781570 • $9.99 US/$12.99 CAN

House of Assassins
9781982124458 • $8.99 US/$11.99 CAN

Destroyer of Worlds
9781982125462 • $8.99 US/$11.99 CAN

Tower of Silence
9781982192532 • $28.00 US/$36.50 CAN

THE GRIMNOIR CHRONICLES

Hard Magic
9781451638240 • $8.99 US/$11.99 CAN.

Spellbound
9781451638592 • $8.99 US/$11.99 CAN.

THE AGE OF RAVENS
with Steve Diamond

Servants of War
HC: 9781982125943 • $25.00 US/$34.00 CAN
PB: 9781982192501 • $9.99 US/$12.99 CAN

MILITARY ADVENTURE
with Mike Kupari

Dead Six
9781451637588 • $7.99 US/$9.99 CAN

Alliance of Shadows
9781481482912 • $7.99 US/$10.99 CAN

Invisible Wars
9781481484336 • $18.00 US/$25.00 CAN